The Daughter Eaters

Mark Young

Funky Ink Press

Copyright © 2020 Mark Young

The right of Mark Young to be identified as the Author
of the Work has been asserted by him in accordance with the
Copyright, Designs and Patents Act 1988

ISBN: 978-0-9955676-5-8

Prologue

The small, lithe, brown-skinned girl couldn't see the sun, but she knew it was rising. The cock out back had started to crow, and any minute now she knew the church bell would start to toll, calling out the faithful to prayer. She rolled over on the rough urine-sodden blanket but was immediately yanked back by the manacle around her wrist; it was connected to a short chain attached to the iron bedstead.

The room she occupied was little more than a cupboard; it had no windows and just one door, always locked. The air in the room was already heavy with oppressive heat. The girl could feel droplets of perspiration sprouting out on her scalp and under her thin arms. She wiped a hand across her forehead to stop the sweat running into her startlingly blue eyes.

Her bones ached and she hurt all over. She had all but given up hope that anyone would come for her. She had even begun to forget the faces of all the people she had loved. All but one: Yolanda. Yolanda had been her last friend after her mother had died. They said Yolanda was only a maid so she shouldn't like her, but she hadn't been able to help it. Maybe Yolanda would come for her.

She heard the heavy footsteps outside in the passageway and she shrank back, dread and fear rippling through her. He always came in the mornings, if he was there. She began to whimper and moan, pulling on the chain, but as the key was placed in the lock and began to turn she seemed to calm, her eyes lost their luster and became dead, as if she were in a trance, which in a way she was. She had learned that this was the only way to survive what was to come.

CHAPTER ONE

The black clad Mexican woman looked around Jonas Calver's New York law office and frowned. She wasn't used to such places. She studied the expensive teak and mahogany furniture, the thick pile carpet, the diplomas on the wall, and then the man behind the desk. All gringos looked pretty much the same to her, but this man seemed to have a kind face. She fidgeted some, eyes downcast, studying her lap as if it might hold the answers to why she was there; she fiddled with some rosary beads.

'Would you like some coffee, Miss Lopez?' Hettie asked from the doorway, pronouncing it "corfee."

Miss Lopez looked up, unsure.

'Go on,' Jonas Calver said. 'Live a little.'

She hesitated, a small frown, then a quick, '*Si*, thank you. Black, no sugar.'

'Good,' Calver said. 'Now we've got that out the way, what can I do for you, Miss Lopez?'

She looked down in her lap again, then up, and met his eyes for the first time. 'It's my sister, Yolanda. I must get her out of jail, or they will kill her,' she blurted out, then stopped abruptly as if surprised by the boldness of her words.

'Okay,' Calver said slowly. He looked up as Hettie came back in with their coffee and began placing the cups down on coasters on the desk.

'Isabel, isn't it?' Calver asked, reaching for his coffee and taking a sip. He liked it scalding hot.

'*Si*,' she replied, picking up her cup as well.

'You like it hot too, huh?'

'Sure,' she nodded, starting to relax.

'Good. Okay, Isabel, so let's start at the beginning. Why are you here, and what do you think I can do for you?'

'Courtney told me to come. She said you have a good heart. That you would sort it out, even though we have no money to pay you.'

Calver groaned inside. Sometimes he wished his part-time investigator would stop sending him hopeless *pro bono* cases, because eventually it would bankrupt the firm and they'd both be out of a job. He sipped his coffee, mulling. Then again, if she'd sent the women, maybe there was something in it.

'So what's Yolanda in prison for, Isabel?'

'She was the maid in the Dinks kidnap murder case.'

Calver raised his right eyebrow quizzically. The Dinks case had been huge for a while, and not just in the US; a rolling 24-hour media circus, but Calver had thought it was long finished. The child's body had never been found but Yolanda Lopez had been arrested and charged with kidnap, to which they'd later added murder, although the evidence for that was flimsy - a tiny amount of blood and hair found at the scene and a jail house "confession". But she was tried and convicted on all charges, two, three years ago and given life without parole. And Calver had recently read that all her appeals had been exhausted.

No one other than Yolanda had ever been charged although the consensus amongst lawyers and law enforcement at the time had been that she couldn't possibly have acted alone. It was a case that had provided endless fodder for the huge online community of nuts and conspiracy theorists, and there were even a couple of true crime books that purported to solve the riddle of what had really happened that night.

Calver leaned back sipping coffee, not noticing it was now tepid. He stared out of his third floor office window across the Brooklyn street to the majestic Brownstones on the other side. Isabel sat quietly too, pensively, sipping her coffee, waiting for the strange gringo to speak.

'What did you mean when you said, "they will kill her," if you don't get her out of jail? Who will kill her?' he asked.

'The other prisoners. They think she's a child killer. They already blind her in one eye. We don't get her out, she gonna die?' she said, crossing herself. She looked up at Calver and, holding his eyes, said, 'she didn't do nothing wrong. She is innocent.'

'Doesn't matter,' Calver said. 'It's the evidence, Isabel. Always the evidence. Especially the evidence the jury hear on the day, and that day is long gone. But anyway, what makes you think I could do anything now? Last I heard all her appeals were run.'

Isabel looked down in her lap again, as if contemplating something. She said, quietly, 'Yolanda, she say Sapphire Dinks is alive. She know it.'

Calver looked at her, expressionless for a moment. He said,

trying to take the edge off his words, 'Isabel, there was a massive search, and a public appeal and no trace was ever found. The prosecution proved that the child had died, although I'll grant you, that's without a body and on what many thought was pretty shaky evidential ground. But even if Sapphire were alive, how could Yolanda possibly know that, stuck in jail? She's dreaming. Needs something to hold onto. It happens when they know they're never going to get out.'

'But she is sure,' Isabel said emphatically, 'and my sister, she don't lie. She believes it. I told Courtney and she say come see you. Courtney say, you need the work,' she added, looking around the office questioningly, as if the decor might confirm Courtney's assertion.

She was right that he needed the work, but did he need this? The story seemed fantastical. After all this time and scrutiny by all those investigators and lawyers, not to mention all those members of the public, the defendant just happens to know that the person she was convicted of kidnapping and murdering was still alive?

Isabel watched the negative doubt spreading across his face and knew her visit had been a waste of time. She slowly rose to her feet, trying to hide the tears; she had perhaps expected this outcome. She looked down at him. 'I am sorry to have wasted your time. I just wanted to try and save my sisters life, that's all,' she said, her dark eyes full of grief.

The intercom on Calver's desk buzzed. He flicked it impatiently. 'Yes, Hettie?'

'Courtney is here, boss. You want I should send her in?'

Calver studied Isabel standing before him, maybe realizing for the first time what it must have taken for her to come into his office and speak to him. 'Fine,' he said to the intercom. Then he nodded and said, 'sit down, Isabel. We're not finished yet.'

###

'*Qué Pasa*, Isabel?' Pascal said as she wandered in, rare smile, chewing on a bagel, coffee cup in her hand.

She placed the cup down on the desk and nodded at Calver. 'You wanted some high-profile work to bring in the punters, well, here it is,' she said.

'Yeah, and what am I supposed to do with it?' he said. 'All her appeals are done, so there's nowhere to go. What d'you want me to do, teleport her out of jail?'

'Look, Calver,' she said. 'Forget the detail for a minute. Just announcing to the world you're taking it on will generate a mountain of media coverage, and jack up your profile, and much as I hate to say it. You need it.'

'Thanks for reminding me,' he said, but he knew she was right. Still, he couldn't see how taking on a hopeless case was going to help.

Pascal watched him for a moment, observing his troubled mien. She moved over to stand at the window, back to the room. She looked out on the street, taking another bite of her bagel, showering crumbs over the recently vacuumed carpet.

Calver turned back to Isabel. 'What did Yolanda's lawyers say when she told them of her suspicions about Sapphire?'

'Her lawyers no good,' she said, her eyes flaming with anger.

'They trick her. Took her money. Now she got nothing. They kept pushing her for movie and book rights to the story. She told them, there is no story. She didn't do nothing wrong, so she don't have no lawyer now.'

Pascal wandered back, bagel finished. She grabbed a chair, swiveling it around so she could sit on it back to front, sliding in, facing Calver, arms folded over the back. 'You hear that, Calver? You any idea how much those kind of deals can be worth? Book, movie rights' she said, laying it on with a trowel. 'There's your funding.'

Calver ignored her, addressing Isabel. 'Where is Yolanda now, and who's holding her papers?'

'She's in Bedford Hills Max security. I am going to see her Wednesday. I got all her legal stuff in my spare bedroom. Never seen so much paper,' she said.

Pascal reached down and squeezed Isabel's hand. Calver said, 'so what does Yolanda say? What makes her think Sapphire Dinks is still alive?'

'She wouldn't tell me, but when I told her about Courtney, and she work for a lawyer, she said to bring her with me, next visit.'

Calver thought for a moment. 'Okay,' he said. 'Can't hurt to take a look. Hettie can get the papers over here, and you,' he said, finally looking at Pascal, 'can run down to Bedford Hills with Isabel, and have a chat with Yolanda. My guess is she's dreaming. Wishful thinking, but see what you think. It's worth a punt, and hell, I've got the time,' he said, looking at his barren desk. He glanced out the window again, then back across the desk at Isabel. He said, 'and Isabel. Don't go getting your hopes up.'

But Isabel couldn't stop the wide smile from spreading across her face.

###

Next day, after dealing with a nothing DUI case downtown, Calver made his way back to the office and bumped into Pascal as she arrived.

'Hettie told me you got Yolanda's papers. Thought I'd take a look before going down to Bedford Hills tomorrow,' she said.

'Sounds like a plan,' Calver said, checking his watch.

They made their way upstairs to an empty side office where they found the huge stack of papers generated by Yolanda's trial. The files cascaded over chairs and desks, lever arch files, cardboard boxes, bible thick papers on treasury tags piled up to the roof. Luckily Calver knew what to look for, so he rummaged through, checking index sheets, and then tracking down the relevant paperwork, so they ended up with a core pile containing statements, exhibits, police and FBI reports and transcripts of testimony given at trial.

When that was sorted they ordered some Pizza and sat back to read, Calver with a yellow legal pad he proceeded to fill with his spidery scrawl. Pascal sat across the desk from him with a laptop, scrolling through old news and media reports, and occasionally reading an item selected for her from the pile by Calver. She made her own notes on screen.

On occasion as Calver went through the papers he would sit back and look across at Pascal as she filtered out the stuff she was scanning; it was somehow soothing to watch her work. She was ex-British intelligence and clever as hell; perhaps not educated to the highest standards, but she made up for that with the most extraordinary capacity for unorthodox, lateral thinking he had ever witnessed. He wondered what scenarios were playing through her mind as she read up on the strange tale of Sapphire Dinks. He thought back to the worries he had had that she wouldn't stay on in the US after they finished what they had come out there for. That work had essentially been getting him out of Rikers jail and acquitted of murder. That done, she had stayed on, just like him, and more than that, she had helped him set up his new law firm with attorney Morganna Fedler. She had then come on board as their investigator and had flourished. Now she was doing mostly investigative work for Morganna, on the civil side, checking out corporations and individuals. Calver turned his eyes back to the papers.

As he did so, Pascal observed him for a moment, wondering what the little smile had been for as he had surreptitiously watched her. She knew Calver got off on her buccaneering street style, but she doubted that he had any real understanding of what made her tick. Not many people did, but she liked Calver, and that was rare in itself, for her to feel such an emotion about anyone. She knew he was glad she had stayed out there with him after the trouble last year. Maybe she should have gone back to her old life in London but there was nothing waiting for her back in the rainy old UK, and the more she experienced the fast pace of New York, the more she was beginning to feel at home there. She scrolled through some more news footage on her laptop, her mind descending back into the mystery of Sapphire Dinks.

Hours later Hettie popped in to say goodnight to them before shutting up the shop and leaving for home. Shortly after, Calver stretched and yawned. 'So, how d'you meet Isabel Lopez, anyway?' he asked.

She looked up. 'Skid row. Soup kitchen for the homeless out in East Harlem. She's a volunteer there. I was looking for some guy Morganna wanted a statement off, and I struck up a conversation with her.'

Calver nodded and rubbed his eyes. 'So, Dinks,' he said. 'What do we think, on a cursory read through? How about you do some scene setting?'

Pascal stretched and leaned back in her chair, eyes closed, almost as if she were preparing to meditate. For a moment she sat completely motionless, silent, then she began to speak in a quiet tone. 'Okay, crime scene: we're talking triple A security on a palatial gated residence, millionaires' row in Manhattan, overlooking Central Park,' she said, eyes still closed. Calver listened and watched her as she continued her soliloquy. 'There resided the Dinks family comprising parents Robert and Maria, baby daughter Sapphire and the maid, Yolanda Lopez.

'The Dinks family were by current standards, old money, mainly derived from railway era patents from the 1950's. Their fortune was then essentially channeled into charitable trusts that Robert administered, benefiting various good causes. So they were, and are, bloody rich. Maria was Robert's second wife. His first wife, and mother of Sapphire, died, but she was interesting,' Pascal said, opening her eyes and reaching for a can of coke.

'She was a pure bred native American women,' she continued.

'A Navajo whose native name was "Johona" or Sunny, in English, and she was a real campaigner: Greenpeace, the environment, marches, the whole nine yards, and she seems to have been the love of Robert's life. Died of a brain tumor. Maria O'Halloran, the current wife, and Sapphires step-mother, is very different; a Chicago born model, and she has her own small fashion house here and in Mexico City, which she built up as her modeling career wound down.'

As Pascal paused, Calver took over. 'So, time of the kidnap, three and a bit years ago, Sapphire was what, six years old? It was September 18th. Robert left the house that morning at around 8 am as he usually did, and never came home that night - he was at a fund raiser - until 2 am in the morning. Maria had a fashion showing and left the house at 6 pm, and wasn't back until around midnight, and in bed by 1 am. They are both solidly alibied, and there is film of Maria at her show,' Calver said, pulling his notepad over and scanning some of the pages, looking for something.

Pascal continued, 'last sighting of Sapphire was around 9 pm when maid Yolanda Lopez looked in the bedroom. Swore on oath she saw the child sleeping peacefully. Next morning she goes to wake the child at the usual time of around 7 am, she's not there, but a ransom note tied around a cheap mobile phone is, and all hell breaks loose.'

Calver read from his notes, 'so ten-hour window for the snatch. What was Yolanda doing during that period?'

'Yolanda lived in maid's quarters, or annexe to the side of the house. It's a two-bedroom kind of granny flat. There was a child intercom that monitored Sapphire's room and fed into the flat and Sapphire had a buzzer she could use to call Yolanda, but we know she almost never used it. Yolanda testified she retired to her flat around 10 pm where she watched TV. She heard Maria arrive back around midnight, then Yolanda went to bed around 12.30. Didn't hear a peep after that,' Pascal said.

'First problem,' Calver said. 'NYPD say the note has disappeared and they only have the phone. The note apparently said, "we require $25 million in Bitcoin, today or Sapphire will die. We know you have the money. We will not negotiate or produce proof of life. If you contact the authorities she will die. You have one chance to save her. We shall phone you at 7 pm to effect the transfer of funds. She will be released unharmed within 24 hours of payment."'

'They didn't call the police,' Pascal said. 'Robert takes the call at 7 pm, transfers the Bitcoin to the digital currency address given. Sapphire is never seen again. When the family finally call the FBI in, 72 hours later, what d'you know? The trail is cold. Later they are able to deduce that the phone call was made from a position within the Met Life stadium out in East Rutherford, New Jersey and was made during a Taylor Swift concert there. So looking at any CCTV around the stadium was pretty pointless.

'You know,' Pascal added. 'These people were some outfit, because the Feds found nothing. Absolutely nothing.'

'I take it you don't think Yolanda did it, then?' Calver said, watching her with a smile.

'You know, I really don't know,' she replied, checking her phone screen. 'We're just scratching the surface here, and there's nothing obvious either way. But my take is these guys were real pro's, and I'm not sure Yolanda fits the profile. Guess I'll find out tomorrow when I see her.'

'Prosecution's case was she was the inside man, not the brains,' Calver said. 'Their whole case was predicated on the basis there was a ring outside, orchestrating the whole thing. I don't believe it could have been done without inside knowledge and help on the night. That's Yolanda. And, where's the money and where's the body?'

'What about the tiny piece of skin and hair found in the bedroom the prosecutor set so much store by?' Pascal asked.

'As the defense said, that could have been caused by her simply banging her head on a table although the fact that Yolanda couldn't recall any such incident leading up to the kidnap was rather damning,' Calver said.

'What about mum and dad?' Pascal asked.

'Motive?' Calver threw out. 'Okay, Robert's dead, but he was immensely wealthy via the trust, and, by all accounts, absolutely devoted to Sapphire. His suicide 18 months after the kidnap attests to that. Guy died of a broken heart.'

'I agree, but what about Maria?'

'She has a successful fashion business. And what? Her own child, or step-child?' Calver said.

'It happens, but I agree, doesn't make sense. And more importantly, the Feds looked at her, real early on, as you'd expect. Went over her every which way and she came out clean as a whistle.'

Calver checked his watch and yawned again. 'Not much more we can do tonight. Get some sleep, Pascal. Then you can be real bright eyed and bushy tailed tomorrow when you go see Yolanda.'

'Gee, thanks, Calver,' she said

CHAPTER TWO

The drive up to Bedford Hills Maximum Security Correctional Facility had been quick, about an hour, paralleling the Hudson River north to Westchester County, and on into the hamlet of Bedford Hills. They didn't speak much on the way up, Pascal driving and Isabel seemingly preoccupied. On arrival they endured the usual stringent checking process, stowing of personal stuff in lockers, production of ID, searches and pat-downs, then traipsing through a succession of heavy metal gates until they finally arrived at the visitor area and handed over their paperwork for another inspection.

When that was all done they were assigned a table, sat down and waited. It was a large hall-like space with tables and chairs, and a couple of vending machines up against the wall near the doors. Pascal was surprised at how few visitors there were, but it gave them plenty of space to spread out. As she looked about she couldn't help remembering her own time in prison in the UK when she had served a sentence for killing her step-father. She shook herself, ridding her mind of the bad memories. But this place somehow didn't seem so bad. She'd read up on it the night before. Built in around 1900, it housed approximately

900 women, and it had a reasonable reputation, for example for allowing inmates to have children there, and offered some good educational programs.

Pascal looked up as a rather slight women with a striking resemblance to Isabel approached their table. She nodded to Isabel whilst carefully studying Pascal.

'Yo Yolanda,' Isabel said. 'This is Courtney, the friend I told you about who works for the criminal attorney, Jonas Calver, in Brooklyn.'

As Yolanda took her seat Pascal noticed her right eye was cloudy and she was clearly unable to see with it. For a short while Yolanda and Isabel spoke quick fire Spanish which Pascal couldn't follow. It sounded like a lot of affectionate banter, maybe about children and family. Then the conversation became more formal and Pascal heard her name mentioned and that of Calver. All the while Yolanda, with intermittent and shy glances, seemed to be weighing Pascal up with her one good eye.

The sisters seemed to run out of things to say to each other, and then Isabel said she would go and get some snacks from the vending machines over by the wall. As she moved away, Pascal said, simply, without preamble, 'why do you think Sapphire is alive, Yolanda?'

Yolanda frowned, scrutinizing Pascal anew with her good eye, immediately intuiting Pascal was not humoring her. She rubbed a hand across her mouth. 'Because someone who has been with her recently, and liked her, wrote and told me so,' she said, pausing to lick her lips. 'This girl write me a note, funny way so the censors don't get it but still enough in there that only someone who knows Sapphire could have wrote it,' she said.

Pascal held Yolanda's eye, unwavering. 'You know how many sightings there have been from cranks?' Pascal said. 'When they set up that hotline and web page the whole thing crashed repeatedly, and they've still got stuff on the internet, so why do you believe what's in a note? They asked for money yet?'

'I believe she's alive,' Yolanda said quietly. 'You know, Sapphire's mother. She Navajo Indian, and she teach Sapphire lullaby from a baby, and the girl's always humming it. Never came out in the media, this stuff. So this person must have been with her recently. You could not know this about her less you spend time with her. She got bright blue eyes and crooked teeth which is what the media always concentrated on, an this person, she never mention that, she just tell of the lullaby.'

Isabel returned with some snacks and drinks, immediately noticing the tension at the table. She quietly handed out some candy bars, not interrupting, watching Pascal leaning back in her chair.

'What exactly did this note say? D'you have it with you?' Pascal asked.

'No. We not allowed to bring stuff in here, but I read it so many times, I know every word.'

'Tell me about it.'

Yolanda bit into a candy bar, collecting her thoughts. 'It came about a month ago. It was on one piece of scrappy paper, no address, and it looked like a child's writing.'

'What did it say?'

Yolanda closed her eyes. 'The note say, "I am scared. I miss my

friend. She sings *Shii Na Sha*. She spell for me. She tell me if I get out
to find Yolanda and you will help us.

Tilly-May."'

Pascal took a sip of coke, all the while watching Yolanda, who
calmly returned Pascal's gaze, waiting. 'How many kids these days
even know how to post a letter, especially to a US prison. It's all text
messages and emails?' Pascal said, almost to herself. 'But then maybe
it's not from a child. Maybe its from some clever guy with an angle.
Then you'll get another note, now you're hooked, asking for money.'

'I don't think so,' Yolanda replied slowly, calmly, convinced.
'That's the name of the lullaby, *Shii Na Sha*. She always humming it.'

Pascal suddenly stood up and walked away from the table
towards the vending machines at the side of the room. After a moment,
Yolanda and Isabel began to speak again, slowly this time, in hushed
tones of Spanish. Pascal looked at the snacks in the vending machine,
not really seeing them, as she weighed up what Yolanda had told her.
She wandered back to the table deep in thought.

'Tilly-May?' Pascal said as she re-took her seat.

'Means nothing to me,' Yolanda said. 'Don't know anyone of
that name.'

'I'm assuming you get your share of crank mail, such a high-
profile case?'

'I do, but they filter most of it out. As I said, I believe this one.
Isabel told me what your boss say. I am not stupid and I don't have no
dreams about saving myself, but I believe Sapphire is alive and she's in
danger, and she needs me. Now, will you help us?'

'Let me ask you something, Yolanda, that may sound silly. Did you kidnap Sapphire?'

Yolanda smiled. 'Hey, we all innocent in here, right? Look, you don't know me but Isabel does. Okay, she family, but she know I don't lie. I would never harm Sapphire. I loved her. You see, me and my husband - he long gone now,' she said wistfully. 'We couldn't have kids, so Sapphire was like a daughter to me, especially after her mother died. Maria, her step-mother was okay, but Sapphire never got over losing her mum.'

Pascal continued to watch Yolanda, her look almost piercing in its intensity, as if she was trying to see into Yolanda's soul, searching for truth. 'Good enough,' Pascal finally said. 'I'll talk to my boss, as it's his call, but before I go we need to talk money and resources as Calver, he don't work for free.'

'And I guess you don't either, right?' Yolanda said with that quick knowing smile again. 'But I got nothing to trade, so I guess Isabel was wrong about you and you can't help us.'

'But you do have something, Yolanda. Film and book rights to the story. Calver can negotiate you fair deals on that stuff and take a cut to fund us in investigating and appealing if we can dig something up. What d'you say?'

Isabel directed a burst of quick fire Spanish at Yolanda. She nodded. 'I don't care about the rights and the money. Take it,' she said. 'But find Sapphire, that's all I want. Meantime I gotta try and stay alive in here,' she said, her face darkening and her eyes taking on a hunted look as she began to withdraw back into her shell.

Pascal stood and shook Yolanda's hand. 'Would you mail the note to us?' Pascal said, handing Yolanda her card. 'We will examine and copy it and return to you.'

'Fine,' Yolanda said. Then she was gone.

###

A few days later Pascal sat across the desk from Calver studying the note received in the mail from Yolanda.

'Shame she didn't get the envelope it came in for a post mark,' Calver said. 'Tilly-May? Not a lot to go on. Gotta be a kid, right? That kind of scrawl?'

'Easy enough to fake a kids handwriting, Calver, or even get a kid to write it for you.'

'You think it's a shakedown?' he said

'I don't know,' she said. 'Not necessarily.'

'So what's your thinking?' Calver said, looking up as Hettie brought in some letters for him to sign.

Pascal's brow furrowed as she thought it through. 'If you wanted to hustle Yolanda, you'd do your homework, and it would be easy enough to check out the Native American angle, like Sapphire's background for example,' she said. 'Depending on your resources you might even be able to get to ex-cons who'd been in Bedford with Yolanda and say picked up some scuttlebutt about Sapphire.'

'Yeah, but as Yolanda told you, you wouldn't know about the lullaby unless you'd been with Sapphire, and it's not something Yolanda would have told anyone. She made that clear when you spoke to her.'

'That the note?' Hettie asked, still standing by the desk

Calver nodded.

'May I?' she asked.

'Sure,' he nodded, handing it to her. 'Come and join the party, why don't you?'

He turned back to Pascal. 'I don't think I buy it as a hustle either,' he said. 'Unless you knew Sapphire was alive, which unless you were the kidnappers, how would you? Why would you try such a long-odds hustle, especially as Yolanda's in jail and got no money; far easier just to sell the story?'

'I agree. A hustle's a long shot.'

'Okay well let's assume it's kosher for now,' Calver said. 'But then the problem is that the text gives us nothing.' He read it through again slowly and out loud, Pascal and Hettie listening carefully:

'"*I am scared. I miss my friend. She sings Shii Na Sha. She spell for me. She tell me if I get out to find Yolanda and you will help us. Tilly-May.*"'

He rubbed his face in frustration. 'No clues in there. Gives us the name of the lullaby, she's scared, misses her friend who told her to find Yolanda who will help them?'

'True enough,' Pascal replied, 'but it does give us a name - Tilly-May. And also, what about the phrase: "if I get out"?'

'Yeah, so the fact we've got the note, suggests, what? She got out?' Calver said. 'But out of where?'

Pascal closed her eyes. 'Let's go back and look at what we got here?' she said. 'When you remove all the bullshit, what we got is a basic kidnap ransom job. So let's just assume the writer of this little note was kidnapped as well, but has escaped.'

'But where does that take us? Not very far,' he said.

'Maybe, but surely first step should be to check out missing girls, using Sapphire as a template; same age, class, ethnicity and location,' Pascal said.

'I'll buy that. Maybe we can come up with a match for this Tilly-May,' Calver said

'You know,' Hettie said, tentatively, puzzled, 'I think there's something here near the bottom of the page,' she said, holding the note up, lightly rubbing the surface. 'Maybe something's traced through from the sheet that was immediately above it on the pad.'

'Let me see?' Pascal said. She got up and took the note over to the window and held it to the light, slowly examining it, back and front, and running her fingers over the surface. She came back to the desk. 'You gotta a pencil, Calver?'

'Sure,' he said, handing one over, intrigued, watching her. 'What you got?'

'Let's see.'

She gently began to shade the pencil over a small area on the bottom right hand corner of the note. Calver hunched forward, watching as letters began to appear, white against the pencil shading. When she finished she slid the note across the desk for Calver to look at. Starting at the edge of the note, the letters revealed the words, "dad Juarez".

Hettie, looking down over his shoulder, said, 'kids' father?'

'Could be.'

'Juarez is a Mexican name,' Pascal said. 'Yolanda's Mexican?'

'We're just going around in circles,' Calver said. 'Mexican connection just gets her in deeper.'

As he spoke the phone in the outer office began to ring. Hettie said, 'that must be your eleven o'clock.'

He nodded. 'Okay, we'll have to come back to this,' he said, reluctantly drawing the meeting to a close.

###

For the next couple of days Pascal was tied up running down a lead in a civil case for Calver's law partner, Morganna Fedler, but most of the time the Dinks case held center stage in her mind.

She found the whistle blowing corporate fraudster hiding in plain sight working in a Deli called Pop's Meat Co in the East Village. After reporting the location to Morganna, it was gone 9 pm. On a whim she called NYPD detective Daly. He had helped her out with Calver's trial the year before. Okay, he hadn't helped her out to start with, he'd tried to nail Calver, but eventually she'd talked him around and he'd ended up helping them out. She liked the guy. He picked up first ring

'Hay, Daly,' she said. 'How d'you fancy buying a tourist a genuine Pastrami on Rye down the East Village?'

'Courtney,' he said, voice neutral.

Maybe he was bugged she hadn't returned his calls a while back. 'Sorry, man,' she said. 'I know you called me, but you know how it is, and I was in like this kind of delicate situation, and time was running and—'

'Where are you?' he asked

'A Deli in the East Village. It's kind of a stake-out, waiting for the boss to show, but man, the food sure looks good, and I was getting kind of hungry.'

'And you lost your wallet and thought of me, right?'

'Don't be like that, Daly. Where are you? Close?'

'Close enough,' he said. 'Stake-out you said. Maybe I better come down, make sure you're not breaking any laws.'

'That's the spirit,' she said. She gave him the address.

Five minutes later she watched him swerve his car out of the traffic and into the curb, lurching to a halt. She was standing at an intersection about 50 meters from the Deli, leaning against a wall. He clambered out the car and ambled over, nodding at her. Big, athletic build, square jaw and blue suit, but he wasn't what he looked - the all American apple pie eating quarter back - he was almost the opposite, quite a subtle guy, as she'd found out. And he didn't miss much with those granite-colored, cold, watchful eyes, that she knew they could also turn warm and soulful, with the right stimulus.

'Who's the mark,' he asked without preamble, looking over at the deli.

'Juanita Vasquez, accountant,' Pascal said. 'Some say for the mob, but we don't want her for that. My lawyer boss wants her as a witness in a civil suit she's running. Claims for 10 million bucks' damages, but Vasquez is also a defendant in criminal proceedings for fraud, and that's why she's skipped bail and is running.'

'How d'you locate her,' he asked, his eyes sizing Pascal up. 'Never mind,' he added, seeing her expression become distant and closed. 'Pastrami on Rye, you said. Let's go.'

They walked over and entered the deli. It was a small joint, two people serving behind the counter, one looked like the proprietor, male and elderly with a solicitous smile, the other was Juanita Vasquez. Hispanic, slim, but too well dressed for the job, and with a skittish look in her eyes. Daly ordered a couple of Pastrami on Rye's whilst Pascal watched the woman up close, surreptitiously comparing her to the photo she had on her phone. It was a match.

They took their sandwiches and a couple of cans of coke outside and sat at a table on the sidewalk. To Pascal's English eyes the sandwich looked gigantic, filled with rolls of succulent beef. She took a huge bite and began munching away. After a moment she paused. 'Wow, Daly,' she said through a mouthful. 'This is seriously good.'

He nodded, amused expression on his face, which turned serious. 'I thought you'd have been hitched by now, Courtney. Wedding bells. You and Jonas Calver,' he said.

She spluttered through a mouthful. 'Daly, you may be a detective but when it comes to amour, you don't know shit. Calver is more like a brother to me. No, you're way off base there boy.'

He nodded, and she thought she detected relief in his expression. 'And you're still here? Not getting homesick?' he asked.

'You know what, Daly,' she said.

He shook his head, amused expression back.

'I love New York.'

'I'm glad to hear it, so that means you'll be staying?' he persisted.

'For the time being. Say, Daly, you ever work a missing persons case?' she asked him

'Back in the day, sure,' he said. 'Why? Oh, now I get it, you want something? That's why you called me. You—'

'That's not why I called you,' she insisted. 'Alright, I thought I might need some help with our lady friend in the deli, but I could handle that myself. No, I thought about you, and I thought why not? You know, Daly, I got no real friends in this town and it can get lonely.'

'You're breaking my heart,' he said, but he was smiling. 'So as your new best friend, maybe I can take you to dinner this week.'

'You already are,' she said. 'But sure, name your day. We'll do it again.'

'I'll call you,' he said. 'So, you gotta a misper, eh? Tell me about it?'

Pascal took a sip of coke to wash the last of her Pastrami down, her eyes watching Vasquez through the window of the deli. 'We got a case, I can't go into details yet, cause its sensitive. Missing young girl called Tilly-May, but that's *all* we got. Don't know where she's from, who her family are, any of that. We just know she's probably between maybe 6 and 9, and taken from her family any time during say, the last 2 or 3 years.'

'Jesus!' he said as he turned to watch the street, his eyes taking on a calculating look. He rubbed his face. 'You're not telling me the half of it, are you? And let me guess something else, what you have told me is almost pure speculation?'

Her face remained immobile, unreadable. 'Look, Daly,' she said. 'I'll tell you as soon as I can. Got to get the okay from the client and Calver.'

He watched her for a long moment. 'It's another girl, isn't it?' he said, nodding his head, and again she was surprised at how quickly he could jump mental barriers and make connections that more conventional minds would never get.

'Maybe.'

He pulled out his cell-phone. 'I'll check that name for you,' he said.

She listened as he phoned in and spoke to a couple of people. After five minutes he said, 'nothing on that name, but thousands of missing girls in that age range every year. Most turn up, but plenty don't. But what if it's a false name?'

'Then we're fucked,' she said. 'But thanks for trying, Daly. I was being straight when I said I'd tell you all about it when I can.' She looked up at the deli. 'Shit!' she said.

Daly smiled. It was a bail bondsman who was leading Vasquez out the door, hands secured.

'Can't you do something, Daly?' Pascal said. 'Morganna will be here soon.

'Sorry, Courtney, I can't interfere with their lawful business,' he said.

Pascal got up and stalked off, cellphone to her ear as she relayed the news to Morganna that her witness had flown the coop, but maybe she'd be able to talk to her in lock-up. When she turned back Daly had gone, but then a text pinged in saying he'd call her.

Later she sat alone in a bar, hunched over looking down into her scotch wondering whether she was so happy in New York after all. The big city could be the loneliest place on earth, if you didn't know anyone, and she'd always found it hard to make friends. Lovers were easy, but friends? She guessed for now Calver was her only friend, and they hardly hung out, unless it was for work.

'Top you up, honey?' the barmaid asked, interrupting her thoughts

Pascal's eyes came back into focus. The girl was tall and lithe, like an amazon, eyes green and smoky. 'Why not,' Pascal said. 'If you join me?'

'Sure,' the girl said, pouring another glass.

'What's that accent?' Pascal asked, intrigued.

'New Orleans, Creole,' she said. 'Like it?'

'Love it.'

As their eyes met the girl laughed and Pascal felt that frisson of attraction passing between them like electricity, but then something else flickered in her brain, a name in the background noise triggering something, a memory in her head. She looked up at the TV over the bar as the commentator said it again, and her eyes re-focused on the screen, this time alert. It was a news strand about the killing of women in a city in northern Mexico.

She watched the screen for a few moments, a cold chill running down her spine. She finished her drink. She looked at the girl lingeringly, longingly, competing forces raging in her head. 'I have to go,' she finally said, sadly.

The girl frowned. 'Your loss, honey,' she said, turning away abruptly.

Pascal left the bar feeling even more lonely, arriving at Calver's rented place a few minutes later, unannounced. He opened the door about to say something, but seeing her expression, decided not to; he ushered her in.

'It's not a person,' she said, without preamble. '"dad Juarez". Its a place.'

'Where?'

'I think its Ciudad Juárez, northern Mexico, just across the border from El Paso.'

'You think that's where Tilly-May is?'

'Could be, but hell, it's the only clue we got and we got to start somewhere.'

'I seem to remember reading something about it,' Calver said, uncertainly. 'Gangs of serial killers, and endless drug wars? That the place?'

Pascal smiled thinly. 'That's the place.'

Calver looked thoughtful. 'I sent the Tilly-May note to a forensics guy I know, to see if there's anything else on it we didn't pick up. He's promised to phone me tomorrow. Come to the office at 11 and we'll see what we got.'

'I'll be there,' she said.

###

Next morning they convened in Calver's office at 11 a m, Hettie hovering surreptitiously by the side of the desk. Calver put the forensic guy on speaker-phone, and after a bit of banter they got down to business. The paper on which the note was written was universal and cheap, no watermark or distinguishing features, and could be purchased virtually anywhere in the world. He confirmed the words "dad Juarez" had been traced through from writing on another sheet of paper placed on top of the note.

'Anything else?' Calver asked.

Hettie leaned forward towards the phone.

The guy coughed. 'Yes,' he said. 'I won't bore you with the tests we subjected the paper to, suffice it to say we found a series of penciled letters that seem to have been rubbed out, but also with some gaps between them, but unfortunately the letters do not appear on the surface to make any sense.'

'What are the letters?' Pascal asked.

'Okay, it looks like, "c-u-gap-gap-gap-u-e." Then second word, "m-o-gap-gap-p-o-gap-gap-t-z-i-n."' He said.

'What's it mean?' Calver asked.

'I have absolutely no idea. That's your problem, my friend, so over to you,' he said. 'Good to speak with you, Jonas. We must catch up sometime,' he added before hanging up.

'So what's it mean?' Hettie asked, echoing Calver. 'And why did she rub it out?'

'Maybe it wasn't her. Maybe someone else was doodling on there,' Pascal said.

'It's a riddle we're not going to solve here and now,' Calver said. 'We don't have enough information.'

'I agree,' Pascal said. 'The only real clue we have is the place name, Ciudad Juarez. And I think we need to move on it now, before someone takes another pop at Yolanda.'

'You want to go down there?' Calver asked

'Of course I do,' she said. 'Yolanda's genuine, I have no doubt about that, but the note? Who knows? So let's find out. Shit, we've got the rights which could be worth a fortune, even if there's nothing in this, so there is no real downside?'

'Apart from your neck, honey,' Hettie said.

'Although,' Calver mused, 'it could even add to the value of the rights - another strand to Yolanda's story, the investigation and what followed.'

'And what about Courtney's safety?' Hettie persisted. 'She go down there, who knows what she'll find and how dangerous it could be.'

'I'll be fine, Hettie,' Pascal said, 'but thanks for your concern.'

Hettie looked at them both as if they were mad. She was about to come back at them but then the phone rang in the outer office. She took a last look at them, shrugged, and went to answer it.

Calver nodded. 'So how you want to play it?'

'I'll have another chat with my friend detective Daly at NYPD and see if I can wrangle some type of contact down there, even just a name. He's already run a missing persons on Tilly-May and drawn a blank. Then I'll see if Isabel fancies a trip to Mexico. My Spanish won't cut it down there.'

'Sounds good,' Calver said. 'I'll go visit Yolanda and get her signed up for the rights and take a statement from her.'

'You know, Calver,' Pascal said, a shadow of concern flitting across her face. 'Maybe we should hold fire on any announcements to the media about this case, just until I've had a scout around. I think it could be dangerous to alert people that someone else is taking another cold hard look at the facts.'

'Agreed,' he said without hesitation.

'Okay,' Pascal said. 'I'm going to go see Isabel, then I'll head down Mexico way.'

'Keep me informed. And Pascal?'

'Yeah.'

'Take care.'

'Always.'

###

They sat around the table in Isabel's cosy kitchen, all blackened pots and pans on the wall, a large crucifix and Madonna shrine in the corner and a big fridge covered with multi-colored post-it notes. Pascal was chewing on a slice of homemade Pizza and Isabel was cradling a small grandchild in her lap. 'Ciudad Juárez?' she repeated. 'Yes, I know it. I have a cousin lives nearby in Chihuahua City, Hernan. He's a carpenter. He often works in Juarez. What's the connection?'

'We think the note from this Tilly-May may have come from there,' Pascal said.

'So Sapphire could be there?'

'Maybe,' Pascal said, evenly, not wanting to get Isabel's hopes up. 'I was thinking you come with me, for the Spanish, but maybe safer you stay here and you introduce me to Hernan. Maybe he can get me a place to stay, as a hotel's no good for what I have in mind?'

'You want me to call him now?'

'Why not, but don't tell him what we're doing. Tell

him…….Tell him, I'm looking for a missing husband.'

For twenty minutes or so Pascal held the sleeping grandchild on her lap whilst Isabel spoke to Hernan in Spanish on the land-line. When she replaced the receiver, she was smiling. 'When he works in Juarez, he stay with his wife's sister. He will get you in there. He will meet you at the airport and he's happy to be your guide if you need it,' she said.

CHAPTER THREE

Ciudad Juárez international airport sits small and serene, a single terminal, sparsely populated with staff who looked like they would rather be somewhere else. Pascal stood around for 30 minutes waiting for an entry visa stamp in her passport, then she was moving towards the exits, traveling light with just a rucksack.

As she came out of the terminal building the heat hit her like a blast from a steel furnace. As she looked around trying to get used to the glare of the sun a tall wiry walnut brown man with a mustache approached her tentatively, with a shy smile. 'Miss Hansen?' he said.

It took her a moment to remember her cover name. 'That's me,' she said. 'Hernan?'

'*Si*. Come. I have the car,' he said. She followed him over to a beat-up old Camaro. She climbed in and they slowly moved off into the light mid-morning traffic.

As they drove the scenery looked to Pascal almost like a moon landscape. Wide open streets, almost deserted apart from the odd car and truck, the highway stretching away into the distance. Virtually all the buildings seemed to be single storey, interspersed with billboards, and there seemed to be endless telegraph poles connected together by huge numbers of cables strung across the streets, and in the distance rust colored mountains as a majestic backdrop.

'I take you to my wife's sister house,' Hernan said in halting English. 'She care for you, *si*?'

'Thank you, Hernan. Isabel sends her love to you and your family.'

'*Gracias Señorita,*' he said. They drove on in companionable silence for a while. Hernan fiddled around with the cars audio system until he found some quiet mariachi music. As Pascal listened, she thought back to the meal she had had with Detective Daly the day before. She had thought long and hard about how much to tell him, because he was clever and would see through it if there was too much bullshit, so she came as clean as she could, but not everything. She half smiled recalling the way his fork of pasta, dripping with tomato sauce had stopped mid-flight, half way towards his mouth when she told him she was looking for Sapphire Dinks. She had played it down by saying they thought Yolanda was dreaming and there was absolutely nothing in it, but if there was any chance, they had to take a look, if only to placate Yolanda. And they were getting paid, with the funding from the film and book rights, so what the hell. Why not, right? She told him that Tilly-May was the young girl that they had a tenuous line on. They believed she might be in Ciudad Juárez and she was going down there to check it out.

He'd said, 'man, I knew you were crazy, but this is insane. You know how dangerous it is down there? You poke your head in a hornet's nest and then think you can just walk away. You'll be a tourist down there. You know what the *Federales* are like and their attitude to women? And Calver? He's gonna let you go down there on your own?'

'Daly, I didn't know you cared?' she'd said with a smile.

But he'd been pretty wound up by then. 'Don't joke, Pascal, cause it could cost you your life.'

'Spare me the melodramatics, Daly,' she'd said. 'If you're so concerned give me a name I can use down there, a contact, preferably from the Drug Enforcement Agency.'

That had got him thinking. They'd knocked back a few more beers while he ruminated, Pascal getting the impression he was dragging things out so he could spend more time with her. He eventually came up with a contact, Hispanic guy who'd worked with him on a trans-border drugs bust in New York couple of years back. Trouble is he thought the guy was based in Mexico City, which was hundreds of miles south of Juarez, but he'd promised to look the guy up and see what he could do.

Before they'd parted he'd asked her what her cover was going to be? That had made her stop and think. The thing she'd told Isabel about looking for a husband wasn't going to cut it, so she'd back and forthed it with Daly some. Eventually they'd come up with: journalist. Catherine Hansen, NYC freelancer with fake Facebook and linkedin profile. She was going back to Juarez to do a follow up article ten years on from her last visit, concentrating on how the city had changed. As part of that process she was to stay with a local family for a while so she could experience life on the street.

Later Daly had called her as she was leaving for the airport. His guy had come through. They had someone in Juarez - no name - he would make contact with her. She should text Daly her address and number when she was in place and then wait. Daly had made it clear that this was a favor from his friend, and whether the guy down there talked to her or helped was up to him and would be outside official DEA business. She was on her own, and God help her.

With the memory of Daly's injunction ringing in her ears Pascal settled her head back against the rest and was soon fast asleep, waking only when the car began to slow as they arrived at their destination.

###

Pascal's first week in her new home went slowly as she tried to acclimatize herself to her surroundings. The small, immaculately clean, two-bedroomed house was situated in San Antonio, a neighborhood to the north west of the city, a kind of shantytown of small breeze-block built single storey houses with small back yards, iron fences, washing lines and innumerable mangy dogs.

Hernan's sister-in-law, Claudia Rodriguez, wasn't there much, seeming to work all hours at the factory, so Pascal spent most of her time with Claudia's teenage daughter, Ana. She was studying tourism at the local college and was excited about having Pascal to stay. They hadn't done much apart from visiting the *El Chamizal* park up on the northernmost border of the city, and mostly Pascal had stayed around the house, researching on her lap-top, pretending to write the article and trying out her Spanish. But now she was starting to get frustrated; she needed to get a line on Tilly-May.

She sat at a plastic table on the jerry-built concrete veranda that stretched out into the tiny, scrubby back yard of the house. She was sipping a coke and watching the street through the back fence. It was mid-morning, the sun rising hot and fast, the street quiet, few cars, a couple of stray dogs patrolling the broken pavements and the odd passerby. She was playing around with a piece of paper on which she had written the indistinct pencil words Calver's forensics guy had discovered on the note from Tilly-May, but she still wasn't getting anywhere with it. She figured she'd looked at it so long she was going cross-eyed.

She looked up as Ana wandered out, cell-phone clamped to her ear, whispering sweet nothings. Must be her boyfriend, Enrique. Ana was seventeen years old, tall and willowy with short black hair and big brown eyes.

Not wanting to listen in on Ana's phone call - she was starting to get the basics of Spanish - she got up and wandered over to the back fence to look out on the street, sipping her coke.

When she wandered back Ana had finished her call and was looking intently at Pascal's doodling on the sheet of paper. 'What's this, a riddle?' she asked in her excellent English. 'You know, Cathy, I love puzzles, crosswords, sudoku.'

'Yeah, it's a puzzle all right. Its driving me nuts,' Pascal said.

'You know what it looks like to me?' Ana said, eyes filled with curiosity. 'Aztec, the ancient South and Central American language. Some call it Nahuatl, and some still speak it. We studied it some at school. Let me take this away and have a look,' she said, waving the sheet of paper at Pascal.

'Be my guest,' Pascal said. They both looked up to watch as Enrique pulled up to the curb in his silver colored open-top jeep. He was about five years older than Ana, slick, with bad-boy stamped all over him. Pascal didn't like him. He climbed languidly out of the jeep and sauntered over to the fence, opening the gate and coming through. He was medium height, slicked over black hair, shades, so you virtually never saw his eyes, and a kind of curl to his lip that seemed to waiver between petulance and arrogance. He greeted Ana and they hugged. He nodded at Pascal.

'Pretty American lady still here, eh?' he said in his heavily accented English.

'Apparently,' Pascal said, rising to her feet.

As she turned to go, he said. 'You know bar work? I talk my boss about you. He say if you want bar work down Gomez Morin Street, go talk to him. Lots of gringo customer?'

It was the most he had ever said to her.

'Hey, why not, Cathy?' Ana said, excited. 'You need to get out of here and see the city, to write that article.'

Pascal on the point of dismissing it out of hand, stopped herself. It did make sense. She needed to get out, as nothing was happening, and maybe some physical movement would shake something loose. She looked at Enrique. 'Why not,' she said. 'Set it up.'

He nodded, arrogant smile back in place. He put a phone to his ear and began to speak rapid Spanish. Ana slid her arm through his as he spoke, smiling all the time at Pascal.

Enrique tapped his phone off and said, 'It's the Cantina Gold on the Boulevard. Take a taxi and he'll see you there at three.'

Cantina Gold looked seedy at 3 pm in the afternoon, but Pascal guessed it probably scrubbed up pretty good when the sun went down. She imagined how the switched off neon lights spread over the contours of the building would make quite a spectacle when lit up against the night skyline. She rapped loud and hard on the outer door to get some attention. Nothing happened; the place seemed stone dead. As she was contemplating searching for a back entrance, an old lady holding a little white dog in her arms materialized in the depths of the building and approached the door. She looked through the glass, sucking on her teeth. There were some metallic sounds as she slipped the bolts and opened the door. She eyed Pascal up and down suspiciously for a moment, then turned and led her through the darkened bar area to the back where she gestured towards a closed door, and then left, all without uttering a single word. Pascal, starting to lose her patience, banged loudly on the door.

A moment later a voice from within, '*Si, entrar.*'

She opened the door and went in. It was a small box-room, one filing cabinet and a desk with a large Mexican guy sitting behind it smoking a cigar. He had a drink on the table and a cell-phone to his ear into which he was speaking quietly. He flicked his eyes over Pascal and gestured to a chair across the desk from him.

She studied him. Frayed cuffs on his white shirt, sweat stains under his arms, dark shadows under his eyes and a general air of despondency, but then a tired smile as he finished his call.

'I crack a joke to Enrique about needing some gringo bar staff with the tourists here and he sends me you,' he said, taking a cloth from his pocket and wiping some sweat from his brow. 'A Journalist he say? But you don't look like one to me,' he said, and she could now see a certain watchfulness in his eyes. The shopworn air was probably a useful front, make people drop their guard.

Before she could answer, he was speaking again, English pretty good. 'You done bar work? You mix a Mojito? Come, show me at the bar,' he said, rising quickly, surprising her, moving past her to the door. She got up and followed him back through the darkened area to the bar, where he flicked the lights.

'I am Monteros. Just Monteros, and this is my bar,' he said, waving his hand around, before adding, 'for now,' with a strange expression on his face.

Pascal held her hand out. 'Catherine Hansen. Nice place,' she said, looking at the incredibly well stocked shelves behind her. There were bottles everywhere, and good expensive labels. And it looked like someone had been in earlier as there was fresh fruit set out, sliced lime, lemon and oranges.

'One Mojito coming up,' she said, dropping her bag and rolling up her sleeves.

Monteros leaned over and pressed a button under the bar and a moment later crunching rock music - the old Robert Palmer classic, Addicted to Love - started playing through speakers all around the room. He held his watch up and shouted, 'Go!'

Pascal was moving as he spoke, whirling smoothly into action, almost like a dancer, her hand sliding a small cut Collins glass off the shelf, then half a fresh lime from the saucer, swiveled onto a plastic juicer into the glass, then some sugar. Handful of fresh mint leaves, five or six dropped in and mashed up against the side. She couldn't see the ice until Monteros slalomed it down the counter to her. Cracked rocks spooned in about a third up the side, large bottle of Bacardi back-handed off the shelf and flipped up, spinning over her shoulder into her other hand, generous slug in, ice crackling away, then topping it all out with soda water. She slid the glass along the bar to Monteros, moved up and dropped the squeezed half lime and a couple of mint leaves on top, then stepped back, done.

Monteros stopped his watch and leaned down and switched the music off. He held the drink up to the light, frosting now showing on the side of the glass. 'Thirty-five seconds. Looks good,' he said. He took a sniff, then a small sip. 'Very good.'

'Should be,' she said. 'I worked bar in Cuba three months, back in the day. They make the best Mojito in the world.'

He looked at her some more, sizing her up. 'Be here at eight to start your first shift,' he said. He nodded and walked off back towards his office.

She watched him go, enjoying the buzz, then she left.

###

Ana seemed subdued when Pascal got back. And when she told her she'd got the job at Cantina Gold, that didn't raise a smile either. Then it came out that Enrique worked the door there, bouncer and security, and maybe Ana wasn't so pleased Pascal would be spending so much time with her boyfriend. Pascal told her that actually she liked girls, which wasn't exactly a lie but it placated Ana somewhat and put a smile back on her face.

Just before Pascal was about to leave for her shift, Ana came into the bedroom looking studious, reading glasses perched on the end of her nose. She was carrying Pascal's scrap of paper with the doodles on. 'Doesn't make sense,' she said.

'What doesn't?'

'Well, I've spent a lot of time messing about with this, down the library and on-line,' she said. 'Lots of different combinations of letters and words. I've substituted likely letters into the gaps, and the only phrase I have come up with is silly. In Nahuatl, it would be: "We will eat your daughter?"'

Pascal's eyes narrowed. 'Explain,' she said, checking her watch. Wouldn't do to be late for her first shift. She heard the taxi hooting outside.

Ana said, 'the only words I can come up with, filling in the gaps, are: "*Cuazque*." Missing letters, a-z-q. Meaning, literally, "we will eat". And "*Mochpochtzin*". Missing letters, c-h, twice. Meaning literally, "your daughter."

Pascal grabbed her bag, starting for the door, mind running on overdrive.

'What's it mean?' Ana asked, puzzled.

'Later,' Pascal said, not wanting to articulate the dark thoughts that were starting to circle around inside her head.

By 10.30 p m Cantina Gold was moderately busy, the after-work crowd having cleared out to make way for the more populous night owls who were beginning to show up in numbers. It was a strange kind of bar; slightly old-fashioned. It stretched out down the side of the street with tables for eating and space in the middle for dancing or just standing, and there were booths as well on the other side of the dance floor.

Behind the bar Pascal was paired with Dominga, a pitch-black girl from Detroit. She seemed friendly but reserved, but she knew her bar work; slick, quick and economical. They had barely spoken other than, Hi, how you doing. Dominga was working at the other end of the bar to Pascal, but as the crowd thinned, they moved closer together. Pascal had seen no sign of the owner, Monteros, but Enrique was there, out front on the door. He seemed to be effective, as there had been no trouble.

Pascal took a sip of her spring water as Dominga hunched up on the bar next to her. 'Glad you can cut it,' the girl said quietly. 'Not like the usual people he puts me with, don't know their ass from their elbow.'

'Thanks,' Pascal said, turning slightly to smile at her. The girl was mid-twenties, voluptuous figure that was well covered in a conservative dark top. 'You been here long?' Pascal asked her

'About three months. Do another couple then back to the States. What are you running from?' she asked with a knowing look.

'Me? I'm a journalist trying to get the inside track on Juarez, for a story.'

'Uh huh. If you say so, honey,' she said, moving back up the bar.

As she did so, Pascal looked over at the door, watching as two guys came in with Enrique tagging along, talking and smiling. There was a kind smoothness about the way the two men moved through the crowd, towards the rear where Monteros's office was situated. They seemed to shake Enrique off with some finesse, despite his rather clingy-looking persistence. He watched them go with a kind of wistful expression on his face. He looked up and caught Pascal watching him, scowled and returned to his post on the door.

Pascal served some more drinks. Twenty minutes later the two guys came out, this time with Monteros in their slipstream, looking like he was kind of pleading with them, his hand on the lead guys arm. Lead guy shook it off and said something that seemed to stop Monteros in his tracks. He dropped his hands, shrugged, watched the two guys for a moment, then turned and made his way back to his office. The two men walked towards the exit and stopped, seeming to change their minds. They turned back and made for the bar, got up on stools and ordered drinks from Dominga.

Pascal looked them over from a few yards away. Lead guy was medium height, kinda chubby with a baby-face, smooth brown skin and a quick unsettling smile. The other guy looked like muscle, big and rangy with a dead, flat, emotionless face that gave the impression you'd need to drive a nail through his kneecap to get his attention.

'Hey, nigger,' lead guy was saying to Dominga, having fun. 'This drink's no good. Change it. I want Remy brandy.' He nodded to the big guy, smiling. He turned back, lifted his glass up and poured the contents on the bar, then placed the glass rim down in the puddle of drink.

Dominga looked frightened. She lifted the glass, wiped the bar, and reached back for a bottle of Remy Martin. Lead guy nodded to the big guy, who said, as if on cue, 'I don't like mine either.' He poured his on the bar as well. Pascal looked outside for Enrique. He was there, watching through the glass, but then he turned his back and walked away. He wasn't going to help any.

Now lead guy had reached over and cupped Dominga's chin in his hand and was drawing her face close to his. He was whispering something to her, and Pascal could see the spittle spraying off his lips. Dominga dropped her hands to her sides in supplication, maybe thinking don't resist, and they'll go away.

But Pascal knew better. She moved up the bar carrying a glass filled with Absolut Peppar vodka, which was all she could find in a hurry. She knew it was meant to be spicy as hell, like the hottest Habaneros peppers. She chucked the contents of the glass in big guys face, and while he was putting his hands up to protect himself she grabbed lead guys hand off Dominga's chin, twisting it over and slamming it down on the bar, so his hand came over the edge. There she wrenched three of his fingers back to breaking point, holding his wrist in a vice like grip, whilst she moved her face to within 3 inches of his. 'You're leaving,' she said, quietly. Then she smashed the end of a bottle off on the bar and held the jagged edge to his neck, adding, 'less you want facial surgery that'll make you look like the Joker.'

There was incredulity in the guy's eyes, flicker of fear, then bravado again. Big guy started to reach into his jacket, but lead guy said, 'No! She's mine, this one. For later. What's your name?'

'Hansen. And yours?' she said.

'Hector Morales. Remember it,' he said, menace back in his voice. Then, casually, 'okay, shows over. We're done here, for now, but this ain't over.'

'Before you go,' Pascal said, increasing the pressure on his wrist, 'put fifty bucks American on the bar for the damage and the drinks.'

There was a flash of fire in his eyes and Pascal thought for a moment she'd overplayed her hand. But after a moment he relaxed and nodded to big guy who took his wallet out and placed some notes on the bar. Pascal released his wrist and the guy stood back and straightened his collar.

'You okay, mister Morales?' Enrique said, subserviently, having sidled up unnoticed by Pascal.

'Beat it,' Morales said without even glancing at him, his eyes staying locked on Pascal. 'We'll be back,' he said. Then they were leaving, walking away towards the exit with Enrique in their wake, jabbering away.

'Who the fuck are you?' Dominga said, looking wonderingly at Pascal. 'I mean, thank you, of course, but I'll tell you, it ain't worth it, trust me. That guy, Morales? He's a Sinaloa captain. You should leave town, honey. Like now.'

'Why? What just happened here, Dominga?' Pascal said, unperturbed.

'You don't know shit, do you?'

'No, I don't. So tell me.'

Dominga studied her, weighing things. She normally kept her mouth shut but she owed Pascal. 'There's a turf war going on in this city, and has been forever, and it's up and down. It's between the Juarez cartel and the Sinaloa cartel and they fight for territory and over Crystal Meth and the drug gateway to the US through El Paso, and every damn thing.'

Dominga's words were no great surprise to Pascal as she'd done some research before coming down, but this was street detail. 'So our boss, Monteros, is Juarez cartel?'

'Not exactly,' Dominga said.

'Explain?'

'Monteros is just a guy who pays protection to the Juarez, and they will probably take the bar off him soon and keep him on as a legitimate figurehead. Enrique is the Juarez place-man, watching, probably dealing on the door as well.'

'So how come Enrique looked so friendly with that Morales? They on opposite teams.'

'Beats me,' Dominga said. She wandered off to serve another punter.

Pascal poured herself a slug of Remy and knocked it back, savoring the smooth fiery liquid as the adrenaline rush started to subside. The words, "we will eat your daughter," reverberated around in her head, but what did it mean?

CHAPTER FOUR

As the taxi pulled away from the curb, Pascal collapsed back in her seat, worn out and glad the shift was over. She yawned as the car made its way through the pre-dawn traffic. After about five minutes she noticed her driver seemed to be paying a lot of attention to his rear-view mirror.

'Hey, buddy, what gives?' she said.

'*Signora*,' he said. 'Maybe you have an admirer?'

'Huh?'

'Nissan Pickup,' he said, gesturing behind.

She turned and looked. It was about ten meters back, a real beat up truck with one visible male occupant. She couldn't make out the face, but didn't think it was any of the guys from the bar. She deliberated for a moment, coming to a quick decision. As they came to a stop at some lights she took a twenty out of her wallet and passed it over the seat to the driver . 'Keep the change,' she said, moving as she spoke; door open and out quick, moving obliquely in shadow, veiled from the sight line of her follower. She flitted between parked cars at the roadside, down the sidewalk, back in on the stationary truck still idling in the traffic. She wrenched the door open, startling the guy. 'What d'you want?' she said, glaring into the gloomy interior. 'Cause I'm real tired, and I don't have time for this bullshit.'

As she peered in trying to make out the drivers features she heard the unmistakable click of a firearm being cocked. The lights from a passing car briefly illuminated the rear seats where another guy sat, gun trained on her. Street lights flashed on the drivers teeth as he smiled. 'Get in, *Signora*,' he said. 'Our boss, he wants to meet you.'

She held his eyes for a long moment, working the odds - they weren't good. She shrugged, climbed up into the cab and slammed the door. 'Who is—'

'No questions,' he said. 'Its not far. Relax.'

Ten minutes later they drew up in front of a large white stucco building with black framed windows. She climbed out of the truck as did the guy from the back. More generic muscle she thought as he expertly patted her down, then ran a small device like a Star Trek Phaser all over her, presumably checking for a wire. Satisfied she was clean, he gestured for her to go up to the front door where he rang the bell. A moment later the door was opened by a maid in black uniform with white trimming. She led Pascal and her escort through a large hallway, ornate chandelier hanging from the ceiling, thick carpets on the floor, on into a smaller room like a study. There were books all along one wall, dark furniture, and a man stood at the side of an open fireplace speaking in muffled tones into a tiny cellphone. He looked up but didn't acknowledge Pascal.

She looked around. Her minder had disappeared. She studied the guy on the phone. He was small, about 5' 9", wearing casual outdoor clothing like a farmer might wear; dark colored trousers, light check shirt, no jewelery, mid-fifties, but slim and fit. The overall impression she got was of ordinariness, someone who would not register if you saw them; someone you probably wouldn't remember.

He finished his call and looked up. 'Who do you work for?' he asked, his voice soft, nonthreatening, no accent.

'Monteros,' she said.

'I don't think so,' he said. 'Monteros is a fool. Try again.'

'Look, I don't know who you are, but it might be nice if after abducting me at gunpoint, you were to introduce yourself. I am a journalist doing a story on this city and I do bar work for Monteros,' she said.

'I am told you accosted my driver without invitation, so it was hardly an abduction. You seem brave, but also reckless and foolish. And incidentally, without my protection, the man you humiliated tonight, Hector Morales, would kill you like swatting a fly. But maybe you're from the DEA?' he said musingly, turning and walking over to a drinks table. 'But the fact that you're Caucasian, and you're accent sounds British, not American, suggests not. The DEA tend only to use Hispanics when they try to infiltrate our ranks,' he said handing Pascal a scotch. 'My name is Alvaro Chavez, by the way' he added, turning away and sipping his drink.

'You're ranks?' Pascal said. 'So if Morales is Sinaloa, you must be the other side, Juarez?'

'The media is fixated with names and gangs, but to me it's just people and territory, and who is strongest, yes?'

Pascal just watched him, waiting. She was obviously there for a reason, but maybe he was just curious about her; he'd ask a few questions and then let her go.

'They showed me a clip of you with Morales and Chico at the bar. I've never seen a woman do that before. It was quite exhilarating, but of course foolhardy and extremely dangerous. Mano e Mano is fine, but when a woman does that to a man in our machismo culture, he will have to kill her to regain face,' he said, sipping his drink, smiling to himself.

'So what do you want with me?' Pascal asked, looking at her watch and yawning - she didn't get some shuteye soon she'd start sleepwalking.

Chavez looked at her, eyes veiled, calculating. 'Monteros works for me, so you work for me, but maybe I've got better work for you, with a lot better pay?'

Pascal, excited, didn't reply, her mind whirring away, logging the possibilities. If she got in, she would have access to street intelligence available nowhere else in the world, and getting a line on Tilly-May might get a whole lot easier.

'But,' Chavez said.

'But?' Pascal echoed him.

'To do what I have in mind, you must show your loyalty to me,' he said.

'And just how would I do that?'

'By killing a man.'

Sunday Pascal had no shift at the bar so she rolled out of bed late, around 10 am. She pulled on some cut-off shorts and a halter top and went out on the porch, tousle-haired from sleep, big mug of coffee in one hand, laptop in the other. The sun beat down on the backyard and there wasn't a cloud in the sky. Mexico was still deeply Catholic so Sunday was a real church day, real quiet, peaceful and today there was no one in the house to hassle her: bliss.

She read some online news as she sipped her coffee, wondering whether she should check in with Calver, but what could she tell him? That she'd got nowhere fast? Not a single line on Tilly-May. She grimaced. Tracking down Sapphire, if she was still alive, seemed further away than ever. And what of the rubbed out Aztec phrase, "we will eat your daughter"? She had no idea what it meant or signified, if anything.

Her mind turned to Alvaro Chavez and the strange meeting she'd had with him a couple of nights ago. She hadn't exactly said anything when he'd talked about killing someone as a loyalty test. Not yes and not no. She was desperate to cultivate the guy, so she'd said nothing. Chavez had said he was going to check her out and would contact her again.

Her cell buzzed loudly on the table. She checked the screen; unidentified caller. Only a very few people had her number in Mexico. She tapped "answer" and held the phone to her ear. 'Yes.'

'Hi,' a quiet voice said. 'Is that Catherine Hansen?'

Pascal didn't recognize the voice. 'Yes,' she said, guarded.

'I am Fernando Ruiz. We have a mutual friend in New York. I think we should meet.'

Must be Daly's guy finally coming through. 'Where?'

He gave her the name of a Cantina and told her to take a taxi. He would be there in one hour.

As Pascal climbed out the cab she ran a critical eye over the joint. It was way out in the east of the city and looked pretty primitive, a ramshackle old-style wooden Cantina with a couple of tables outside on the sidewalk. Inside, no women, a handful of old guys playing dominoes in the corner and a bored middle-aged guy behind the counter digging away at his teeth with a toothpick.

When it looked like the guy wasn't going to serve her, and Pascal was getting ready to light a fire under him, a voice behind her said, '*dos tequila por favor, Pablo. La señora está conmigo.*'

She turned to look at the speaker who had come up silently behind her. First thing she noticed was the cowboy hat; a huge gray colored stetson with a black band. The guy underneath it was medium height with brown eyes that had crinkle marks around them suggesting laughter, but he wasn't smiling. He looked kind of solemn but not unfriendly.

'Fernando Ruiz, I presume?' she said.

He smiled. 'In person, and you are without doubt, Miss Hansen.'

She nodded, holding out her hand which he shook. 'Lets go outside,' he said, picking up the two Tequila glasses from the bar with the bottle and moving off before she could reply. She followed, sizing him up some more. He looked athletic, wearing old style ripped 501 Levi's which seemed to fit a bit too snuggly, and on his feet ornately patterned cowboy boots. All he was missing was some spurs, Pascal mused, old cowboy movies flickering through her memory.

They sat and both took a shot of Tequila. He studied her, light street sounds in the background, the faraway rumble of traffic on the freeway.

'Daly didn't say much about you, and what he did say sounded like bullshit,' he said.

She sensed an undercurrent of hostility, restrained anger, and she wondered why. 'What's your problem, Ruiz?' she asked calmly.

'What's my problem? My problem is amateurs coming down to Mexico and fouling things up for the pros. That's my problem. So why don't you tell me what you're really doing here, and if I don't like it, and you can bet I won't, you can hightail it back to where you came from?'

Pascal straightened up in her chair. 'I'm not going anywhere, Ruiz. Daly thought you might be able to help me, but I guess he was wrong. Thanks for the drink, *muchachos*,' she said, tossing it back in one and rising to her feet.

For a moment there was something in Ruiz's eyes, but then it was gone and he was smiling again. 'Sit down,' he said, pouring some more Tequila into her glass. 'Just sussing you out, seeing what you're made of. Relax.'

She studied him. It didn't sound convincing and there was something indefinably troubling about the guy, a niggling shadow behind the eyes, but maybe it was nothing, or just something you inevitably picked up doing that kind of work, where essentially you had to mistrust everyone. But then she couldn't afford to be picky; she needed all the help she could get, so she nodded and slowly retook her seat.

'Good, and *Salud!*' he said, clinking his glass against hers. 'So, okay, Miss Hanson,' he added, crooked smile. 'You tell me what you're doing here. The real story, or the one for the birds. Up to you.'

She deliberated for a moment, holding his eyes. They remained firm and steady, so she told him the story, or a story. She was an investigator for a lawyer, and she was looking for a missing girl. She gave him no real details and kept it tight and sparse; nothing about the note, just what he needed to know to make it sound kosher. She told him about Cantina Gold and her run in with Morales and Chavez, and Chavez's loyalty test, at which point his eyes had widened but he hadn't interrupted. She didn't mention the name Sapphire Dinks.

When she'd finished, Ruiz said, 'Daly told me you're ex-British intelligence. That true?'

'Yeah.'

'Well you'll need to be. You go any further with this.'

'You know these guys? Morales? Chavez?'

'Yeah. We know them.'

'And?'

'And what?' Ruiz said pushing his hat back on his head, frowning.

'So talk to me,' Pascal said.

He smiled as he poured some more Tequila. He was attractive

when he smiled, Pascal thought, his mouth kind of lop-sided giving him a faintly piratical air. His face turned serious. 'If you want to know what's really going on, I'll tell you, and it ain't the crap the media have peddled for years.'

'So tell me,' she said. 'I've got the time. Tell me about Juarez?'

He sighed and ran his tongue along the salty rim of his glass. He leaned back in the chair and pushed his hat back on his head some more. 'Back in 2008 when the financial crash hit Mexico, Juarez lost around 90,000 jobs, so we got a shed load of very desperate people. Around the same time, the Sinaloa cartel started to move in here to try and take the drug routes from the Juarez cartel. Both sides deployed street gangs in a vicious war that saw the murder rate explode. 2010, probably the worst year, there were nearly 4,000 murders here. Can you believe that?'

Pascal didn't think he wanted an answer; but she had done her homework and she knew the score. Ruiz ploughed on. 'Murder almost on an industrial scale. It went on for about five years before the people and the police started to fight back. By 2015 they'd got the murder rate down to well under a thousand, and they'd nailed some of the bigger fish. We at the DEA helped with some of that. But then in 2016 the violence started to rise again. I guess it never really went away, they were just being a bit more discreet. But now it was breaking out on the streets again.'

'So what caused it?' Pascal asked.

'It's hard to say. There's been a splintering of the cartels and infighting between smaller groups, generally about local drug sales of crystal meth. But then you have at the higher level the fact that Ciudad Juarez is a major entry point for drugs into the US through the border with El Paso. You control the Juarez-El Paso drugs corridor into the US, its essentially a license to print money, so it's a pretty big prize. And as I said there's been a fragmentation of the gangs whilst at the same time they have diversified into extortion, kidnapping, human trafficking and retail drug sales; they call it *narcomenudeo*. And typically these smaller groups are more predatory and this just leads to even more violence. For us at the DEA it's very difficult to work out who works for who and who is doing what. You've got La Linea and the Barrio Azteca gang allied to Juarez and then you've got the Jalisco New Generation allied to Sinaloa and then even smaller street cells and groups spread out around the city.'

'You mentioned kidnapping and human trafficking?'

'What can I tell you? They all do it. Small and big.'

'Children?'

'Sure. Anything.'

'So what do you know about Alvaro Chavez?'

'Very little. He's believed to be a captain in the Juarez cartel. I've never seen him. In fact I don't think we've even got a picture of him. Low profile and clever; keeps out of the limelight. And that test you mention is not unusual, especially where their looking at outsider non-Mexicans.'

Ruiz looked at his watch. 'Look, Catherine, I've got to go in a minute, so maybe we can carry this on some other time. And listen, I don't want you going and doing anything drastic, less you run it by me first.'

Pascal just looked at him. He hesitated, looking slightly apologetic. 'Okay, okay. I can't stop you doing anything, but I am trying to help you, so would you please consider consulting me before you do anything? Maybe I'll be able to help you.'

'No problem,' she lied. She'd have to think about that. 'One last thing,' she added. 'You ever hear the phrase, "We will eat your daughter?" It's just something we picked up around the disappearance of this girl. It's probably nothing. In fact the original words are in Aztec, the old language, or what I think they call here, Nahuatl.'

'The daughter eaters, huh?' he said, voice neutral, but his expression was thoughtful. 'Look, I'll ask around, and then why don't we meet for dinner tonight, then we can talk?'

'What about your wife?' Pascal asked, to cover her mounting excitement.

'I don't have anyone. Too dangerous, if you work undercover. Makes you vulnerable.'

Pascal nodded. Seemed sad. 'Fine,' she said as they rose to their feet.

He said, 'I'll call you or text later to set up dinner.'

She watched him walking away down the street, trying to get a feel for the guy and not really getting anywhere, but not caring too much because maybe she was going to get a line on something.

As Ruiz rounded the street corner he had a cheap burner to his ear, rapid Spanish punctuating the air.

CHAPTER FIVE

As she watched Ruiz rounding the corner, dust hanging in the air, Pascal remained standing outside the Cantina looking to hail a taxi but then her cell was buzzing again. Boy was she popular today. She scanned the phone screen; it was a short text message that read: *'heres your mark'*. There was an attachment with the text which she opened. It seemed to be a high-quality video clip of a man standing in a warehouse in front of five other men, each wired to the front of a stationary forklift truck.

As a taxi responded to Pascal's raised arm, she turned it into a shooing motion. She sat back down outside the Cantina to watch the clip. As the barman poked his head out the door she said, without looking up, *'Tequila, Pablo, por favor.'* He nodded like she was a regular and went back to fetch the bottle. Pascal watched the ten-minute clip and that was enough. She recognized the guy as Morales' helper at the bar, the big dead-eyed guy, Chico, who she'd chucked the drink at. The clip showed him walking up and down in front of the line of men, in his hand, a huge hunting knife, and all the time he smiled. The men were young Mexicans, some begging and pleading, others looking fatalistic, knowing what was coming. Then Chico slowly walked back down the line, stopping at each man to pull his head back by the hair, and then slash the razor sharp knife across the neck. As the blood spurted out of each boy's neck artery, Chico moved onto the next man until all five were left slumped, dripping with blood, held in place only by the wires connected to the forklifts.

Pascal's cell was buzzing again. 'Yeah,' she snapped.

'Don't be like that, *Chiquita*,' the voice said. 'Mr Chavez, he say, you take out Chico, the guy on the clip, then you come see him.' She listened, but he'd gone. Silence, the connection dead.

She reluctantly watched the clip again, this time looking for signs that it might be a simulation, but you couldn't fake the throat cutting and the blood spurt. It was genuine. She picked up the Tequila bottle and took a long swig. She placed twenty bucks on the table and hailed a cab, and this time she took it.

###

Back at the house in San Antonio Pascal watched and re-watched the video clip, slowly becoming de-sensitized to the imagery until it no longer completely sickened her. So now she could try and view it objectively and dispassionately. As she slo-mowed it again, no longer involuntarily wincing each time the knife flashed red, Ruiz's call came in to set up the dinner date for that evening. He was sombre and non-committal, just giving her the time - 9 pm - and the place - The Great American Steakhouse.

###

Pascal alighted from her cab outside the restaurant at about five past nine. She looked up at the facade wondering why Ruiz had chosen such a place. Had she really come all this way to Mexico so she could eat ersatz American fast-food imports. But inside it wasn't bad, dark and intimate, low lights, small tables, and at the side deep red upholstered booths occupied by a smattering of well dressed stylish looking folk, chatting and eating.

Ruiz was already sitting at a table and he hailed her as she approached. 'Drink?' he said, lopsided grin.

'Scotch and water,' she said

He nodded to the waiter.

'Jesus!' she said, looking at the menu. 'Are these prices for real, Ruiz? You on the take, buddy?' she winked.

He looked offended for a second, but then recovered. 'Daly warned me about your British humor,' he said.

They ordered steaks. As they waited for their food Ruiz gave Pascal a brief biography. His father had been Mexican and his mother American, both now dead. Born in El Paso 37 years ago, he had dual nationality and had been in the DEA for 15 years, the last 10 in Chihuahua county, mostly in Ciudad Juarez, monitoring the border with

El Paso.

As their food arrived Ruiz said, 'tell me about this missing girl?'

Pascal contemplated her bloody steak, then started cutting away at it. She needed to tell Ruiz just enough so he'd help, but not enough for him to work out the identity of who they were really looking for. She needed to weave a composite of Tilly-May and Sapphire, synthesizing what little she knew of their back stories together into one, and see if it would shake anything loose, or trip something in Ruiz's mind. 'We don't have much to go on. She went missing from New York about three and a half years ago, but we think she, or a proxy, recently made contact; a scrappy piece of paper through the post with the name Tilly-May on it. Its possibly a scam and a precursor to a shakedown, but the parents, who have no faith in the authorities, want it followed up, so here I am.'

Ruiz watched her, waiting, as she chewed on some steak.

'So I took a good long look at that scrappy piece of paper,' she continued. 'And it did reveal some rubbed out or hidden words. And that's what gave me the lead to Ciudad Juarez, but also the phrase I mentioned to you, "we will eat your daughters". That phrase is only our best guess at what the words mean, because firstly the original words have missing letters that we have tried to fill in, and secondly we think the words were in Aztec or Nahuatl, so it's a translation.'

'So you could actually be way off beam,' Ruiz said. 'Could just be doodles on the back of an envelope, or something completely different.'

'That's true, but you seemed to think the phrase might mean something,' Pascal said, raising her eyes and looking at him questioningly.

He pursed his lips and speared a small piece of bloody meat with his fork. 'How much do you know about the so called *feminicidio* in Northern Mexico?'

'I did my homework before coming down here. Hundreds of women and young girls have been killed in Juarez since 1993, and it became something of an international world story, primarily because of the courage and dogged determination of the mothers of some of the disappeared. If the authorities had had their way, no one would ever have heard about it, and even now they appear to play only lip service to investigating dead and missing girls. Many of the victims were and are from poor and often rural backgrounds, and there is obviously a class and racial aspect to it, many of the girls were dark skinned. There was a big trial in 2015 which the authorities touted as being some kind of major breakthrough when it was nothing of the kind. My take was you had a terrible triumvirate of police, politicians and drug lords, combining together to thwart any serious investigation. They created a kind of rolling conveyor belt of scapegoating. The girls were all prostitutes and deserved what they got, then they lined up low level soldiers to take the fall, or the blame was pinned on people already dead or serving time, often with planted evidence, so none of the big fish ever suffered.'

'Not a bad summation,' Ruiz said, nodding and sipping some red wine. 'You know the UN said femicide is a pandemic in Mexico. 8, 9 women killed every day. You see all those pink crosses around Juarez? They're all missing girls. City's even produced a phone App called, "*Noy Estoy Sola*", you are not alone, case they get in trouble.'

Ruiz sipped some more wine, Pascal kept her mouth shut, hoping he'd open up some more.

'And you're right about that big trial in 2015. It was a crock. Never got close to the big guys. You know who they convicted? A load of street punks, five guys from the Azteca gang who are part of the La Linea crime cartel. Girls were abducted, then forced to work as hookers in a shit-hole knocking shop called "Club Verde" and then later murdered, dumped in a mass grave, twenty-one of them, 'bout an hour from the city. Thing is, a load of people knew those missing girls were working at that place, but no one said a thing. That's what fear does to people. And you know what? It's still going on today.'

'So tell me about the daughter eaters or whatever it is. Is it something? Does it exist? Does it mean anything to you?' Pascal asked.

'Until about three months ago I would have said no, but then I did hear something.'

'What did you hear?'

Ruiz sipped some more wine, watching Pascal, maybe assessing her, calculating what line to take. He lifted the bottle of red wine and topped up her glass.

'Before getting to that, we need to go back a while, and you need to understand the basic context of what happens around here. There have always been rumors of gangs of serial killers here, mostly I think based on lots of salacious media hype. I think the killings here arose from a unique environment of cultural machismo, or ingrained misogyny mixed in with massive corruption and lawlessness. You add in very powerful drug cartels fighting for territory and you have the perfect environment for what happens here. I think there probably may have been a gang back in the day, that possibly mutated into something else, an organization that deals in much younger girls, children.'

Pascal sipped her wine, trying to keep her excitement under wraps. 'Go on,' she said.

'I have absolutely no proof of any of this, and of course the DEA are not principally concerned with vice or people trafficking, just narcotics.

'But,' she prompted him.

'So going back, about three years ago I was working undercover, trying to infiltrate a street gang, part of La Linea, and I got real close to a guy for a short period, before they made me. Then the guy was disappeared, but during the period I was with him, couple of times I crashed at his place and he was living with this girl. She was 12 years old. When I first arrived I thought she was his daughter or sister, but she wasn't.'

'What was she?' Pascal asked.

'She was his women essentially. He even offered her to me one night, and I had to gracefully decline. Most of the time he had her manacled on an ankle chain. But then this one time, he got called out unexpectedly and I got talking to her.'

'And?'

'She told me her story.'

'Come on, Ruiz, quit stalling, get to the point will you?' Pascal said.

He smiled. 'You want some dessert?' he kidded her.

She just looked at him.

'She said she was abducted in Mexico City when she was 8 and taken to Juarez, raped, then pimped out for cash, big cash. She said girls often disappeared when they were no longer valuable. She was lucky, if I can put it like that. One of the soldiers took a fancy to her, actually looked to me like he had fallen in love with her and taken her out of the system; most weren't so lucky. Remember,' he said. 'DEA's primary concern is narcotics, so this arrangement with the girl was not really of interest to us on a professional basis.'

'But you must have been interested, surely?' Pascal said. 'Any criminal activity that funded the cartel must have been of interest to you? Tell me what you surmised?'

'Okay, you want to know what I believe?'

'Ruiz, why the fuck do you think I'm sitting here?'

He smiled his crooked grin, hailed the waiter and ordered another bottle of red wine. Then he began to talk again. 'I believe there may be a small group specializing in pimping quality young children. It's made up of guys who were foot soldiers, probably in the late 90's when the Juarez *feminicide* really took off, and now they've come of age. I'm sure it started out with guys who liked sex with children and realized they could get away with almost anything. They had something of a system in place for abducting adults, and they just adopted the same strategy with kids. Then when the major cartels started to fracture and split up and there was a lot of diversification into extortion, abduction and kidnapping, and people trafficking as well as drugs, this group diversified into abducting, ransoming and pimping children as a serious business.'

'That's a theory, Ruiz. Probably a good one, but what do you know?'

'I put that together from talking to the girl, Sonia. Her boyfriend was obviously part of a group who were involved, but she was way too frightened to say much, but the one thing she did say, and this tells you why there's nothing out there about this: there's *nothing* online. Nothing, and that's apparently one of their basic rules. Probably learned it from *Al-Qaeda*. They never use the internet or mobiles for their activities or any communications, and that is strictly enforced. Any breaches and they're gone.'

'I wondered about that, why there's nothing out there.'

'So essentially it could be like a kind of private club, based on word of mouth, recommendation and the old mafia blood oath of *Omertà*. Almost like a secret society,' Ruiz said.

'So what's with this daughter eaters tag, given what you say about how shy they are?'

'Slip of the tongue, I think, and I'm only speculating. I thought about it some after we spoke, and then remembered something we got in a wiretap about 3 months ago that made no sense at the time. It was a conversation about some senior guy in the cartel visiting from Mexico City and them wanting to lay on something special for him. This visitor obviously liked young girls, and one of the guys talking, said, "talk to the daughter eaters", and laughed. I only remembered it, because it didn't make sense at the time - just thought it was a silly throw away comment - until you mentioned the phrase yourself, or something close to it, in relation to this missing Tilly-May girl.

'One other point that may tie in with your thing,' Ruiz said, pouring some more wine from the fresh bottle into their glasses. 'Sonia said it wasn't just Mexican girls. She said she saw an American girl once.'

Pascal slowly swirled red wine around her glass, deep in contemplation. Then she drained her glass. 'I need to think about this, but couple of obvious questions: where's Sonia now and who is the guy on the wiretap who mentions the daughter eaters?'

'Sonia's long gone, disappeared along with the boyfriend. My guess is they're probably in a mass grave somewhere out in the desert, or been melted down in an acid vat. That's the usual scenario these days. But the guy on the wiretap is still around. Raul Soto is a street punk with the Barrio Azteca gang. Probably not too hard to find, but there's no way he or anyone else is going to talk to you. You start asking questions, you'll end up like Sonia and her boyfriend.'

'Okay, but if I got in with Chavez's group, you could say I'd also be getting in with Raul Soto, because the Azteca's are affiliated with the Juarez, right?'

'How the fuck are you,' Ruiz said, incredulous, 'with your cut-glass British accent and pale white skin, going to get the fuck into one of the most dangerous drug cartels in the world?'

'Take a look at this,' she said, tapping play on her smart phone and sliding it across the table.

Ruiz silently watched the clip of Chico killing the five guys. He replayed it, then leaned back in his chair, suddenly looking old and worn out. He sipped wine, his eyes scrunched up in thought. 'Chavez, right?' he said. 'I thought you might be kidding me about him, just trying to impress me so I'd talk to you.'

'Nope. They're serious. They want me to kill this Chico animal, and then maybe I'm in with them?'

'Just out of interest,' he said, crooked smile back in place. 'You actually prepared to pop this guy, just to get in?'

She didn't answer, just held his gaze, eyes ice cold.

Ruiz nodded, looking shaken. 'You know,' he said, 'I doubt Chavez's group is part of this Daughter Eater crew, if it exists, so it might not help you.'

'If I get in, I can maybe get close to Soto, but I doubt I'll have much time. They'll never trust me, and I doubt they plan on me living any longer than Chico, but it's the only game in town. I gotta give it a shot.'

'You really are crazy, aren't you?' Ruiz said. 'What? You're just gonna walk up to this guy and pop him? These guys may look stupid, but Chico's been around a long time, and that don't happen 'less you're real careful. These guys are under threat 24/7, so they don't expose themselves to unnecessary risk, and this guys no street punk. He'll have guys protecting him, including bent *Federales* and cops.'

'I don't give a shit about that, Ruiz,' Pascal said, eyes flashing. 'There's a little girl out there being abused by these fucking animals and I'm going to do something about it, starting with Chico. Now, you can help me, or you can cover your ears and walk away. All I want is a location where I can find this piece of shit, and then I'm gonna hammer a fucking great nail through his skull. You reading me?'

'Loud and clear,' Ruiz said, 'but why not use your head and do the obvious. Ask Chavez?'

In the end Pascal didn't need to, because Chico came to her.

CHAPTER SIX

The work had been grueling, the bar packed to the rafters, so when Pascal finally emerged at the end of her shift and climbed into the cab Enrique had hailed, she was half asleep. Part way in she realized something was wrong. Chico was sitting there with a gun trained on her, and then Enrique was shoving her in the back so that she tumbled into the car. Enrique slammed the door behind her and there was the sound of burning rubber as they screeched away from the curb.

As she straightened up, without warning, Chico, with the gun turned sideways, slammed it into her face. She heard her nose crack and felt the gunmetal against her mouth, mashing against her teeth. As she tried to recover, a man in the front passenger seat leaned over, pulled her arms out and snapped handcuffs on her. In all it had taken about five seconds. Decoyed, immobilized and secured without a squeak - professional as hell.

She felt blood dripping from her nose and mouth. She lifted her manacled hands and wiped her face, then turned to look at Chico. The gun had gone and he was sat calm, his giant frame relaxed. There was no triumphalism in his expression, he just looked bored, another pointer to the fact that the guy was a pro. As Pascal's sluggish brain began to function again, the video clip of Chico cutting the throats of the five Mexicans ran on a loop in the back of her mind.

'Where you taking me?' she mumbled through her mangled teeth.

'Mr Morales, he always keep his promises. He say you his, and it will be so. No more talk,' he said. He took out a gold cigarette case, selected a smoke and lit up.

Pascal looked out the window. They were traveling east, moving out of the bright lights into a less built up area with little traffic, but many warehouses and darkened factories. After around half an hour they pulled into a yard in front of a large white building that looked like an aircraft hangar. There was only one other vehicle parked there, a sleek expensive looking black SUV, empty. The only light showing was coming from a small annex at the side of the building that looked like an office.

Chico gestured, and said, 'out.'

The other guy opened the door and pulled her out of the car and onto her feet. She stumbled against him, to test their responses. He immediately stepped back to let her fall and she heard Chico's gun click as he readied to fire. She stood up as Chico came around the car to her. He said, 'no more tricks,' and viciously punched her already bloody and broken nose. She couldn't help the scream escaping from her compressed lips. She staggered back, just managing to remain standing.

The other guy grabbed her and began to walk her towards the lighted annex. Inside it was a small empty office reception area with a long front desk and some tables with chairs. They led her through, down a short corridor and into the warehouse area. It was half stacked with pallets on which were wooden boxes, and in the background some forklift trucks. It looked like the place where Chico had taken out the five guys. It was dimly lit with a few spotlights, but there was a lighted area in the middle where an empty chair stood. They took her over to it and sat her down. A tie was placed around both ankles securing her. Chico handed the other guy his gun and walked away towards the office. The other guy moved some distance off to keep watch. He lit a cigarette and started looking at his cell phone.

Pascal's nose ached as waves of throbbing pain reverberated through it. She could feel blood in her nostrils, clogging them and then running down her face and dripping off her chin into her lap and onto her manacled hands. She tentatively explored the inside of her mouth with the tip of her tongue. She could feel a tiny chip on an incisor but otherwise her teeth felt solid. She looked down at her hands and the cuffs, examining them minutely. They looked like the standard double lock Smith and Wesson model used by a lot of Law enforcement in the US and other places.

As she examined them she worked through her abduction stage by stage, analyzing each action. She'd thought these guys were pro's but maybe they weren't. Why hadn't they searched her, even a cursory pat-down? They knew she wouldn't take a weapon into work at the bar, and they had the gun and she was handcuffed so maybe they felt they didn't need to, but that was sloppy.

She heard the sound of a door opening and Morales moved into the light, slowly walking towards her. He nodded, dismissing the other guy, who immediately walked away towards the office.

As Morales came to a halt in front of her, he looked down, smiling, his baby face looking smooth and untroubled. 'Before you die, Cathy. It is Cathy, isn't it?' he said, lightly. 'I wanted you to know that it's me who is ending your life. I am taking it, and your soul. But before you die, you must beg for my forgiveness, and you will.'

'Fuck you,' Pascal said, trying to keep her spirits up.

'Hector! We's waiting,' a female voice called out plaintively from the lighted doorway that Morales had just come through. Pascal looked over and could see two scantily clad young women hanging in the doorway.

'In a moment, my dear. Kiss your sister. I will be with you shortly,' he said.

'My,' Pascal said. 'I bet those gals can't hardly wait for your tiny dick, Hector. And I bet you need to throw in a bit of torture as well, just to get it up, right?'

Morales' expression didn't change at the sexual slight, but Pascal knew virtually all men were susceptible to such jibes, and his actions confirmed it. He reached down and gently took hold of her bloody nose. She didn't scream outright but she couldn't stop the small moan that escaped her lips as Morales started to squeeze the bone. The pain was excruciating. Tears popped out of her eyes unbidden and began to run down her cheeks, mingling with the blood.

There was a sound behind them. It was Chico returning; he was driving a kind of miniature lawn mower tractor with a small trailer behind it. On the trailer was a large container like a garden water-butt with a chainsaw leaning against it. Chico came to a halt a few meters away from them. Morales let go of Pascal's nose and moved a few steps away. Pascal slumped down, drawing deep breaths, trying to quell the pain in her nose.

Chico brought the chainsaw over, expression inscrutable. 'You want me to start chopping her now, Mr Morales?' he asked.

'You see the vat, Cathy?' Morales asked Pascal, ignoring Chico's question. 'As he cuts, Chico will throw your body parts into the acid so they will dissolve and leave no trace. You ever been cut up alive, Cathy?'

Pascal just looked at him, all her bravado gone. She was scared now.

Chico took out some masking tape. Morales said, looking at Pascal, 'to stop the screaming, Chiquita. You see, I don't want to be disturbed whilst I am breaking in those two young sisters, but don't worry, I will come back before you die, so you can see me.'

Chico put tape across Pascal's mouth as Morales walked away towards the lighted doorway and the two waiting women.

As the door closed behind Morales, Chico put the chainsaw down, leaned back against the trailer and took out his gold cigarette case. He watched Pascal as he selected a cigarette and lit up, his face, as it always seemed to be, completely unreadable. After a moment he held the cigarette out towards her, gesturing.

Pascal didn't smoke but she nodded her head. Anything to give her some time. Chico pealed back the tape and put a cigarette in her mouth and held his lighter to it. She sucked in the smoke trying not to cough, knowing she'd have to exhale through her mouth, her nose completely blocked. She said, 'I have a tape of you, Chico, killing five men in this very place.' She said it calmly and then looked away. 'It's on my phone, right side jeans pocket.'

Chico watched her for a moment, then moved towards her. The contours of the phone stuck out the side of her jeans. He worked his fingers in, pulled it out and powered it up. He held it in front of Pascal, and she directed him to the on screen icon. He tapped it, leaned up and watched.

'You one brave guy, Chico. Taking on five unarmed hog-tied boys who can't fight back. Why don't you give me a knife, and we go at it, just you and me? What d'you say?' Pascal said. As she spoke she surreptitiously felt the outside of the small coin pocket on the right hand side of her jeans, praying it would be there. She let out a breath of relief as she felt the outlines of the bobby pin she always carried, case she had to pin her hair back.

'Where you get this?' Chico asked.

'Alvaro Chavez. He wants me to kill you,' she said.

That got a reaction. His eyes narrowed, then he laughed unconvincingly. He looked at her again quizzically, as he considered how she might have got the clip without the help of someone like Chavez. 'You wait,' he said, moving away in the direction Morales had gone.

As he moved off Pascal had her cuffed hands over the small coin pocket. She managed to get her fingers in and slowly tugged out the bobby-pin, all the time praying and telling herself to stay calm. With the pin out she bent and fashioned it so it was straight, with the plastic tip removed. She stopped for a second, rolling back time to the training session she had attended around six years ago, some kind of field-craft crap she hadn't taken seriously at the time, but wished she had now. She knew the cuffs were a double lock model, so she'd have to go into the housing twice.

She heard a scream in the distance and stopped for a second, looking over at the door, but it remained closed and quiet. She inserted the straight part of the pin into the upper portion of the lock, straining to find a way of maneuvering her hands so she could achieve the gentle touch needed. She gently felt her way in, probing until she felt contact inside the housing with the locking mechanism. Working away from the cuff's direction of travel, she applied pressure slowly, praying all the time. She felt slight movement, then a kind of snagging. She cursed, removing the pin and straightening the bent end, then reinserting it slowly, going through the same process, telling herself to stay calm. Now she felt the heat in the warehouse for the first time, sweat starting to form and run down her forehead like rivulets of condensed steam. She applied pressure again, gently increasing it, trying to mimic the movement of the key. She felt slight movement, a click as she felt the double lock mechanism release, and then an indescribable wash of relief. She drew some deep breaths, but she knew it was only the first stage. Now she had to try and release that final single lock.

She straightened her bobby-pin, inserted it again into the upper portion of the lock, about half way in and then bent the pin to the left, creating a bend. Out, then in once more, past the bend, bending it to the left again. She withdrew the pin and nodded to herself as she studied the resultant S shape. She held her breath as she carefully reinserted the pin, gently feeling her way in until she felt contact inside the housing with the locking mechanism. As she started to gently probe, she heard the door open, and she froze. Chico was silhouetted in the lighted doorway for a second, then he was moving towards her. She kept her hands in place in her lap, not moving.

Chico stood over her, looking down. 'Mr Morales, he say I should start, soften you up with some cuts, then he going to question you, when he finish in there,' he said, gesturing towards the closed door. He held her phone up. 'You hanging with Chavez, Huh? I think it maybe better you don't talk to Mr Morales too much, he might get ideas,' he said. 'Tell me what you know now, I'll make it quick, straight through the neck. You won't feel nothing. When Mr Morales, he come out, I'll say the chainsaw slip.'

Pascal held his gaze, her eyes pleading, trying to squeeze out more time, because the bobby-pin seemed to have become jammed in the housing. She tried to subtly wiggle the pin without drawing Chico's attention to what she was doing, but her hands were slippery with sweat and the cuffs constrained her movement. She felt like screaming in frustration. She eased the pin in the housing, trying a different angle, praying.

Chico walked back and picked up the chainsaw and pulled the starter string. It fired into life with a throaty roar like the sound of a small motorbike starting up. He stood in front of her, loosely cradling the chainsaw in his hands, then moving it up towards her neck, same calm unruffled expression on his face as if he were about to carve the Sunday roast.

Pascal knew her time was up. It had been mostly a good life and she thanked God for the time she had been given. She looked up at Chico, determined not to flinch in meeting death. She prepared herself as the buzzing saw blades moved towards her neck. She felt like she was floating but she was calm. When she felt the bobby-pin move she thought her mind was playing tricks, a last macabre joke, but then she felt the tension bar go completely. As the cuffs came open she launched herself from the chair in one smooth motion, grabbing the handle of the chainsaw and changing its direction, swinging the long moving blade around in an arc, then into Chico's side. It cut straight through his thin shirt and into his body, blood and small bits of flesh churning up from the blade as he let out a piercing scream. The saw cut straight in from the side towards his belly button, only coming to a halt as the blade snagged in his spine. The sound of the motor rose and whined as it labored and strained to cut through the bone, the sound competing with Chico's dying moans.

He sagged on the blade as it slipped from Pascal's bloody hands onto the floor, engine now whirring to a halt. There was silence apart from Chico making weak gurgling sounds in the back of his throat. He would be dead within minutes. Pascal removed the ankle ties. She looked over at the door where Morales was. It remained closed and quiet. She looked over at the office, wondering where the other guy had got to, all the time calculating and assessing. She picked up her phone and took a couple of photos of Chico.

She tore off a long strip of his bloody frayed shirt from where the saw blade had cut and felt around in his pockets until she found and retrieved his lighter. She moved to the small tractor and slowly undid the fuel cap and fed the long strip of cloth in, dousing it in petrol, then withdrawing it so a long wick hung down from the open cap. She climbed onto the tractor seat and turned the ignition. It started at once. She sat motionless for a couple of beats, thinking. She moved the tractor slowly forward and around so it faced the lighted office area. She pulled her belt off and secured the steering wheel so the tractor would travel in a straight line. She took a last look around then began slowly driving the tractor towards the office area. Ten feet away she flicked the lighter, but as she applied the flame to the rag hanging from the fuel tank, she saw Morales appear in the other doorway and start shooting. Pascal jumped from the tractor as it crashed through the doorway and continued on its way pulling part of the brickwork down behind it with the trailer, then smashing through into the office.

As the other guy ran in from the office area past Pascal, she slipped inside, racing past the still moving tractor to the outer door and out to the black SUV in the yard. As she reached the vehicle there was an explosion and the office area erupted in a fireball of flame and smoke.

She climbed into the SUV, glad to see the keys dangling from the ignition. She burned rubber leaving the lot, then settled down to a steady speed. As she drove, she reached up and tentatively felt her bloody nose; it still hurt mightily but now it was a dull, throbbing ache. She figured she better get to a hospital and get that bone set quick, less she wanted to end up looking like Smokin' Joe Frazier.

She drove west trying to retrace their journey out, and now she could hear the sound of sirens in the distance. She hit the main drag and after 15 minutes was back in a built-up area with plenty of cabs. She parked up the SUV in a side street and sat for a while with her phone, composing a text message. It was a reply to the one she had received with the clip of Chico killing the 5 Mexicans. In the end the text was just two words: *"mission accomplished"*. She attached a photo of

Chico's bloody, lifeless, almost cut in half body, and pressed send.

She got out the SUV and started looking for a cab as faint pink tendrils of sunrise starting to creep up the horizon. She felt like she wanted to sleep for a week.

CHAPTER SEVEN

In the end it felt like she did sleep for a week, but after 6 days with Alvaro Chavez at least her nose was starting to heal up. After the explosion and a frantic rush to the hospital, a harried A & E doctor had managed to set the bone and told her, give it time and it would be good as new. A few days later Chavez had shown up at the bar with an offer for her and her bandaged nose; a thousand bucks a week plus room and board. The job was vaguely described as security, to be in a group protecting and oscillating around the Man. Essentially she would be a bodyguard.

She knew it was quite possible Chavez had never expected her to survive coming up against Chico, but with him dead, Chavez had to find her a place. Her impression of Chavez was that he cultivated a kind of eccentric side and his employment of a supposedly tough white female killer played into the image he had of himself. And her induction into Chavez's group acted as a provocation to Morales and his Sinaloa cohorts that might unhinge them enough to do something stupid in retaliation and give Chavez an edge in the unending turf war.

Her job was basically to constantly scan for evolving dangers arising around the Man, but the trouble was Chavez seemed to be a real homebody. So, much of her time was spent hanging around the White House as it was jokingly called, the place where she had originally been taken to meet Chavez. But in the evenings he invariably moved about, never sleeping at one place for more than a couple of nights, but these places were close together in a tight geographical zone. Sometimes his nights abode would be palatial, other times a hovel.

She had managed to speak to Ruiz just once, as she wasn't allowed to carry her own phone, so when Chavez asked her to buy some cigarettes when they were out one time, she'd bought some and a burner. Ruiz had been desperate to pump her but there'd been no time. He'd told her there'd been no media coverage of Chico's killing or the explosion, nor a police report, so Morales had obviously hushed it up. No, he had no line on Raul Soto, the guy on the wiretap. When he'd asked whether she'd made any progress, she'd about run out of time and had to hang up, neatly avoiding having to tell him she'd got nowhere either. That was partly on purpose. She had made a conscious decision not to ask any questions to start with, as it would immediately put her under suspicion, and so she had rigidly adhered to that for a week, but now time was up and she needed to start digging. She had to get a line on Tilly-May.

One place Chavez did like to go regularly was the Great Sand Dunes Casino. It was a big place, looked like a multi-storey car park from outside, but inside it was dark and buzzing, flickering with neon and night sounds, and tonight Pascal was there with Chavez and just one other guy, Jorge. She and Jorge were meant to be discrete, in the background, to give Chavez as much freedom as possible without prejudicing his safety. So they were stood around five meters either side of him, mingling with the punters as he moved around. The guy liked blackjack and was pretty good at it, and tonight he was stood at the table, playing.

Jorge was mid-twenties with kind of innocent looking eyes, but he was a guy with hidden steel who couldn't be pushed around. He was one of the better soldiers, he had some education and reasonable English, and often asked her about New York, and she had tried to cultivate him. She looked over at him now, his eyes smoothly scanning the crowd, alert and doing his job. She moved over towards him, and said, 'anything?'

He looked up, surprised she'd moved off station. 'Quiet, man. But lots of nice ladies, no,' he said, looking appreciatively at some flashily dressed hostess who was showing way too much flesh.

Pascal smiled and said, 'down boy.'

He smiled quickly and nodded, then into serious mode again, eyes moving over the crowd once more.

'You know, Jorge,' she said tentatively, 'I got a good Mexican friend in New York. She's a maid, not much money, not enough to come back anyway, even for holiday.'

'Yeah?' he said, to make conversation.

'Yeah, and she asked me, when she knew I was coming here, to see if I could locate her dead sisters' boy. He came down ten years ago, and they lost touch. He lived in Chihuahua city and Juarez she thinks. I said I'd give it a shot.'

'Uhm,' he said, not really engaged. 'That all you got to go on? What's his name?'

'Raul Soto. And she said he might be in a gang.'

'Don't know the name,' he said. 'What gang? She say?'

'La Linea.'

He nodded, thinking. 'I's tight with some of them. Want me to ask around?'

'Would you?' she said, taking his hand. 'It would mean a lot to me, and to her.'

'Sure,' he said. 'No problem.' He looked up. 'Better fade, bosses coming.'

She backed away into the crowd as Chavez walked over juggling a handful of chips.

###

A few days later Jorge came through. He'd been off for a while, she didn't know where, and then he was back on with her. They were standing in a street market where Chavez had stopped to buy some fruit. She and Jorge were a couple of meters away, scanning the crowd. Jorge said, unprompted, 'I found your guy, Soto. He don't know you but he want to meet.' Jorge's usually warm brown eyes looked cold today. 'I don't think you straight with me. Soto's mother, she alive and well in Tijuana, so what's the game?'

Pascal made a split second decision. 'I'm looking for a little girl who's gone missing. I know Soto is not involved but I think he may know where I can find her.'

Jorge thought for a moment. 'That's your business,' he said, serious. 'But you fool enough to meet him, ain't no way you'll come back. Shit, he out in Diaz Ordaz *colonia*, a busted barrio west side of the city, real bad place. I heard he hiding out there from some guys for a killing. You go down there, maybe he'll see you, but you won't come back.'

'Thanks, Jorge,' she said, but he turned away. She'd offended him which made her sad, as he seemed like a nice guy stuck in the wrong business. 'Hey, Jorge. I didn't mean to disrespect you or abuse our friendship, but I didn't know any other way to get a lead. I think you have a little daughter. I'm trying to save someone like her; maybe you understand?'

He looked away for a long moment, watching Chavez as he paid the fruit vendor some notes. He seemed to nod to himself as if he had decided something. He said, 'I told Chavez, so maybe you should get out, away, like now.' He handed her a scrap of paper. 'That's an address, neighborhood bar Cantina in Diaz Ordaz where you likely find Soto.'

'Thank you. I won't forget you,' she said, and she meant it, but he was already walking away to the car.

Later, back at the White House, it was pretty clear she was being watched. When she had opened the front door, a figure had immediately appeared on the sidewalk with a menacing look. She nodded and closed the door as if it had just been part of her security sweep. She guessed quite soon they'd all get in the car to go someplace, but it would be a one way trip for her. It was time to leave the Chavez household.

She went to the kitchen to get a cold drink, floor plan of the house spread out in her head as she mentally checked possible exit routes. Best bet was the toilet on the first floor. She knew it had a small window, a ledge outside and a drainpipe not too far away. If she tried that route, she would not be able to take anything with her, as they would watch her enter the toilet and carrying any kind of bag would be a red flag. So clothes and wallet, basically.

She finished her orange juice, checked her pockets for wallet and keys, then made her way up to the first floor landing. There were a couple of guys there; she nodded and walked past the door to the toilet and then came to halt as if she had just decided she needed to take a leak. She walked back to the toilet door, grimacing and smiling at the two guys. They both nodded, one smiling as she went in and closed the door. She pushed the solid looking lock home, then immediately moved to the small window. It was an old style vertical sliding sash, small gap but she reckoned she could squeeze out if she could open it. She tried it, but it seemed glued shut, immovable.

She went to the door to listen, couldn't hear anything. They'd give her ten minutes maybe, if they thought she was taking a dump. She turned the tap on to create some noise and went back to the window, then she noticed a concealed bolt at the side. It slid open easily, and the sash came up without a sound. She looked out, sun going down, but it was still light. Maybe she should have waited for nightfall, but she just had a premonition she had to get out now. She looked down. The garden stretched out, lawn and immaculate flower beds, and then a couple of guys at either end lazily patrolling, both looking at cell phones. She took a breath and silently climbed out on the ledge and began to slowly edge her way along towards the drainpipe about two meters away.

The ledge was about 6 inches wide, so movement was relatively easy. She checked her watch. Ten minutes had now elapsed since she'd entered the toilet. She grasped the drainpipe, looked down, pulled herself off the ledge, against the pipe, and began lowering herself. She heard banging on the toilet door, followed by shouts, and she increased her rate of descent; if she fell now it wouldn't be too bad but would make a noise. She looked over her shoulder and saw one of the men running towards the house, head down, the other was looking up at the window where the noise was coming from but hadn't yet seen her clinging to the drainpipe.

As she dropped the last couple of meters onto the paved area, turning as she hit the ground, the other guy was there, moving in on her, hand inside his jacket reaching for a weapon. She carried on moving into a kind of football charge, hitting him with her shoulder, trapping his hand in his jacket and bowling him over onto his back. She stood over him and stamped down hard on his face hearing a crunch as his nose and jaw cracked and shattered, cutting off his screams. She slid the gun out of his jacket holster as she went into a roll, noticing it was a Sig Saur 9mil., bullets starting rain in on her, screaming and ricocheting off the paving stones. She scrambled up and ran for her life. As she rounded the side of the house there were two guys on the gate, three vehicles parked up. The flatbed truck was used by everyone, so she calculated it was most likely to have keys in and she was right. As she opened the door more bullets struck the vehicle. She turned as two men came out the house both firing at her; she leveled the Sig and dropped them both, moving into the driving seat as they hit the ground, more fire now coming from upstairs windows. Car in gear, she swerved in a wide arc spraying gravel out, turning, to give her space to pick up speed, then towards the closed gate, ducking down as she roared towards it, bullets from the gate guys pinging off the vehicle, windscreen shattering all over her.

One guy managed to jump out of the way, but the truck hit the other one before it smashed through the iron gates, bumping and turning hard right onto the main drag, Pascal fighting to control the vehicle as it slewed across a lane just missing an oil tanker, horns blaring all around her. She fought the wheel, holding on for her life as the vehicle careened and wobbled, then gradually subsided, righting itself and coming back under control, speed dropping quickly, and then she was sedately motoring again, her breathing slowly coming back to normal, her mind already analyzing the next step.

Maybe at last she was going to get a line on someone who might know something. Time would tell, if she could stay alive long enough to find out.

###

She sat in the beat up truck Ruiz had loaned her, looking at the shanty-houses spread out across the hillside that was Diaz Ordaz. She had a photo of Soto pinned against the dash and she was watching the street. It was a poor run-down area even by Mexican standards, but there were flashes of color in the flowers and the bright murals, and even some green areas, as if the people were trying to fight back against the bleakness.

She had been watching the place for two days now, regularly moving around and changing her appearance, often lying on her seat, out of sight with periscope mirror trained on the building. So far he hadn't shown and she was beginning to wonder about the information Jorge had given her. It was the right address, and Ruiz had confirmed it was a meeting place for gang members. You'd only know it was there because it had a large black door poking out between a cheap liquor store on one side and an open unit selling used car parts on the other.

She rubbed her face. She felt like she'd go cross-eyed if she had to watch for much longer. As she yawned again with tiredness a memory of Yolanda Lopez flashed through her mind. The small dignified and courageous woman sitting across from her in Bedford Max prison, patient and trusting, her eye cloudy and sightless. Pascal knew she had to crack on, whatever it took. Her mind wandered. And what about Jonas Calver? Maybe it was time to call him, give him an up-date? But what could she tell him? Zilch? She'd be embarrassed to tell him how little progress she'd made. That call would have to wait.

As her eyes swept casually over the target zone for about the millionth time Soto suddenly emerged from out of the black doorway. She hadn't seen him go in so maybe there was a rear entrance somewhere. He looked nervy as hell, scanning the street cautiously and then starting to walk down the sidewalk. Pascal checked her face in the mirror. She had darkened her skin, trying to make herself look like a native Mexican, her short hair now dyed pitch black. She got out of the truck and began to follow Soto, keeping well back among the sparse number of pedestrians. Then it got a bit easier as he was talking on the phone, less interested in what was going on around him, ensconced in his conversation as he continued walking. Pascal crossed the road to the other side, keeping him in sight.

He turned right into a side road, so Pascal sped up, and as she reached the junction she caught a glimpse of him entering a building down the end of the street. She could just make out faded lettering on the wall that said it was the Cafe Flamingo. Pascal leaned back against the wall, thinking, continuing to watch the place. Half way down the street, opposite side of the road was a rundown Cantina with a couple of empty tables outside. She made her way down to it, took one of the tables, ordering a coffee from the girl behind the counter. She now had an unrestricted view of Cafe Flamingo which was around fifty meters away on the other side of the street. Her table was behind some large potted cactus plants which also shielded her from anyone who might be looking over at the Cantina from Cafe Flamingo.

She studied the building. It was three stories high, standing alone and it kind of dominated the street. Run-down as hell with faded yellow peeling paint and broken plaster, it had a continuous balcony, or walkway around the second floor. Occasionally she could see people walking around it and poking their heads over the side.

Pascal dug her burner out and texted Ruiz asking for any Intel he might have on the place. She sipped coffee, watching. It was mid-afternoon, siesta time so the street was quiet and felt kind of drowsy, as if everyone was taking a nap, which they probably were. But Ruiz wasn't; her phone buzzed with a reply that read: *"its a whorehouse!"*

She looked up to see the door opening and Soto leaving, but he stopped in the doorway to kiss a girl on the mouth - she looked about twelve years old. The door closed and Soto moved back up the street. Pascal leaned back behind the cactus plants, deliberating. She knew where to find Soto now. Maybe Cafe Flamingo would give her more than following the guy and trying to pump him? She decided to stay put. She smiled as the rough contours of a plan started to form up in her mind, a plan that would call for a substantial involvement from Ruiz.

CHAPTER EIGHT

'Absolutely not,' Ruiz spluttered. 'I'm DEA, not sex crimes, and this is way outside my area of expertise.' They were sat in Ruiz's beat-up truck, temporarily loaned out to Pascal. She was sitting in the driver's seat, and they were parked up around the corner from Cafe Flamingo.

'Man, you don't have to *do* anything,' Pascal said. 'Just go in and talk, say you're looking for something special. Sex with a female child and you like it real rough, and you'll pay top dollar for it. How difficult is that?' she asked.

'And then what?' he responded, still rattled. 'What's that going to give you? It's no secret they likely offer that kind of service. So what? And they'll check me out, and I don't want that. Sorry, but it ain't gonna happen,' Ruiz said.

Pascal nodded. She couldn't really blame him. 'You know how long I've been in Juarez, Ruiz? And I still don't have a damn thing. If I don't get something soon I might as well pack up and go home. Leave that little girl to get raped, murdered and chucked away like a piece of garbage.'

Ruiz looked into the distance, crooked half smile on his face. He said, 'you don't give up do you?' He drew on a cigarette, watching the street, ruminating, smoke drifting up from his nostrils. Then he said, quickly, 'okay, I'll go in, but nothing fancy. I'll be a dumb punter, ask for a girl, question her and get out. Best I can do.'

She leaned up and kissed him on the cheek.

###

They saw no need to hang around so Ruiz went home and got changed. He came back significantly dressed up, looking flashy, a mouthy guy with more money than sense. At 9.30 pm. he poured some whiskey on his hands and rubbed it on his face and into the stubble around his jaw.

He climbed out of the truck and Pascal wished him luck. He nodded and moved off into the night. She settled down to wait. Dog tired and despite the gentle street sounds and bustle around the truck she soon fell into a deep sleep. She was woken by a tapping on the passenger side window. She checked the dash clock: 1.10 am. She opened the door and let Ruiz in. He looked sombre. 'Let's get outta here,' he said.

###

They sat at a table on the sidewalk downtown sipping black espresso. Ruiz looked bushed and washed out. He ran a hand through his hair and raised his tired eyes to look at Pascal. 'She's there you know, Tilly-

May,' he said casually.

She felt a surge of excitement. At last, something. 'Tell me what happened?' she said.

He rubbed the stubble on his chin. 'It was easy in the end,' he said. 'A quiet night. Not too many punters. I played drunk, so they kind of left me to stew, but kept the booze coming. Maybe they figured on rolling me and taking the wallet, but I poured most of the drink off in a potted plant. In the end I got lucky, and maybe it's true what they say about like attracting like, because the girl who lighted on me was a real lush.'

'What happened?'

'This Carlita, who sat with me, she was pretty drunk, but they didn't know it to start with. She was taking a lot of my drink, and her mouth was getting pretty loose. Boy I had to sit and listen to her whining, seemed like forever,' he said, his eyes going flat as he remembered. 'We were on the second floor, and its essentially a conventional brothel. Girls mingling with punters, plenty of booze and music, people pairing off and going to rooms after speaking to the madam, big butch girl called Brigida. Talking to Carlita, I said I heard guys who liked the young stuff talk about a little girl called Tilly-May. She didn't even blink. Said Tilly was a real special girl, because she was upstairs, on the third floor, a place guys like me would never get to see, and she surprised I'd heard about Tilly. Maybe I moved in high circles?

'Anyway, by then she's starting to get maudlin, saying Tilly was a real good girl. Then she took this little wallet out her pocket and showed me an old style photo, said they'd been let out by their minders to go shopping. Tilly and some others had sneaked in a photo booth, and Tilly-May had got the picture. But by then I noticed Brigida was watching us, talking to one of the guys who looked like the house muscle. So I pre-empted them and got up to leave, but before I did I asked to use the john as an excuse to have a nose. I wandered along the landing to see if you could get to the third floor, but couldn't find a staircase, and couple of security guys appeared real quick. When I asked a couple of questions, they got heavy, hustled me downstairs and kicked me out with a boot in the ass, saying don't come back. I don't think Carlita will give them anything useful because she was pickled, and I was just another drunk punter.'

He finished speaking, looking tired. Pascal took a sip of espresso, watching him over the rim of her cup, caution fighting excitement. His story just seemed a little too pat - Tilly-May suddenly appears out of nowhere. But then again maybe it was just Karma and she was getting paranoid. Hell, after consistently coming up empty, she'd been given a solid lead. Maybe she should just grab it and stop trying to pick holes in it. Her eyes re-focused on Ruiz.

He was watching her. He held his fist out, turned it over, opening it, revealing a small black and white photo. 'I palmed it,' he said. 'I'm told its Tilly-May.'

She picked up the photo and studied it. It was a slightly out of focus picture of a pretty little girl's face, smiling into the camera. She looked about 8 years old. The features were discernible but not crystal clear, and she wondered about that; not a great photo for ID purposes.

After a moment Ruiz said, 'so what you gonna do?'

She looked out at the early morning streets and then over

towards the mountains in the distance, her eyes turning inward as she thought about that question. After a moment, she said, 'I need to get into the building and get her out,' *and ask her about Sapphire*, but she didn't say that. Something inside her, a gut instinct or intuition, told her to keep that to herself. She knew detective Daly would not have revealed what little she had told him about Sapphire, so no one here knew why she was really there, and she aimed to keep it that way.

'I won't say you're fucking crazy again,' Ruiz said. 'But you are. How you going to get in and out with the girl? It's like fort Knox in there?'

'With your help, amigo. Can you draw me a floor plan?'

He looked at her, mouth agape.

###

The plan Ruiz managed to sketch out was a rough pencil drawn affair, much of it clearly based on speculation and memory, but it had the basics. Pascal watched Cafe Flamingo for one more session, sipping tequila and imbibing the night air, drawing in a feel for the area and its denizens. She was particularly interested in a large tree that grew tall and reached up to the second floor balcony, its branches at some points obscuring the middle section of the building from the street. As far as she could see it was the only logical covert way in. In keeping with its run-down appearance, Cafe Flamingo didn't appear to have any CCTV in or around it and it was possible there were no cameras. Perhaps the reputation of the place was enough to scare off potential snoopers.

Based on her observation, Pascal reckoned there was a sweet spot between around 4.00 to 5.30 am when the place went really quiet, wound down and the lights went out. Trouble was, the third floor seemed hermetically sealed as no lights showed up there at any time.

She checked her watch: 4.20 am. She rose from the table on the sidewalk, left a tip and went back to the truck parked up around the corner. There she donned her black night gear; she took along only a roll of duct tape, a hunting knife and some rope wrapped around her waist. At the foot of the tree, she put on a woolly black cap and pulled it down around her ears.

It seemed eerily quiet, the building shrouded in darkness, just a stray dog occasionally barking and distant sounds of traffic. She looked up at the tree, eyes traveling up the trunk, then over the branches that stretched out and touched the balcony. Then she began to climb.

There were small branches sticking out at the base of the tree and the trunk was thick with large grooves in the bark providing hand grips for her small fingers. It was almost like climbing a ladder and she was soon up to just below the balcony. There she sat for around five minutes just listening and acclimatising. There was no sound of movement on the walk-around balcony.

She examined the branches which up there suddenly seemed puny and insufficient to carry her weight. She looked down; a fall from there would at the least seriously injure her if not kill. She looked up; there was a branch up there, stretching out around 6 feet above the balcony. She started to climb again.

She arrived and looked out along the branch and down onto the empty walkway. The branch looked pretty flimsy towards the end. She lowered her head, feeling the living wood under her cheek. She closed her eyes for a moment, resting, willing up the courage. Her problem was that the one fear she had in life was not violence, but heights. She swallowed hard and started edging her way out along the branch. The distance to the balcony was only about seven feet but it looked like a mile. Half way across, the bough started to dip and she froze. She half expected to hear the crack of the branch breaking but it held. But if she moved any further, it was likely to go. She seemed stuck.

She calmed her breathing, trying to get it regular and slow her racing heart. She heard movement from the balcony, a scrape as if a door were opening. There were quiet steps and she looked down. It was one of the guys she had seen hanging around the doorway to the Cafe. It looked like he was doing a security sweep. He stopped right beneath her, and leaned over the balcony, looking down. She could hear his breathing. If he glanced up, he would be looking right into her eyes. She held her breath.

He stepped back and was moving again, and another guy was there. Looked like they patrolled in two's and were meeting up underneath Pascal. They didn't speak just moved away a few feet and slid a door open and went back inside, closing the door behind them.

Pascal knew now how she could get onto the balcony, if the branch would hold. She needed to move quickly along it in one movement and try and get her weight to the end of the bough as at swung down onto the balcony, before it broke under her weight in the middle. It was a trade-off between tension, mass and velocity. It sounded great in theory.

There was a very slight breeze that seemed to come in waves

that blew the branches upward. She watched the leaves waiting for it to come, then as she heard the rustling sound she was scrambling along the branch, her stomach churning as the bough began to dip, then she heard the crack as it went and she was coming down fast. She hit the top of the balcony wall hard, air knocked from her lungs, then she was rolling with the movement over the side and into the walkway, continuing until she came to a stop against the sliding doors. She remained completely still, lying on her back breathing hard and listening. Someone must have heard something, surely? She waited as her breathing and heart rate came down. Nothing stirred.

She rose to her feet, looking at the sliding glass door. There was a curtain behind it and no gaps for her to see through. She slid the door open silently, listening intently, then reached in and moved the curtain. To her left she was looking down an empty corridor with a couple of doors each side. As she carefully examined the area, she wondered where the two guys were and then dismissed the thought; she didn't have time to worry. The longer she stayed inside the more at risk she was of discovery. She stepped into the corridor and noticed a door to her right just before the end of the corridor. She moved to the door and opened it. It looked like a back service stairway going up to the third floor. She stepped into the stairwell and began to climb.

At the top, another doorway. She opened it a jar and looked through; another corridor, this time with a number of doors off either side. She stopped there and rested, listening and thinking. There were 8 doors, 4 either side and it looked like the only option was to go down and check each one until she found Tilly-May, if she was there. Not scientific or subtle but she didn't think there was any other way. She moved to the first door, listening. She turned the door knob and looked in through the crack. Two beds and two sleeping girls, neither was Tilly-May, too old, and wrong size. She moved to the next door. She guessed security was probably lax up here because the security on the access ways was so heavy.

Second room, two more girls, this time one was awake, sitting on her bed with her back to the door. Neither one was Tilly-May, wrong hair color. Pascal silently closed the door and moved on. As she got to the next door, she heard footsteps coming from the end of the corridor around the corner. She silently entered the room, closing the door behind her and leaning against it, then standing to one side. Two beds again, and two girls both sleeping, one's face obscured in the pillow; she waited. Then the door was opening; she flattened herself against the wall holding her breath. A shard of light from the corridor extended across the floor, held a moment as someone looked in, then the door was closing again, and Pascal was slowly exhaling her breath.

As she moved toward the bed her excitement was rising; she looked down at the girl's partially obscured face and knew it was Tilly-May. She moved to the other bed and looked down at the girl, a teenager, around 15 she guessed, snoring lightly. Pascal thought for a moment, running through the options. She had no choice really if she was to try and get Tilly-May out. She dug out her roll of duct tape, all the while studying the lightly snoring girl. She drew off a length of tape, slowly, without making a sound, bit through with her teeth, then stood over the girl, waiting for her to breath in. As she did so Pascal lent down and firmly placed the tape across the girl's mouth. As she came awake, Pascal held her finger up to the girl's face, indicating silence. There was intense fear in the girl's eyes as she came awake, turning to a drowsy kind of shock as she took in Pascal's appearance. Pascal whispered, 'relax. I'm not going to hurt you.'

She got up and moved over to Tilly-May's sleeping form. Pascal took out a dog-eared copy of Tilly-May's hand-written note and lightly tapped the girl's shoulder, finger to her lips. She came awake quick, eyes hunted, then like the other girl a kind of mild surprise followed by a sort of deadness. Pascal wondered whether they were on some type of drug as they seemed sluggish but maybe it was just the usual groggy feeling of first waking from a long sleep.

Pascal held the note in front of the girl and her eyes widened; she was about to speak, so Pascal put her hand over the girl's mouth. 'Quiet,' she said. 'I'm going to get you out of here, but you must be quiet, whisper.'

The girl nodded, eyes full of wonder. Pascal removed her hand. 'Yolanda?' the girl whispered. 'Sapphire said you would come.'

'No, I'm not Yolanda. I'm Courtney. Is Sapphire here?'

The girl shook her head.

'Okay, I'm going to get you out, but you must be quiet and do everything I say.'

The girl nodded meekly, grabbing Pascal's hand and pulling it to her mouth to kiss it. Pascal heard a sound behind her as the other girl came off the bed, going for the door. Pascal swung her leg across sweeping the girls feet from under and she went down. Tilly-May said, 'she's not my friend. She's here to watch me.'

Pascal nodded. She hauled the girl back onto the bed, then she unwound the rope from around her waist. She tied the girl's hands and

feet to the four bed posts so she would have trouble moving, then she re
-covered her with the blankets, so just her hair was showing on the
pillow. Then she got Tilly up and placed her pillows under the blankets
on her bed to look like a sleeping form. It wouldn't fool them for long.

'Is there any way out of here other than the front door?' Pascal
asked.

'There's a lift at the back only stops at this floor and the ground
floor where the cars are parked. They bring supplies in from there. You
can get on it here but there's always men downstairs watching.'

'Good,' Pascal said. 'Let's go. Which way to the lift?'

'Down the corridor, then right, and it's at the end.'

Pascal nodded, slipped the door open and checked the corridor.
She pushed Tilly out in front of her, moved out, closed the door, and
hustled her silently down the corridor.

It seemed too easy, but it was the witching hour, and she guessed
that the incidence of any real threats to the place, other than the odd
drunk or fight between punters, was low. And that lack of threat
eventually degraded security and the watchfulness of those on guard.
That's what she told herself, anyway.

In the lift going down Pascal put her woolly cap back on and
pulled it down, then took out her hunting knife. Tilly-May's eyes
widened, but she didn't look scared. She grabbed Pascal's other hand
and squeezed it.

'Get behind me,' Pascal said, 'and do exactly as I say. I'm
guessing they'll see the lift is coming down. When the door opens, *run*.
I want you to find a car with keys in the ignition. Can you do that for
me?'

'I'll try,' she said. 'But what about you? You can't fight them all. You're just a girl. They'll kill you.'

Pascal smiled. 'Don't worry,' she said. 'I eat guys like that for breakfast.'

Tilly-May giggled, and then the lift doors were opening.

There were two of them standing there, casually watching as the doors slid open. Pascal knew she'd get only one chance to hit them hard before they could recover. She shouted, '*run*,' at Tilly-May, as she launched herself at the two guys. The one on the right took the hunting knife up to the hilt in his stomach. Pascal left it there, continuing her momentum into the other guy as he tried to pull his gun, so they went over in a heap, the gun skittering away across the concrete floor.

Pascal was up first, football kicking the guy in the face as he tried to get up, hearing a satisfying crack in his neck as his head snapped back. She ran, stooping to pick up the gun as she moved, but she couldn't see Tilly-May. She heard a shout from the right, 'Courtney, over here.' And there she was, standing beside a small blue ford fiesta. Pascal wrenched the door open, and said, 'get in,' turning the ignition as she spoke.

As she accelerated away towards the exit, another guy appeared, running to stand across the lane, raising his gun. She hit him dead center, throwing his body over the car as she smashed through the barrier and out onto the street, picking up speed, reaching the junction and turning right onto the main drag.

###

The hotel was cheap and anonymous, part of a national budget franchise chain, six stories high, tucked away in the south of the city. Pascal booked herself in as a backpacker, a mother traveling with her young daughter. When they got to the room on the fifth floor they both crashed out on the double bed and fell asleep instantly.

About mid-morning Pascal rose and phoned down for some breakfast. She opened the doors out onto the tiny balcony and moved a small table and two chairs out there, went back in and sat down near the bed. She dug out her phone and checked it. A load of miscalls from Ruiz - he could wait. She turned and watched Tilly-May for a while as she slept, amazed that the child's face could look so calm and untroubled after all she'd been through. Her skin was smooth and unblemished, light brown in color; maybe she was part Hispanic although her accent when she spoke was pure American. Her hair was light brown, cut short, and she had brown eyes and a mass of freckles. A fly alighted on her nose as she slept, her hand involuntarily flipping out and casually swatting it away, a light frown dimpling her face. Pascal smiled, then took a photo of her.

When she looked back, Tilly-May was awake, watching her, looking confused, maybe halfway between relieved and scared.

'Good morning,' Pascal said, smiling at her.

'You won't take me back, will you?' she asked.

'Of course not. You're safe now,' Pascal said. There was a knock at the door. 'And I've got us some breakfast. Would you like some?'

Pascal went to the door and ushered the lady in with their breakfast on a tray.

Later they sat out on the balcony and ate. Pascal was desperate to question her but knew if she moved too quickly it might make her clam up. But in the end it was Tilly-May who starting talking, unprompted. 'Sapphire was my best friend,' she said, nodding to herself, looking old beyond her years. 'She's two years younger and not very grown up, so I looked after her. But then they took her away, Gutman, the fat man took her, and now I don't know where she is,' she said, wistfully.

Pascal pulled her into a hug, looking down, watching the girl. 'Where are you from, originally Tilly-May?' she asked her.

'Beverley Hills, Los Angeles,' she replied. 'And my names not Tilly-May.'

Pascal's phone buzzed: Ruiz. She better take it this time. She rose, tapping him on, raising the phone to her ear and walking back inside the room.

'Jesus! Where you been? You get the girl. What happened?'

'Whoa there. Slow down,' Pascal said. 'I got the girl and we're fine, holed up in a hotel. Say, you ever hear of a guy called, Gutman?' she asked.

There was silence for a couple of beats. Pascal thought the connection might have gone down, but then he was on again. 'What was that name again?' he asked.

'Gutman.'

'Look, maybe I should come down there now and see you, and we can talk.'

'Fine,' Pascal said, and gave him the name and address of the hotel. He said he was near and would be there in fifteen. As she disconnected and walked back out onto the balcony, she wondered idly why he hadn't answered her question about the man Gutman.

She told Tilly-May a friend, Ruiz, was coming but that she mustn't talk about Sapphire as this friend didn't know anything about her. The child looked troubled by this so Pascal hugged her again. 'So what is your real name, Tilly-May?' she said.

'Lucy,' she whispered. 'Lucy Collins.'

'Well, Lucy, I want to rescue your friend Sapphire. I know it's horrible to talk about what you've both been through but I need to know as much as possible so I can help. Do you understand?'

'I understand, Courtney. I want to find her too. She can't look after herself on her own,' Tilly-May said, her small face intense and serious.

'Who is this Gutman? Might she be with him?'

Tilly-May scowled. 'He's the worst,' she said softly. 'He has a Hacienda in the desert, and Sapphire was there most of the time, because he liked her more. I was mostly at Cafe Flamingo, at parties for old men.'

The way she spoke was so matter of fact it scared Pascal. She wanted to stop the girl from revisiting such painful memories, but she knew the only way in was to get the detail, however much that might hurt, because every second could count.

Tilly-May seemed to understand. She said, haltingly, taking stuttering breaths, 'they hurt me so much, and there were so many I have forgotten. Always hurting me, wanting more, and when I didn't know what they wanted they would beat me, until I couldn't cry anymore.' She stopped and smiled softly. 'But now it's over, yes?'

'Yes, it's over,' Pascal said, looking over the balcony and watching as Ruiz' beaten up old truck drew into the car park. He had two male passengers with him this time but they stayed in the vehicle when Ruiz got out and made his way to the entrance.

'Stay on the balcony, will you, sweetheart?' Pascal said, going back into the room and closing the French doors behind her.

As Ruiz knocked, she opened the door and scanned him quickly, noticing the underarm bulge of a firearm. He smiled his crooked smile. She turned and began to walk away, saying, 'what's with the—' but she never got to finish her sentence because Ruiz smashed a ball-bearing filled cosh down on the back of her head and she went down.

Must have been only a few moments before she was moaning and shaking her head, coming around, her eyes bleary. She slowly took in the scene. One large guy from the truck was holding Tilly-May, the other one was stooping down over Pascal, securing her hands with wrist ties.

Tilly-May looked like a ghost, her face deathly pale. She gazed at Pascal's bound wrists and dejected expression. The girl seemed to slump in the large man's hands, but it was a ploy to deceive him. She easily broke from his grasp and then she was running, but to Pascal it seemed almost to be in slow-motion. She slipped through the French doors and as the child reached the balcony wall Pascal screamed, '*no*,' as she jumped. Pascal's scream echoed and ended abruptly with the sound of Tilly-May's small body hitting the sidewalk five stories below.

She scrambled to the balcony and looked down. Tilly-May's body seemed peaceful now. She could even have been sleeping if it wasn't for the long tail of pooling blood spreading around her head. Behind Pascal, Ruiz said, 'too bad. But she was spoiled goods.'

Pascal had her arms over his head before the words had left his mouth, tightening them around his neck like a vice, pulling with everything she had, screaming, but they clubbed her again from behind and she went down, out cold.

When they revived her with a slap and glass of water thrown over her face, her heavy-lidded eyes looked flat and empty. She said, tonelessly, 'I will kill you, Ruiz, however long it takes. That's a promise.'

He laughed. 'I don't think so. Less you can come back to life and dig yourself out of a mass grave. Let's go.'

Before the police arrived they left, two soldiers in the front, one driving, and Pascal in the back with Ruiz.

CHAPTER NINE

In the truck for a while, numb with grief and guilt, Pascal couldn't think straight. She had known something was wrong when Ruiz had arrived - he was carrying for Christ sakes. Why had she turned her back on him? A child had died because she had been sloppy and half-asleep, and now she'd have to live with it. She wanted to scream the world down and cry forever, but she knew she had to keep a lid on it because Sapphire was still out there. And that was something to hold onto, as well as her cold coruscating anger for Ruiz. Tilly-May had endured so much in her young life, and she had been within touching distance of freedom, and then she'd had it taken it away from her by a dirty cop. She was acutely aware of Ruiz sitting beside her, his smell, sweaty and sour. She wanted to attack him now and kill him, but she knew if she was to have a chance of redemption, a chance to get Sapphire and make Ruiz pay, she needed to suppress her anger and try to engage him.

She collected herself together mentally, the old mantra playing in her head: never give up. 'So, what turned you, Ruiz?' she asked idly, barely disguising her contempt. 'Go on, surprise me. Money? Little girls?'

'All of it,' he said, half smile, as if he'd been waiting for her to ask. 'You know how much the DEA pay? Slave labor man, and I got tired of it. Tired of watching millions and millions of dollars pouring through like a river and never being able to touch it. But now I can. What kind of a schmuck is gonna give thirty years to the agency and then get what, a gold watch? Not this monkey. And the perks, man. You've got no idea.'

But Pascal was struck by the haunted look in his eyes as he spoke; it didn't seem to fit the glib and predictable rationale for his betrayal. 'So what about all the ordinary men and women who do believe in the agency and justice?' she asked. 'And what about the little girls, abducted, raped and murdered, and their families never knowing what happened, never being able to grieve?'

She held his eyes for a long moment. ' You ain't worth shit, Ruiz, because you got no code and you got no honor. Just another dirty cop,' she said. 'Gutman buy you, did he?'

For a second Pascal thought she saw something in Ruiz's eyes. Pain, guilt, remorse, but whatever it was, it was gone in an instant. 'Solomon Gutiérrez to you,' he said flatly. 'He runs it all, and you're about to meet him.'

Pascal looked out of the window as she covertly tested the ties around her wrist. There was no give. The vehicle slowed as it came out of the desert, approaching what looked like a ranch, a substantial white single storey stucco property spread out on a large plot. The building was set around a courtyard with fountains, and further out there were corrals with some fine looking horses, and at the extremity a bell-tower.

Ruiz led Pascal into the house; he seemed to know his way

around. He led her into a large living room with an empty open stone fireplace. On the walls were heavy oils showing figures from Mexico's past, mostly in uniform. There were also animal heads amongst the pictures, mounted, sticking out of the wall, buffalo and elk, and there were thick rugs scattered over the stone floor. A large man, tall and wide sat at an antique desk working on some papers, large flat-screen monitors facing him, showing what looked like real-time stock prices.

The man remained seated but said to Ruiz, without looking up,'leave us.' Pascal studied the guy. He was fat, no other word for it. Sitting down you couldn't see it all, and his well cut white suit did a good job of disguising it, but it was there. His face was jowly, thick and fleshy, with sensuous lips below a small thin mustache. His black eyes seemed empty and expressionless, but watchful.

'I am Gutiérrez,' he said. 'You come to look for the Dinks child, no?'

Pascal's surprise was evidenced by an almost imperceptible widening of her eyes, but he picked up on it with a nod to himself. 'I have followed your noisy progress since you arrived here in Mexico, and of course, Ruiz has told me certain things about you. There could be only one reason why you are here. Fortunately you work alone with only the lawyer in New York, and I am satisfied you have communicated nothing of what you have learned to him or the outside world. So damage is containable,' he said, finally looking up at her. 'But, as I think you say in America, she is too hot to handle now, and regrettably I must end it,' he added.

He got up and seemed to glide to a set of double doors, and now she could really see how fat he was. Shape wise he was like one of those spinning tops, all the mass concentrated around his waist. He opened the double doors and stood to one side.

Pascal looked through; the room was unlit, but she could make out the shape of a small child sitting on a chair looking at pictures in a book. She moved closer. Her heart jumped. It looked like Sapphire Dinks. The fat man clapped his hands and switched the light on, and the child jumped to her feet. Pascal noticed the manacle around her ankle, on a chain attached to the wall. The child looked skinny and underfed, her bright blue eyes were blank but focused on the fat man, seemingly indifferent to Pascal.

'Sapphire?' Pascal said, but it was as if the child was deaf.

'She can't hear you, only me. Luckily I have rather strange, mild sexual tastes. She has suffered little, her life not so different to any poor Mexican child growing up in the Barrios. I have enjoyed her company for many months, but your arrival must end that. So, if you and the child were now to disappear the matter is resolved,' he said.

'So tell me about the Daughter Eaters,' Pascal said casually.

This time it was his eyes that registered something, a faint glimmer in the depths, but he smiled pleasantly. 'I'm sorry, I have not heard that name before?'

'Nice try, Gutman, but you can't kid a kidder,' she said.

He watched her some more, still smiling. He moved to the double doors and closed them again, blocking off Pascal's view of the child once more. Gutman glided over to a well stocked drinks table. 'Hah, so perhaps a little light entertainment is in order?' he said. 'You've bought yourself some time, but only a little. Drink?'

'Sure. Why not. I'll have a scotch,' she said.

He slowly mixed the drink and handed it to her. 'If you know anything, tell me,' he said. 'If you convince me you have real knowledge, we'll talk.'

Pascal sipped her drink. 'Why you so worried about what I might know? You're going to kill us anyway?'

He moved his massive bulk over to the chair and sat again, still contemplating her solemnly. 'You have a certain quality about you, my dear. You're about to die but you show no fear. That is uncommon. It says you are more than you seem on the surface, a person not to be underestimated. I would be foolish not to try to ascertain what knowledge you have.'

'And what if I tell you to go fuck yourself?' Pascal said, sipping her scotch.

His eyes darkened briefly. 'Spare me profanity,' he said distastefully, but then smiled again. 'Ah yes, you're baiting me, of course. But seriously, Courtney. May I call you Courtney?' he asked, impervious to any answer she might give. 'I'm sure you're curious, so tell me what you know, and if its more than just speculation, perhaps I will satisfy that curiosity. A bargain.'

'I'm hungry,' Pascal said. 'Get me a Big Mac style burger with onions and fries and one for the girl - she looks famished - then maybe I'll talk.'

Gutman raised a phone from the desk and spoke briefly in Spanish. 'It's on its way. Sit down,' he said indicating a comfortable armchair. 'As for Sapphire, she barely eats anything these days, but she will have one also.'

Pascal let that pass. 'Okay, a bargain,' she said. 'But to see each side carries out its obligations, and as you currently have all the power, I'll give you a bit, then you give me a bit?'

'Fine. But you see again, you use the word currently as if there is a way out for you. You are uncommonly self assured and confident,' he said.

'So they tell me,' she said.

A door opened and a Mexican woman entered carrying a tray that she put down on a small table which she drew up to Pascal's chair. '*Mucho Gracias*,' Pascal said, winking at the woman.

As the maid took one of the plates off the tray and went through the double doors which she closed behind her, Pascal said, 'I have the secret name you use, or others use, and that was enough to stop you in your tracks. So I've already given you something. Tell me how you got to where you are?'

Gutman shrugged impressively, his huge frame juddering. 'I was a street punk, but I had a brain, but that's not enough. You have to love violence and prove yourself time and again if you want to really move up in the cartel. So twenty five or so years ago I began developing a sideline,' he said.

Pascal finished munching a mouthful of beef, bread, onions and gherkins, and said, 'abducting, torturing, raping and murdering young women, yes?'

'No! Never. I offered a service to paying customers and developed a sound business model from that. And I wasn't alone, I was just more organized and determined, and I endured. Others didn't.'

Pascal wiped her lips with a napkin and took a shot of scotch.

Gutman had a smile on his face as if he were remembering the old days. 'We used to go on safari with rich punters looking for game, scouring the barrios for young meat to ravish,' he said.

'Sounds a gas,' Pascal said. 'Taking from poor families their most precious thing, their children, and killing them.'

'Pah!' Gutman said. 'They breed like rabbits, the poor. We were the wolves, they the sheep, and it was a natural phenomenon.'

Pascal guessed Gutman was probably clinically insane, making him even more dangerous. But she wanted facts so no point in winding him up.

'You know, Courtney,' he continued. 'In twenty-five years you are the first person to cause me trouble,' he said with a beaming smile. 'In the early years the cartels tolerated me, then they used me themselves, as did the *federales*. In Mexico I am now essentially untouchable, until you appeared. Your abduction of the child from Cafe Flamingo was daring and courageous, albeit that I allowed it to happen. Of course your intervention also cost me the life of one of my men who we had to put out of his misery.'

'My heart bleeds for you,' Pascal said. 'The girl, before she died told me her name and where she was from. Tell me about her. Was she abducted to order?'

'I don't believe she told you anything before her unfortunate end,' he said.

'Her name's Lucy and she was from L.A. and I'm guessing she came from at least a middle class family, so it would no doubt take the FBI about 5 seconds to ID her from missing persons,' Pascal said.

Gutman licked his lips again. 'What can it hurt now to tell you a snippet or two?' he said. 'She was one of our first forays across the border,' he said with satisfaction. 'A complete success and most lucrative. A big name Hollywood producer had become infatuated with the girl. She was the daughter of an actress he cast in his film in order to get access to the child. When that didn't work, he came to me.'

Pascal studied the man, almost fascinated, as if he were some type of exotic spider held in the bottom of a jar. 'So why was she still alive? I thought your fucked up psychopath clients paid to kill?' she said.

'Not all, but part of the deal we strike is that the target will cease to be soon after the contract is fulfilled, whatever the particular peccadillces of the client.'

Pascal nodded, watching the guy. 'I get it. The target still has value to you, even after your high roller has tortured and raped her. You can still use her in Cafe Flamingo or for whatever, to sweeten a deal with a police chief or a politician. Risky though with a gringo kid, right?'

'Not at all. Their origin is disguised. Like all great businesses, we sweat and make full use of our economic assets before we retire them.'

'Most commendable,' Pascal said. 'But what about Cafe Flamingo? Surely the place is rather obvious, if say your high roller clients are seen going there, and with the assets as you call them, all in plain sight?'

'Not at all my dear. The third floor of Cafe Flamingo is essentially sealed to the outside world, with extremely tight security on any access and egress points. And we have a heliport on the roof where special clients arrive and leave at night unobserved and untroubled, thanks to the cooperation of our local law enforcement who all regularly partake of our wares at the club.'

'You certainly seem to have got it all worked out,' Pascal said, frowning.

'Indeed, but I can see something still troubles you?' he said.

'Yeah,' she said. 'Tell me about protection.'

He laughed. 'I can see you are still trying to amass information, my dear, but it will do you no good, even if you could escape and tell your story. I own all the politicians in Chihuahua County, and that extends all the way to Mexico City, the police, *Federales* and I've told you about the cartels.'

'Well that's all well and good, but I'm not talking about Mexico. Mexico's essentially a failed narco state, virtually run by the cartels, and the fact that you may own some of these people is no surprise to me. What I'm talking about is protection in the USA. Fernando Ruiz is a lower echelon nobody in the DEA so he's not going to protect you against kidnap and murder charges in the States. You're are certainly not a fool, so before you extended your kidnap to order activities across the border you must have done so with protection in place. If not, you would be placing yourself up shit creek without a paddle. US law enforcement wouldn't hesitate to indict you for kidnap and then extradite you to stand trial. You've already admitted you kidnapped a US national, a minor, took her across a national border, and it was apparently done at the behest of a US national. That's serious stuff in anybodies book.'

Gutman clapped his hands with pleasure. 'You know, in different circumstances, my dear, I would not hesitate to offer you a senior role in my organization, but we must deal the hand God grants us.' He studied her face with satisfaction. 'Since you are no longer a risk to me, and we do have a bargain after all,' he said, chortling away. 'I will indulge your curiosity. Yes, you are right. You dismissively and insultingly characterized Mexico as being a hotbed of corruption, but the US is no different. Everyone has a price, and I can afford to pay it. We have a client who is a US senator,' he said, and now Pascal could see he was lost in a kind of reverie of power, his eyes far away. A smile spread over Gutman's face. He turned to Pascal. 'And, my dear, he isn't just a senator, he's also a very close confidant of the director of the FBI. Perhaps that answers your question?'

Pascal's first thought was that he was bragging, but that didn't really stack up. Gutman was egotistical but also very clever and she doubted he would embark on kidnapping US citizens unless he was protected, so his story could be true.

Gutman watched her face, enjoying her expression as she concluded he was probably telling the truth. 'So you see, my dear, even if you were free to cross the border and tell your little story, it wouldn't help you, because it isn't just the senator we have in our pocket.'

Pascal knew if he was telling the truth, she had nowhere to run, even if she could break free. They had her every which way, and now the clock was almost run-down. Time for a last question, about the thing that had brought her there, the thing that was now likely going to take her life. 'So tell me about the kidnap of Sapphire Dinks, Gutman? Treat it as my last dying wish if you like.'

'Alas my dear, I have to disappoint you,' he said, waving a hand. 'Not because I don't want to tell you, but because I am afraid I didn't organize her kidnapping, although I did greatly benefit from it. One detail I can tell you though is that Sapphire won't be able to tell you anything either, because she was drugged for the kidnap. So I am afraid you will be taking that particular mystery to your grave'

Pascal watched his face, initially not believing him, but her disbelief quickly fading. Why would he lie? He had nothing to gain from it, and his expression was relaxed, unconcerned whether she believed him or not.

He nodded. 'I understand your distress, my dear. To go through all that you have been through and still not know, and then to die with your prize, Sapphire, the person you were seeking to save, must be a bitter pill indeed for you to swallow, but I believe it must be God's will. Now!' he said, clapping his hands, 'I have pressing business to attend to so we must cut short our most interesting chat. I am satisfied you have communicated nothing of what you know to the outside world. We know you have had no contact with the New York lawyer, Calver.'

He stood up and walked to the double doors and opened them again and went through. He knelt down by Sapphire and released the manacle from around her ankle and lead her back into the room. The child still looked as if she were in a trance, but she had a smear of ketchup on her chin, suggesting she may have eaten the burger. The other door opened and Ruiz came back with the driver. The fat man must have pressed a hidden button somewhere. He said, 'it is fitting that our DEA man should take you both for a long drive into the desert,' he said, taking a last lingering look at Sapphire. 'Adieu.' He nodded.

The soldier pushed them out of the room, and a moment later they were back in the truck, but this time with Sapphire in the front seat next to the driver and Pascal in the back with Ruiz. Sapphire's hands were free and they had removed her ankle chain. Pascal whispered, 'put your seat belt on, honey,' as if she were on the school run. Ruiz laughed, but Sapphire did as she was told.

As they moved back into the desert, Pascal began studying the topography. She had no real plan in mind. Things looked so bleak. Ruiz may have come over all relaxed but he was trained and sharp, and both he and the driver had guns, and her hands were tied. But she had to try something, anything, to try and save Sapphire. She started looking for the right place. Trouble was the desert here was just endless flat scrubland, and she didn't know how far they were going, although Gutman had said they were going on a long drive. She settled back to wait

For a long time they traveled in silence, the desert flat and unchanging, the engine sound quiet and monotonous. But then the vehicle almost imperceptibly began to climb and there were small rocky outcrops erupting out of the desert; this looked better. There was no other traffic, the road - or more properly track - was deserted, other than their silent wraith like progress. So far she hadn't paid much attention to Sapphire, too busy angling for a way out, but now she did. The child mostly had her back to Pascal but from what she could see, Sapphire's small jaw line looked firm and her short blonde hair looked fine, although a bit straggly. She seemed to still be in a kind of trance, unaware of her surroundings and what was going on, maybe cocooned in her own world. Maybe that was a good thing, for the moment.

Pascal sat up straighter, edging a bit closer to the back of the driver's head, trying not to alert Ruiz, who was looking at texts on his cellphone. Pascal said to the child, 'Sapphire, I have spoken to Yolanda, and she sends her love. Sing me your lullaby, sweetie.'

Sapphire had stiffened in her seat when she heard Yolanda's name. Then incredibly the child began to hum quietly to herself. Pascal felt a frisson of excitement. She glanced out the window again and now they were driving up between rising rock walls, with gaps to their right where the desert stretched down at the side to the valley floor. Pascal reckoned she was unlikely to find a better place, but it was incredibly dangerous because of the sheer drop into the valley on the right, unprotected by road barriers, but if she didn't make her move soon, they'd die. But then again, they were going to die anyway, so what the hell.

She took a deep breath, pretending to cough, then shot her hands up and over the drivers head and down around his neck, getting the wrist ties in just the right place beneath his chin, then violently jerking up and hearing the satisfying crack as the guys neck vertebrae snapped. The truck immediately went into a swerve, veering towards rocky outcrops on the left, bouncing off these, careening over towards the sheer edge on the right, but then miraculously veering back and smashing hard into rocks on the left again, screeching along the jagged rock face, metal screaming. The truck hit a bump in the road and turned over, sliding along on its roof for what seemed like forever, before coming to a juddering halt, wheels spinning in the air, engine caterwauling in a high-pitched whine.

Pascal was underneath Ruiz. He was moaning, blood dripping down from a gash to his head. Sapphire was hanging upside down in her seat belt still singing her lullaby. Pascal felt dazed. She took some deep breaths. She started to crawl from under Ruiz and out through the smashed truck window, worming her way out onto the desert floor.

Ruiz started to moan again, saying, 'help me. I think my leg's broken.'

Pascal ignored him. She moved forward on her knees, reached into the driver's side and switched the ignition off, then moved around to Sapphire's side and began to untangle her belt and drag her out.

She pulled Sapphire over to a rock and sat her down. She looked okay. Pascal studied her surroundings. The truck was off the road at the side, and they were on an outcrop overlooking the valley, and still there was no traffic. Pascal looked at her watch, but it was broken. She checked the sky, sun sinking below the horizon; late afternoon. She heard more moaning and could see that Ruiz had managed to drag himself out of the truck and now lay on his back.

Pascal went back over to the now silent truck and climbed back in, rummaging around to see if she could find anything useful. She dug through the dead driver's pockets, digging out a gun and a knife. She cut her wrist ties.

Two gunshots rang out in quick succession, sounding like thunderclaps in the silence. Pascal scrambled out. Sapphire was standing over Ruiz with a Glock hanging in her hand. It must have still been on him.

'Get that fucking kid away from me,' Ruiz screamed.

Pascal ran to Sapphire who now held the gun loosely in her hand, her face blank. Pascal could see where the two bullets had hit an old broken tree trunk by Ruiz's side. 'Give me the gun, sweetheart,' Pascal said, voice quiet and even. It didn't seem as if the girl heard her, but she dropped the gun and plumped herself down where she was. She sat, running her fingers through the sand, continuing to hum her lullaby.

Pascal dropped down next to her, checking the gun was safe. She put her arms around her and rocked her gently. At first the child felt brittle and still, but gradually she began to soften and relax into Pascal's embrace. Her breathing slowed and she was asleep. Pascal looked over at Ruiz; he seemed to have passed out as well, which was fine with her.

Half an hour later Pascal had managed to raise the truck, using the jack. She had rolled some large rocks underneath, gradually raising it up to a height where she could have a go at rocking it right side up. She took a sip of spring water from a bottle she had found in the truck, then she put her shoulder against the underside and started to heave, straining upward, veins and muscles bulging, eyes popping out, great spurts of air venting. The truck began gently rocking, inching up, and then with one final heave it was over, bouncing and crashing onto its wheels. Pascal collapsed back on the ground and lay there for a while getting her breath back.

She mopped some sweat off her brow, got up and was moving again. She tried the engine and it started first time. She switched it off and went and got Sapphire and seated her in the front. She went back and looked at Ruiz, lying unconscious next to the body of the driver. She looked at him for a long time but couldn't quite bring herself to actually kill him in cold blood despite all he had done. If Ruiz had personally killed Tilly-May, she wouldn't have hesitated, but he hadn't, although he was clearly part of what eventually killed her. She went and got a bottle of water and wedged it between his legs.

Ten minutes later she sat in the truck, examining the two cell phones she had recovered. Ruiz's looked dead and broken, but the driver's smart phone was fully charged and working. She got out and placed Ruiz's phone with the water bottle, took a last look at him, still sleeping, and got back in the truck. She glanced at Sapphire who was now in a deep, peaceful sleep. Pascal rubbed a hand over her face, suddenly feeling intensely tired, but this wasn't the time for sleep. One last thing to do. She dialed up the New York number from memory and waited, listening to the buzzing tone as she looked around and contemplated, through the waning red sunset, the majestic desert scenery splayed out across the valley.

Calver's booming voice came through in her ear like he was standing next to her. Pascal spoke uninterrupted for four and a half minutes, leaving nothing out. Apart from a few low whistles, Calver remained silent, listening intently. When she finished, they were both quiet for a moment before Pascal spoke again. 'Why don't I just bring her in, maybe go to the US consulate. Tell the world we've got her back, solved one of the all time classic mysteries?'

'Two reasons I can think of straight up,' Calver said immediately. 'And you sound as if you know them already, and just want me to confirm your fears.'

'Maybe. So spell it out?'

'First, what this Gutman guy said about protection. We can easily believe everything he said about Mexico. Guys protected, head to toe, so you need to be real careful everything you do down there. As to the US, you said you weren't sure whether you believed him, so I don't think you can risk putting your head above the parapet until we know whether he has the FBI or anyone else in his pocket. I know it sounds incredible, but who knows? If he does, we - sorry - you, are in real trouble. I just think coming out publicly before we know what's ranged against us is dumb. As well as that, thinking it through; this case is a cause celebre, so as soon as we show out, what happens? We get buried under an avalanche of 24/7 media interest, and worse, we'll lose control of Sapphire, who'll be taken into custody while they sort things out, so we'd be outside, looking in.'

'And your second point?' she said wearily.

'It's a legal point that you may not have appreciated. If we produce Sapphire, Yolanda's murder conviction should fall, but it doesn't mean the kidnap charge will. You see, you say you believe this Gutman guy when he says he didn't kidnap Sapphire. Not only that, he also says Sapphire can't help either, because apparently she was drugged during the kidnap. She can't tell us squat. So essentially we're back to square one. We don't know what happened, so we can't prove Yolanda wasn't in on the kidnap. My guess, unless they could get anything out of Sapphire, Yolanda remains convicted of kidnap and she stays in jail for life.'

'Shit,' Pascal said. 'I hadn't realized that. So you're not just pretty face after all, Calver?' she said with a wan smile. 'So what you're saying is we essentially still need evidence?'

'That's the way it looks,' Calver said. 'We haven't solved anything. The mystery remains.'

'Yeah, and if we come out publicly, the people who did it will double down, burrow deeper, and be even harder to nail.'

'That's what I think,' Calver said. 'We'll never smoke them out if we go public now. Much easier if they don't know we're coming. I know it's your ass on the line so you need to decide, but I think you should get to a safe place and lie low. See what happens. Gutman is going find out you've flown the coop with Sapphire pretty soon, and then we'll maybe see something.' He paused. 'You sound whacked, Pascal. Get out the desert and find somewhere to hole up. Then you'll have time to think as well. When we know where we are, we can act.'

'Check,' she said, eyes half closed as sleep stole up on her. She snapped the phone off, shaking herself awake. She sprinkled some water on her face, started up the truck and slowly edged back out onto the road.

CHAPTER TEN

Jonas Calver sat across the table from Yolanda. It was an unscheduled visit arranged at short notice after he had got off the phone with Pascal. He had said nothing to Isabel on the drive down to Bedford Hills about Pascal's endeavors in Mexico, and now he sat and waited patiently for Isabel and Yolanda to finish chatting.

Yolanda seemed like she was trying to put on a brave face for her sister, but she didn't look good; not quite emaciated but thin, with hollow dark rings under her eyes and her voice quiet and subdued, as if she were afraid of being overheard.

The Spanish chatter descended into silence. Isabel said she'd get some snacks and got up to go to the vending machine. As she moved away, Calver said, 'you were right, Yolanda. Sapphire is alive.'

It looked as if she hadn't heard for a beat, then her eyes went wide, and she lurched forward in her seat grabbing Calver's arms on the table. 'How? Where is—'

'*No contact*,' a guard said sharply, suddenly looming out of nowhere, glowering down at her.

She slowly released Calver's arm, smiling. 'Sorry,' she said.

'What's all the excitement,' Isabel said, arriving back and seeing Yolanda's expression.

'Jonas says they've found her,' Yolanda said. 'They've found my baby.'

'What? Where?' Isabel said, looking at Calver, not believing it.

'It's true,' he said. 'I spoke to Courtney in Mexico and she has Sapphire with her, and Sapphire is okay.'

Both women were now smiling widely, Yolanda with a stray tear running down her cheek. Isabel was first to recover. 'So what do we do now? How do we get Yolanda out of here?' she said.

'Well, first things first,' Calver said, serious again. 'We don't go public, at least not yet.'

'But why? Are they in danger? Why don't they just tell the authorities and bring Sapphire back? I don't understand,' Yolanda said.

'I don't either, yet,' Calver said, deciding to skirt the truth and avoid detail until he knew more. 'It was a bad line, and they were stuck out in the desert somewhere. She's going to get them to a safe place and then call again and then we'll talk in detail. She still has some problems down there. And if there were to be any questions about her identity from the Mexican authorities, things could get sticky. So let's take it one step at a time. First, I need to talk to Courtney some more on a secure audible line. Then I'll know more concrete detail, and so will you.'

Yolanda said, 'she thinks the people put me here are still out there, waiting.'

Isabel said, 'I think she's right to be cautious, at least until we get them back safe in the States.'

'What makes you think they'll be safe here?' Yolanda said.

'Look, no point going off half-cock,' Calver said. 'Let's get all the information from her about their situation, and then we can make informed decisions. But one thing I think we can do is get on with filing the appeal against Yolanda's conviction,' Calver said, looking at her. 'But we'll do it low key for now. Just file the papers without any fanfare. It will take a while to filter through the system, and by then we should be ready for any blow-back.'

Isabel was smiling again. 'Good. So we're going to get Yolanda out. How does she appeal? I thought she had no more chances?'

'We make a S2255 Habeas Corpus motion to the court asking them to vacate the sentence.'

'And what's a S2255, or whatever you called it?' Isabel asked.

'It's a motion to the court who convicted Yolanda to vacate the judgment on the basis that we have new evidence that wasn't available at the time of conviction. That is, that the person she is alleged to have murdered is in fact still alive,' Calver said, staying silent about the kidnap element of her conviction.

'Go for it,' Yolanda said, smiling and taking a bite out of her Hershey bar.

'Yeah,' Isabel said. 'Go for it.'

###

It was another cheap rooming house, this time in the south of the city. Sapphire lay on the floor watching cartoons on the TV. They'd been there the night and now it was late afternoon, the waning sun still hot through the open window, dappling shadows across the simply furnished room. Pascal lay on the bed, head propped up against the pillows, laptop open, one eye on the screen, the other on the silent girl splayed out on the floor.

Pascal had texted Calver the hotel number and expected a call anytime. So far she had held off trying to question Sapphire because she didn't think it would get her anywhere. The girl seemed to be in a kind of trance and mostly stayed silent. Physically she seemed okay, but mentally, who knew. Pascal would give her some time to get accustomed to being free and safe, and then maybe she'd talk some.

What to do next though was key. Maybe they should just hole up where they were until things died down. It was a cinch word would be out on the street now. Gutiérrez's boys as well as the Barrio Azteca gang from Cafe Flamingo would be out looking for them, and it was their city and their country, and she and Sapphire stuck out like a sore thumb. And there was the truck as well; she'd had to use it to get back to the city, and eventually it would be found where she'd dumped it in a car park.

'Mama!' she heard Sapphire say. She looked over at the girl, engrossed in the TV screen, and at last there was a smile on her face. The cartoons were gone and now she was watching a National Geographic style documentary showing native American Indians in paint and feathers doing some kind of tribal dance.

Pascal got up and went and sat with the child. She put her arms around her and lent back against the foot of the bed, gently stroking her hair. For a minute they sat quietly watching. Then Pascal murmured, in the child's ear, 'Sapphire, tell me about your Mama's people?'

'They Navajo,' she whispered, wonder in her voice as she watched the screen.

Pascal lent down and kissed her cheek again. Sapphire looked up and put her arms up around Pascal's neck and shyly kissed her back on the cheek. She whispered, 'this is what I did with Mama.' Then she stiffened.

Pascal glanced back at the screen to see a photo of Tilly-May. It was a local TV station news report, and there was an outside shot of the hotel block and then another from some distance away, of the small body lying on the sidewalk in a pool of blood. Sapphire was hyperventilating, unable to get her breath, clinging to Pascal and making a keening noise. Pascal held her close, stroking her, saying, 'it's okay, it's okay.' She grabbed the TV remote to change the channel, but then there was a shot of Pascal herself, so she turned the sound up and tried to follow the Spanish in the tail end of the report. It gave Pascal's alias name of Catherine Hansen and seemed to say she was being sought in connection with the child's death, and that was it. As the channel moved onto another story, Pascal processed options that seemed to be narrowing by the minute. So now the authorities were looking for her as well. Thank God she had given another false name when signing in.

She looked down at Sapphire, slowly realizing that the child had pulled out of her embrace and was looking at her in a strange way. Pascal got up and went to the bathroom. Earlier she had seen there was still some stuff in the wall cabinet left by previous guests. It was the kind of place where they rarely put any serious effort into cleaning the rooms. There were some sleeping tablets there. She studied the label, took one out and went back with a glass of water.

Sapphire was sitting staring at nothing, disconsolate. She looked up with that same strange expression on her face. Pascal gave her the tablet and she swallowed it quickly with the water. She said, quietly, 'You're a liar, just like all the others. Your name's not Courtney, and you killed my friend Tilly-May.'

'That's not true, Sapphire,' Pascal said, trying to stay calm and keep the desperation out of her voice. 'You have to believe me. I came here to try to get you both back.'

Sapphire looked away from her and back at the TV screen, her eyes drooping, half-closing and then she wasn't listening anymore. Pascal lifted her up and carried her over to the bed and lay her down. She watched her for a moment, observing the calm little face, peaceful again. Then the desk phone rang.

Calver again. She listened, watching the child. 'Detective Daly's been asking me about the DEA agent, Ruiz? They've obviously picked up he's missing, and he wants to speak to you.'

Pascal felt a surge of anger and impotence. She drew a deep breath to keep from screaming. Didn't she have enough on her plate? 'Hey, Calver. I've now got an APB out on me here with the *Federales* for Tilly-May's death, and I got drug cartels coming out of my ass, so fuck Daly. I could do with some help here, you know,' she said, voice tight.

There was silence on the line, then softer, 'Hey, Courtney, sorry. Wasn't thinking, but Daly was pretty heavy. Serious shit. He was talking FBI.'

'Great,' Pascal said. 'I got the girl, but nowhere to run.'

'Yeah,' Calver said, 'look, I've seen Yolanda and I filed the Habeas Corpus motion to get Yolanda a new hearing based on new evidence.'

'Yeah, well, you're the lawyer but maybe that wasn't such a great idea,' Pascal said. 'They pick up on the filing, won't take 'em long to join up the dots and work out who our mystery witness is.'

'Maybe, but it'll take time, and we have to break cover eventually. Can't keep the kid on ice too long either or we could get charged with something?'

'Great,' Pascal said again. 'When d'you see Daly?'

'Yesterday, after I'd filed the motion. Why?'

'It's too soon for them to have got a warrant for phone taps, but from now on we talk on burners, yeah?'

'Check. Look, sorry for being a dick,' Calver said. 'Who the hell do we trust now?'

'No one,' Pascal said. 'Until we know more. And you're a lawyer, Calver, so you better be extra careful about what you say, like lying to law enforcement. So the less we talk for the moment the better. Anyone who tries to help me is going to get dragged in. I've been thinking about what we discussed. I believe for now, it's best for me and the kid to go underground and somehow make our way back and stay hidden until we can come up with a plan for revealing Sapphire without getting everyone jailed or killed. Best I can come up with for the moment.'

'Okay, Courtney. How is the kid anyway?'

'Not so good. She thinks I killed her friend, Tilly-May.'

'Wow. How you going to get out of that one?'

'I'll tell you when I know,' Pascal said, tired now, the strain of the last few days finally catching up with her, making her feel like she was drowning. 'Okay, Calver. Go out and get a burner and text the number. I'll get back to you when I know what the hell I'm going to do.'

'Okay, Courtney. Stay safe,' he said, finishing the call.

Pascal looked over at Sapphire who was now lightly snoring, wondering how she'd be when she woke up.

###

Solomon Gutiérrez was sitting at his grand mahogany desk cutting into a bloody steak the size of a magazine cover when an aide scurried into the room and whispered something hurriedly into his ear. He whispered something back then clapped his hands at the two young Mexican girls who were playing at his feet. They immediately got up and left the room.

A moment later the doors were pushed open and two men came in half-carrying, half pulling a stumbling and injured Fernando Ruiz. He was covered in dust, and thick blood had congealed through his right trouser leg and there were bruises and blood on his face. He seemed to be having trouble keeping his eyes open.

Gutiérrez waved the men over to a chair where they deposited Ruiz. A moment later Gutiérrez stood over the injured man, looking down at him whilst gently swirling brandy around in a large balloon glass.

He asked his men for a report and they told him that when Ruiz and his driver had failed to call in they had sent out a routine patrol to check the route. 'We thought they might have gone back to the city for some fun and not called in,' his under boss said. 'Couldn't get them on cell-phones. It took a long time to find him because the vehicle was gone and he was laid up on the road behind some rocks. He crawled out when he heard the vehicle on our third sweep. Ruiz was pretty far gone - he's been out there couple of days - and his driver was dead. Their vehicle and the woman and girl were gone, so we brought Ruiz and the dead driver back. Both their guns and the driver's cellphone are missing.'

Gutiérrez waived the men out. 'Tell me what happened, Fernando?' he said.

Ruiz looked up, his bloody eyes slowly focusing on Gutiérrez. 'Water,' he croaked, 'and a doctor.'

'All in good time, my friend,' the big man said, bending down and carefully running his hand over Ruiz's right leg. 'You know,' he said, 'as a young man I worked in a hospital for a while.'

He effortlessly ripped the blood-soaked trouser leg material away from Ruiz's calf and looked at the wound. His fingers as he felt down the leg were surprisingly gentle. He probed up and down, at one point making Ruiz gasp in pain. Gutiérrez stood up. 'You have a nasty gash there my friend, but I don't think the bone is broken, maybe a fracture.'

He held the large glass of brandy to Ruiz's lips and watched as the man greedily sucked some into his mouth, then coughed and retched.

'Tell me what happened, my friend. A doctor is on the way who will attend to your leg.'

Ruiz rubbed his face, trying not to wince. The pain in his leg was becoming unbearable. 'The girl bushwhacked us,' he said slowly, struggling to get the words out. 'Strangled the driver with her wrist ties. Broke his fucking neck while he was still driving, for christsakes. We could have gone over the edge, but the car stayed up and turned over. Then the kid almost shot me with my own gun.'

Gutiérrez nodded, then walked away to stand at the grand window. He looked out on the corral, studying the horses as they slowly moved around. He sipped some brandy, then moved back to stand over Ruiz again, who was now slumped over, eyes closed. 'Where will the girl go? What will she do?' he asked.

Ruiz looked up. 'There's a lot of people out looking for her now I guess,' he said, grinding the words out. 'The kid from Cafe Flamingo who went over the balcony, she's in the frame for that, and if that kid was a US citizen, means she's in trouble both sides of the border.'

'What would you do, my friend? In such a situation,' Gutiérrez asked.

'I'd probably try and get across the border covertly with this kid - whoever she is,' he said, finally looking up at Gutiérrez, leaving that clear question hanging in the air between them.

There was a discrete knock at the door and an aide poked his head in to say the doctor had arrived. Ruiz looked up, surprised, not having believed they had called a doctor for him.

Gutiérrez smiled. 'You see. I am as good as my word. Now, can you retrieve this situation, if the good doctor can patch you up, which I am sure he can?'

Ruiz nodded, desperate to have the doctor look at his leg and quell the pain.

'Of course,' Gutiérrez continued, 'it's in your interest to stop the girl. If you don't, she will no doubt be talking to the DEA about your serial betrayal of the agency, no?'

Before Ruiz could respond the doctor was there with his small black bag. He spent twenty minutes with Ruiz and gave him an injection for the pain. Gutiérrez told the doctor they had a well equipped surgery. If he would wait whilst he finished speaking to Ruiz, the doctor could then set the leg or do whatever he needed to do. The doctor nodded obsequiously and left.

'So?' Gutiérrez said.

Ruiz already looked better, eyes focused, color coming back into his cheeks. He nodded. 'It shouldn't be too hard to find her,' he said, his mind already working the angles.

'Good. I have put the word out on the street also, but I believe you must engage the services and resources of your employer, the DEA.'

'I agree, and that's no problem,' Ruiz said. 'Get me a phone and I'll start working it while the doc fixes my leg.'

'Excellent,' Gutiérrez said, clapping his hands again. The doors opened and the same two men came in and Gutiérrez told them to take Ruiz to the surgery and give him a decent untraceable phone to use there.

###

Hundreds of miles south in Mexico City the man sat at a table outside a roadside cafe, phone to his ear. 'I told you never to call me on this number,' he hissed.

'I'm sorry,' she said, calm as ever. 'But they've filed an appeal. New evidence, a witness. And the only witness they could bring to court who could hurt us would be the brat, but how can that be, if she's dead?'

The man held his surprise in check. He surveyed the empty tables around him, the cloth awning gently swinging above him in the light wind, his two bodyguards standing a few meters away, watching the street and every movement in it. 'How do you know these things? It would be a big story if true, and yet there is silence?'

'Oh its true all right. Just been filed, low key. I have a line into the federal prosecutor's office. Okay, I'm assuming the witness is the brat, but who else could it be?'

The man took a sip of his bitter espresso, thinking hard for a moment. Then he said, 'Do nothing. I will inquire and speak to you again in 24 hours.' He cut the connection and then sat for a while thinking deeply, going back in time and then going through the history of what had happened. The kid should have been disposed of in Juarez, his territory, and maybe she had been, and the witness was someone else. He needed to find out what the hell was going on down there. He couldn't put it directly to his underlings, he'd have to come at them obliquely and then hit them with the name.

He signaled his bodyguard. The man brought him another

cellphone; he pressed speed dial. The only number on the phone connected him with his under boss, Alvaro Chavez up in Ciudad Juarez.

Chavez took the call with trepidation. Dante Figueroa was one of the top five or six guys in the Juarez cartel. Chavez listened to the quiet voice, so understated and yet so frightening. At first all he seemed to want, unusually, was a simple situation report on what had been happening on the ground, but then he asked if anything out of the ordinary had occurred.

Chavez's mind scrambled to work out what the boss might be getting at so he could process a response that would protect him. The only thing he could think of was the girl. At first his voice failed him, then he coughed to cover it and started again. 'There has been a little turbulence here, sir,' he said, his voice faltering again but then firming up. 'An American, or British in fact, woman came here recently, posing as a journalist. Catherine Hansen. She worked at one of our bars and came into conflict with a captain in Sinaloa, Morales, and I took the decision to use her against him.'

'And what did you do?'

'It was a test. I suggested she kill Morales' guy, Chico, if she wanted to join us. It was to smoke her out,' he said uncertainly.

Figueroa remained silent, so Chavez quickly carried on. 'She did kill him, defending herself and I used her as a bodyguard for a while, but it was clear her interest lay in underage prostitution that some of our gangs run here.'

'And?' Figueroa said, no longer patient.

'Somehow she got into one of the establishments operated by one of these outfits, Cafe Flamingo, and took a young girl out.'

'So what did you do?' Figueroa asked, voice still calm, but Chavez could sense rage bubbling beneath the surface.

'We observed from a distance, obviously to make sure there would be no adverse consequences for our operations,' Chavez said, rather proud of his choice of words under pressure.

'And what did you observe?' Figueroa asked testily.

Chavez answered haltingly, 'it appears they made use of a dirty DEA cop, Fernando Ruiz, who was friendly with the woman, to trap her, but things did not go to plan. The young girl died.'

'Tell me about Gutman,' Figueroa said suddenly, unbalancing Chavez who had no idea Figueroa knew about the fat man.

Chavez sighed. Maybe they would have mercy on him if he told them all. 'We tolerated Gutiérrez whilst his activities did not harm us. He runs an underage prostitution ring and it seems he's had an American child living with him for months if not longer, almost like a wife,' he said, distastefully. 'It seems that she may have been this Catherine Hansen's target from the start. There are rumors circulating on the street suggesting she has got the child, after some type of confrontation.'

'So the child taken from the Flamingo died, but this woman, this Hansen, then managed to take a second child, this American child, away from Gutiérrez?' Figueroa said, his highly analytical mind scything through Chavez's halting prevarications.

'I believe that is so, sir.'

'And now this Hansen woman and the American child are, where?' Figueroa said, ominously.

'I'm sorry, I don't know, but I can find her instantly, if she's still here. I did not understand her importance to you,' Chavez said desperately. *'El Jefe.* If I had known—'

'Enough,' Figueroa said. 'Are the authorities looking for this Hansen?'

'Yes, in connection with the death of the first child and I am sure the *Federales* with DEA may also be looking for her because it seems this Ruiz may also be missing or dead.'

'Chavez, would you like a chance to redeem yourself?'

'Of course. Anything.'

'Good. Find this Hansen woman and the child and bring them to me, immediately. Do not concern yourself with who these people are or why I want them. And one last thing. This hunt must be kept secret. Now, do you have any way of finding her quickly?'

Chavez desperately processed the little he knew of the woman, looking for anything he could give the boss, then something tripped in his mind. 'She was close to one of my boys, Jorge, and I think we can start there.'

'Good. Get to it,' Figueroa said, terminating the call and signaling for another cellphone. He called a discrete private enquiry agency in New York City that he had used in the past and asked them to check the identity of a Catherine Hansen. They said they would have something for him in 24 hours.

CHAPTER ELEVEN

In an empty warehouse in Ciudad Juarez Hector Morales wandered around behind the man sitting strapped to a chair. The man's face was a bloody mess, one eye purple and closed, next to it a black empty socket gaped where the other eye had been, and on the dusty blood splattered floor lay the mans severed left hand. He had nothing left to tell. Morales nodded to the guy with the chain saw. The man flashed his too white smile and gunned the small petrol engine into life then tilted the saw blade into the seated man's neck decapitating his head in a spray of blood and bone.

As the head tumbled onto the floor Morales grinned and wiped his brow with a silk handkerchief. 'So what we got?' he said.

Another man moved out of the shadows, Morales number two, and Chico's replacement. 'The Hanson woman was taken to Gutiérrez's place by a DEA guy, Ruiz. She seems to have abducted an American kid there and disappeared in the desert. Looks like she was after the kid all along, but get this: Dante Figueroa, a top five Juarez lieutenant, hiding out in Mexico City, seems to want them found real bad.'

'Why?

'We don't know.'

'Maybe we better find out,' Morales said, rubbing his fingers, remembering the way the Hanson woman had humiliated him at Cantina Gold, almost busted his hand and then taken Chico out as well. 'Find out who this Hansen woman really is and why they want the kid. If Figueroa wants her, then maybe we want her too. We get a hostage valuable enough to the Juarez, then maybe we can fuck them over, muscle some more of their trade here,' he said, his mind already calculating the kudos he could get from his bosses for executing such a plan.

'I'm on it boss.'

Pascal checked her watch, wondering when Calver would text her the number of his new phone. She took out the cellphone she had taken from the driver in the desert. She'd turn it on once more for the info then ditch it.

She looked over at Sapphire, watching cartoons again. Since waking she had remained resolutely silent, simply ignoring Pascal, but one or two times Pascal had glanced over and caught Sapphire watching her with a strange enigmatic expression on her face. Now she looked up again and Sapphire was watching her with that same look. Sapphire said, 'why did they put Yolanda in prison? She didn't do anything.'

'I know, sweetheart. That's why I'm here, because you can prove what they say about Yolanda is wrong, and we can get her out.

Wouldn't you like to do that?'

'Yes,' she said, firmly.

Pascal studied her earnest young face. Maybe it was time to start probing a bit more deeply, and maybe there wouldn't be a better time than now when she was fired up to help Yolanda. 'Sapphire, can you remember what happened when they took you away from your home, from your family and Yolanda?'

She didn't hesitate. It was almost as if she had been waiting to be asked. 'Someone put me to sleep I think for a long long time. I was at home with my toys, then I woke up and it was dark, and I was in a box, and then I was asleep again. Then I woke up and I was pulled out of the box in Mexico.' Sapphire was biting her lip, her face intensely serious, as if she were trying to solve some complicated puzzle.

Pascal went over and sat with the child, putting her arms around her and cuddling her. At first there was mild resistance, then she relaxed into Pascal's embrace. 'Friends again?' Pascal said.

'I didn't really think you killed Tilly-May,' Sapphire whispered. She mumbled shyly into Pascal's chest, 'friends.'

Pascal kept the easy smile on her face but underneath she was tense as hell. A finger was beginning to point in a very specific direction as far as the abduction was concerned, but it was never clever to jump to hasty conclusions.

She checked her watch and tapped on the dead drivers cellphone. There were a mass of text messages and missed calls. Pascal ignored them, hunting for the text from Calver with the number of his burner. She found it and wrote the number down on a piece of paper, then scrolled through the remaining messages, all in Spanish, apart from two she spotted in English, both addressed to "Catherine Hansen", but from different senders. How the fuck did anyone know she had the guys phone? She better ditch it.

The first message was from Jorge, her old friend and co-bodyguard she'd worked with for Alvaro Chavez. It read, *'hey, Cathy, call me this number I can help.'*

The other was from Hector Morales. It read, *'Chiquita, we need to talk. Forget the past. We can help you against the Juarez.'*

Pascal quickly switched the phone off. Decision time; they couldn't stay where they were, but neither could they hop around Ciudad Juarez, because sooner or later they'd get picked up. They needed to get out of Mexico, back to the States, and Morales was probably their best bet, notwithstanding the fact that he would clearly try to double cross them.

###

He answered first ring. 'I've been expecting your call,' Morales said. 'It's nice to—'

'Can you get us out,' Pascal said, in no mood for banter.

'Of course, Chiquita, but we need to meet.'

'No chance. You run a people smuggling operation, yes?'

'Yes, but we need to meet and make arrangements, it's not—'

'Bullshit. You run those poor suckers over the border like sheep, and most of them never make it. Me and a child will go in your next run. All I need from you is the rendezvous point. And one detail you need to know, Morales. I'll be packing, and anyone tries to mess with me or the child, I'll blow their fucking head off. You got that?'

'I will call you back in 1 hour,' Morales said, voice tight. The phone went dead.

Pascal knew Morales would now be busy arranging a set-up. Why else would he help her? He got nothing for helping them cross the border, other than the chance to abduct her and the child for his own purposes, but it was the only way she could think of to get across quick. It was high risk, but it seemed the best option when they were being hunted on so many fronts.

An hour later Morales called again. As luck would have it, and wouldn't you just know it, there was a run planned that night. He told Pascal to be in El Chamizal park in the north of the city at 8 pm where they would be collected. They should dress simply and carry little. Pascal told him they'd be there and tapped the phone off.

'Would you like to go on an adventure, sweetie?' she asked Sapphire.

The child had got tired of cartoons and was now sat at a table drawing and seemed so engrossed she didn't hear Pascal. Pascal smiled. She tussled Sapphire's hair. As the girl looked up, Pascal said, 'I'm popping out to get us some stuff. Then we're going to go on a journey, a journey home.'

'To see Yolanda?' Sapphire asked.

'You bet. And we're going to get her out of prison. No. You're going to get her out of prison.'

'Really?' Sapphire said.

'Really,' Pascal said firmly. 'Now, I'm going out to get us some stuff for our trip. Do not answer the door to anyone but me. I'll tell them on the desk. You got that?'

'Yes, Courtney,' she said gravely.

When Pascal got back it was gone 4 pm and Sapphire was asleep in front of the TV.

It had been a busy afternoon for Pascal. One highlight of her time with Chavez had been a visit to an arms dealer's warehouse where Chavez had examined and bought some small arms for his men. Pascal had been impressed by the sellers very detailed technical knowledge of the armaments and the fact the guy was clearly an independent who owed no allegiance to any cartel - he sold to all of them. So that afternoon she had gone back to see him. The guy had been suspicious to start with but after she'd been searched he was happy to sell her anything she wanted, provided she had the cash. In the event she wanted only one thing, which she had seen on her first visit, and which was still there, but she also bought some ammo and a shoulder rig for her hand guns.

She didn't disturb Sapphire, but instead quietly began her preparations. First she dug out the two 9mm Glock's she'd taken off Ruiz and the driver, cleaned and checked their action before loading them up with the ammo she'd bought. She took out the knife she'd got off the driver and sharpened it. Next she tried on the cross-over shoulder rig. She holstered the guns, one under each arm, then practiced smoothly withdrawing the weapons and leveling them on herself in the mirror. Catching her face unawares, she mimed blowing herself away and winked at her reflection. She dug out the belt she'd bought with a pouch on it and checked it would take the knife, her passport and currency. Lastly she pulled out of the bag the weapon she had bought from the dealer. It was in two pieces and quite old, almost antique, with one projectile to go with it. She assembled it on the bed, aiming and testing the action, before leaving it lying on the cover.

Finished with the weaponry, she laid out on the bed the other stuff she'd bought; two sets of cheap clothing for each, one drab and dark, the other more colorful; also some make-up wares that would have done a theatrical troupe proud, plus a couple of wigs, one for a child and one for an adult. She had no set plan but knew from long experience in the field, being able to change your appearance and identity quickly could often grab you an edge. She looked at the stuff laid out then went and took a shower.

Coming out of the bathroom, hair in a towel turban she checked Sapphire was still sleeping. She went to the tiny optional self-catering kitchen annex and washed and sliced some potato and onion and chucked them in a frying pan on a gas ring on a low heat. She beat 6 eggs in a dish and added salt, pepper and a dash of milk, moved to the fridge and cracked open a Bud, took a long drag, savoring the cool malty taste as she stood at the hob slowly turning the potato and onions in the pan. Lastly she poured in the beaten eggs and left the pan to slowly cook.

Going back to the living room she stopped suddenly on the threshold. Sapphire was sitting rigid, staring at the TV as if she had seen a ghost. Pascal checked the screen hoping it wasn't more pictures of Tilly-May, but this time it was just a CNN story about US politics, speculation that Texas senator, Victor Diaz, would be seeking the Republican nomination for a presidential run. 'What is it, Sweetie?'

Pascal asked her.

'That man,' she whispered. 'He's the one who hurt me.'

Pascal's switched off the TV; better keep the damn thing off if it was going to send her into a fit every time she watched it. She pulled Sapphire into a hug.

As she held the child, her mind turned over what Gutman had told her. It did now look like he had been telling the truth. The child was highly unlikely to lie about such a thing. Pascal knew a bit about Diaz. He was one of a new generation of Hispanic Senators. Family values were at the core of their appeal, and his right wing credentials were impeccable. Pascal recalled, from having watched some of the open meetings, that Diaz was one of the ranking members of the powerful United States Senate Select Committee on Intelligence. He was clearly a guy who had serious juice in Washington.

The thought that such a man, in such a position, who was under unrelenting public scrutiny 24/7 could be involved in abusing kidnapped children just didn't seem credible, unless the guy was seriously unhinged, or got off on suicidal risk. She'd have to think about it, but for now, they needed to get out, and trying to subject Sapphire to the third degree wasn't an option; it would have to wait.

It was 6.30 pm when Pascal finally dished up the Spanish omelet, and for once Sapphire seemed hungry, clearing her plate. Pascal got her to shower, then they both dressed in the cheap, drab, dark clothing, examining how each other looked as they did so. As Pascal finished fastening her belt, Sapphire wandered over to the bed.

'What's this, Courtney?' she said, holding up the weapon Pascal had bought earlier. 'It looks like my trombone I used to have at home?'

Pascal quickly moved to the girl and gently retrieved the weapon. 'This, sweetie, is a very old Russian Rocket Propelled Grenade launcher, or RPG,' she said, breaking the weapon down into its two parts.

Sapphire's eyes glowed with excitement as she examined it. 'Whatever is it for, Courtney?' she said.

'Oh, it's just in case we run into a little trouble on our adventure,' she said, casually.

Sapphire regarded her quizzically, not quite convinced at the explanation, but finally nodding her head and moving to sit on the bed. Pascal unwrapped two different colored rucksacks, put one inside the other along with their remaining stuff, including the RPG and its strangely shaped charge, then strapped it onto Sapphires back to see if she could manage it if she had to. She just about could. Pascal hesitated a moment before taking out one of the Glock's from her holster and stowing it in there as well, Sapphire standing dutifully with her back to her.

Pascal lifted the rucksack off Sapphire and put it over her own shoulder. They took a last lingering look around the room then left.

###

Out at his hacienda Gutiérrez stood at the large open and empty fireplace, phone to his ear, listening to Ruiz's report on progress. The man was full of bravado now, saying he was on the point of catching the woman and the girl, but Gutiérrez didn't trust him; how could he? A man who would betray his own? But then again, whilst their respective interests coincided, it was expedient to allow Ruiz to pursue the matter. After all, maybe he was telling the truth, who could know.

Gutiérrez terminated the call and moved to the long window. He stood there for a long while looking out towards the mountains. It wasn't just Ruiz's loyalty that worried him, the mans competence was also suspect, especially recently with the debacle over first the girl from Cafe Flamingo, and then Sapphire. Gutiérrez pondered, his gaze turned inward away from the mountains as he finely weighed risk, probability and possible outcomes. Protection of his business, which was in essence the entirety of who he was, was paramount, and his business was his clients and the protection of their anonymity. If he could not guarantee that, there was no business. And ironically, in this regard, he did hold certain ethics; so should he forewarn the client who was most at risk from Sapphire Dinks, if she should suddenly materialize? Or should he try and contain the problem locally and deal with it utilizing his own resources? But then again the client in question was extremely powerful and could bring a huge range of assets and resources to the problem.

The dilemma vexed Gutiérrez for a further ten minutes during which a tortuous debate went back and forth in his head. Time was clearly of the essence and it was unlikely they would get second chances. Logic dictated he should mobilize all assets available in solving the problem even if that might cause him some small embarrassment. The alternative was unthinkable.

He went to his desk and lifted a land line telephone that was very rarely used. It was only part land line, then satellite, routed through various territories around the world; it was untraceable and scrambled.

Each client had been given a special password that would be used only in an emergency requiring contact. Gutiérrez had never had to use the system before. He dialed the number, waited a moment, listening, then said, 'give me senator Victor Diaz. It's extremely urgent. Tell him........tell him its Jupiter. He will take the call.'

###

It was 7.45 pm as they approached the park in the twilight, the streets still busy with people and cars. Pascal knew she would have to ad-lib as she had no idea how Morales was going to set things up. She knew a bit about people smuggling because she had read up on it as part of her research before coming to Mexico. She'd waded through a shit load of stuff, including research papers from the University of Texas and US Immigration. If it was a real run, and she expected it would be, it would not be organized by the cartel or Morales, it would be run by the smuggling outfit. They would pay a toll to Morales to run it through his drug territory, and that gave her some scope for creating a bit of mayhem, something she'd surely have to do to get through. She glanced around at Sapphire sitting calmly in the back seat humming to herself. She looked okay - she'd need to be.

Pascal knew all runs were different but generally comprised the same outline. You had the *chequeadores*, or caretakers watching the border looking for any opportunity to cross when the patrols were otherwise engaged. These guys used various techniques, sometimes setting up observation posts on hotel balconies or in cars and using night vision equipment. They would have details of border guard patrols and shift patterns, and they would be in constant contact via radios with the *Coyotes*, the actual smuggler guys who would be ready to move on the border as soon as they got the word. If necessary they would also use *Cuidanderos* who would set up a diversion, like throwing rocks at a border patrol if it got too close. Sometimes it would take more than one attempt to get through.

So somewhere in the park Pascal reckoned there would be a group of migrants, probably from very poor central or south American countries, sitting huddled, scared and waiting for their pick up.

Pascal paid off the cab and led Sapphire into the park. There were still plenty of people out enjoying themselves. Pascal caught Sapphire smiling as she watched a couple with a young girl and a small dog on a lead. They walked on, Pascal constantly scanning around them.

They passed through a small campsite area and then could see in the near distance a small group of seven or eight people sitting at wooden tables in a roofed over area adjoining some public toilets. The people looked out of place, their clothing and body language; they didn't look like people enjoying a trip to the park. As she watched them a large dirty white camper van drew up alongside the group. Looked like the people smugglers had arrived. Pascal gestured at Sapphire to halt and they stood for a moment in some trees as Pascal carefully scanned every inch of the terrain.

The area was quite deserted now apart from the group and the camper van, and the light was beginning to fade. Further out from the group, around 100 meters away she could just see the front of an SUV sticking out from some trees. As she scanned it a memory was triggered. She re-read the plate, and then it hit her; it was the same vehicle she had used to escape from Chavez's warehouse when she had taken out Chico. She had dumped the vehicle in a car park, and they must have recovered it.

As Pascal studied the set-up, her mind worked the angles and slowly a rough and ready plan began to form in her head. Chavez and his crew would never expect her to ID the vehicle; it probably never crossed their minds. More importantly she was betting he would wait for her to be cooped up in the camper van before showing his hand. That way there was less chance of her escaping.

Pascal told Sapphire to keep watch on the group. As Sapphire turned back to watch, Pascal removed the rucksack and separated out their stuff. She put the RPG and charge in her rucksack and the rest in the other one which she strapped onto Sapphire's back. She took a last look around and checked the SUV was still there. She said, 'okay, sweetie, let's go.'

As they walked on toward the group something else suddenly hit Pascal: Sapphire had been watching Spanish speaking cartoons for hours on TV but she had never thought to ask her, so now she did. 'Do you speak Spanish, Sapphire?'

The girl looked up at her as if she were an idiot. 'Of course I do, silly. Yolanda taught me some and they only speak it here.'

Pascal felt like slapping herself, but now they were almost at the tables and the group were eying them up suspiciously. Pascal guessed they might be Guatemalan, maybe Honduran. She whispered to Sapphire, 'ask them if we might join them.'

The girl addressed them in polite Spanish. They seemed a bit taken aback, but then smiled at her and nodded.

As they joined the group, two guys alighted from the Camper van and approached the table. The *Coyotes* had arrived. Pascal checked her watch; it was 8.10 pm.

She studied them. A leader, tall and thin with a mustache, and a smaller younger teen, both dressed in combat trousers, singlets and loose waistcoats, and both packing. The lead guy carried a radio in his hand from which static and voices could be heard. Probably waiting on a call from the *chequeadores* that the coast was clear for a run.

The lead guy took out a smart phone and seemed to be scrolling through pictures, checking off each member of the group. He looked at Pascal and smiled. 'You the two special ones?' he said in broken English, big smile revealing a gold tooth at the front.

Pascal nodded. He held her gaze for a moment, looked at Sapphire, nodded again, and said, 'in the truck, now. Vamoose.'

Pascal stood with Sapphire and let the group board first, all the time watching the two guys. Lead guy was talking on the cellphone nodding his head, still quite leisurely .

Pascal lent down and whispered to Sapphire, 'get in the camper van, sweetie, and wait for me.'

Sapphire, her expression serious, studied Pascal's face for a moment in the twilight. She said, 'you mustn't kill any more people, Courtney. It's wrong.'

There was no answer to that. Pascal nodded and kissed her, and she climbed up the steps into the camper van. Pascal trotted up to lead guy and said, 'I must use toilet,' gesturing towards the small building at the side. '*Necesito el inodoro.*'

The guy frowned and checked his watch. He didn't want to agree, but as he'd referred to them as "special", she reckoned they wanted her on the van. The guy nodded reluctantly, saying, 'okay, but quick, or we leave without you.'

Pascal ran to the building, already undoing the rucksack. She went down the side of the small structure and peaked around the corner at the SUV still parked behind trees, just the front visible. As she studied the vehicle, the engine started up. She quickly removed and assembled the two piece RPG. She studied the long shaped charge which she hadn't really looked at before but now she could see how old it was and the signs of rust. She pushed the projectile into place in the barrel, praying it would still work and not blow her up. She crouched down, holding the launcher on her shoulder. As the vehicle slowly began to move out of the trees towards the camper van, Pascal sighted on it, holding the long barrel firm. As the vehicle loomed and centered in her sights she pulled the trigger, but just as she did so the vehicle began to accelerate. Pascal didn't wait, she dropped the RPG where it was and began running towards the camper van. As she ran she heard the explosion and looked back to see the smoking SUV. The charge had hit the back of the vehicle which was now in flames, various men milling around the front.

As she got to the top of the camper van steps she screamed, '*go,*' but the driver seemed frozen, spellbound by the spectacle of the burning vehicle. But lead guy wasn't so easily impressed; he violently shook the man and told him to get the hell out of there. Pascal had calculated that whatever their relationship to Chavez they would not want to hang around after the explosion to talk to law enforcement. She also knew that the Coyotes generally paid a toll to the cartel and got some or all their money on delivery, so they were not going to hold things up for the cartel unless they were forced to.

The engine roared and the vehicle began moving and then they were accelerating away, bouncing on the uneven surface as the large van picked up speed.

###

Pascal took a seat next to Sapphire and hugged her. A little later as the van moved away from the park they heard sirens approaching, then saw the flashing lights as law enforcement and emergency service vehicles raced past them.

Pascal said to Sapphire, 'see. I don't always have to shoot people. Sometimes I just blow-up their cars.'

Sapphire's face took on that serious look that Pascal was getting used to, but the girl stayed silent.

The other folks in the van seemed to have recovered from the earlier excitement and were now starting to talk quietly amongst themselves, looking around and gesturing. One leaned forward and spoke quietly to Sapphire.

'What's he say?' Pascal asked.

Sapphire looked embarrassed. 'He said, he liked the fireworks, and, and…. you really kick-ass.'

Ten minutes later the van slowed as it paralleled the border.

They could see El Paso in the distance looming in the twilight. They were now driving in what looked like a storm drain or dry canal bed, moving slowly, wall to their right. It was partly brick and partly fencing, covered with razor wire, lights and the odd camera. All the while lead guy who sat at the front with the driver had the radio as if bolted to his ear, listening to squawks and chatter. Then they stopped.

Here it was darker, fewer lights, a bricked up area of wall. The driver switched the engine off. They sat silent there, even the radio deathly quiet. There was a short verbal exchange on the radio and the lead guy nodded to the driver. He got up and said something to two of the migrants, gesturing at a couple of ladders lying along the floor. They each took an end and started to move, carrying the ladders out of the door onto the concrete floor of the incline, then up to lay them against the wall towering over them.

Lead guy then spoke to them, Sapphire quietly translating for Pascal. He said go silently over the wall, where another Coyote was waiting for them. He would take them to a load house, a safe house. There was nothing to worry about.

They got up and moved, single file, like a snake, down the steps and up towards the ladder. A loud squawking on the radio, and lead guy was gesturing for them to stop. They could hear an engine the other side, some way away. Pascal watched through the fenced part. The vehicle looked like border patrol and had now stopped about 200 meters away. Lead guy spoke quietly into the radio, whilst they all stood, most holding their breath and praying.

They heard shouts from the vehicle, and now Pascal could see a small group of people had appeared on their side of the fence. They were chucking stones at the border patrol and shouting insults at them. Pascal heard a sound like light mortar fire and then she could see the smoke bombs going off amongst the stone throwers. Lead guy turned to them and said, 'go,' and then they were scurrying up the ladder.

CHAPTER TWELVE

As they clambered down on the other side they were in shadow but could still hear the border patrol getting into it with the *Cuidanderos* decoy. As they descended, they could see two battered old SUV's attended by a couple of *Coyotes*, slim anonymous guys in baseball caps waving them down and into the vehicles.

Pascal and Sapphire took a seat in the second SUV with six migrants, the main bulk going in the other vehicle. They slowly moved away in darkness, low speed, no lights, a silent two car convoy.

Pascal felt uneasy; it all seemed a little too slick. If it was that easy what was all the fuss about? All you needed was a truck, walkie talkie and a ladder, and seemingly anyone could get to the promised land? She knew Morales had intended to double-cross her from the outset, but the smuggling operation was clearly independent of him, although subservient to him, but how subservient? Who knew? But maybe she was being too cautious - again - over thinking everything as she tended to do. She looked up and studied the driver's profile. With the visor of his cap hooding his face and in the half-light she couldn't see much, but he looked clean-cut and American; he was wearing a head mike that he was speaking quietly into but with the engine noise she couldn't hear what he was saying.

She turned to look at Sapphire sitting quietly beside her, her small hands gripped tight in her lap, her face set in a determined mien as if she was concentrating on some deep and difficult problem.

'Penny for them,' Pascal said, but Sapphire didn't seem to hear her. She tried again, louder. 'What are you thinking about, sweetie?'

'Why can't we just call 911, the police, and tell them I am alive and well, so they let Yolanda out?' she said, a small frown creasing her brow. 'And why are we hiding? Why couldn't we come here openly? I am free now, aren't I?'

The child was very quick witted and bright. Pascal wondered how much she should tell her, but before she could speak, Sapphire was asking more questions.

'Is it because of Tilly-May, or that man on TV,' she said, eyes hooded and dark. 'The man who hurt me?'

Pascal sighed. Probably not clever to lie to her because she'd see through it and telling her enough to make her stay wary and vigilant made sense. 'It's all of that, I am afraid,' Pascal said. 'The man on TV is very powerful, and I want to be sure we are safe, before we talk to anyone, as a precaution. Does that make sense?'

Sapphire nodded slowly. 'I guess,' she said, unsure.

'Look. Don't worry so much,' Pascal said with a bright smile. 'It's only for a short while. As soon as I know we're a hundred per cent safe, we'll tell everyone you have come back. We'll get Yolanda out of prison and you can go home. Deal?' she said.

The child nodded, but Pascal could tell she was still worrying.

They were both jittery, their nerves jangling but it would have to wait a little longer. She looked back out of the window, willing the SUV on. They had left the barren border area and were now approaching the suburbs of El Paso, traveling past odd buildings that seemed little different from those they had just left behind across the border.

As they passed through another barren red desert area, free of buildings, they came around a sharp bend and there it was up ahead: a road block. She hadn't consciously expected it, but subconsciously and in some way, intuitively, she had. The positioning was clever and strategic, the abruptness of the bend meant it was too late to do anything.

As the vehicle slowed Pascal looked out of the window studying the set-up. There were some arc-lights suspended over the empty road, and a couple of sleek looking dark official vehicles drawn up around the barriers and then a large truck. It appeared that they were only blocking some of the traffic, a few random vehicles that had been parked up on the shoulder but were now moving off leaving the space empty. Now both SUV's were being directed to that area.

As their vehicle slowed, Pascal studied the people behind the barriers expecting to see the green uniforms with the yellow and black insignia of the US border patrol, but these guys were in black flack jackets with large white letters stenciled on the back: DEA.

Pascal glanced at Sapphire and squeezed her hand. She looked calm but the other migrants looked frightened. The driver turned to them and said, 'stay calm folks. This is a bust. Do as you're told and no one gets hurt.' He repeated his words in fluent Spanish. He turned to Pascal. 'You. Up,' he said.

She slowly rose to her feet. He approached and patted her down, removing the Glock from her underarm holster, and hefting it in his hand. She expected him to query the other empty holster, but he didn't. He gestured to them and said, 'out.'

They climbed out of the SUV onto the tarmac and joined the other migrants standing in a huddle, a couple of black-clad guys hemming them in. From around the edge of the truck appeared another man and this one walked with a limp and a stick. As he emerged into the light Pascal's heart sank. It was Ruiz, and he was smiling, grimly. 'Hey. How you doing?' he said.

He turned to the other migrants and told them they would be repatriated unless they had a legal right to enter the US. They were led away, leaving Pascal and Sapphire alone in the glare of the arc lights. Pascal's eyes swept the area; the barriers were being hastily removed and piled into the truck along with the migrants. The truck loaded, it pulled out leaving Ruiz and three grunts holding their guns on Pascal.

It crossed Pascal's mind that it would be very easy for Ruiz to finish the job here, and that thought was reinforced when Ruiz told two of the guys to take the other car and they would follow. He turned back to her. 'You should have finished me when you had the chance. Too late now. You'll be held in El Paso while you're processed, and then we'll take a view. And just who the fuck is this kid?' he said, looking closely at Sapphire. 'I mean, she's the reason you're here, right?'

Pascal was amazed he still didn't know. Sapphire started to speak, saying, 'my name is—'

'She's just a missing girl like Tilly-May,' Pascal said quickly, drowning out Sapphire's response.

Ruiz shrugged, unconcerned. 'Okay, well get in the car, and this time you're gonna have my gun trained on you all the way. One move and its bye bye,' he said, pushing Pascal into the back seat. He got in beside her, gun held on her, unwavering. Sapphire got into the front seat alongside the grunt who was to drive. Then they were moving off.

'No need for a seatbelt this time, eh, sweetheart,' Ruiz said to Sapphire with a wink. 'Your crazy friend's not gonna turn this car over.'

Sapphire ignored Ruiz, and simply stared straight ahead at the oncoming road.

Pascal watched Ruiz out of the corner of her eye. He seemed relaxed, but she could tell he was hyper alert, perhaps not unreasonably after their last run-in. The chances of him suffering a lapse in concentration this time around seemed pretty slim. She'd just have to keep thinking, watching and waiting, but she couldn't leave it too long because maybe it was his intention to finish the job and kill them, although it wouldn't be quite so easy this side of the border. As well as that, she reckoned the men who had accompanied him were genuine DEA, although she couldn't be sure about that, but if so it might make things more difficult for him.

'So, Ruiz, how d'you get onto us so quick, and set up the block?' she asked.

'Hey, I'm dirty, right?' he said, crooked smile. 'I get whispers from both sides. I got the best street Intel there is. You know,' he said, voice going serious. 'You're so clever, you ever consider the fact I might just be that rarest of the rare, a double double? Or is that too complicated for you? Maybe I was playing a part when Tilly-May jumped. Remember, I didn't kill her. And you ever consider the fact I might not have been taking you and the kid to your death in the desert, before you turned the car over?'

Pascal watched him for a long moment, her face blank. She didn't buy it, and she wasn't about to trust him.

He held her eyes, waiting, then shrugged when she didn't respond. As she turned to look out of the window, she became aware of frequent pinging sounds coming from inside his jacket. Sounded like his cellphone and a load of text messages coming in, then it was a ringtone, a call, then another. Ruiz scowled and removed the phone with one hand, gun staying rock solid on Pascal, in the other. He laid the phone on his knee, reading the screen with one eye, the other on Pascal. The phone rang again, probably going to voice mail, Pascal figured.

'My but you're popular, Ruiz,' she said, riding him. 'Why don't you answer, could be your bosses at the DEA, or maybe your real boss, Gutman. Don't mind us birds, we won't listen.'

Sapphire chuckled in the front seat.

Ruiz's eyes blazed for a second, then he grinned to cover it, but Pascal could tell he was getting ratty - good. She wondered who all the calls were from. Someone, or maybe more than one person, clearly wanted to talk to him pretty urgently, and he wasn't answering.

He scowled again, turned the phone off, then, one handed, with some difficulty, removed the Sim card.

Pascal raised her eyebrows theatrically at him but said nothing They heard a siren growl behind them and saw the flashing blue light through the window and at the side as two El Paso PD black and whites surrounded them; the one at the side moved smoothly past them and pulled in, bringing them to a halt.

'That's all we need,' Ruiz muttered. 'Dumb-ass cops on a traffic stop - assholes.'

Pascal's eyes narrowed as she looked around at the set-up. 'Yeah? I wouldn't so sure of that, Ruiz,' she said. 'Take a look around. See the big dark car with the blacked out windows laying back? That looks official to me. I don't think there's anything routine about this stop. Maybe you should'a answered your phone, man,'

Before he could answer, they were told to get out the car with their hands up.

They carefully did as they were ordered, Ruiz holding his DEA card out. They stood in a huddle, couple of patrolmen watching them as the dark vehicle drew up in a cloud of gravel and dust; two occupants, guy in plainclothes and a goon in blue and black law enforcement style attire. Pascal looked around. Again, the stop location appeared to have been carefully chosen. It was an open section of road on a wide bend where there were no buildings. There were rocky outcrops to the left and open scrubby desert to the right, and very little traffic.

Pascal watched the guy as he climbed out of the vehicle. He was tall, with a blonde buzz-cut bullet head and he looked like a marine. He said to the patrolmen, 'Thank you officers, for assisting. We'll take it from here.'

They nodded and got back in their vehicles to leave. The guy turned to Ruiz. 'I'm FBI agent John O'Hara, and we're taking over here,' he said, his voice punchy and authoritative. 'I have a warrant for the arrest of your prisoner, going by the name Catherine Hansen, for the murder of a child identified as Tilly-May, who may have been a US citizen.'

'Now wait a minute,' Ruiz said. 'What's your authority?'

'This,' O'Hara said, brandishing a piece of paper.

Ruiz grabbed it. Pascal could see it was a warrant.

'We checked with the DEA, Ruiz, and your stop wasn't even official. We and they tried calling you. You running something here, buddy?' O'Hara said, knowingly.

'No way, man,' Ruiz said. 'I heard about the warrant and didn't have time to stop and log the take-down. I got her didn't I?'

'Yeah. Thanks man,' O'Hara said. 'And as I said, we'll take it from here.'

'No problem,' Ruiz said. 'Mind if I tag along, for the ride?'

O'Hara looked like he was going to object but then his cell trilled, and he snapped it to his ear, listening. 'Yes, senator,' he said just loud enough for Pascal to hear, almost standing to attention, before moving out of earshot.

So, what the hell was going on here, Pascal wondered. If O'Hara had assistance from El Paso PD then he had to be running it through official channels, didn't he? And they'd already secured a warrant for Tilly-May, rigged for murder, which supported it being official, but how in hell could they know and act so quickly? The fix must well and truly be in, and the fact that O'Hara was in direct contact with a senator, pointed only one way: Victor Diaz.

She knew in that moment that if US law enforcement got her into custody, she would never get out, partly because they were dirty, but also because of the system. While those thoughts passed through her mind, she maneuvered behind Sapphire, her eye on the rucksack. O'Hara walked back towards them with a determined look on his face.

He said to Ruiz, 'we'll meet you back at the El Paso field office.'

Ruiz looked as if he was going to argue, but then thought better of it. He got back in the car with his side kick. As the vehicle pulled away Ruiz leaned out of the window and said, hopefully, 'we'll see you back there then, man.'

As Pascal watched Ruiz's car disappear, she said to no one in particular, 'somehow, I don't think so.'

She smoothly drew the Glock out of the rucksack, and said, 'so how is Senator Victor Diaz these days?'

As she leveled the gun she was surprised by how quickly the FBI grunt moved, almost instantly raising his weapon and drawing a line on her. She took him out with a shot through the shoulder, avoiding the Kevlar jacket. He spun around and dropped, but now O'Hara was pulling his weapon, again surprising Pascal with his speed. She shoved Sapphire and shouted, 'run,', but in that moment, O'Hara fired.

She felt like she had been hit by a sledgehammer, but as she went down she managed to get off one round into O'Hara and he went down as well. Now all three lay on the side of the road in the swirling dust.

A shadow fell across Pascal, and then she could feel small hands running over her. 'Are you all right, Courtney? You're bleeding, a lot,' Sapphire said, crouching over her, voice full of worry.

Pascal raised herself on her elbow and looked down. There was blood all over the right side of her midriff. It felt numb right now, but she knew the pain would come. She looked around; the FBI grunt was trying to raise himself up and O'Hara looked out cold. Pascal told Sapphire to get the FBI guys gun which was lying a few feet from him.

She scurried away and grabbed it.

Pascal raised her Glock at the FBI grunt and said, 'throw your cellphone and car keys here.' The guy watched for a moment, but when he saw her finger tighten on the trigger, he quickly gave them up; Sapphire brought them over.

They were at the road side, and there didn't seem to be any traffic. Pascal managed to get up and stagger over to O'Hara, gritting her teeth, her hand held over her stomach, ineffectually trying to staunch the flow of blood.

O'Hara was unconscious. The bullet seemed to have creased his shoulder, and there wasn't much bleeding, but there was a gash on his head. Looked like he had hit it on a rock when he went down. Pascal took his cellphone and gun.

She dragged herself over to the FBI grunt and phoned emergency services so he could hear her. She asked for ambulance and told them gunshot wounds. The FBI guy gave her the location. Pascal told Sapphire to get in the car, then she dragged herself into the driver's seat, blood dripping onto the car floor. As she turned the ignition, she felt faint, eyes drooping, but she knew she had to get them out of there.

She put the car in gear and then burned out of the rough scrub, spraying gravel and almost hitting a car that had to take evasive action to avoid them, then they were on the road heading for El Paso. She looked for signposts as she knew they had to get away from the city, get off the main routes, ditch the car as the FBI guy would give out the details immediately. Now she could hear the sirens in the distance. If there was a warrant, and she didn't doubt O'Hara's word on that, law enforcement countrywide would be looking for them, and shooting two

FBI guys wouldn't help. One slim positive thought shimmered through Pascal's ailing mind; maybe the roadblock was off the books as well, even with El Paso PD? Ruiz set-up clearly was, to protect his back, because she knew he was dirty and would spill if arrested by anyone else, but what about O'Hara? Was his attempted arrest kosher? The warrant suggested it had to be but who knew? As her blood seeped out and her strength dwindled, she gave up trying to get her head around it.

###

Half an hour later they sat in the car, in darkness. It was a big BMW official FBI vehicle and it had a small green first aid box. Earlier they had stopped at a convenience store and Pascal had sent Sapphire in to get water, snacks and aspirin. Pascal had pulled the big car off the main road onto a desert track and followed it into the wilderness, then off road across country for fifty meters into some trees.

She switched on the cabin light and turned to Sapphire. The girl seemed to have retreated into herself, maybe she was in shock. She was fiddling with the driver's smartphone, looking at the screen but not seeming to see it. They'd have to ditch it soon before the feds could use it for tracking. Pascal reached down and pulled her blood drenched tee shirt up. She heard Sapphire gasp, broken from her trance by the sight of the wound. It looked bad, but it wasn't in a dangerous position in terms of internal organs. Blood loss and infection were the main concern, and if she didn't get medical attention soon it would go bad; trouble was any official medical involvement would generate an immediate police report because it was a gunshot wound. So if they attempted to travel in the vehicle or get official medical attention, Pascal would be arrested in a heartbeat.

She wondered if she was going into shock herself; she was shivering but it wasn't cold, and she was struggling to keep her eyes open. The wound still oozed blood and the clothing around it was drenched.

'Courtney, we need to go to the hospital, or you'll die,' Sapphire said, voice desperate and full of fear.

Pascal shook her head. 'Can't do that,' she said, gritting her teeth. 'Ruiz set me up for Tilly-May. I'll be arrested like Yolanda, and never get out. And they can't leave you to be a witness, either.'

'So what do we do? We can't stay here.'

'No. We can't stay here,' Pascal whispered, strength fading fast. She closed her eyes as if she were asleep. They were both silent, just the quiet sounds of the desert around them.

After a moment Sapphire said, tentatively, 'we could go to my mother's people.'

'Where's that?' Pascal asked idly, thinking the girl was daydreaming of a fairy tale escape.

'Gallup, New Mexico. Many Navajo people live there. Grandma is there. She would help us.'

With an effort Pascal slowly turned her head to look at Sapphire. Her mind was sluggish, but she knew they were sitting right on the border of the state of New Mexico. She said, 'check it on google will you, sweetie? Distance.'

Sapphire, excited, grabbed the smartphone up, tapping and

watching the screen. 'Three hundred eighty miles, under six hours driving, IS 25 North, IS 40 west.'

Pascal sighed, thinking whether in her condition it was doable. The big car was great, but they couldn't use it, because there was an APB out on it, and they'd be picked up, probably within a couple of miles. As her mind worked on the problem she whispered to Sapphire, 'have a go with the water and wipes. See if you can clean the wound.'

Sapphire got to work, gently wiping and dabbing, slowly cleaning layers of congealed blood away. When it was clean, Sapphire looked in the first aid kit and got some antiseptic cream and smeared it around the wound. Then she applied a gauze pad and bandages, pulling Pascal up from the seat, making her wince, then winding the bandage around her.

When she finished Pascal was sweating profusely, beads of perspiration standing out on her forehead and running down into her eyes. She blinked, looking down at the neat bandaging and could see it already turning red. She quickly covered it so Sapphire wouldn't see.

'Sapphire, check Greyhound or any coach routes running near here to Gallup, will you,' Pascal said.

Sapphire tapped at the smartphone. A moment later she said, breathless, 'it's not far, look, Courtney, a station. Sixty-eight dollars and going in about an hour.'

Pascal studied the screen and location, wondering whether she could make it. She'd have to. They'd have to chance using the car for that short distance, and would have to dump it close to the stop, which would mean soon as the Feds found it they would be checking everything, buses, trains, cars, but they'd have to risk it. There really was no other way.

Pascal started the car and slowly backed out of the trees. She felt weak, almost like she was floating, eyes drooping again, but she knew she mustn't succumb even though it's what she wanted more than anything else in the world. She shook her head and floored the accelerator, the big car bounding forward, throwing up clouds of desert dust into the dry night air.

###

About a mile from the stop they had some luck. They were driving through outer suburbs, run down and poor, lots of squats, boarded up premises interspersed with the odd bright-lit store. They passed what looked like a group of street drinkers on a corner, five guys and a woman, some looking worse than others. Pascal looked them over as she slowly rolled by. As she came to a junction, she noticed a taxi rank, her mind working desperately slowly, an idea forming in her head. She slowed and did a wide turn across the road, causing some horns to blare in her wake.

She stopped short of the group and told Sapphire to take their stuff and walk up to the taxi's and wait on the bench she had seen there, and not speak to strangers. The child looked at her quizzically, concern in her eyes. Pascal smiled as best she could, and said, 'it's okay, sweetie, I'm not going to kill anyone. Off you go.'

Sapphire nodded uncertainly, but got out the car, then walked away up towards the junction. Pascal drove the short distance down the road drawing up next to the group. She turned the engine off and got out the car, staggering a bit, dizzy, and had to take hold of a lamp post to steady herself. She rested, her elbow held over her wound to hide the blood. She paused taking a breath whilst the group watched her, talking quietly amongst themselves.

Pascal summoned up a smile. 'Guys,' she said. 'I'm in a bind, on the run from a violent husband, and this car you see here, is hot.' She dangled the keys in front of them.

They all raised their heads, interested. One of them, mid-twenties although he looked years older had a kind of keen, feral look. He eyed up the car, then Pascal. 'Is that so?' he said. He looked far from drunk, eyes working over the vehicle. 'And what's that to us?'

'Maybe your lucky day,' she said, tossing him the keys. 'Just do me and yourself a favor. Drive it well away from here before you unload it.'

The guys eyes went back and forth between Pascal and the vehicle. 'No problem,' he said. 'But are you okay, lady, 'cause you don't look so good.'

'I'm fine,' she whispered, moving away from the group. Whether he did move the car away or not was up to him, but she reckoned on balance he probably would. He could get good money for a car like that, even hot. Anyway, it might slow down the FBI some. As she looked up with the last vestiges of her strength, she wondered if she could make it to the junction. She gritted her teeth and said to herself, one foot in front of the other. As she started to walk a taxi pulled up with Sapphire sitting in the front seat. Pascal didn't tell her off, just sank gratefully back into the back seat and closed her eyes.

The bus station was a one stop shop that seemed deserted; just an unattended ticket window, but it did have restrooms and importantly, no CCTV. They sat down outside on some benches while Pascal attempted to order her thoughts. She knew she didn't have much time left; if she didn't get some rest and medical attention soon, she wasn't going to make it. She looked at Sapphire, calmly looking around the streets, trusting completely in Pascal. She knew she had to try. She opened her pouch, dug out some cash and explained to Sapphire what they were going to do and why.

Five minutes later Pascal had managed to drag herself and Sapphire to the ticket window. She rapped on it, pulling her face into the best, friendly and calm expression she could muster. Sapphire held her arm around her, under Pascal's jacket, partly holding her up.

After a couple of moments, a large middle-aged Hispanic guy waddled out of a back room and slid in behind the ticket window. Pascal asked for two tickets for Los Angeles. The guy mumbled they were lucky, the coach would be there in ten minutes but they'd have to change. On queue Sapphire said loudly, 'Catherine, I want to go to Disneyland.'

As the guy handed over the tickets, Pascal said they'd see. The guy watched them for a moment then retired back into his room at the back. Pascal looked up out of the window and watched as the coach pulled in. She told Sapphire to go in the restroom and followed her in, almost all her energy gone. She moved into a cubical and collapsed down on the toilet. Sapphire came in and held her hand, her small earnest face full of worry. Pascal whispered to Sapphire what needed to be done. She nodded and began taking out the change of clothes, make-up and wigs. She sorted the clothing and then began undressing Pascal.

Ten minutes later Sapphire studied her handiwork and nodded approval. She was now a brunette and Pascal a blonde, both colorfully dressed. Now for the last part. Pascal told Sapphire to go outside and wait out of sight for the Gallup coach.

Pascal got herself out of the restroom back up to the counter. She donned shades, then rapped on the ticket window. Same routine; the guy reappeared, this time grumbling about passengers suddenly turning up at all hours. With the last vestiges of her energy Pascal tried to put on an approximation of a Tennessee Hillbilly accent, and asked for two tickets to Gallup, for her and her husband who would be along. When the guy passed the tickets through the window she almost collapsed, but managed to hang on, waiting until he had retired back to his room before dragging herself outside. As she sat down on the bench her strength went, her eyes closed and she was out cold.

An hour later she woke up sweating and moaning softly. She was sat at the back of a moving coach. Sapphire sat beside her squeezing her hand. She looked down and there was a thick blanket over her knees, and she wondered where it had come from. Sapphire smiled as Pascal's eyes opened; she lent up and wiped Pascal's brow with a handkerchief. 'Are you okay, Courtney?' she asked.

'I am now, sweetie,' she said, although she knew she wasn't. 'However did you get us on here? You're amazing.'

Sapphire laughed. 'It was easy. I told them you weren't well and that you'd taken your medicine and needed to sleep, so the driver helped me get you on here, and a lady up front lent me this blanket for you. Simples.'

Pascal kissed her. 'Could I have some of the water, please?'

Sapphire handed her the bottle and she took a sip. She looked at her watch. She didn't want to look at the wound; she knew it was still bleeding although not as much as before, and it felt numb. She took two aspirin she had been keeping and swallowed them with another sip of water. She checked her watch again, her eyes very heavy, sleep always beckoning. 'How many hours until we reach Gallup?' she asked, drowsy.

'About six I think. Try to sleep, Courtney. When we get there, Grandma will fix your wound. She's the daughter of a medicine man.'

Pascal smiled as she drifted into sleep

CHAPTER THIRTEEN

She answered immediately as if she had been waiting for his call. He could hear her breathing almost as if she were standing there with him. He sat at the same table outside the same cafe in Mexico City, gimlet eyed bodyguards a couple of meters away watching every move in the street.

'It's not good news, *mi corazón*,' he told her. 'It seems you were right, the kid did not die, and Yolanda Lopez's lawyer, he sent an undercover investigator down here to search for her. My guy in New York says this investigators real name is Courtney Pascal. She's ex-British intelligence. May even still freelance for them. She's the one splashed over the media couple of years ago when she saved the Queen of England, took out a guy with a bomb. My guy is still digging, but word is, handle with care. Seems she's one smart cookie. She lifted the kid, then got over the border and blew straight through an FBI roadblock, but they clipped her. She's wounded with a warrant on her head, so I'd guess it's only a matter of time before they pick her up.'

'This is bad,' she said. 'I'm talking to the trustees right now, and it was already delicate, trying to release funds without a body, and now this. I still don't understand how that Indio brat could still be alive. You prom—'

'Hey, you're not thinking straight, *nena*. Money will be the least of your worries. If that kid surfaces, you'll be looking at kidnap and attempted murder. They'll throw away the key.'

'So what do we do?'

'We find this Pascal and the kid before anyone else does, and then we bury them in the desert where no one will find them.'

'And how do we that?'

'With the help of the FBI and the US Marshals Service.'

'Explain,' she said, coolly.'

'There's a warrant out for this Pascal or Hansen or whatever she calls herself, for the death of another kid down here. It looks like a frame, but the point is it means the FBI and the Marshals are all hunting her, and we've got a guy inside so we can piggy-back a ride. All we've got to do is grab her before they do. We'll get her and the kid.'

'I hope so,' she said, then paused a beat, thinking. 'But why is there still no coverage in the media? Doesn't make sense, unless…?'

'Unless they haven't joined up the dots,' Dante finished the sentence for her. 'They're looking for this Pascal for the first kid and haven't looked to identify the kid with her- yet.'

'So maybe we got a bit of time still?' she mused. 'You know the Federal Prosecutor here in New York? He made his name on the back of the Dinks case, before joining the District Attorneys office. I got to know him some, if you know what I mean, during the trial.'

'And,' Dante said testily.

'And I don't think he's going to want this case coming back on him. Could make him look real bad, especially as he cut some corners in railroading Yolanda Lopez. You want me to talk to him?'

Dante sipped his coffee, thinking. She'd surprised him again with her audacious cleverness, her ability to spot a weakness and then go all out to exploit it. 'Let's keep that on ice for now. If we can't get a line on them quick, that's a fall-back,' he said, already worrying she was so strong willed she'd go ahead and cosy up to the DA anyway.

'Okay,' she said. Then, as if as an afterthought, she added, 'and just remember, Dante. Its a common misconception that the US doesn't have an extradition treaty with Mexico. It does, and its effective. So, if I go down, so do you.'

As the cup in Dante's hand shattered from the pressure of his grip, his bodyguards went into defensive crouches, believing they were under attack. Dante, surprised, looked down at the shattered remnants of the cup. After a moment he pulled out a crisp white handkerchief and slowly began to wipe his hand.

###

John O'Hara sat at the chiefs desk in the El Paso combined FBI, DEA field office out in South Mesa Hills. He was still smarting from being bested by the girl, anger simmering just below the surface of his calm demeanor. He irritably adjusted the dark blue sling around his shoulder as he listened and watched the grunts working through the leads. The bullet had only creased him. It was the bang on the head when he fell that was the shitter. Knocked him cold. Mild concussion the medic had said. But he wasn't about to let a few scratches deflect him from taking down the bitch. He knew he'd hurt her bad, a belly shot, so she wouldn't get far, not with the kid in tow.

But the girl had surprised him with her fearlessness and marksmanship under pressure. He was convinced she'd tried to wound and not kill, and that was the mark of someone very confident in their abilities. Two shoulder shots on the move in close quarters under fire. He wouldn't under estimate her again.

His mind turned to Senator Diaz and the call he had just taken. Diaz wouldn't talk over the phone and wanted to meet right now, away from the field office, which was fine with O'Hara. He too wanted to know what all the fuss was about. Why the two anonymous fugitives were so important, and why he had personally been chosen by Diaz to pursue them.

As he picked up his keys, one of the local grunts came in. 'They found the car, sir,' he said. He was chewing some tobacco as he spoke, so O'Hara could hardly understand him.

'Where?'

'Six hundred fifty miles east in Dallas.'

'What have they got?'

'It was a traffic stop. Driver was local, said he'd just bought the car from some guy for five hundred bucks. When we got heavy, he gave a us a description, but it wasn't Hansen and the kid. Just some low-life. Maybe they dumped the car and the guy found it?'

'So what are they doing now?' O'Hara asked.

'They're looking at CCTV. See if they can pick up the guy sold the car. Nothing yet.'

'We've got something,' a new guy coming into the room said. He nodded at O'Hara, and announced himself. 'Bill Patton, US Marshals Service. We picked up the car on CCTV on IS10 about 120 miles out of El Paso, one male driver, and they got a picture of him. It's going through facial recognition now, see if he shows up anywhere.'

'Good, but what about in El Paso?' O'Hara asked. 'Anything? 'Cause she obviously unloaded the car here.'

'Nothing so far, sir,' the Marshal said.

'Okay, keep me posted,' O'Hara said as he made his way out.

###

Pascal woke to the sound of a curtain flapping lightly in the wind. Her eyes fluttered, then she could see the window, open ajar, bright sunshine playing through the thin curtain onto the single bed in which she lay. It had clean white sheets and felt like a warm cocoon that she never wanted to leave. She tried to raise herself on her elbow but gave up - it was way too hard. She closed her eyes again and was instantly asleep.

She slept through undisturbed another twelve hours. When she awoke again, she felt weak and tearful. She moved her hands down her body and felt the thick bandages around her stomach, and then memory started to filter back; ladders, walls, Ruiz and O'Hara, gunshots and a mad escape across country.

She looked around the small simply furnished bedroom. Bare floorboards with a rug next to the bed, a dressing-table and a wardrobe. There was an old poster on the wall announcing a demonstration against a mining company.

There was a creak and the door opened a crack, somebody looking in, then it closed again. A few moments later it burst open and Sapphire was there, standing in the doorway, and there seemed to be a shadow behind her, and Pascal could just make out another person, barely taller than Sapphire. They both came into the room.

Sapphire said, 'this is grandma. Her name is Sialea-lea, but people call her, Sia. I just call her Grandma. She's the one tended your wound.'

Pascal looked at the small, compact woman. Her face was mahogany brown, skin taught over high cheekbones showing barely a line. Eyes brown, looking a thousand years old, but clear and wide with a hint of warmth. Her hair was gray, pulled back in a ponytail, and she wore a simple white peasant blouse and skirt that looked like rawhide.

Pascal smiled and said, simply, 'thank you.'

Sia nodded. 'I was glad to help.'

Pascal was surprised for some reason, that she spoke English. 'How long have I been out? When did we get here?'

'You've been out nearly three days,' Sapphire said. 'Grandma got the bullet out and sewed you up. They wanted to get a town doctor, but I said no. Hope I did right?'

'You both did great, and—' she stopped mid-sentence, wincing with pain as she tried to sit up.

Grandma said, 'you need to stay still, or you'll pull the stitches and start the bleed again.'

Pascal grimaced and relaxed back into the pillows. 'Where are we?' she asked.

'This is grandma's place, couple of miles outside Gallup. We're safe here,' Sapphire said, looking uncertainly at her grandmother. 'I've told grandma everything,' she added.

Pascal nodded. 'I am sorry to bring trouble to your door, Sia,' she said, trying out the strange name. 'But we had nowhere else to go.'

'We're well used to trouble here,' Grandma said with a grim smile. 'But you didn't bring trouble. You bought a gift: Sapphire. I thought she was gone, like my daughter, but you brought her back to me. I will never be able to repay you enough for that.'

'Well I reckon saving my life is payment enough, if any were due,' Pascal said. As her mind started to function again, she added, 'you got wifi here; cellphone signals?'

'Of course we have, silly,' Sapphire said. 'Where do you think we are, the moon?'

Grandma said, 'you need to eat some food even if you don't want it. I'll fix you something.'

'Thank you,' Pascal said. She lay back on the pillows, weak and tired again, eyes fluttering then closing.

###

Ruiz sat at a corner desk the El Paso field office had allocated him. His expression was bland but underneath his nerves were screaming. He rubbed his knee, the dull ache from when she had turned the car over in the desert still plaguing him, all playing into his fear and anger. Silencing the girl was all that mattered, before she could open her mouth and destroy him. And they were giving him the cold shoulder in the field office, not just O'Hara, the FBI acting boss, who seemed to have disappeared, but the grunts as well. And the way O'Hara had just waltzed up and taken the bust. It made him look stupid, but worse it had taken control of the girl away from him. Okay, she was on the lam, but having the Feds come in was a disaster. However much it hurt, he needed to get back in with them, so he could monitor what was coming in. Ruiz's anger and fear propelled him out of his chair, almost causing his knee to collapse. He stopped and leaned against the desk, composing himself. He picked up his walking stick and made his way into the main office.

'Hey, Ruiz. I was just coming to see you,' one of the grunts said, unconvincingly.

'Yeah, I'll bet,' Ruiz muttered. 'What you got?'

'Facial recognition came through,' he said. 'Guy's an El Paso street punk with a load of low level priors. A nobody. Guy folded quick when he knew it was the feds. Description he gave sounded like the girl but she's flying solo. No kid with her. Guy said she gave him the car and walked away.'

'So where is she?' Ruiz said.

'Beats me,' the grunt said, smiling.

Ruiz bit back on his anger. The guy was fucking with him, but he needed to play it cool if he wanted to nail the girl. 'Where was it? Where he bagged the car?'

'Here in El Paso, the suburbs.'

'So what we doing about it?'

'Nothing yet. We were waiting for O'Hara to get back, and for your input. You bought this mess to us, and we already hit our overtime limits for the month. What d'you want?'

'I want you guys on the street, fanning out from where he took the car, asking questions.'

###

O'Hara was let into the hotel room by a guy on the door wearing an earpiece. Diaz was sitting at a table near French windows that opened out onto a balcony. Outside the El Paso heat simmered and shimmered. Diaz was eating a late breakfast, toast and coffee and he had a laptop open on the table feeding in online news.

'John. Good to see you,' he said, looking up. 'Thanks for coming so quick. Want some coffee?'

O'Hara nodded.

Smooth, easy charm and charisma, and that's why the folks voted for him in such large numbers. Diaz was distinguished looking with a square jawed rectangular face with steady brown eyes and black, slicked across hair, graying at the temples. When he stood to hand O'Hara his coffee, they were eye to eye, which put him around 6' 2".

'John, what went wrong?' Diaz asked, his eyes turning cold, all warmth drained away.

'Well when we got there, Ruiz, the DEA guy, had already effected the stop. Guys a clown. Hadn't even checked them for firearms. Okay, my fault in assuming an experienced DEA agent would have done that, but he didn't. So the woman had a Glock in the kids

187

rucksack, and she pulls it, and she was damn fast and accurate, creased us both but I hit her with a belly-shot. I mean, who the fuck is she anyway?' O'Hara said, then remembering who he was talking to, added, 'sorry, senator.'

Diaz waved the apology away 'Shit happens, right, John?' he said. 'You know, son. You were personally chosen for me by the FBI director himself. Got to know him real well as a result of my work on the senate oversight committee. You're his recommendation. Hell, he even agreed to second you to my staff.'

'I won't let you down again, sir' O'Hara said.

'I know you won't, son, 'cause I'm told your one of the directors best. So I need you to get out there and hunt her down. Forget what's gone before.'

'But what's this woman's importance, sir? I was given the warrant and told to apprehend her and the child, but isn't that a job for the US marshals?'

'Come and sit down,' Diaz said, putting his arm around O'Hara and leading him back to the table. 'You've probably read the speculation that I may seek the GOP nomination, and I'll tell you, it's a real possibility, but there are powerful people out there who don't want that to happen, and they will stoop so low to blacken my name you wouldn't believe it.

'You've seen the warrant, it's for the arrest of this Hansen woman for the murder of a child in Mexico. Now, everybody knows all the good works I've done down there. The visits to the orphanages and the assistance programs I've pushed. Well, now they're trying to twist that. Trying to link me, *me*, with abuse of kids down there. Can you believe that, John?' he asked, his face thunderously angry and self-righteous.

'This Hansen woman is at the heart of it, John; she's the key to allowing them to try and smear me in this way. I've even heard they've been coaching the child to make false claims against me, just to derail my run. These despicable people are hinting that I, a US senator, may have had a liaison with this child, but they won't break cover and come out and say it straight, unless and until the woman and child surface and are apprehended. So d'you see what's at stake here, John?'

O'Hara's eyes seemed to change, go flat and Diaz smiled as he watched him.

O'Hara didn't notice Diaz's change of expression. He said, slowly almost as if he were talking to himself, 'so maybe, if they were never apprehended at all. If they were to disappear, that would be justice all round?'

'You got it in one, John. I knew we'd work well together,' Diaz said.

As O'Hara nodded his cell rang out loud. Diaz smiled and said, 'take it,' as he moved out onto the balcony. When he came back a moment later O'Hara was finishing up the call. 'Field office say they've got a lead. Our felons got on an LA bound greyhound bus.' O'Hara smiled. 'And the woman's belly-shot, so they won't get far.'

Diaz held out his hand to finish the meeting. They shook. 'Keep me informed,' he said.

As O'Hara left the room, Diaz was already on another call, this time to his *consiglieri* and putative campaign manager, Paul Santiago. 'Paul, I just sent the attack dog out,' he said.

'Victor, are you sure that was wise?' Santiago replied, cautious as ever. 'We need to keep control of this. No loose cannons.'

'You worry too much, Paul. Okay, the guy's stone crazy, but he'll make this shit storm disappear quicker than a Vegas card sharp. And I'm in with the FBI director - he wants me on the hill - so, any blow-back, we get to finesse it from inside.'

There was a pause then Santiago said, tentatively, 'Victor, I've never asked you, because I didn't want to know, but now I need to, if you're gonna seek the nomination, cause I think we both know you are. Is there anything I need to know?'

Diaz was silent for a moment; the biggest prize of all that he'd worked all his life for was coming tantalizingly close now. Most of his life he'd fought against what he'd thought was a weakness, a sick desire to rape children, and the ultimate, to kill as well. But since he'd began to amass power, a base, his senate seat, and now maybe the greatest prize of all, he questioned whether his desires were so outlandish. Mostly he had been happy to rape and murder cheap Indio Mexican children who no one but their continuously breeding parents would miss. But in the way of such things, that had become a commonplace, and so he had sought something more, and the Daughter Eaters had provided that as well, and really he didn't want that to end because he knew he couldn't stop, and why should he, now all the power was flowing his way. So containment was what was needed now, and ace FBI agent O'Hara could provide that. Maybe, he thought, he, Victor Diaz, could one day be POTUS. He smiled at the thought. He could become Nietzsche's true Ubermensch, come to save the world with a new morality.

'Victor?' Santiago prompted him.

'Hey, Pauli, you know the score, and you always have. You hitched yourself to my star long ago and its too late to start getting squeamish. You want a berth on the hill, you gotta take me as I am, warts and all, and protect the project. Now, are we cool?'

Santiago chuckled. 'We're cool, boss,' he said, and the phone clicked off.

CHAPTER FOURTEEN

Pascal sat out on Sia's veranda watching the horses. There were three, a sorrel and two bays, and they all stood solemnly watching her over the wooden fence. Maybe they were expecting some food, but she didn't have any. She sipped some iced tea from a tall glass, rocking her chair back on her its rear legs so it rested against the wall of the house. It felt good to just sit and feel safe for once.

She looked out across the corral to the dusty desert flat-lands stretching away and then rising up into a low range of hills, all dusty reds and browns with cactus and scrub bushes sprouting here and there. It was hot and humid but comfortable in the shade of the veranda awning.

She looked down at her bare midriff and the angry looking diagonal scar that ran like a slash down to her pelvic bone. The wounds of war. It was healing well and so was she, but there was still weakness, and when she had to stand up, she was unsteady on her feet, and there were spells of dizziness, but they were fading. Whilst convalescing she had emptied her mind of what had gone before, to aid her recovery, but now her mind was starting to re-configure, regroup and go back.

O'Hara was FBI and he'd had an official warrant. That meant US Marshall's would be looking for her as well. And Ruiz was DEA, so that made three US law enforcement agencies all out looking for her. She thought about the decoy ticket purchase for L.A. It was so obvious it was unlikely to fool them for long, and then it would be a case of how quickly they could pick up the trail to Gallup, New Mexico.

As she mulled this, Sapphire wandered out onto the veranda with a glass of orange juice.

'How are you, Courtney?' she said gravely.

'Good, thanks to you and your amazing grandma,' she said.

Sapphire looked radiant, and Pascal was amazed at how resilient children could be. The girl wore a brown headband with white and red shapes on it, her dirty-blonde hair pulled back behind her ears; underneath, her serious blue eyes regarded Pascal, looking striking against the contrast of her rapidly darkening skin. She wore shorts that showed of her lissom brown legs and Pascal thought she looked like a frisky young colt.

'Courtney, I saw you looking at the horses,' she said, half smile on her face. 'Maybe you'd like to go riding? We could go up into the hills? If your wound can take it.'

Pascal checked her face to see if she was kidding, but she looked serious. 'You know what, Sweetie. I'd love that,' she said. She knew that conventional medical wisdom would probably not advocate going riding as a good way of recuperating, but she had always found her body's constitution was unlike other peoples, and she contrarily almost never followed medical advice; it had always seemed to work for her.

'Cool. I'll go get them saddled up. We can take a picnic, and you can tell me what's going to happen next,' she said, a shadow of a frown flickering across her face.

Pascal watched the girl walk away towards the barn where the saddles were kept and wondered what the hell she was going to tell her.

###

The only time Pascal had ever been on a horse was before she got expelled from her posh private school, and then it had been jolly jodhpurs, hard black hats, boots and dressage, which had kind of spoiled it for her. She knew she was going to end up with a sore butt, but she also had a feeling she was going enjoy it, as long as her wound stayed quiet, and Sia had given her a corset to wear to help with that.

Sia had waved them off with a rucksack of food and water, and admonishments to be careful, follow the trails and not stay out too long. Then they had been gently walking their horses out of the gate, across the track and into the rough scrub-land that bordered the farm.

For a while they rode single file along a path, not speaking. It was hot, and Pascal was sweating lightly in the early morning sun. Sia had given her a wide-brimmed Stetson to keep the sun off her; made her feel like a real cowboy. They picked their way through a rock strewn area and the gradient became steeper, starting to rise. They went up through a narrow draw, rocks one side and overgrown brush on the other, always rising, the horses starting to work at the terrain.

Twenty minutes later they were into a clearing and the lower valley was spread out below, and now they could walk the horses side by side. Again, there was no talk, both just enjoying the quietness and the stunning beauty of their surroundings. They stopped to look down over the valley, the horses lowering their heads to pick at the meager grass.

'It's nice here with grandma, isn't it, Courtney?' Sapphire said, almost as if she wanted reassurance.

'Of course it is, sweetie. Why wouldn't it be?' Pascal said.

'Oh, you know. Maria, my step-mum didn't like me seeing grandma after mum died, and like dad would never stand up to Maria. So I never got to come here much.'

'Well you're here now, Sweetie, and I can see why you loved it so much, and your grandma. She's quite a woman.'

Sapphire turned in her saddle to look at Pascal. 'What's going to happen now, Courtney? 'Cause we're in danger, right?'

Pascal looked back at her. 'Yeah, we're in danger all right, but now I'm getting better, I'm working on it. I'll find a way to make us safe.'

'What. What happened to me,' Sapphire said, struggling to get the words out, swallowing hard. 'I know—'

'Hey. You don't have to go back and re-live—'

'Yes I do,' she said firmly. 'I need to do that to help you,' she added with certainty and wisdom beyond her years.

Pascal watched her and felt her heart welling up. 'How much do you remember?' she asked.

'Just about all of it,' she replied, her eyes haunted and frightened.

'I don't know, Sapphire,' Pascal said, worry creasing her brow.

'Re-living that stuff is going to screw you up. No question.'

'That maybe so, but you need to know what happened to me, to get us out of here. And hey, I'm tougher than you think.'

Pascal held her eyes for a long moment. Sapphire stared back calmly, her gaze unwavering. Pascal nodded. 'Okay. Let's make camp here, on the ledge. Have something to eat, and then we'll….. talk.'

Sapphire smiled and dismounted. 'I'll picket the horses. You can get us some tucker.'

###

They sat, backs against a large rock, looking out over the valley. They could see Grandma's spread looking like a matchbox way off. There were only a few other neighbor places strewn out across the valley, all someway away from Grandma's ranch. Pascal chewed on some dried brown meat that didn't look particularly tasty, but was. 'What the hell is this stuff?' she said, taking a lump out of her mouth and examining it.

'That's grandma's special beef jerky. Like it?'

'Love it, bit salty though. Pass the water, will you.'

She handed her the canteen. As Pascal put it to her lips, Sapphire said, 'so where do you want me to start? What d'you want to know?'

'Everything you can remember, right from when you were taken. And Sapphire?'

'Yeah.'

'You start feeling bad, like you don't want to say stuff. We stop.

You got that?'

'I got it, but it's time to tell it.'

Pascal nodded. Sapphire looked across the valley at grandma's house, the sun catching a glint on one of the windows. She held out her hand for the water canteen, took a swig and wiped her mouth. She hugged her knees to her chest and began to speak.

'The day it started I know I was happy, but I can't remember why. I think I had just turned six. Maria was excited, because she had a show that evening, and Papa was out as usual. It was normal really. In the late afternoon after I got back from school, I watched stuff on the TV. Yolanda was around doing chores, cleaning up and we horsed around and had a few jokes. Then later I ate with Maria, which was unusual, it was usually Yolanda. I remember because we had my favorite which was cup of noodles. You just pour in boiling water. Then Maria put me to bed, and that was it.'

Sapphire looked up from studying the ground, then down across the valley again, silent for a moment as she gathered her thoughts. She continued: 'I still don't know what happened. The next bit is jumbled, and I can't exactly tell which bits are dreams and which bits happened. I think I woke up and I thought I was in a coffin. I couldn't push the lid off and I shouted, and the lid was lifted, but the light blinded me, and it's a blur, and then it goes dark again and I must have slept.

'When I woke again, I was in a small dirty room. It was hot and I was naked and chained to an old iron bed. I shouted but no one came. Then I cried and cried and screamed and still no one came. There was no sound from outside and I didn't know what to do,' she said.

She stopped there, got up abruptly and walked over to the

horses. Both nuzzled into her, smelling her, looking for food. She patted and stroked them, whispering to them, and then walked back and sat down again. 'I must have fallen asleep. When I woke up there was some food on a plate on the table next to the bed. It was like a wrap, or a Tortilla with chicken salad inside and it was delicious, and there was diet coke as well. That was the last nice thing that happened to me for a long long time, eating that chicken Tortilla,' she said, scuffing her heel in the red earth.

###

'It's way too obvious,' O'Hara said.

The local FBI agent nodded as if he understood. 'Well, that's what the guy said, sir.'

They were sat in the field office in a room O'Hara had commandeered, and he had his feet up on the desk as the grunt reported to him. 'So let me get this right,' O'Hara said, just getting warmed up. 'The little girl calls the woman "Catherine", loudly right in front of the ticket guy as they buy a double for L.A, right?'

'Right.'

'Ticket guy say anything about the state of the woman? Was she bleeding?'

'When I pressed him, sir, he did say she looked pretty wasted, white face like she was sick and maybe about to keel over, and she had her hand pressed against her stomach like it was painful.'

'They got any CCTV of the bus stop?'

'No sir. It's a one stop hole in the wall.'

'We checked L.A. and the incoming coaches?'

'Doing it now, sir. So far, nothing.'

O'Hara gamed it in his head; maybe it was a double bluff, and they had gone to L.A. Clever thing to do, and this chick was clever; ram the obvious down the watcher's throat. You can't see the piece on the board because its staring you in the face. O'Hara dismissed the grunt with a wave, then stopped him at the door. 'He didn't actually watch them get on the coach, or any coach, right?' O'Hara said.

'That's right sir. Guys got a cubby-hole at the back of the ticket office where he seems to spend all his time. Probably a porn hound'

'So they could have got on any coach. Get me a schedule, will you? All coaches arriving and leaving, with destinations, two hours either side of the L.A. bus. And find out all the tickets he sold during the same period. Can't be many.'

'I'm on it, sir.'

As the grunt left O'Hara's office, Ruiz was loitering outside and fell into step beside him, gritting his teeth as he tried to keep up. The grunt was more than happy, given his sky-high case load, to deputize Ruiz to go back to the coach stop and get the stuff O'Hara had asked for.

###

'On the third day an old lady all in black came into my room,' Sapphire said, continuing her story, her voice soft and controlled. 'She didn't speak to me, just replaced the bucket I had been using and took away my empty plate. I shouted at her, but she ignored me and left the room.'

Sapphire got up and began to shuffle her feet. She leaned back against the large rock they had been sitting against, and she looked up at the sky. Pascal watched her, worrying about what this was doing to her, but all too aware it was the only way they were going to get out from under.

Sapphire kept her head tilted up, watching the sky overhead as she continued to speak. 'I slept some more and when I awoke there was more food and a drink, but this time I think it may have been drugged, because there's a blank space after I eat the food and drink. This time when I woke up, I was in a nightmare.'

Sapphire started to shiver. She hugged herself, arms crossed over her chest, her back pressed against the rock. Pascal scrambled to her feet and embraced her. It was getting too scary for the girl. Better to backtrack to less frightening times and try and work out what had happened. 'It's okay,' Pascal said. 'Let's stop here a while, because I want to go back to the night it all started, when Maria made you a meal and you ate together.'

Sapphire nodded, already calmer, the tremors fading away.

'Earlier you said Yolanda normally fixed something for you to eat in the evening. But that evening it was Maria. Can you remember why?' Pascal asked her.

'Sure. She had a show and was excited,' Sapphire said, but it came out a little too quick. She looked puzzled, as if she were trying to solve a riddle.

'Sapphire, I want to ask you something, but I don't want to

upset you again,' Pascal said, gently.

'It's okay,' she said, her tone sad and resigned. 'I know what she did now. But I didn't want to believe it.'

'What did she do?'

'She must have put something in my food or drink to make me go to sleep.'

'Why?'

'I don't know.'

Pascal pulled her closer and kissed her cheek. 'It's okay,' she said.

'I thought she loved me, you know. But she couldn't have, could she?' Sapphire said.

'You know, Sapphire, people do things for strange reasons and we don't always know what those reasons are. Maria may have been threatened or tricked herself. We don't know, but we need to find out.'

'How?'

'By looking at the detail, and at what you can tell me.'

'But what else can I tell you?'

'Before that night, how was it at home? I know you lived there with your father, Maria and Yolanda. Did anything change leading up to that night? Did you see anything odd or strange?'

'Nothing. Papa was so busy, never home, and I didn't see much of Maria. It was usually just me and Yolanda,' Sapphire said, frowning as she thought back, trying to pin down ghosts. She turned away from Pascal and wandered over to the horses again. She stroked the Bay's nose, whispering in his flapping ear. She turned back, looking over her shoulder at Pascal, and said, 'I did see Maria with a strange man once though, couple of weeks before. I didn't think anything of it at the time and I'd forgotten, but when you just asked about seeing anything, it came back to me. Just popped into my head.'

Pascal felt a small surge of excitement. 'Tell me what you saw?' she said.

Sapphire patted the horse and came back to the rock and sat down. 'It was Yolanda's day off, and they sent me back from school early that day. I can't remember why. When I came in the house, they didn't hear me.'

'Who?'

'It was Maria and a man I'd never seen before.'

'What were they doing?'

'They were laughing, in the kitchen. Maria was in just a bathrobe that wasn't done up around the waist, which shocked me, and her hair was wet. When they saw me, Maria shouted at me but the man calmed her and smiled at me. I was frightened.'

'What happened?'

'Maria said he was an old friend visiting unexpectedly, and he left quickly. I could tell she was angry, and she didn't speak to me for a while. She said only that I mustn't tell Papa as he would get upset.'

'Tell me about the man?'

'He was very handsome. I think now, he was a Mexican. He had dark hair and nice eyes and he smiled a lot. As he was leaving and they were in the hall I heard her call him, "Dante".'

'Did you ever see him again? Or did she ever mention him again?'

'No.'

Time to go, Pascal thought. The girl looked washed out and tired. 'Maybe we should be getting back. We can talk some more tonight?'

Sapphire smiled, relieved. They collected up their stuff, got the horses ready, mounted up and moved back out onto the trail.

###

Hettie stood in the doorway of Calver's office, warning look on her face. 'I have a couple of people here, say they're from the government, but wont say what it's about,' she said.

Calver nodded, unsurprised. 'Show them in,' he said.

Two of them, a man and a woman, dressed in dark cut suits. All they were missing were the shades. They came in, the woman moving into the background, guy taking the floor, front of Calver's desk. He wanted to look tough, but it didn't quite come off; face too thin, eyes a bit too close together, but the guy worked at it.

'Agent Calhoun,' he said. 'FBI, and this is agent Monroe,' he added, gesturing to the small compact blonde behind him. They both simultaneously flashed ID's.

'Welcome, guys. Take a seat. Want some coffee? We do the best in Brooklyn,' Calver said.

They remained standing. 'We'd like to know where Courtney Pascal is. We have reason to believe she may be using an alias, Catherine Hansen. There's a warrant out for the arrest of Hansen. If they are one and the same person, then she's a fugitive from justice, and she works for you,' Calhoun said.

Calver flicked a switch on his intercom. 'One coffee please, Hettie,' he said. He looked up at Calhoun. 'What makes you think I know her, or where she might be?'

'Don't fuck with us, Calver. We know she was working for you down in Mexico. The charge sheet just gets longer by the day; murder, attempted murder of an FBI agent, assault with a deadly weapon, resisting arrest. She needs to face justice and go to gaol, and you can join her if you're not going to cooperate,' Calhoun said, angry red spots showing on his cheeks.

As Hettie bought in Calver's coffee on a tray, agent Monroe stepped away from the wall behind Calhoun. 'Look counselor, we know she works for you, and so you likely have a good idea of where she is right now. We'd just like to clear the ID issue up and she can go on her merry way. Cooperation now will help later on. It's only a matter of time. You know how it works,' she said.

Amateur good cop, bad cop Calver thought as he spooned in one sugar and stirred his coffee. 'It's no secret Pascal works for me,' he said, taking a sip and nodding approval; it was piping hot and just right. 'I spoke to her couple of days ago. She's not stupid. She gave absolutely no indication of where she was. If you want me to hazard a guess at her location at the time of that call, I would say probably Mexico, on the border with El Paso. But I'm sure you know that already.'

'Yeah, we do,' Calhoun said. 'What we want to know, is where she is now?'

'I can't help you with that,' Calver said, looking up at them with his best cold hard stare. 'But what I can tell you is that whether or not she's using an alias, the chances of her murdering a child are zero. So that charge is bullshit, and you probably know it. Classic frame. Now, I never make threats, but I'll tell you this on her behalf. She really is the wrong kind of person to fuck with.'

'Get this,' Calhoun said to Monroe out of the corner of his mouth. 'This two bit shyster wants to threaten the FBI.'

'I made no threat, and I've told you all I know. Now I'd like you to leave.'

Monroe leaned down over the desk fixing Calver in the glare of her eyes. 'If you learn of Miss Pascal's current whereabouts, be sure to notify us immediately,' she said. 'Here's my card.'

'Yeah, you got 24 hours, Calver,' Calhoun said. 'Or we'll be back to arrest you for obstructing justice.'

'Fuck you,' Calver said to their retreating backs.

CHAPTER FIFTEEN

Sia's home was spacious with big airy rooms, simply furnished. The land on which the house stood had been in the family a long time and the home had been built in stages over the years, a bit here a bit there, bedrooms, then a barn and corrals and now it was quite a spread. The kitchen was a large room dominated by a big wooden table in the middle, set by a long window. Sia had promised she would make them a traditional Navajo dish for supper, and she had: Mutton stew with corn and squash with fry bread tortilla on the side. Now they sat around the table, eating, the evening sun dipping into the range of hills on the horizon, the last tendrils of its light dappling in through the window and slanting across their faces.

As they ate Sia told Pascal about her problems with a mining company who were hassling her, wanting to buy her land, and not wanting to take no for an answer. 'You know they took millions of tons of uranium from the land round here, starting in the 1940's, for the atom bomb,' she said, ladling out a second helping of stew for Pascal. 'I'm not anxious to give them another go. All they know how to do is take. Never how to nurture the land and give back to it. We always gave offerings to the earth for what it gave to us. The miners just ruin it for everyone and leave a mess,' she said.

Pascal nodded, liking the spirited little women, impressed by her feelings for the land and her wish to conserve it.

'What's the matter, Sapphire?' Sia suddenly said, looking at the girl. 'Why are you so quiet?'

Sapphire forced a smile, toying with her food. 'I was remembering how it was here with mum. All the fun we had before she died.'

Grandma took her hand. 'Her spirit is still here, and you are here too, and she would have been proud that you made it back. I know a little from Courtney, what you have been through. Maybe it was like the Trail of Tears the Nations experienced, but you are like your mother. You are strong inside.'

Sapphire looked down at her barely touched plate of stew. 'You said you know a little about what I went through, grandma, but I want you to know it all,' she said. She quickly looked up at Pascal. 'Courtney, we need to finish it, what we started in the hills.'

'Sapphire, you don't—' Pascal started to say.

'No. It's okay. If Grandma's here, it's easy to talk. Does that make sense?' she said.

Pascal nodded. 'Of course. I understand.'

'You remember when we first met, Courtney?'

'Yes. Out at Gutman's ranch, in the desert.'

'That's right. Well, after the lady in the black shawl who came in to clean my room, he was the next person I met.'

'Tell us what happened?'

She took a sip of water, concentrating. 'When I woke up the next time I was in the main house, sitting in a chair in the living room, and Gutman was there talking on the phone. They had dressed me and there were some cookies on a plate and a coke, so I had some.

'When he finished his call, he didn't say anything for a while. He just sat and watched me. I wasn't frightened. Then he said, and I remember his words because they sounded so strange, and not even scary. He said, "you know, your kidnappers say I must kill you quick and leave no trace, but I say no, because I have plans for you."'

'I thought it was silly and it was like we were playing a game. He told me to come over to him, to his big desk and he made me sit on his knee. I still wasn't scared, and he didn't try to touch me. I just sat on his knee like I did with papa sometimes.

'He said, "you are going to be meeting some very important people, and you must do what they say. You must please them, and in exchange, you get to live." Then he showed me these old-fashioned photographs of men that were lying on his desk, and all the time he made nasty but funny comments about them. They all looked so old, and I still thought we were playing a game, like I did with Yolanda.

'Then he said, "would you like a friend to play with? A young girl like yourself?" and he smiled, and it seemed like a kind smile, so I said yes, and a few second later the old lady in black brought a young girl into the room.'

'Tilly-May?' Pascal said.

'Yes. That's how I met Tilly. You see, I was so pleased to have someone my age, to talk to and play with, and she was nice. She told me what happened there. What to expect, but it didn't make sense to me then. I just wanted to play with her.

'We shared a room and we were allowed the run of the house. Gutman left for a while. There were men outside but just Tilly, me and the old woman inside. We never tried to escape, we just played games and talked.

'But after a few days I was getting bored and that's when Tilly started to tell me things, scary things. She said I would have to go into a room with an old man and he would hurt me, but that I mustn't cry out or it would get even worse and I might even disappear. I didn't know what to make of that, but then Gutman came back and they moved us.'

'To Cafe Flamingo?' Pascal said.

'Yes. And I guess it was something like Tilly told it, but it didn't happen straight away. There were some other Mexican girls there who we didn't mix much with. They kept us apart. Then a few days after we arrived, there was a lot of things happening, and they were cleaning the place up. They dressed us up in funny clothes and had a woman come in and put special make-up on us. That was fun, but what came after wasn't'

'You want to take a break, Sweetie?' Pascal asked her.

'No. I'm fine, but I wouldn't mind some of your green tea, grandma,' she said.

'I'll make us all some. You carry on with your story, and I can listen while I make it,' Grandma said.

Sapphire continued. 'We never saw the men, but we knew somehow that they were watching us, maybe through the big mirror on the wall. Then you got chosen, but I got chosen by one man. I think it was much worse for Tilly, because it was lots of different men for her, and some hurt her so bad. And then she died,' she whispered, desperately trying not to cry.

'Look maybe we better stop now,' Pascal said, deep lines of worry etching into her face.

'*No!*' Sapphire said, angrily wiping away her tears. 'I need to finish this.'

Grandma put a cup of tea down in front of Sapphire, and gently gripped her shoulder. 'I think you're right,' she said. 'You do need to finish it, let it out. Cleanse yourself.'

'The man we saw on TV, Courtney,' Sapphire continued, doggedly

'Texas Senator, Victor Diaz?'

'Yes. That was the man who chose me.'

There was silence for a beat, then Sia said, 'sorry folks, but I need to go to the john.'

It broke the tension. Pascal smiled and Sapphire said, 'yeah, me too, grandma.'

A few minutes later as they waited for Sapphire to come back from the toilet, Sia said, 'd'you believe she was kidnapped to order?'

Pascal studied the old woman, surprised that rather than emotionally wringing her hands about Sapphire's ordeal, she had been calmly analyzing what had happened.

'I've thought about that, and it's possible, but I don't think so,' Pascal said. 'Gutman's operation does kidnap to order sometimes, but I don't think that's what happened here. I think someone else kidnapped her and she came into his hands somehow, so in a way it was just opportunistic in some way. Unfortunately I didn't get time to question him about how Sapphire ended up with him.'

Sia nodded, then said, tentatively, 'we don't need to know the details of what this Diaz did to Sapphire, do we? I think we are wise enough in the ways of men to know what will have been done to her. It would break my heart to make her re-live it in our home.'

Pascal nodded. 'I agree, but one day she will have to go through it with law enforcement, so these people can be punished. But not now. What I need now is the details: how they operated, and the time lines.'

'Why?'

'Because I'm going to nail them, all of them, that's why, and in order to do that I need the detail,' she said calmly.

Sia smiled grimly, watching Pascal, impressed by her cool detached way and her lack of fear. She would have made a great warrior back in the day. Sia said, 'Why don't we just reveal to the world that we have her? Then we can get poor Yolanda out of prison and Sapphire can go home to New York?'

'Because I don't think she'd ever get to New York. If it was just the kidnappers, whoever they are, who were looking for her, I wouldn't be so worried, but Senator Diaz? That's something else. He's a coming man, very influential already, and he sits on one of the most powerful congressional oversight committees: intelligence, where he has day-to-day contact with the guys who run the whole edifice and all its branches: FBI, Homeland Security, CIA, DEA, Justice department, US Marshals. You want to bring Sapphire out of the shadows, with a guy like that pulling all the strings?'

Sia swallowed, looking shaken.

'And that's only half the story. I'm a fugitive from justice, because they're trying to frame me, so that puts me in danger but also means they can negate anything we might try and release to the media about the story.'

'So what can you do?' Sia asked.

'That is what I have to work out.'

As Sapphire returned and took her seat, Pascal said to her, 'Your Grandma and I will never get close to knowing what you went through at the hands of these people, but I am not going to ask you about that now. You may be asked about it in the future, but we are not going to do that today, okay?'

Sapphire nodded, looking pensive, perhaps relieved.

'What I want to know instead,' Pascal continued. 'Is how often you had to see Diaz. What was the process, who arranged it and where it took place?'

'That's easy. I saw him only once, in a room on the third floor of Cafe Flamingo. Through all the time, that was the worst. It was all night, went on forever and I thought it would never end,' she said, her voice catching in her throat. She swallowed. 'After that one time, I was kept by Gutman at the Hacienda and only had to see him. He never hurt me like Diaz, but he made me do things that made me feel sick and like I wanted to die.'

Pascal studied the girl. She looked like she was in a trance, remembering bad things. Probably time to stop, but Pascal took a chance with one more question. 'Did you ever see Diaz again?' she asked.

'Yes. Once,' Sapphire replied. Her eyes turned inward as she thought back. 'It was out at the hacienda. Me and Tilly had a new friend called Tamara, but she was only there a few days. She was so scared and missed her mother. She was only seven years old, from Washington she said. When they moved us to another room, they took her away, but as I was walking down the corridor I looked down from the landing and saw Diaz coming into the house. I never saw Tamara or Diaz again after that day.'

It was now pitch dark outside. They heard the ghostly howl of a Coyote out on the mesa. Sapphire shivered. She said, 'so what are we going to do now, Courtney?'

Pascal rubbed her sore midriff. 'Let's all get some sleep. Tomorrow's a new day and we can start planning the fight back,' she said.

Sia said, 'I'll second that.'

###

'The fugitives got lucky,' the FBI grunt mumbled.

'What do you mean?' O'Hara said, his face darkening. They were in the field office and O'Hara had his feet on the desk again.

'The coach driver. He was a relief guy. Called in when they're short staffed, but this guys a bozo. A drunk. Gets paid; goes on one. Found him in some dive in L.A. They had to sober him up, and he couldn't remember anything. Not even driving the coach let alone passengers getting on or off on the way. Dead end. Sorry boss,' the grunt said, already moving away, anxious to get out of range.

O'Hara cracked his fingers. So they got lucky, a break. Or was it? He shouted after the guy, 'who spoke to the driver? Took the statement?'

The grunt stopped at the door. 'It was the DEA guy, Ruiz.'

'Get him in here. And bring me those schedules for the other coaches, arriving and departing. And who's checking hire cars, cabs and stolen vehicles around the stop?'

The grunt just looked at him, mouth working, trying to come up with a good answer. O'Hara watched him, a rattler watching a swamp rat. 'What's your name, agent? he asked, quietly.

'Michaels, sir.'

'Well, agent Michaels. I'm putting you in charge of checking vehicles around the coach stop - cabs, hires, carjacks and thefts - and I want answers within the hour. You got that? Less you want to go back to writing reports in the back office.'

'I'll get on it right away, sir.'

'And get Ruiz in here.'

Moments later Ruiz ambled in looking the worse for wear, a day's stubble, bloodshot eyes and dressed like he was auditioning for the part of a street drinker. He lent back against the door jamb and folded his arms. 'Michaels said you wanted to see me?'

'That's right. This is now a joint FBI US Marshals operation, so we don't need the DEA. So I want you to brief me on your involvement going back with the fugitives, and what you got from the coach driver, and then you can hand over all your stuff and crawl back under whatever rock you crawled out from.'

'You're Diaz's boy, right, O'Hara?' Ruiz said, examining his fingernails. 'And, correct me if I'm wrong, but you have no authority over me. DEA have a legitimate interest in this fugitive in relation to an ongoing investigation relating to drug trafficking coming out of Mexico. She worked with us and we need to debrief her. In addition, I have every right to work out of this field office. If you don't wish to work with the DEA and pool our resources, that's your choice, but if it were to get back to the powers that be, that you're not playing ball. Well……?'

'You threatening me, Ruiz?' O'Hara said.

'No way, man. I'm just shooting the breeze with a valued colleague.'

O'Hara watched him, wanting to crush the guy, but keeping his face immobile, keeping that friendly good o'l' boy look in place.

Ruiz pushed himself up off the door jamb into the room. 'Look, O'Hara. I don't like you and you don't like me, but its better if we work together on this, at least for now, yeah? And what Michaels told you about the coach driver? It's kosher. Company only called the guy in occasionally, when they were short. He gets paid and goes on a bender. He can't tell us anything. Seriously.'

O'Hara nodded. Maybe he could use Ruiz for now, then unload him down the line with an accident or friendly fire incident. He swung his legs off the desk, leaned up and bawled out the open door, 'get us two coffees will you, Markeson.' Then to Ruiz, 'pull up a chair, Ruiz. You can tell me what you know about our fugitive. It might help us get a line on her. Welcome aboard.'

Ruiz nodded, not taken in by O'Hara's sudden change of attitude. He took a seat as Markeson bought in a couple of cups of coffee and placed them down on the desk.

###

Pascal sat at Sia's beat-up old desk-top computer and checked out a defunct email address she hadn't used in years. She had to clear out about five thousand spam messages. Her finger hovered over the new message button as she tried to pull up from memory the old email address for Christoff. As it materialized in her mind, she slowly typed it into the space.

She glanced out of the window; it was dawn and Sia was already outside feeding the horses. Sapphire was still in bed asleep. Pascal sipped some freshly ground coffee she'd found in the pot. The injury and recovery had slowed her down, and not just physically, but now she was back in play mentally. First step, logically, was to get all the information she could and there was only one go to guy for that - Christoff, but they hadn't spoken in a while, following a silly argument. He'd gone off in a huff and they hadn't spoken, and then it had gone the way of lots of such relationships; you keep saying you're going to give them a call and you don't and then it becomes difficult to be the one to make the first move. And now it would be, oh, she's only contacting me because she needs help. Fuck it! She finished typing in his address.

She knew he'd gone back to MI6, working part-time - he was semi-retired - out of the UK consulate on Third Avenue in New York. They'd worked together in the past when she'd worked for MI5 and subsequently he'd come over to the US to help with Calver's defense problems the year before and then, like her, he'd stayed on.

She'd thought about phoning, but it was too risky.

She began typing. She said she was in trouble and needed help. She didn't sketch out the background detail, but said she was particularly interested in background information on New York Socialite and fashionista, Maria Dinks and possible links with a guy known only as "Dante", almost certainly a Mexican national. She included Sapphires brief description of the guy. Then she asked him to check missing children, a Lucy Collins from Beverley Hills L.A. and a Tamara, no surname, from Washington. She gave their estimated ages and dates they disappeared. Then she added a coda that if he had the time, did he have any snippets of information about Texas senator Victor Diaz. She intuited that whatever Christoff's feelings, the names mentioned would certainly arouse his professional curiosity. She finished up by saying how sorry she was for the break in their friendship which she had allowed to develop by not calling. If he could help maybe he could email back with a number.

She re-read what she had written, then hit send.

CHAPTER SIXTEEN

Hettie said, 'it's Michael Daniels on line two.'

Calver said as he picked up, 'who's Michael Daniels?'

Hettie shouted through the open office door, 'he's the federal prosecutor for New York.'

Calver sighed. He'd been wondering how long it would take them to pick up on it. He said, 'Jonas Calver. What can I do for you, Mr Daniels?'

'You can start by telling me what this Dinks shit is about,' he said, voice tight. 'You're now apparently the attorney of record on appeal. So what gives, counselor? You dig up the second shooter on the grassy knoll? What've we got here?'

'We got what it says on the appeal notice, counselor.'

'Come on, Calver, don't play dumb. I haven't seen it yet, it's still mired in the court, so all I know is that it's been filed. So what have you got? If it's any good, maybe we can talk.'

Calver looked out the window across the street at the Brooklyn Brownstones. Yep, they were still there, standing tall and sturdy. He rubbed his chin, thinking, wondering how long it would be before

Justice joined up the dots linking the warrant out for Catherine Hansen -
or Pascal if they'd figured it out yet - and the FBI's visit to his office,
and the contents of his appeal. He was confident they would work out
who the witness was in pretty short order, but he owed it to Pascal to try
and spin the thing out as long as he could; try and give her an edge. She
was right; he probably shouldn't have filed yet, but it was what it was.
'We're concerned for the safety of our witness and that's why we're
asking for the identity details to be sealed for now,' he said.

'Come on, Calver. We're the government, not the mafia. What
d'you think we're gonna do? Whack your witness? We don't do that
anymore.'

'Maybe you don't, but there are some pretty powerful people out
there who do, and as soon as they get wind of what we got here, they
might just try.'

'You're some drama queen, Calver. This case is old news, and
the evidence for conviction of Yolanda Lopez was rock solid, but, okay,
let me humor you. What about protective custody for your witness?'

Calver thought hard and fast. 'It's a possibility, but I'm not quite
ready to talk to you yet. Give me 48 hours.'

'Done. I'll call you back, but if the media pick up on this and ID
your witness, there's going to be a shit storm.'

As if he didn't know that, and it gave the lie to the prosecutor's
false jibe about Dinks being old news. Was it hell. He needed to talk to
Pascal.

###

Sia brought her old-style rust colored SUV around to the front so they could go into Gallup and get some provisions. They piled in, Pascal up front with Sia, and Sapphire in the back. Pascal enjoyed the scenery as they drove, harsh orangy colored scrub desert interspersed with stunning rock formations that rose into the sky and took the breath away. It took about fifteen minutes to get into the small city.

Gallup had wide sidewalks with even wider streets but seemed strangely quiet. Sia pulled them into a car park outside a large looking convenience store. She said, 'I need to go in the bank. You and Sapphire can go in the store. You want anything, they'll have it there.'

In the store Pascal bought a couple of cheap burners, then she had a look at the hunting rifles. Sapphire studied an array of smart phones in a locked cabinet. After fifteen minutes, they left the store to go find Sia. As they arrived at the entrance to the bank, Sia was stood on the sidewalk with her back against the wall, speaking to a man in a suit. A uniformed cop stood to one side, hands on hips, his prowl car pulled up at the curb, door hanging open and blue light lazily oscillating on the top.

Pascal held back. If she intervened the cop would ask who she was, and the only ID she had was for Catherine Hansen, so it would flag up instantly. Sapphire was tugging on her hand, so Pascal explained the problem. Sapphire nodded and smiled. 'Grandma can look after herself,' she said. And it looked like she could, because after a few moments the cop got back in his car and left.

Sia noticed them approaching and nodded. The man turned to look at them, sizing them up. He was big, towering over Sia. For a second his look was angry, but it passed quickly to be replaced by a false smile. He said, 'morning ladies.' He began to move away saying over his shoulder to Sia, 'you should think about what I said, and back off because my boss ain't the patient kind.'

Sia looked stressed, but shouted after him, 'I've given you my answer, so you can tell your boss to stick it in his pipe and smoke it.'

The big guy didn't answer, just ambled away down the sidewalk, got in a big black car and drove away. Sia said, 'come on, let's go home.'

On the way back Sia told Pascal about the run-in and some of the background. 'I been doing voluntary work for a while now. Advocacy and protesting, mostly about police brutality against Native Americans and about there being way too many liquor licenses being granted around here. You know,' she said turning to Pascal, hands on the wheel, a keen look in her eye, 'this small city has one of the highest concentrations of liquor licenses per person of any city in the US, and it generates a river of blood money. I've been calling for and making a nuisance of myself with others, trying to change things but the liquor industry here, and their protectors, most of them corrupt and dirty law enforcement, don't like it, and they're trying to stop me.'

Pascal smiled, warming again to the fiery little grandmother. 'Is there a link? I mean can you prove a link between police brutality and liquor licenses?' Pascal asked, starting to get interested.

'It's not so much that. Maybe I didn't express myself so well because I'm angry at the moment. It's more a question of unexplained deaths, and many of them are the result of police prejudice and brutality, but others are simply people drinking way too much cheap freely available booze. Then they get run-down by traffic or die of exposure in the winter as they got nowhere to go to sleep.'

'What can you do?' Pascal asked.

'We can organize, protest and challenge new licenses and generally make trouble. Challenge them at every level. Question every death in police custody, get campaigns going online and run farm sales, music, you name it. We been fighting this fight for 200 years and we're not going to stop now.'

'Go grandma,' Sapphire chirped from the backseat.

'In fact, Courtney,' Sia said, getting into her stride, 'I've got some of our victims and supporters coming around tonight for supper so you can meet some of them.'

'I'd like that,' Pascal said, but she was already thinking about Christoff and whether he'd come through; she'd check her emails when she got back

###

'Gallup,' O'Hara said, looking up from the coach schedules he had been scrutinizing. 'Looks the most likely destination. There were only two other coaches in the time slot, and they were local.'

'What and where is Gallup?' Ruiz said, sipping coffee, watching O'Hara sitting at the desk.

'It's a small town in New Mexico,' Michaels said, hovering by the door. He'd brought the coach schedules in and was surreptitiously trying to edge his way out, but couldn't resist sharing his knowledge

'Wait!' O'Hara said, stopping him in his tracks. 'What d'you know about this place?'

'Last year I did some covert work in Window Rock, Arizona, which is about 25 miles from Gallup,' Michaels said.

'So tell us about it. What kind of a shit hole is it, and why would they go there?' O'Hara said.

'I don't know, boss. Gallup is the kind of center of the Navajo Nation; it's a small town, pop of around 20,000, bordered I think on three sides with Indian nation reservations. And as you say, boss, it is a shit hole, so I don't know why they'd go there.'

'But then,' Ruiz said, 'maybe that makes it a good place to hide?'

'What assets we got out that way?' O'Hara asked quietly.

Pascal sat at the table in the living room and powered up Sia's old desk-top. She went straight to her email account inbox. Nothing there, but there was something in her spam folder - Christoff had come through. She read it:

"Lovely to hear from you Courtney. We've both been idiots, so lets put it behind us. Your query and the names you mention intrigued me, and I could certainly do with being intrigued! I wont bore you with what they've got me doing here, but lets just say its less than scintillating. Yes do give me a call and quick - my numbers set out below.

Ciao Christoff"

Pascal pulled out her new burner and texted the number to Christoff. Five minutes later the burner buzzed and danced on the table. She grabbed it up. After some pleasantries about old times Christoff cut to the chase. 'Okay, the bad news first. I've got nothing on Maria Dinks and Victor Diaz over and above what's out there already. But I'll carry on digging and see what I can find.'

'And the good news?'

'Dante. I think he might just be Dante Figueroa?'

'Who he?'

'He, my young friend, just happens to be one of the top guys in the Juarez drug cartel.'

Pascal whistled. 'How sure are you, and what the fuck is he doing with Maria Dinks?'

'Well that, of course, is the million dollar question. As to how sure I am? Pretty sure. There are very few pictures of the guy, but I accessed by back channels, if you know what I mean, a file on him held by the DEA. One of the places he showed up at was a fashion shoot in New York, and they got a picture of him there. At the time US authorities had no reason to arrest or question him, but they did watch him.'

'Let me guess? Maria Dinks was showing there?'

'You got it.'

'What about the missing girls?'

'A Lucy Collins disappeared from Beverley Hills nearly four years ago when she was 8. No trace was ever found and there were no suspects. One theory was that she may have drowned, washed out to sea as she was swimming at the beach when she disappeared. It made a bit of a splash at the time, if you'll excuse the pun, because her mother was a quite a well known aspiring actress.'

'What about Tamara?' Pascal asked.

'A Tamara Hunt disappeared from a swish private school in Washington around two years ago. She was 6. Again, no trace, but this time it seemed clear she was abducted, but again they seemed to have no leads. They picked up a drifter, a known sexual offender with a conviction for child rape but had to let him go because of a lack of evidence, not least - no body. But, funnily enough there is a connection with senator Victor Diaz,' Christoff said.

'And what's that?'

'His daughter went to the same school, and he made a public appeal on behalf of the family, asking anyone with information to contact the police, and begging the child to return to her family.'

There was silence between them for a couple of beats. Then Christoff said, 'd'you want to let me in on what the hell you've got yourself into this time?'

'It's a long story.'

'It always is.'

'I've found Sapphire Dinks, alive. She's with me and we're hiding out wondering how the hell I'm going to get her into protective custody I can trust. And that's without me being arrested and charged with murder.'

'Boy, you sure pick 'em, but it sounds exciting,' he said gleefully. 'Want any help?'

'You kidding me? Why d'you think I reached out to you?'

Christoff sighed. 'I'm glad you did. But what have you got here? Is there some kind of organized ring abducting young girls?' he asked.

'It's complicated, but yes. But I don't think Dinks was originally part of it but chasing her I seem to have stumbled onto it.'

'Okay,' Christoff said, slowly. 'So how d'you want to play it and do you want to give me your location?'

She thought for a moment. 'Much as I'd like you here, Christoff, I think I've got enough support for now. Better you stay in New York and keep digging. You might want to talk to Jonas Calver, but watch out. The Feds are waking up to what's happening and they're trying to get a line on me through Calver, so they'll be watching and monitoring him.'

'Understood.'

'Okay. That's all for now. And, Christoff - thanks.'

'Hey, it's a pleasure. And don't wait so long to get back to me next time.'

'Don't worry,' she said. She switched the burner off, smiling. Talking to him had given her a definite lift.

###

They came in ones and twos, straggling in, some on horses that they tethered to a rail, some on foot. In the house they made up a small group congregated around Sia's large living room. Pascal stood at the back, studying them; they were mostly older folk, a few women sprinkled amongst them. Some looked pretty far gone; emaciated frames with too bright eyes full of an old longing for that next drink. Maybe they'd come for the free coffee and beef jerky, but maybe not; the general murmuring amongst them began to take form. They were discussing the proposed opening of another liquor store in Gallup and there seemed to be a lot of anger and outrage.

'These big fancy liquor stores. They killing our people. What we going to do about it?' a large stout mahogany brown man said to nods from the group.

'Let's firebomb the fuckers,' said another, to whoops and a smattering of laughter.

'No,' Sia said quietly, standing at the front of the group. 'No violence.'

More background grumbling. 'Why not? It's the only thing they and their cop minders understand,' a tall muscled young man said. Pascal had noticed him earlier, because of his youth, poise and confidence. He was over 6 feet tall, light brown skin, about twenty-five with long black hair pulled back in a ponytail. His cheekbones were like high light ridges of rock. He was dressed in baggy jeans and a black top and on his feet he wore wonderfully soft looking brown moccasins that ran up and laced around his shin almost to the knee.

'Hey. Cool it, Greyeagle, you hothead,' one of the women said.

He smiled and it dazzled - white teeth with a dimple. Pascal looked over at Sapphire sitting perched on a small chair in the corner of the room. Her eyes were shining as she watched Greyeagle. Pascal sighed and moved away into the kitchen to grab a secret scotch - Sia said they had to hide the alcohol, to avoid temptation.

When Pascal went back in, they were breaking up. They had decided to attend the council licensing meeting to make protest.

###

Next morning Sapphire and Pascal were up early. They stood in the empty corral dressed in old tee shirts and tracksuit bottoms with rope belts. Sapphire had been nagging Pascal to teach her judo, and Pascal had finally agreed. She would show her some light and gentle moves now that her wound was on the mend.

Pascal studied the young girl critically, looking her up and down, assessing her stance and posture. 'Okay, sweetie,' she said. 'I'm going to show you a simple throw that's one of the basics. It's called, Uki Goshi, but you can call it floating hip.'

Sapphire glowed with excitement, looking small and incongruous in her loose fitting garments pulled in tight at the waist, her blue eyes shining bright out of her sun browned face.

'In judo, you can use the belt of your opponent, like this,' Pascal said, her hand shooting out like lighting and grabbing the belt.

Sapphire laughed nervously. 'Wow, Courtney! How can you move so quick? Show me. I want to learn it all.'

'In time, it will come. I need to go slow because of the wound but that way you can see the moves and pick it up nice and slow,' Pascal said, gripping Sapphire's shoulder with one hand, the other going to her waist. 'Now, you grip me in the same way.'

'Then we step like this,' Pascal said, and they began to move slowly backwards and forwards towards each other almost like they were dancing. Sapphire giggled.

'Now, I am going to throw you, slowly so you can see what's happening. Don't worry, I won't drop you,' Pascal said, sliding slowly sideways and letting Sapphire slide gently over her hip. Then she lifted Sapphire over, but instead of throwing her down on the ground she cradled her up into a hug and then released her

As she did so they heard clapping sounds. Greyeagle from the night before sat astride a horse watching them from about ten meters away. He had come up unobserved and soundlessly. Today his hair hung down around his face, no hat but a patterned headband, and he wore a light brown kind of buckskin jacket and trousers with cowboy boots. Pascal thought he looked like an extra from an old style western, but with style and a certain kind of cool. She also noticed the rifle stock sticking out of the saddle sheaf.

'Good morning,' he said.

'Good morning,' Sapphire shot straight back, followed by, 'would you like some breakfast?' before Pascal could say anything.

He smiled at her and nodded at Pascal. 'No, thank you. I've eaten already.'

'Nice piece of kit,' Pascal said, nodding at the rifle. 'What is it?'

'It's a Dragunov,' he said.

'Sniper rifle?'

'Yep,' he nodded.

As he spoke, they heard the sound of an approaching vehicle, and they all looked up. In the distance a small dust-cloud surrounded a dark SUV as it approached along the desert road that fronted the ranch.

About a hundred meters from them it started to slow.

Pascal watching, eyes beginning to narrow, started to turn to Sapphire to tell her to get in the house, but by then the vehicle was slowing to a stop in front of them. The windows were blacked out but the front one whirred down and a head leaned out.

'Sorry to bother you folks, but we're lost,' he said, his eyes slowly running over Pascal and Sapphire. He looked like a cop, but not a desert county cop, more like city plain clothes. Clean-cut, eyes watchful. There was another guy next to him, but Pascal couldn't see him.

'Where you headed?' Greyeagle asked them.

The driver leaned out to look at Greyeagle, still sitting astride his horse. 'Window Rock,' the guy said.

Greyeagle spat. 'You're going the wrong way, mister. You need to turn around and go back. There's a sign a few miles back, surprised you didn't see it,' he said

The guy made as if to come back, but the other unseen guy mumbled something to him. He nodded, and said, 'thanks for the directions. Sorry to have bothered you. You have a nice day now.'

He took a last lingering look at Pascal and Sapphire. The window slid back up and then the car was moving off in a wide arc of dust, around and back the way it had come.

No one said anything for a moment as they watched the vehicle disappear into the hinterland, dust billowing out behind it.

'Funny looking tourists,' Greyeagle muttered, and spat again.

'Do you have to do that?' Sapphire asked, crinkling her nose in disapproval. 'It's a disgusting habit.'

'Don't be rude, Sapphire,' Pascal said mildly. Then, 'no, I don't think they're tourists either.'

'In fact,' Greyeagle said. 'If I didn't know better, I'd say they were looking for some people, and just hit the jackpot. Who the hell are you anyway?'

'We're—'

'Sapphire, go in the house now, will you sweetie,' Pascal said, cutting her off.

Sapphire looked set to argue but when she saw Pascal's expression decided against it. She turned and reluctantly trudged back towards the house, all the way casting furtive looks back at Greyeagle.

He smiled. 'Nice kid,' he said. 'Look, I'm not prying. Keep your secrets, but any friend of Sia's is a friend of mine, so if you're in trouble and want any help, just ask. That guy just now. He gave me a real bad feeling, and he'll be back, probably tooled up next time.'

Pascal studied Greyeagle, sitting casually astride his horse. He looked completely relaxed and completely at one with the harsh desert landscape around him. He returned her stare, calmly, unblinking. Pascal nodded. 'Come on. Let's talk, because you're right. They'll be coming back, and we need to be ready when they do.

CHAPTER SEVENTEEN

'Looks like it's them, sir,' Michaels said, handing O'Hara a blow-up, which he passed on to Ruiz. 'Ronnie got the snap through the side window,' he added

'It's them alright,' Ruiz nodded. 'How d'you track them?'

'Seems the little girl took a taxi off the coach. Sounds like the Hansen woman was virtually unconscious from the gun shot wound. The wino redskin cab driver spilled the lot for five bucks. He drove them out to a little ranch couple miles outside the town. It's registered to a Navajo nation woman.'

'Good work, Michaels,' O'Hara said, nodding in dismissal.

The guy stood for a moment, perhaps expecting more of a pat on the back. Ruiz smiled pityingly as he left the room.

O'Hara, feet on the desk again, smiled up at Ruiz. 'We'll get a chopper up there and go in at 3 am, you, me and a team of four; night vision goggles, the works. If you want to set that up, I've got some phone calls to make,' O'Hara said.

Ruiz hesitated.

'What?' O'Hara barked.

'I'd like another DEA guy along with me, so make that a team of five,' Ruiz said, guessing O'Hara wanted to get him out in the desert on his own.

'Sorry old buddy. I'm leading this operation. It stays at four, unless you want to sit this one out?' O'Hara said, knowing smile playing on his lips.

Ruiz nodded, smiling too, thinking, 'fuck you, asshole.' He'd need eyes in the back of his head out in the desert, but he'd have to run with it for now. As he moved out of the room O'Hara was lifting the phone to his ear.

'Get me Senator Diaz,' he said.

###

They sat around the kitchen table talking quietly. 'I knew they'd come,' Pascal said. 'I just didn't think it would be so soon. I'm sorry, Sia,'

'Don't be,' she said. 'Better to face it now.'

'Who are, they?' Greyeagle asked.

'They're nominally the feds, but it's a rogue operation,' Pascal said. 'Off the books so there'll be no oversight, or qualms.'

'So what do we do?' Sia said.

Pascal looked out of the window, unseeing, her mind working through the options. 'Forget the feds, or whoever they are for a moment,' she said. 'We either run or we fight. Our primary objective is to get Sapphire to safety, but we've got a situation here where we can't trust the authorities because we don't know which one of them is dirty and which is clean. We need to get Sapphire into some kind of protective custody that we can trust, so she can be produced as a witness in a court in New York, if it has to go that far. That's the only way we get Yolanda out from under. And I won't lie, it's the only way I'll get out from under as well.'

'But if you run, they'll follow. They'll track you down and then you'll just have to do it all over again somewhere else,' Greyeagle said. 'Surely it's better to stand and fight now, and win.'

'Yeah, but how do we win, given the objectives?' Pascal said. Then her burner started dancing on the table. She snatched it up. 'Yeah?'

It was Calver. She stood up and walked through into the lounge.

'It's okay,' he said. 'Isabel's phone. I borrowed it. Look, I've had the federal prosecutor on about the appeal, trying to squeeze out who the witness is. They obviously haven't joined up the dots yet, but they will. He's offering protective custody. I said I'd get back to him within 48 hours?'

'I don't trust them. He may be kosher, but it only takes one guy,' Pascal said.

'I agree your assessment, but it narrows down the options somewhat.'

'Yeah, well look, Calver, I'm afraid its whole lot worse than you think. They've found us and they'll be coming soon.'

'Fuck!'

'My sentiments exactly.'

They were both silent for a beat.

She spoke first. 'In a way its real simple: we need to nail the real kidnappers and keep Sapphire alive while we do so.'

'That's simple? How you gonna do it?'

'I'm on it,' she said, looking at her watch. 'Gotta go. I'll be in touch.'

She snapped the phone off and moved back into the kitchen.

###

They all looked up as she came back and took her seat at the table. When she didn't say anything, Greyeagle said, 'So you got a snake, Sia. What d'you do?'

'You chop it's head off,' Sapphire shot back before Sia could answer.

'Bright girl. That's right,' he said, nodding and turning to Pascal. 'That's right,' he said again. 'So who's the head?'

'O'Hara,' Pascal said.

Greyeagle got up and walked to the percolator and poured himself some more black coffee. 'You know,' he said, pensively. 'I was in sniper school at Fort Bragg before I crashed out the service.'

Pascal eyed him up, assessing him anew. He had the shape and build of a soldier and he looked super fit.

'You got night sights for that Dragunov rig?' she said.

'You bet.'

'What are you thinking, Courtney?' Sia said, a slight undercurrent in her voice.

'That ledge?' Pascal said, almost as if she were talking to

235

herself. Then to Sia, 'the ledge overlooking the ranch that Sapphire and I rode up to and had our picnic at.'

'Yeah, it's called Table Rock.'

'That's right,' Greyeagle said looking over at Pascal. 'And it's got a beautiful unrestricted view of the ranch.'

'Or field of fire,' Pascal said. 'What's the range?'

'Bout a mile as the crow flies. Easy peasy,' Greyeagle said.

###

They flew in low over the hills in the ghostly light of the still bright moon, the chop chop chop of the rotor blades cutting through the clear desert air and echoing across the valley. Inside the chopper, three men each side, O'Hara and Ruiz at the front facing each other, nearest the door, faces blacked up, night goggles pushed up on their heads. Next to them sat the grunts, checking their weapons, faces blank, showing no fear.

The pilot spoke through their earpieces, 'coming into DZ, ETA two minutes.'

O'Hara stood up abruptly and moved to the doorway. He watched as the small ranch house came into view. It was shrouded in darkness, apart from the fading moonlight and a single light showing in the veranda that fronted the house. Hit 'em hard and fast while they were still rubbing the sleep from their eyes, he'd told the grunts. The belly shot would have slowed the girl down; shit she was still convalescing. See how quick the bitch would be this time when he got her in his sights. He smiled to himself.

Then the chopper was coming in fast down front of the house and they were readying for the jump onto the hard packed earth. There they would spread out, encircling and moving in on the house.

About a mile away, Sia, Sapphire and Greyeagle lay stretched out on the ledge looking down, watching the helicopter as it swooped in. Behind them three horses and a couple of mules, laden with clothing and provisions, stood tethered to a rock.

Greyeagle held the Dragunov sniper rifle out in front of him, its long barrel resting on a rock he had positioned earlier. He looked again through the night sight and focused on the veranda light. He made a tiny adjustment to the dial, then sighted again on the open door of the helicopter as it alighted in front of the house. Pascal had said that O'Hara would be first out. She had also described Ruiz in detail, height and build, in case they'd brought him along, and told Greyeagle not to take him out, as she might need him. All the others were expendable. Kill or be killed she'd said; if they didn't take them out, they would all be killed, she had absolutely no doubt about that.

O'Hara's blacked up face suddenly loomed large in Greyeagle's sights and he pulled the trigger straight away, cross hairs on the nose. But as he fired, O'Hara was jumping from the chopper, and the bullet missed the head striking the chest. It was a cinch he was wearing a Kevlar vest, but the slug caught him in mid-air, lifting him back and smashing his body against the side of the chopper where he slid down onto the ground and lay prone. But by then there was another slug in the breach and another face in the sight, but it was Ruiz rabbit-hopping onto the ground with the bad leg Pascal had told him about, then running in a kind of limping crouch towards the house.

Greyeagle moved his sight onto the next guy jumping from the doorway, pulled the trigger and watched the spurt of blood jet from the guy's head as he fell forwards out onto the ground. He took out the next one as well, but the other two got out into cover, dragging O'Hara with them, and then the chopper was lifting off and pulling away in a wide arc, back the way it had come. Three down, three on the plot.

As the chopper's sound faded into the waning moonlight, the tableaux before Greyeagle drifted into eerie silence. He wondered whether to go down there, but Courtney had been insistent, he must stay where he was with Sia and Sapphire.

###

As the first guy silently edged his way into the living room, Pascal could just see his shadow silhouetted by the weak moonlight filtering through the French window. As he stopped to listen, night goggles slowly traversing the room, Pascal smoothly rose up from behind the couch and threw the ten inch razor sharp knife Greyeagle had given her. It took the guy in the neck, going straight through and cutting the jugular on the way; even in the dark Pascal could see the rich fountain of blood spurting into the night air as he went down in a heap.

She walked silently over, flicking her pencil light on him. She rolled him over and pulled the head-rig off, light point running over his face and down his arms. The guy was Hispanic and covered in Tats, a racing cert he was no FBI agent. She swept her hand under the couch and located the fire-axe she had placed there earlier. She heard the tinkling sound of breaking glass coming from the front of the house. She stealthily moved towards it. As the guy came in through the broken door, she swung the fire-axe around in a wide arc, holding it sideways on and delivered the blade dead center of the guys face, across the nose, splitting his head wide open like a coconut.

As the guy dropped to the floor she moved across to the front door and pushed it open, then stepped back into the shadows. She shouted out, 'Hey, Ruiz. I figure you're the only one standing, old buddy. You can lay down your arms and come in and talk, or get your head blown off by my sharpshooter friend on the ridge. What's it to be?'

There was silence in the night air. Pascal waited. She looked up across the valley at the rocky outcrop, shrouded in shadow. She knew they'd be up there, Greyeagle with the night sight trained on the darkened doorway. She heard movement, a light sound of a foot scuffing on earth, then a faint clink of metal, coming from the corral. As she looked over Ruiz rose up from behind the horse's water trough and stood with his hands raised.

'Good call,' she said. 'Where's O'Hara?'

'Here,' Ruiz said. 'He's still out cold.'

'Keep your hands up,' Pascal said as she walked towards him. She raised the burner to her mouth as she walked and said, 'good work, Greyeagle. Change of plan. Plots secure, so bring them back down.'

She looked down at O'Hara, pulled the Glock from her waist band and pointed it at him. His eyes fluttered open and he smiled. 'That was mighty fine shooting, specially at night,' he said rubbing his chest. 'What was the range?'

'Bout a mile,' she said.

'Who the fuck is he?' O'Hara said, wincing and pulling the Kevlar tunic away and looking down at his chest.

'You can meet him in a minute,' she said, then to Ruiz, 'cuff him and bring him in the house.' She handed him some cuffs taken off the last grunt she had killed. 'And guys. Please don't fuck with me because you're both expendable and I'd actually like to kill both of you right now.'

As Ruiz put the cuffs on, Greyeagle rode in. He gestured back over his shoulder. 'They're following, slowly.'

Pascal nodded and told Ruiz to bring O'Hara in the house. 'We'll put him in the basement for now. I've checked it out and its secure.' As Greyeagle came over Pascal gave him a brief hug. 'Great shooting, man,' she said, then, 'can you search this guy,' nodding at O'Hara. 'Make sure he's got no hidden Com's, then shove him in the basement.'

'You got it, ma'am,' Greyeagle said, eying up O'Hara. 'It was a sweet shot. Had him dead center, but the dummy moved last minute. Never mind, eh? It's good not to take a life sometimes, even when they deserve to die'

Pascal smiled and turned to Ruiz. 'You, come with me,' she said, and led him to the house.

In New York, Federal Prosecutor Michael Daniels sat in Calver's office gingerly holding a cup of coffee Hettie had just handed him. He watched Calver across the desk, waiting. Calver looked up. 'What if I told you, Daniels, hypothetically of course and off the record, that Sapphire Dinks is alive and well and we can produce her,' he said.

'Bullshit!' Daniels said, but his expression didn't quite go with the exclamation. He put his cup down, stood up and walked over to the window. He gazed across the road at the Brooklyn Brownstones, his back to the room.

'Course, you weren't the original prosecutor, were you?' Calver continued, quietly, subtly trying to plant the seed and manipulate the guys emotions and ego. 'So, hardly your fault the case has all gone to hell. In fact, you could make quite a name for yourself, solving the riddle, righting a wrong and clearing up the mess.'

Daniels remained standing at the window. Calver waited, guessing the guy was busy mapping out stellar career trajectories in his head. Daniels turned around and walked back, sat down and raised the cup to his lips and took a sip. 'You want, what, counselor? A retrial?' he said.

'What Yolanda Lopez wants is justice, exoneration from false charges, and her life back - freedom,' Calver said.

'And a multi-million dollar settlement from the government, right? Ain't gonna happen on my watch,' Daniels said, pausing to take another sip of his coffee. 'Anyway, what does the kid say, assuming, hypothetically of course and off the record, that she's still around. Her materializing out of the wide blue yonder gets Lopez, maybe, an acquittal on the murder charge. Nothing else. Attempted murder and kidnap stay so she stays locked up. All depends of course on whether the kid is alive and what she has to say.'

Calver didn't say anything.

'So what about protective custody, if she's in danger,' Daniels continued. 'Then we can talk to her, maybe sort this whole mess out?'

'Yeah, well, problem is, I don't know where she is, hypothetically. And the person who may have her trusts you lot about as far as she can throw you. Tell you what,' Calver said brightly as if he had just thought of it. 'Why don't you just agree to a retrial; as you know we've lodged our 2255 habeas Corpus appeal in the Southern District Court. Don't oppose it. Let's bring it on, let justice take its course, and in the meantime, we'll see if we can produce her and maybe she can talk to you and we won't need a trial, hypothetically. And don't forget, you cooperate now, if the government has to pay damages, this sensible behavior on your part is likely to lower any award that might be made.'

'You know what I heard this morning from an FBI agent we're working with on federal indictments, Calver?' Daniels said. 'Funny thing, there's a warrant out for a Catherine Hansen, following the murder of a child in Mexico, and the feds now believe this Hansen woman is in fact your investigator, Courtney Pascal. Seems she maybe on the run in the US now, and apparently she has another child with her. How about that?'

'Tell you what,' Calver said, his face immobile, as each man watched the other warily. 'Why don't we both have a think, and then talk some more. Course,' Calver added mildly, 'the elephant in the room is the media. They're going to get a hold of this any second, but maybe they can be used.'

Daniels stood up, stony-faced. He walked to the door and turned back. 'You just better hope, Calver, the FBI and the US Marshals service don't get a hold of your gal first, cause if they do, all bets are off, and you'll need to get yourself a new investigator, 'cause they'll throw away the key. But if she stays outside the net, maybe, just maybe, we'll need to talk some more.'

Calver nodded. 'Good enough,' he said, as Daniels stalked out the room.

CHAPTER EIGHTEEN

Pascal and Ruiz sat on the veranda as the sun came up. Sapphire and Sia had gone back to bed and Greyeagle had taken the bodies of the dead grunts, who Ruiz had confirmed were ex-drug gang mercenaries, out in Sia's SUV into the desert to burn and bury the ashes.

Pascal was quietly speaking to Christoff through the burner she held to ear whilst she watched Ruiz. He was sat sprawled in a rocker, its front feet off the floor, back tilted against the side of the house. His eyes were calm and unreadable as he surveyed the desert spread out before him.

Pascal listened as Christoff told her of his recent phone call with Calver. 'He thinks the federal prosecutor, Daniels, might be persuaded not to oppose his habeas corpus appeal brief, and go straight to a retrial, if. Big if, they don't pick you up first,' Christoff said.

Pascal stood up and walked to the rail around the edge of the veranda. She looked out at the horses in the corral standing motionless, silhouetted against the red desert skyline, looking timeless. 'So I've gotta stay out, on the run, maybe get my head blown off by some trigger happy cop while the lawyers dicker. Great,' she said wearily.

Christoff said nothing for a beat, then, 'well, I can't help you with that, but I have got a snippet of news about Maria Dinks.'

Pascal's face brightened. 'What you got, *kemo sabe*?'

'Don't see how it's going to help you, but Maria's got a glitzy fashion show listed in Mexico City in two days' time. I had a look at her fashion house and it's basically centered on New York and Mexico City, small offices and outlets in both.'

Pascal turned back from the veranda rail and noticed Sapphire had wandered out in her nightgown and was now sitting looking out across the valley, her face taught and unsmiling. 'Okay, Christoff. Good work. Keep digging and stay in touch, ciao,' she said.

'*Kemo sabe*?' Sapphire said accusingly, looking at Pascal with an angry look. 'D'you know what an insult that is to Native Americans? D'you even know what it means?'

'Uh-oh,' Ruiz chipped in happily. 'Sounds like you've upset her, laying out that tired old Hollywood racial stereotyping.'

'Shut up, Ruiz,' Pascal said, turning to Sapphire. 'I'm very sorry. I didn't mean to cause offense. Pure ignorance on my part. Anyway, what does it mean in Navajo? I thought it was a term of endearment.'

Sapphire's expression suggested Pascal's attempt to appease her hadn't worked. 'It means, "soggy shrub," if you must know,' she said. 'Now, I'm going to feed the horses. I'm sure I'll get more intelligent conversation with them,' she said, turning and stamping her way off the veranda.

Ruiz clapped his hands, laughed and tilted his chair back against the wall again. 'That's one sassy kid you got there,' he said. 'You know, in Spanish *kemo sabe* means, "he who doesn't understand," and I reckon you don't understand kids.'

'Yeah, but I don't rape and murder them,' she said, her face like stone.

Ruiz grin froze on his face and he looked down in his lap, silent as she watched him. Then his face relaxed and the look passed as quickly as it had come. He looked up at her. 'So why am I being spared?' he said, rubbing the stubble on his chin, confident crooked grin back in place. 'You're not getting squeamish are you, Pascal? That is your name isn't it? And what about O'Hara? You don't finish that fucker here and now, he'll just keep coming.'

'Ain't that a fact, Ruiz,' she said mildly. 'But fuck O'Hara, for the moment, let's talk about you, shall we, and how you can help me and help yourself.'

'I don't see what you got to offer, Pascal. There's a warrant out for you and US Marshals and FBI are all out looking, notwithstanding O'Hara's little black Op. And any hick county cop stops you and runs a check, you're fucked.'

'Yeah, but not in Mexico I'm not,' she said quietly.

'You're kidding me, right?' Ruiz said, watching her, concern starting to dislodge the smile on his face. 'You go through all that shit to get out, and now you want to go back? For what?'

'All the answers are down there, amigo, and you're coming along to help,' she said, looking at him pointedly.

'You're fucking serious aren't you?' he said.

'You bet I am. I got the kid out of danger and the country, but now I need to go back and finish the job, because the answers are all down there, not in New York. Long as the girl is safe for now, I can go back.

'One way or the other, Ruiz, you're going to jail,' she continued. 'But if you help me, now, all the way down the line, no tricks, no double crosses, I might just be persuaded to support you rather than burying you in a federal jail for the rest of your life. You help, you know the system, you could shave a whole lot of years off your sentence, you might even cut a deal on giving evidence against your co-conspirators and get no time at all. That'll be up to you. It's the only way out for you, to have any kind of a normal life in the future, and I think you know it. And I'll tell you this, because Tilly-May jumped, and you didn't personally kill her, although you are responsible in your own way, I'm not going to kill you.'

This time it was Ruiz who stood up and limped to the veranda rail to look out over the desert. He stood there for a while, silent, leaning against a veranda post, deep in thought. In the corral, Sapphire could be seen with the horses, feeding them and talking to them, snippets of her words drifting back over the thin desert air. Ruiz turned and limped back to his chair and sat down again. 'I'm not agreeing nothing,' he said emphatically. 'But, tell me what you think you'll find down there, and how it's going to help?'

'Okay, Ruiz. But, if you're going to help, and you are, you need to know the significance of the girl, so I'll tell you. She's Sapphire Dinks.' She sat back and watched Ruiz's face.

It was blank for a moment, then surprised as he processed the information, then he whistled slowly under his breath. 'Sapphire Dinks, and everyone thinking she was murdered. I followed the trial at the time. So, so let me get this straight,' he said tentatively, still thinking it through. 'You're acting for the lawyer, trying to get that. What's her name? Yolanda Lopez who was convicted of the kidnapping, and…..murder, out of gaol. So the kid turning up nixes the murder charge.'

'That's right, but that's all it does. The other charges remain, unless I. No, let's make that, we, can break the case open and find evidence exonerating Yolanda. Sapphire can't do it. She doesn't know enough, but she has given us sufficient to work out what probably happened, but I need to go back to Mexico to prove it.'

Ruiz leaned forward in his chair getting interested despite himself. 'What's your hypothesis and what are you hoping to find down Mexico way?'

Now Pascal leaned her chair back, lifting the front legs of the floor, the chair back resting up against the house wall. She watched Sapphire who was now riding one of the horses bareback around the corral, looking incredibly cool and self- possessed. The girl was slowly healing, but it would be a long road back.

Pascal smiled watching the girl, then frowned as her mind came back to Ruiz's questions. 'We believe,' she said slowly, 'that Sapphire's step-mother, Maria organized the kidnap, together with a guy I have no doubt your crew at the DEA will have heard of.'

Ruiz whistled again. 'What, her own kid?' he said incredulously.

'Step-kid.'

'Even so. Shit! Greed's a terrible thing, right, and I should know. Who's the guy?' Ruiz said.

'First, we don't know what motivated Maria, something we're

hopefully gonna find out. The guy is Dante Figueroa.'

Ruiz just looked at her, no expression, then doubt was clouding his face. 'I don't believe it,' he said. 'Why would one of the top captains in the Juarez cartel - and these are guys who seek out and live in the shadows. Why would such a guy, who incidentally makes millions of dollars out of drug dealing, want to kidnap a very high profile kid, who to boot, is a US national, meaning it would bring down on him all the heat of US law enforcement?'

'That's exactly why you can help me, because you asked that question.

'And, Ruiz, the Daughter Eaters are down there…..' she said, her eyebrow arched in a question mark. 'Aren't they? And we take them down, who do we get? That's right: Victor Diaz.'

'I knew it,' he said, smiling again. 'It's not just the kid, is it? You want all that glory as well, don't you, for bagging Diaz, right? You're no different to the rest of us mere mortals.'

She let the dig the pass, recognizing it as Ruiz's attempt to wind her up.

'You know something, Pascal?' he asked after a moment.

'I know plenty, Ruiz, but go on, surprise me.'

'I'm one fucked up, cynical world weary motherfucker, but you've just intrigued the hell out of me, but I'm still not going to Mexico.'

'You're going, Ruiz,' she said, lifting the Glock and taking a bead on his forehead. 'In two days', Maria Dinks has a fashion show in Mexico City, and you and me, pal, are going to be there.'

###

They all stood outside. Pascal checked O'Hara's cuffs again. He smiled and said, 'how long you think these clowns can keep me trussed up like this? I get free. And I will, I'll kill 'em all, and then I'll come looking for you and your new buddy Ruiz.'

Sapphire passed Pascal a piece of masking tape she had just bitten off with her teeth. 'Shut the fuck up, O'Hara, you're making me sleepy,' Pascal said as she pressed the tape down over his mouth. Greyeagle manhandled O'Hara onto one of the horses.

Pascal and Ruiz stood and surveyed the little group. Sia, Sapphire, Greyeagle and now O'Hara were all sitting astride their horses, with two mules behind them, laden with provisions. Ruiz whispered in Pascal's ear, 'this is a very bad idea. One slip, and that guy *will* kill them all.'

Pascal turned to him, eyes flashing. 'You think I don't know that? But what else can I do. I don't want to kill him now, because it would be murder, and I've got enough on my plate without another charge,' she whispered back angrily. 'Greyeagle can handle him, and its only for a short time until I can get the goods in Mexico and come back and take her to New York.'

Ruiz shrugged and walked over and patted one of the mules. Pascal said to Sia, 'I'm sorry, Sia, for putting you through this but I just don't think you'd be safe here for the moment. It'll only be for a short while, while we sort this mess out.'

'Hey, don't worry,' Sia said, smiling serenely. 'I'm looking forward to it, and so is Sapphire. We're going out in the desert and we're going to live just the way our people did 150 years ago.'

Finally Pascal turned to Greyeagle, sitting on his horse, stroking the butt of what looked like another rifle. 'Just think of O'Hara like he's a rattle snake, seriously,' she said, holding his eyes. 'One slip up, just one, and he will strike and kill you all. You've gotta watch him every second. You got that?'

'I got it,' Greyeagle said. 'I met some of these crazy gung-ho mutherfucka types when I was at Bragg. They don't think conventional, so they're difficult to predict, but I'll watch him.'

Greyeagle looked up at the sun, calculating daylight hours remaining, looked around at his group, then back at Pascal and Ruiz, standing watching them. 'Don't worry my friends, we are going out into the desert, and that's my country, our country,' he said, looking over at Sia with a wide smile. 'I'll take them to my people, and we'll move around some, as you said, until you're back. We'll check in every 24 hours unless there's an emergency. And I got contact details for your guys Christoff and Jonas Calver in case we can't get a hold of you.'

As Greyeagle lifted up his reins Pascal rushed over to Sapphire and grabbed her hands on the saddle pommel, looking up at her. 'Be careful, sweetie,' she said. 'Look after your Grandma, and I will come back for you.'

Sapphire patted her hand. 'I know you will, Courtney. And don't worry, we're warriors. We always have been.'

Pascal watched the troop as they slowly walked their horses out across the road fronting the ranch, and out into the desert scrub land beyond. As Pascal raised the burner to her ear to order a cab, Ruiz said,

'I hope you know what the fuck you're doing, because I sure as hell don't.'

###

They stood outside the Fronton Mexico building looking up at the pink colored art deco styling. Pascal was wearing huge dark glasses almost covering her entire face, topped off with a voguish black cap, and Ruiz looked debonair in an elegant powder blue suit. They joined the throng of exotically clad people as they streamed into the building, all heading for the fashion show.

Pascal and Ruiz each wore accredited passes that Ruiz had managed to wangle via the DEA and their links to the *Federales*. Both agencies were playing ball and supporting what was now Ruiz's operation because he had assured them that they would get a chance to tag one of their most elusive targets, Dante Figueroa. Ruiz had assured them he had solid information from an impeccable source that Figueroa would be there. Just to get a picture of the guy would be worth it to the *Federales*, and maybe they could drop a tail on him or better still, stick a bug up his ass. Ruiz's story had also got them into Mexico, no questions asked. His story to the DEA was that he was working on a case where he had uncovered a lead on a dirty agent so there must be no liaison with other agencies such as FBI and US Marshals for the time being.

They followed the crowd through the ornate recently refurbished building that doubled as a casino and creative arts outlet, hustling their way through the ostentatious pack of preening poseurs until they got to their seats at the side of the runway.

Pascal held a cheap phone in her hand scrolling pictures of Maria Dinks and looking around for her. She was just one of the exhibitors and Pascal knew it would be difficult to try and talk to her, at least while her show was on. Whatever they said to her, Dinks would almost certainly scream for security, but they had to try. Pascal settled down to wait, but all the time, in the pit of her stomach, was a feeling of fear and dread, eating away at her. What if she had been wrong to send them off with O'Hara? What if.....? She had to stop thinking about it, but then in slow motion the image of Tilly-May going over the balcony was playing in her head. She had to get a grip. For reassurance, she replayed the conversation she had had with Greyeagle and Sapphire the day before. They were out in the desert and sounded okay. There were no problems from O'Hara or anyone else. But Pascal knew that as every minute crawled by, they were in mortal danger. She had to finish up quick and get back.

As she looked up Maria Dinks was suddenly there, on the stage, taking a bow. Pascal realized that the fashions that had just been parading down the runway must have been hers. She nudged Ruiz but he'd already clocked Dinks and was watching her.

'You stay out here and see if you can spot Dante, because we don't want to get on the wrong side of the *Federales*,' she said. 'I'll go see if I can corner our girl.'

Pascal got up and moved away towards the curtains at the back of the runway, which Maria Dinks had just passed through. Out back it seemed like chaos, lots of semi-clad women milling around, photographers, guys and girls, some carrying items of clothing, holding them as if they were precious jewels, some carrying clip-boards or hand-helds, and all against a backdrop of shouting and energy. Pascal scanned the crowd and saw Dinks moving quickly towards a corridor at the back of the room, accompanied by a small girl who was talking to her and scrolling through a handheld tablet as they walked. Pascal jostled her way through the crowd and followed them down the corridor.

She could see they had stopped outside a door and were talking. Pascal stopped also and pretended she was having an animated conversation on her phone while surreptitiously watching and being buffeted by people passing by either side. The conversation finished, the girl departed, and Dinks went in the door and shut it behind her.

Pascal approached, still pretending to speak on her phone. She stopped outside the door and tried to listen but couldn't hear anything above the noise of the crowd. She turned her phone over and scrolled to a detailed close-up picture she had recently taken of Sapphire. She put her hand on the handle, hesitated, then opened the door and went in.

As she silently entered, Maria Dinks abruptly raised her head up from the table at which she was sitting. Pascal could see the remains of a line of coke. Dinks, unworried, said, 'get the fuck outta here, honey. This is for authorized persons only. That means designers.'

The room was small like a spare office or store room but much of it was taken up with half-clothed mannequins.

Pascal held the phone out towards Dinks with the picture of Sapphire, and said, 'we need to talk, *honey*.'

There wasn't a ripple in Dink's expression, but Pascal knew instantly that she had recognized the image.

CHAPTER NINETEEN

'Recognize her?' Pascal said.

'I'm afraid not,' Maria Dinks answered, her face blank. She feigned studying the image more closely. 'Its a very poor picture. You take it? Who's it supposed to be?' she asked, smiling.

Pascal studied her. She was rather striking with pale skin and thick black spiky hair sticking up on her head, her eyes too bright now, but confident looking. She wore an elegant outfit, light brown and understated, but classy.

Pascal knew she had no time for subtlety. 'So, Maria, why?' she asked, her gaze zooming in on Maria's pin sharp eyes. 'You seem to have it all; a real career for starters, not the usual rich housewife's hobby, and you're genuinely talented, and living a millionaire lifestyle. So why would you get involved in kidnapping your own step-kid, and with a crew whose plan was always to kill her?'

'You don't know what you're talking about,' she said, 'and I'd like you to leave,' she added, face tight but also knowing.

And now Pascal could see she had a smart phone in her lap under the table, and had been texting. A knock at the door and it opened, face appearing around the edge. It was the small girl assistant.

'Get security will you, Rachel, and have them escort miss Pascal here, out of the building, please.'

Pascal kept her face blank, trying not to show the shock she felt at Maria knowing who she was.

Maria repeated her words in quick fire Spanish, and the girl nodded and disappeared to fetch security.

'Oh, don't look so shocked, Courtney. I've been expecting you, and of course I recognize the picture. I know all about you. In fact I'm honored to meet such a famous personage, saver of the Queen of England no less and fearless fighter of crime. Your reputation precedes you my dear. But I'm afraid its not needed in this instance, because there is nothing for you to find, as the police so emphatically concluded in their original investigation. But I am incredibly pleased you seem to have found my step daughter and I would like her returned to the custody of my family in New York, immediately. Or it will be you who will be facing kidnap charges, along with, what's the current list?' she said with a pitying smile. 'Murder, attempted murder and assault with a deadly weapon?'

She stood up from the table and walked over to Pascal, took her arms and looked into her face. She had eyes like a cat, the irises orange, glowing, and now there was a subtle hint of triumphalism in them. She said, 'thank you for finding Sapphire. If I were to speculate,' she added playfully, enjoying herself now, 'if she's alive, she was probably drugged that fateful evening so long ago, so I'm sure her recollection of what happened has been most illuminating for you, no?'

As she finished two burly Mexican security guards entered.

Maria looked in Pascal's eyes for a long moment then leaned forward and violently kissed her on the lips. 'Ciao,' she said as she walked out the room.

Pascal slowly wiped her mouth, looking vacantly at the security guards. They watched her warily. They came over, each took an arm and walked her out.

###

Pascal and Ruiz sat in the hire car pulled up at the curb, the Mexico City traffic trundling by. 'So what happened in there?' Ruiz finally asked.

'She blew me out,' Pascal said, irritation in her voice. 'Knew I was coming, wasn't even surprised, and she was ready, primed. That is one cool, calculating, cold hearted bitch. She was playing with me,' Pascal said, almost incredulous. 'Pretended to speculate that if Sapphire was alive, she must have been drugged during the kidnap so wouldn't be able to tell us anything? Can you believe that?'

'Yeah, I can, because Dante never showed,' Ruiz said. 'So we better keep a damn low profile because I don't think we're going to be on the *Federales* Christmas list, if you know what I mean.'

As Ruiz finished speaking Pascal's burner lit up and buzzed. 'Greyeagle,' she said, excitedly, as she clamped the phone to her ear. She listened for a short while, finishing the call with a reminder to check in again in 24 hours.

'They're fine,' she said to Ruiz's questioning look. 'Way out in the desert, miles from anywhere. No sign of anyone searching for them. O'Hara's hogtied and quiet. So far so good.'

'So what the fuck do we do now?' Ruiz said.

'Good question,' she answered, deep in thought. After a moment, she said, 'Maria's a blow out. We're not going to get anything out of her, and she's untouchable in Mexico, and probably the States too, because as she says, we got nothing on her.'

'Yeah, and Dante will have gone to ground as well. Probably even harder to get a line on him now,' Ruiz said.

'Fuck!' Pascal said, rubbing her eyes. As she did so an image, unbidden, popped into her head. It was of Yolanda's face, tired and frightened, her blind, cloudy eye, looking but not seeing. Pascal thought of her for a moment, buried away in the Bedford Correctional Facility, hoping and praying.

She shrugged her shoulders and smiled a tired smile. 'We're going back to Ciudad Juarez, that's where we'll solve this.'

Ruiz turned to her, about to bitch, but then he too sighed, nodded and started the car.

###

In the New Mexico desert O'Hara pretended to sleep, but in his head he was analyzing the results of his new policy of cooperation, which included cutting out the smart comments. That is, when they left his mouth untaped, which wasn't often, but was increasing as a result of his new found politeness. And when they asked him to do anything like eat, get on a horse or go for a shit, he would do it with a kind of grudging but uncomplaining mien. He didn't believe Greyeagle, who seemed to be one smart switched on redskin, was taken in, but the girl and the old lady seemed to be beginning to thaw, especially the girl.

He would keep working at it. He could see through his slitted eyes Greyeagle sitting by the fire, slowly turning on a spit some kind of wild turkey he'd shot, and he had to admit it smelled damn good. They were camped in a kind of culvert, red rock walls each side and brush at the end like a kind of natural screen where the horses and mules were tethered. The two tents were pitched either side of the fire, one for the girls, the other for Greyeagle and him, where he could be watched. And he was watched. Greyeagle, even when he wasn't looking his way, seemed to be aware of what O'Hara was doing, maybe even what he was thinking, and it was kind of unnerving, even for an ex-special forces veteran.

To get free, he was going to have to be lucky and come up with something special. Key was to be totally focused, without showing it, so he would be ready to grab it when that tiny chance presented itself, and he was sure it would. He knew Diaz wouldn't be worrying yet, it was too early. So there would be no search parties. Hell, the operation was off the books so no one would know he was missing anyway. He was on this own, but that was fine. He worked best that way.

As he watched the girl emerge from the brush and go over to Greyeagle to take over the spit turning, he thought about Ruiz and Pascal. He couldn't make Ruiz out. The guy was dirty through and through, so why had he just thrown in his lot with the woman? Didn't make any sense. Guy like that could never live with any kind of a deal he might get from the government, given what he'd done. Maybe he was playing an angle? And the girl, or woman he supposed, it was way beyond personal with her now. She'd fucked him over twice and both times he'd completely underestimated her. Wouldn't happen again.

He looked up as the girl came over with a plate of some strips of tasty looking meat from the cooked bird. He smiled, trying to keep the sleaze out of his expression. It was the kind of look he imagined he might have used to greet a daughter if he had had one. He sat up, his back against the tree, hands cuffed behind him, as she flopped down with the plate.

She looked serious but not unfriendly as she forked a strip of meat and held it up towards his mouth. O'Hara leaned forward and took it and began to chew. She watched him, slightly awestruck, he thought.

'Man, that's some damn good turkey,' he said, licking his lips. 'Makes me think its Thanksgiving. Where you learn to cook like that?'

'Greyeagle cooked it, but I can cook as well.'

'I bet you can,' he said as she forked some more and popped it in his mouth.

'Greyeagle says you're a bad man, and very dangerous, but you don't look dangerous to me,' she said, thoughtfully. 'Courtney's not scared of you. She's not scared of anyone. She's teaching me judo.'

'Hey, maybe you could try out some of your moves on me,' he said as Greyeagle loomed behind her.

Greyeagle took the plate off her and said, 'better you stay away from him and let me do that.'

She nodded and smiled. 'Okay, Greyeagle, whatever you say,' she said, moving away back towards the fire where Sia was now sitting and eating.

O'Hara grinned, forgetting his plan for a moment, oozing sleaze. 'You gonna cut yourself a slice of that kiddies tight young pussy, chief?' he said. 'I can see she ain't about to fight you off. Go for it, man. I won't tell.'

'Nice try, O'Hara, but it's never gonna work with me,' Greyeagle said patiently. He placed the plate on the ground, took out the masking tape and put a strip over O'Hara's mouth. 'But no more food or talk for you, my man, until you can learn some manners,' he added before walking back to join the others.

O'Hara watched them, feeling a surge of emotion. Forget Greyeagle. It would never work with him. But he had connected with the girl on some level that he couldn't articulate. He was maybe something dark but also fascinating for her that she wanted to look at and find out about but knew she shouldn't. He would be ready to exploit that, soon as he got the chance. Then he'd kill them all and go looking for Pascal and Ruiz.

###

'You were right,' Maria said into her phone, walking alongside her assistant as they escorted her designs out back to the waiting vans.

'What happened?' Dante asked. In fact he was only 3 miles away, sitting at his usual table, sipping Perrier water, bodyguards either side looking on.

'She turned up, caught me snorting a line,' she said, soft laugh.

'Showed me a recent picture of the brat, but that's about it. She's not so smart. Fact is, they don't have a damn thing, apart from the brat. If you think about it, it changes nothing for us. Yolanda Lopez is still in the frame. Kid tells them nothing, because she doesn't know anything. She was Gaga like the lady, on the night.'

'I'm not so sure,' he replied carefully, brooding. He flicked his fingers at the waiter for an espresso. 'You see, I don't see it like that. It was finished, and now it's not. I had a guy at the show, watching, and there were *Federales* crawling all over it, and somehow I don't think they were fashionistas.'

'What are you saying?' she said, and now there was a tinge of doubt in her voice.

'I think they were watching for me, and if I'm right, what does that tell you?'

'I don't believe they've connected us,' she said, but there was less confidence in her voice.

'Why not? The kid saw us together, her own mother, or stepmother, half naked, playing around with a stranger. That kind of scene tends to leave an impression on a young child. She will have been able to describe me, and I've been racking my brains trying to remember.'

'What?'

'I'm pretty sure you called me, "Dante" in front of her.'

'Shit!'

'You say that Pascal is not so smart. Well she's ex-British intelligence, meaning she'll have contacts in law enforcement all over. Won't take a genius to join up the dots. And that's what I think they've done, and that's why they were there, waiting for me.'

Maria was silent, now leaning against a wall watching her creations being ferried away in a couple of white vans. 'You know what I think?' she finally said.

'No. Tell me.'

'I think we should go on the attack. No sense waiting for them to figure something out.'

'What do you suggest,' he said

'The media.'

'What d'you mean?' he said, thinking she'd gone crazy.

'Look, there's a fucking manhunt going on for Pascal and the kid, but at the same time there is no coverage in the media. Why? This kidnap murder case was a huge story and yet there's not a peep out there, that the murder victim has just turned up alive.'

Dante sipped his bitter espresso marveling again at her ability to dig down and find a kernel of truth even when she was under pressure. 'But I still don't understand how the media can help us,' he said.

'First, I don't think the keystone cops chasing Pascal know its Sapphire Dinks who is with her, yet, it's just another unidentified kid. Now, there are two possibilities there; either they're just plain dumb, and you can never rule that out when it comes to US law enforcement. But it could also be because someone out there doesn't want her identity known either, someone powerful, who can put a blanket on something like this.

'Secondly, what would a genuinely grieving mother do if her murdered daughter suddenly turned up alive in the custody of a fugitive felon?'

Dante remained silent, waiting for Maria to answer her own question. He signaled the waiter for a brandy. It was rare for him to drink alcohol. His bodyguards looked askance, wondering who the hell their boss was talking to.

'She would be screaming the house down to get her child back safe, and the media would be driving the story,' Maria said. 'Add in the fact it's a cause celebre crime mystery of the decade, and you can jack that media interest by a factor of a million.'

'That may all be true, but so what? How does it help us?' Dante said, trying to follow her logic.

'Two things, my sweet. Media interest will mean everyone out there is looking for her, and it may flush out whoever imposed a blanket on this. Other thing is, we can try and control the story to start with. Key thing; when they find her. What happens? She's my daughter, so where does she go? Where's her place? They can't imprison her, and as I was exonerated by the police and prosecutors, and they have no evidence against me, she comes back to me. She must be handed back into my custody as her parent to look after, and that's the story we push when we approach the media. My child is out there with a fugitive felon and I want her back.'

'That's beautiful, *corrida*,' Dante said, something close to awe in his voice.

'No. That's genius.'

'It means,' he continued, developing his thoughts as he spoke, 'you'd have control of her, and you could decide on who gets access, like, say the cops if they got interested again.'

'That's right, but I'm more worried about Daniels, the Federal

Prosecutor, and the appeal. I heard through my source he may go for a retrial for Yolanda, but if I say Sapphire is not going to testify, they might just drop the murder charge, and leave the kidnap conviction in place. Yolanda can't prove she wasn't involved, and they can't prove I was, so Yolanda stays cooped up in gaol. Stalemate.

'But we may need to get a tame psychiatrist to say it would be harmful to Sapphire, given what she's been through, to be questioned by the FBI or required to testify in any retrial.'

'No problem. I can line up a head doctor anytime. Then we control access to the kid.'

'Yeah, but it's even sweeter than that. Having the kid back also means I'll get free access to her trust money as her parent and legal guardian, which so far the Trustees have blocked.'

'Even better. So how you going to play it?' he said.

'I know the fashion critic on the New York Times slightly. I'll ask her to hook me up with someone who can turbo charge the story, not that it'll need it, and then get it out there. What about you? What are you going to do?'

'I think it's time I paid a little visit to Ciudad Juarez, to straighten them out down there,' he said with a wolfish smile.

Soon after they ended the call.

CHAPTER TWENTY

Dante stood in Cantina Gold, Monteros's bar on the Boulevard in Ciudad Juarez, meditatively reading through some text messages. He finished and closed his phone. Beside him stood his captain, Alvaro Chavez, visibly nervous and sweating.

'Have a drink, my friend,' Dante said, gesturing along the bar at Dominga who stood patiently polishing a glass.

Chavez nodded at her. 'Scotch, no water,' he said, voice clipped and tight. She reached back behind her for a bottle of Johnny Walker and drew him a shot. 'Make it a double,' he said, and she shook out another into the glass.

Chavez raised it to his lips and took the lot in two gulps, gently replacing the glass back on the bar. Dominga moved away. The place was empty and shuttered.

Chavez wondered whether to tell Dante the news he had just heard, or hold it back and see which way the wind was blowing; release it when it might have more value for him. But no, it was never clever to try to anticipate the boss.

'Alvaro, you look worried,' Dante said suddenly, his smile

deceptively avuncular. 'Calm yourself and talk to me, old friend. I have been away a while and I need to catch up. Troubling rumors have been reaching us of disruption in production, and squabbles with our competitors. So, control needs to be re-asserted, and punishment meted out to those who would try to disrupt our business, yes?'

'Yes, sir. We are glad you're are back here to guide us. Sir, before I report, there is information I have just received, that may interest you greatly,' Chavez said nervously.

'And what would that be, my friend?'

'The woman, or girl, perhaps, you asked about before, Catherine Hansen?'

'Yes? speak, man,' Dante said, suddenly agitated.

'Well, she's back here.'

'What d'you mean?' Dante asked, believing he had misheard him.

'The Hansen woman is back here in Juarez, sir.

'What d'you mean, back here?' he said, roughly grabbing Chavez by the shoulders, digging his fingers in hard. 'Where is she?' he demanded, his eyes glowing.

'We don't know, sir,' Chavez said quietly as Dante removed the grip from his shoulders. He continued, 'it was just a chance sighting this morning. Jorge who worked with her when they were my bodyguards, happened to see her driving by in a hire car.'

'Why didn't he follow her?'

'He tried, but he was in traffic going the other way, by the time he got around, she'd gone. But sir, she'll be very easy to track down in this city, no problem.'

Dante signaled Dominga. 'Brandy,' he said, voice scratchy. He sipped the drink, his eyes lingering on Dominga's firm body. He turned to Chavez again. 'Find out where she is, put a watch on, then report to me. Do not approach her or let her know we are watching. Tell them: anyone screws up, they will take a bath - in the acid. Go,' he said.

As Chavez left - he couldn't get out of there fast enough - Dante turned to Dominga. He suddenly realized he needed a woman, urgently, that instant. 'Come,' he said, looking at her hard in the face, wanting her to resist. She held his gaze for a moment, seeing what was in his eyes. She nodded, knowing she had no choice. She slowly walked around the bar as he sat back on the stool watching her.

###

Pascal scrolled her burner checking for calls and messages. They'd booked into a little obscure backstreet pension Ruiz had suggested. It was right on the border line between the warring Juarez and Sinaloa factions and might mean they'd get overlooked for a while. Pascal, chewing on a tortilla, switched on the TV and plumped down on the bed, flicking channels with the remote.

Ruiz had gone out. She'd debated for a while whether she should stick to him, keep him under the gun 24/7, but soon realized she couldn't really do that. Either he'd bought into her logic and was now working to undo the wrongs of the past, or he was irredeemably bad and would try and fuck her over. She tended to the former but would not lower her guard. He'd said, reasonably enough, he needed to check in and square things with his bosses at the DEA and find out what had been happening. He said he'd be back in a couple of hours and she should stay out of sight. When he went out, he was wearing a bandanna, huge shades and a vast sombrero, looking like a lost tourist seeking out the Mexican way.

As Pascal flicked TV channels, she caught a familiar sight and went rigid, desperately scrolling back to CNN to catch the story. It was old pictures of the Dinks kidnap case from when it first broke. She quickly upped the volume, tuning in and listening intently to the excited reporter's voice over:

'…… *Maria Dinks was too overcome with emotion to speak herself and that quote was from her spokesperson. CNN have not yet been able to verify the story and we await comment from the FBI, although the Mayor of New York has just tweeted, "its wonderful news if true." Sources say Sapphire Dinks was first located in Mexico and is currently somewhere in the US. Further news on this sensational breaking story will follow. Don't go away while we take a short break…….*'

Pascal got up and paced the room, then went and lent back against the wall, eyes closed. What the fuck was going on? Was it just finally a leak? As simple as that? Her gut told her, no. Maria apparently being too emotional to speak was a clue. And that maybe fitted in with what she'd said at the fashion show. She wanted the child back for obvious reasons, control, and so she was going on the attack, slickly positioning herself with the media and public as grieving mother, to pursue that end. Pascal couldn't help admiring the woman's chutzpah.

As she pushed herself away from the wall, she suddenly stopped mid movement, a chill running down her spine - Greyeagle had never checked in. What with the traveling, booking in and worrying about Ruiz she had completely forgotten it. Her mind awash with images of O'Hara and the desert, she checked her watch. Greyeagle was four hours late.

###

Greyeagle had to sleep sometime O'Hara thought sourly as he watched the guy sitting like a stone statue, but there wasn't much evidence of it. And it was hard to tell whether the guy was asleep or just meditating. Even when his eyes were closed, he looked alert.

O'Hara looked down at his cuffed hands and the rough welts on his wrists where he had tried, in a fit of rage, to break them open. If he could disable Greyeagle, he knew he could handle the girl and her grandmother, even with the handcuffs on. As he looked around, the girl appeared from behind him carrying some brush for the fire. She stopped and looked down at him, face immobile.

'Hi,' O'Hara said, smiling as genuinely as he knew how. 'How you doing today?'

'Fine,' she said, 'and how are you?'

'I'm okay. Getting a little bored, as I like to be active just like you,' he said, turning on the country boy charm he'd learned growing up in backwoods Kentucky. 'You know I could help get firewood, even in my cuffs. I'm sure Greyeagle would be glad of the help.'

She looked over at Greyeagle, her face conflicted. O'Hara figured she was getting bored as well and might like a little harmless mischief. But it sure wouldn't be harmless if he had his way. He slowly rose to his feet, sliding his back up the tree trunk to give him support. She didn't seem to notice.

'Look, you show me the brush wood and I can carry it back. I can't do any harm with the cuffs on,' he said, moving a few steps and praying Greyeagle really was sleeping.

As the girl seemed to hesitate, O'Hara was eying up a football sized rock sitting a little way behind Greyeagle. If he could get anywhere near it without the girl screaming, he might have a chance, assuming the guy was sleeping, and it looked like he was, but then he could wake any second.

'Well, if you don't want my help,' O'Hara said quietly, mock sad, 'I'll just sit back down and carry on being bored.'

She smiled a half smile. 'Okay,' she said. 'You carry this brush over to the fire, and come back here, and then we'll see.'

He nodded, excitement rising. 'No problem,' he said reaching out his cuffed hands to take the brushwood from her. He waited watching her. 'Okay,' he said, gently. 'I'll take it over then?'

'Go ahead,' she said, smiling at being able to order him about.

He moved away cautiously, watching Greyeagle and the rock all the while. As he got level, he dropped the brushwood and lunged for the rock like it was a ball and he was back on the football pitch, scooping it up for a home run. There was a millisecond delay before the girl screamed and that was enough time for O'Hara to swing the rock two handed into the side of Greyeagle's head as he was rising and turning at the same time. The blow knocked Greyeagle back sprawling onto the ground, and O'Hara was on him, using the cuffs to bear down on Greyeagle's neck, slowly throttling him.

###

Calver was sat at his desk watching the news when Daniels call came through.

'I see the Mayor's keen on a retrial,' Calver said mildly, goading the guy.

'That fucking media hound?' Daniels said. 'They say the most dangerous place in New York is getting between that klutz and a microphone,' he added.

'I didn't leak it, in case you're wondering,' Calver said.

'No, I know. Question is: what happens now? I mean, do you have the girl, and can you produce her?'

Calver sat holding the phone, contemplating the Brooklyn Brownstones across the street, options and strategies tumbling through his mind. Question was: why the hell would Maria Dinks tell the world her stepdaughter had been found when the child might turn up in the custody of law enforcement and incriminate her? Bigger question: what should he tell Daniels, when he actually didn't have a clue where the child was and hadn't been able to talk to Pascal in 24 hours? If he guaranteed Daniels that he had Sapphire, the guy might go straight for a retrial instead of opposing it, but surely he'd want to see the child first? But maybe not, with pressure from the media and the Mayor's office rising by the minute. But then if he told Daniels he could produce Sapphire, and then didn't, it would leave Yolanda twisting in the wind in an even worse position than she had been in before.

'I don't have custody of her,' he finally said, 'and I cannot tell you where she currently is, because I don't have that information. But I will go out on a limb and say, we will produce her for any retrial.'

Daniels on the other end of the line was silent. 'I'll take it under advisement,' he said, and cut the connection.

Stars exploded in O'Hara's head. He fell sideways, stunned from a blow delivered by Sapphire to the back of his head with a small rock. But he was still alert and managed to scramble up almost immediately. Greyeagle lay on his back, half strangled and sluggish but now he had a pistol in his hand, slowly raising it to fire. O'Hara hesitated for a millisecond, turned and ran.

As he crashed and stumbled through the brush, trying to keep his balance he heard a crack of thunder and the light dimmed as rare black storm clouds blotted out the sky. Luck was with him this time he thought grimly. He heard gunfire and could feel bullets zipping around him as he ran. A refrain kept running through his head: go for the shitter, because the rain would cover his tracks. Now he was in thick, dense brush and the bullets stopped. He immediately started to double back on himself, as the rain came sheeting down.

Around a hundred meters from the camp they had set up a latrine in a natural trench at the bottom of which was marshy swamp kind of material. They reckoned it had probably been used for that purpose by travelers and nomads for hundreds of years. Now he studied it from brush a few meters away. With an exceptional tracker like Greyeagle, and with him in cuffs, he would have no chance in open country, and they had the guns and the horses. Soon as the squall let up and Greyeagle was recovered they would be out looking for him, but not, he gambled, there.

He moved out of the brush watching the pitching rain eradicate his footprints almost as soon as he lifted his feet. He looked down in the trench at the swamp like sludge that he knew contained feces and urine. As he put the hollow bamboo like shoot into his mouth, he smiled thinking that this was nothing compared to what they had put him through in special forces survival training. He climbed down into the trench and immersed himself in the raw sewage, gritting his teeth and inuring himself to the foul stench.

###

Pascal stood biting her lip, burner pressed so hard to the side of her head it left a mark. She waited, listening to the ring tone, praying. She watched Ruiz who'd just returned, stood opposite her, his eyes hooded and unreadable.

Then Greyeagle was answering sounding faint and distant.

'What happened? Why didn't you call in?' she asked quick fire, almost shouting into the phone.

'We had a bit of a problem,' he drawled. 'O'Hara's broken out, but I'll find him. Can't of gone far. He's still cuffed, and he's got no gun.'

'No,' Pascal said, immediately. 'Get out of there now. Don't wait around. Are there any settlements, people around there, nearby?'

'Not really, its transient, people coming and going. So there could be people a mile away or no one for twenty miles, depends. Look, why don't I track him and bring him back?' Greyeagle said, wanting to restore his pride.

'No. If it was just you, fine, but with Sapphire and Sia there, we can't risk it. I know you could handle him, Greyeagle, but the guy is a trained professional and we can't take any chances, so I want you to get out now, fast.

'And, Greyeagle. We got another problem. The media know about Sapphire, that she's the missing girl from the kidnap case. So, I'm afraid the whole world and his dog are going to be out there looking for you.'

Greyeagle said nothing as he absorbed the news.

'So if you can think of anywhere to lay low for a while, that would be good. The media are likely to hit Gallup hard when they join up the dots, and make the family connection, so they'll be there, as well as O'Hara, when he gets the cuffs off. But main thing is just to get away from where you are now. Will you do that?'

After a moment, he said, grudgingly, 'okay. I've got somewhere

in mind we can go hole up. But some day I want another crack at that
sneaky son of a bitch O'Hara.'

'I have a feeling you might just get your wish, Greyeagle,' she
said cryptically. 'But right now, just get going.'

'I'm on it.'

Pascal clipped the phone off.

'So, Fernando,' she said, turning to him. 'You heard most of
that. O'Hara's busted out but he's still unarmed and cuffed, middle of
nowhere, out in the desert. What's he gonna do?'

Ruiz crossed his arms, thinking. 'He'll pursue the girl, the target,
whatever, but he'll need to get free of the cuffs, get to a phone and
weapons. And that Greyeagle is not some country hick, so O'Hara
won't take any chances. My guess, he'll take what he needs from the
first people he comes across, and just better hope they cooperate, cause
he'll kill 'em as easy as blinking if they don't.'

'So,' Pascal said, nodding, pretty much agreeing with him. 'No
need for us to go screaming down there, at least for now.'

'I agree,' Ruiz nodded. 'So, how about you telling me why
we're in Juarez - what's the grand plan?'

'Gutman,' she said. 'He's the starting point. Solomon Gutierrez.
After Tilly-May died at the hotel, you took me at gun point out to see
him, remember' she said, her eyes turning hard.

'Yeah, I remember,' he said, voice weary. 'How can I forget?
Listen, I'm going to have to live with what I've done, and I'm trying to
make a start here with you, so how about you cutting me some slack and
laying off the constant digs. I know what I've done?'

'I can do that,' she said. 'But, amigo, you're going to have to tell me all you know about Gutman. Why you took me to see him and exactly what your relationship was with him?'

Ruiz walked over to the sideboard and lifted up a new bottle of Tequila and hefted in his hand.

'Good idea,' she said, removing a fresh lime from her pocket and tossing it to him. He silently made their drinks and passed one to her. They moved out onto the small balcony overlooking the drab backstreet that was festooned with lines of washing gently moving in the breeze.

Ruiz sipped his drink, contemplative.

'Time you're taking, buddy, it's making me think your trying to come up with a story,' Pascal quipped.

'No, it's not that,' he said wistfully. 'I went so bad so quick, and did so much wrong that it's hard to start trying to unravel it all.'

'I understand,' she said, 'but we haven't got time for navel gazing.'

Ruiz knocked his tequila back, grimaced and wiped his mouth. He looked down at the floor thinking. 'I went to Gutman for money. Simple as that. But I mean real money. You know I got property in Mexico and the States,' he said with a kind of shopworn pride.

'And? What else did he supply you with?' she asked.

He looked away. 'You know what I said, when Tilly-May went over the balcony?'

'How could I forget it. You said it was "too bad", and you laughed. Then you said, "she was spoiled goods", meaning it didn't matter that she died.'

'Yeah, well, I wasn't exactly speaking true. I said it because I wanted to hurt you. You came down here arrogant as hell and blew my world up. I had a sweet thing going on. But you made me stop and look at myself and I hated what I saw. Okay,' he said looking shamefaced. 'I do like young girls, and I know it's no excuse, but we're talking thirteen, fourteen, fifteen. Some countries that's legal. I know it's wrong and most people are disgusted and I'm ashamed, but Gutman was clever, he got me addicted. End of the day, we're all weak, and we can't always resist temptation.'

'You make it sound like these girls had a choice, Ruiz. Let's be clear; they were abducted and if you had sex with them, it was rape. And what happened to them afterword's?'

'I don't know. Most of them I regularly saw around top floor of the Cafe Flamingo,' he said unconvincingly. 'But I'll tell you this. I never killed any girl I went with,' he said with a flash of anger.

Pascal watched him, thinking now really wasn't the time to grill him about this stuff. That would come later. But Ruiz was still trying to rationalize his behavior. He continued, 'As I said, Gutman was clever and subtle. He barely ever had to use violence. Like all such guys he found out a person's weakness and then mercilessly used it against them.'

Pascal nodded. 'Did you ever see anything connected to Senator Diaz?' she asked.

'Never, but then again, Gutman was incredibly secretive. No ego. No showing off. Every part of what he did was self-contained and compartmentalized, so guys he used didn't know a fraction of what was going on. Communications were all verbal, everybody and every location was continually scanned for listening devices, bugs, you name it. No cell phones or computerized devices of any kind were allowed anywhere near Gutman or his operation, it was all basically in his head.'

Pascal took another shot of tequila. 'Okay, Ruiz, tell me what you do know, and then we'll move on to what you think you know.'

He nodded, his expression grim. He went and sat down.

CHAPTER TWENTY-ONE

Greyeagle walked his horse back into the camp. The side of his head hurt where the rock had struck him, but it had been a glancing blow and there was no fracture. As he approached Sia, she looked up from tightening the saddle strap on her horse. They had been packing up the camp and now the mules were all loaded and the horses ready. Greyeagle shook his head. 'Not a trace,' he said. 'Rain must have washed out any tracks, and there's no sign around about here, so I'm guessing he's long gone.'

'So why don't we just stay here, if he's gone?' she said.

'Courtney said no, we should go, so let's mount up,' he said. 'Might as well head back towards the ranch while we decide what to do, and I'll see if I can raise Courtney.'

A short while later they filed out of the culvert

###

O'Hara stood in the trench, looking over the edge, his feet still submerged in the stinking morass. He was coated in thick brown sludge, only his eye whites showing, making him look like an extra from a horror flick. He was looking back towards the camp. Only Greyeagle had been up there for a cursory look and that had been a good hour ago. Since then there hadn't been a sound, but now he could hear birds chirping around the camp area.

He waited another twenty minutes, motionless, watching. When he was satisfied they were gone he cautiously climbed over the edge and into the brush, moving silently. Five minutes later he stood in the empty camp area carefully going over the ground. He moved to the exit of the culvert and walked out some way to study the terrain. The fresh tracks suggested they had gone back the way they had come, maybe heading back towards the ranch.

He crouched down on his haunches, scooping up a handful of fine sand and letting it run through his fingers. He sniffed the wind, smiled, stood up and started to walk resolutely in the opposite direction to that Greyeagle had taken.

They had drunk most of the Tequila. Ruiz sat in a chair while Pascal roamed around the room.

'See, that's the problem, I been trying to tell you,' Ruiz said. 'I was never in the inner circle, if there ever was an inner circle with Gutman. So I can't give you detail.'

Pascal nodded. 'So tell me what happened at Cafe Flamingo

when you went in and then told me you'd found Tilly-May. Was that all bullshit - a set up?'

Ruiz got up and walked out on the balcony and stood at the rail, looking down on the sun dappled back alley. He felt hunted and deeply uncomfortable. He wiped his brow and moved back into the room. 'Some of it was made up, yeah,' he said, unhappily. 'What else could I do? I was worried you were going to make me as dirty. Gutman told me what to tell you. He also allowed you to get in and get the girl, because he wanted to see what you were going to do. When you got her out and then holed up in the hotel, he told me to go and get you and bring you out to the ranch. I know,' he said, looking shamefaced, 'that it's no excuse, but we had no orders to kill Tilly-May. And I would never have agreed to it, even if I was ordered to. You have to believe that,' he said.

'So taking me and Sapphire out on that long drive in the desert was what? A joy ride? What were you going to do at the end of it?' she said, knowing almost as soon as the words left her mouth it was the wrong thing to say.

She watched his face, surprised at the frozen look of horrified fascination she saw there. A tear ran down his face mingling with sweat. He angrily wiped it away. He looked down at his hands, pensive for a moment. 'D'you think Tilly-May's family will get the body back and be told what happened?'

Pascal bit her lip to stop herself tearing into Ruiz again. 'So much regret and grief, Ruiz, but it's a bit late in the day for that.'

'Well you got Sapphire in the end, didn't you?' he said with a flare of frustrated anger. Then, more softly, 'look, I don't know what more I can tell you,' he said.

'Okay, let's forget about the past for now 'cause I have a very simple question for you,' she said with the beginnings of a smile. 'Can you get back in with Gutman?'

He snorted. 'You're fucking crazy' he said, eyes wild. 'You know that? All the way down the line, you always choose the crazy option.'

'Why crazy?' she said. 'If you've still got an in with Gutman, we've got to use it. Is there any reason why he should doubt you now, or be suspicious?

'Oh, only the fact that you and Sapphire are now a major rolling 24/7 news story, for which he'll no doubt blame me. How d'you get around that?'

'By using it to construct a believable cover story.'

'You're crazy,' he said again, grudgingly, but with a little less vehemence.

'You could go back in, Ruiz, do some good, and really wipe the slate,' she said, getting into it. 'Maybe atone in your own way for some of what's gone down. You want redemption? Absolution, Ruiz? You gotta go through the fire, and the fire is the fat man, Gutman.'

'Man, you really know how to push the buttons, don't you?' he said.

'Up to you, amigo. You want your soul back or not?' She shrugged.

'Okay, Pascal,' he said wearily, getting up and stretching, 'let's play your make believe game. How do you propose to get me in? I just go waltzing back? I never checked in with him after the roadblock stop on the border, so he'll be suspicious as hell, maybe believing I've crossed him. And I was never a regular visitor at the ranch, so I'd need a very good reason to go out there.'

Pascal sat down and took a shot of Tequila. 'Okay, let me worry about the media point. You work up a good cover story for where you've been - say a DEA operation that took you away - then get back on the street and talk to people, contacts, see what you can pick up about Gutman, any rumors, you know the score, Ruiz. Then you come back here, talk to me, and we work up a plan.'

'I guess I can do that,' he said.

'Good. No time like the present. Let's get on it,' she said, jumping up and finishing off her tequila. He watched her, shaking his head with disapproval, but unable to come up with a suitably cutting retort.

Hettie stood at the door of Calver's office. 'Put the TV on, Jonas. Mayor's making an announcement on the Dinks case.'

Calver flicked the remote at the TV in the corner, scrolled channels until he came to the right one. The screen showed the New York Mayor at the microphone in a press conference, cameras zapping and flashing around him as he spoke. To one side of the him stood Michael Daniels the Federal prosecutor and to the other a demure looking Maria Dinks.

'.....so in light of this wonderful news, that one of this city's missing daughters is alive, and close to freedom, we can now hear from the chief prosecutor Michael Daniels, but I'd just like to say, we all want justice in this long running saga and I'm confident Michael Daniels is going to give it to us. Michael,' the Mayor said, gesturing to him.

Daniels nodded and spoke to camera. 'Yes, thank you mayor. Sapphire Dinks was originally located in Mexico and very recently brought into the US by a female adult using the name, Catherine Hanson, although her real name is Courtney Pascal. She is currently being sought by US Marshals and the FBI in connection with charges of kidnap, murder and attempted murder. She is dangerous and should not be approached. Here is a recent picture of her. If anyone knows the whereabouts of these individuals, they should contact us immediately.

'We now believe Sapphire Dinks may be or have been in Gallup, New Mexico where her Grandmother lives, and urgent inquiries are being made there as we speak. I have no doubt we shall shortly have recovered Sapphire and then she can be returned to the loving custody of her mother Maria Dinks,' he said casting a nod at Maria, who offered a saintly smile to the cameras.

'Now, turning to justice, there has been a lot of speculation, much of it wide of mark and of a wild conspiracy theory variety, about Yolanda Lopez's trial, and whether, as many believe, there were other parties involved in the kidnap. Well, in the light of the discovery of Sapphire Dinks, and the fact of Yolanda Lopez's recent request for a retrial, in the interests of justice, we are going to accede to that request, and ask for it to be brought on as a matter of urgency. In the meantime, we remain convinced of Yolanda Lopez's guilt in respect of the kidnap, and although we will be dropping the charge of murder, we are currently considering bringing charges of attempted murder against her. Thank you.'

'Son of a bitch!' Calver fumed at the screen. 'He's been bumped into that,' he added, to Hettie who still stood at the door. 'He hasn't even spoken to the kid so how the hell can he say he's still convinced of Yolanda's guilt? Politics,' he added, with distaste.

'Hey, don't complain,' Hettie said. 'You just got her a retrial, and her life story's probably just gone up in value by about a zillion dollars.' Hettie came farther into the room and stood looking down at Calver. 'But aren't you worried about, Courtney? What they said? Where is she, and where's Sapphire?'

'Courtney can look after herself,' he muttered. 'But, yeah, I am worried, and I'd sure like to know where the hell they are too. Maybe she'll call,' he added doubtfully.

'Yeah, maybe she'll call,' Hettie echoed him. 'I'll get you some hot coffee, Jonas. You look like you could do with it.'

'You and me both, Hettie.'

###

O'Hara jogged on through the desert scrub. As he ran, he remembered Afghanistan and the heat there and how he had honed himself in that harsh environment, turning himself into a super-fit killing machine. He smiled to himself; nothing could stop him now and he felt no pain.

He looked around as he ran, studying the terrain and the horizon. He'd been moving for many hours and expected to cut a road or settlement of some kind soon.

He almost missed the browny-red colored shack as it was so well camouflaged, mingling seamlessly into the desert, set back amongst some scrubby trees. He came to a halt and crouched down in dense bushes about a hundred meters away, watching intently. His eyes crawled over the structure and the area immediately surrounding it. Nothing moved. He began to edge stealthily towards it, slowly, keeping low to the ground, watching all the time.

About twenty meters off, he settled down behind a rock outcrop, that he could peer around. The place seemed empty. There was no movement or sound. He looked down at his hands. It would be good to get the cuffs off and get some food and water. He debated waiting for nightfall, but that was hours away. He looked at the shack; it was a small two room kind of lean-to set up against a rock face that provided its back wall.

As he rose up and edged around the rock outcrop to approach the place, he heard a loud click behind him. He stopped and slowly straightened up and started to turn, when a voice said, 'stay right where you are, mister. I got two barrels stuffed full of buckshot pointed right at your back, an like to cut you clean in half if'n you've a mind to mess with me.'

The voice was strong but aged. O'Hara breathed out. He said, cautiously, 'I have no bad intentions. I am an FBI agent in trouble. I was abducted and handcuffed by a convicted felon fleeing justice, but I managed to escape, and now I need your urgent help. I have ID in my pocket. Please check.'

O'Hara heard the sound of spitting. 'I ain't no friend of the

Federal Government, son, and they're no friend of mine,' the man said.

'Look friend, all I need is one phone call, and they'll come and pick me up, and I'll be out of your hair. And man, I could use a drink of water right now. Water and a phone. That's all I'm asking. What d'you say?'

'You a military man?' he asked.

'Yes sir I was. Screamin' Eagles, to hell and back.'

'Come on in then, boy. Why didn't you say? But keep your hands where I can see them. My name's Jessie. I been out here nigh on 45 years, since I got back from Nam.'

O'Hara turned slowly to look at him. The guy looked to be in his early seventies, but fit. Long gray hair pulled back in a ponytail, and an unkempt goatee, but his eyes looked watchful and alert. He gestured towards the shack and O'Hara started moving, saying over his shoulder, 'if you got an axe, maybe you can get these cuffs off me.'

'We'll talk a little first, son. You can have your water and I'll have a look at your ID.'

'Sounds good,' O'Hara said, wondering whether he'd have to kill the guy.

###

They had been riding single file for a while, the gradient subtly steepening, but always rising, the sun at their back, now beginning to wane. As Sapphire rode on her mind was in turmoil, riven by feelings of guilt because she had been the one to let O'Hara free to almost kill

Greyeagle and then escape. Greyeagle was so silent it was impossible to know what he thought about anything, but he must be mad at her.

She knew the blow to his head would have hurt like crazy, but he never let on, and she guessed it was his pride that was hurting the most. In the end she had to say something, unable to keep it in any longer. She gently tapped the sides of her sorrel mare urging the horse forward until it came alongside Greyeagle's mount.

For a while they rode in silence, Greyeagle not even acknowledging her presence beside him. When she could stand it no longer, she said, 'I just wanted to say, I'm very sorry for what happened. It was all my fault that he got free and hurt you.'

It seemed like Greyeagle hadn't heard her as he said nothing for a couple of minutes as they rode on side by side. 'It wasn't your fault,' he finally murmured. 'You're a child and he was like a cornered mountain lion. We are lucky you hit him, because,' he added, turning to look at her. 'He would have killed us all if you hadn't.'

He leaned down and stroked the neck of his horse, then looked up and studied the sky, his eyes crinkling. 'I believe you are wise beyond your years,' he continued. 'I see it in your eyes and in the way you conduct yourself. And despite what I believe you have endured, you still retain your innocence and humanity. O'Hara sensed this and tried to use it for his own purpose.'

Sapphire said nothing, trying to work out what Greyeagle's words meant, but knowing intuitively it was something good, and that he didn't blame her. 'So, still friends?' she said tentatively.

'Of course. You are my sister.'

That wasn't exactly what she wanted to hear, but it was a start.

She looked around the hilly scrub they were rising through. 'So, Greyeagle, where are we going? What did Courtney say? Is she coming back?' she asked.

'So many questions. But it's a good thing to be curious and inquisitive. We are almost there, if it's still as I remember it from when I was a child.'

'What is it, where we're going?'

'It's an old worked out, long disused silver mine, if its still there undisturbed,' he said, looking around the terrain, checking his bearings. They were approaching a steep rise and the horses and mules were laboring at the gradient. They came to the brow, and then stood on the ridge, looking down.

Sia came up, leading the mules. They sat looking down at the small short valley splayed out before them. At the other end of it they could see some dilapidated wooden shacks, all overgrown with scrub and bushes, set up against rising rock formations. Beside the wooden shacks there were various sized cave openings in the rock face, some having rubbish and debris blocking their entrances. Out front of the shacks in a dusty brush free area stood a long wooden trough and a what looked like a well and some broken fencing for a corral.

They sat for a moment taking it all in. Greyeagle said, 'okay, we're going to make camp here for a while, but first I'm going down to check it out. You stay here under cover until I get back.'

They moved back across the ridge as Greyeagle's horse picked its way down towards the mine.

###

O'Hara sat at a scarred wooden table in the old guys shack sipping water, two- handed, from a broken cup, as Jesse examined his ID.

'Looks genuine, son', Jesse said, checking the laminated card and then tossing it on to the tabletop whilst still carefully appraising O'Hara. It was clear something about O'Hara still troubled him. He got up, went to a cupboard built over the sink, rummaged around, and came back with an old, primitive looking cellphone. 'Gift from my niece,' he said, flatly. 'Hardly use it, 'cept for emergencies. But you give me a number to call, to vouch for you, son. Then I'll cut you free and we can get real friendly.'

'No problem,' O'Hara said, trying to keep the frustration out of his voice. The guy was way too careful, and it was costing him valuable time. When he got free the guy was going to pay for it. O'Hara patiently read out the number for his boss at the FBI, a guy who knew just enough about his mission for Diaz to vouch for him without asking any difficult questions.

The old man held the cell phone gingerly to his ear as O'Hara fed him the detail required to get him put through to the boss. After a short conversation, Jesse got up and held the phone to O'Hara's ear so he could hear and talk. There was a brief two-way that finished with O'Hara saying, 'yes sir. Once this civic minded citizen has cut me free, I will phone you back and we can arrange an extraction. Roger that.'

A short while later outside the shack O'Hara knelt with the cuffs held across a wooden chopping block. Jesse stood over him with an axe. He licked his finger and tested the blade, cocking his head to one side and nodding to himself. He examined the short area of metal connecting the two cuffs and tried a few practice swings at the target.

'Okay, son. Brace yourself,' he said, and then swung the axe blade down on the metal connection. There was clinking sound and the cuffs separated.

O'Hara slowly rose to his feet, holding the red mist at bay, smile still on his face. He needed to pump the old guy first and find out what assets he had at the shack. It was always easier to do it voluntarily than trying to sweat it. Besides, he didn't have the time. He needed to run Greyeagle and the girl to ground and finish the mission.

CHAPTER TWENTY-TWO

'So what have you got?' Pascal asked, watching Ruiz as he stood with his back to her, making coffee with sachets and pouring in water from an electric kettle. He had just come in from a night on the street and he looked tired and despondent.

'Not much,' he said, blowing on the coffee to cool it, and taking a tentative sip. He sighed contentedly, enjoying its rejuvenatory effects. 'It was like I'd never been away, really,' he said. 'There's no word on the street about me, and I've worked up a story of a DEA operation that took me away for a few days, which I think will hold. But here's the thing, Pascal, even if we get around the little detail of 24/7 media coverage about you and Sapphire and the nationwide manhunt, what is it you think I can do, even if Gutman does take me back into his confidence? We know he kidnapped, ransomed and pimped out little girls, some of whom were murdered. So what will you get from Gutman that we don't already know, and how's it going to help us?'

'Truthful answer, Ruiz. I don't know,' she said.

'Great.'

'Look. Sapphire was kidnapped and taken to Mexico and then

handed on to Gutman. From what Sapphire has told me it seems clear that it was intended she would die, but by some fluke, she didn't. She was abused by Gutman himself and almost certainly also brutally raped by Victor Diaz, a prominent US senator and now putative POTUS. Now, Sapphire is not a great witness when it comes to her original kidnap because she was drugged. But she has given me enough information for me to conclude there was probably a conspiracy between Dante Figueroa and Maria Dinks to carry out the kidnap and bag that $25 million dollar ransom.

'You were there at the Mexico City Fronton fashion show. Maria Dinks is a brick wall and is now positioning herself to get custody of Sapphire if they get her back, and control access to her and will probably prevent her testifying. Classic fox guarding the henhouse. So we're not going to get shit out of Maria, which leaves us with Dante, a senior figure in the Juarez cartel who's protected 24/7. No one's seen him and we don't know where the fuck he is. You getting the picture here, Ruiz?'

'Yeah, I'm getting the picture. You have no evidence whatsoever against Maria or Dante for the kidnap, and without that your client, Yolanda Lopez, stays in jail.'

'Correct.'

'Okay, I can see that, but what I can't see is where Gutman can help. He's after the event. Kidnaps all done. Then they turn to him.'

'How do you know that?'

'Okay, I don't, but it seems a pretty slim chance that he knows anything that will exonerate Yolanda Lopez, and even if he does, he's not going to tell us. Thin stuff for me to risk my life over,' Ruiz said calmly, watching her.

'You still don't get it do you, Ruiz?' she said doggedly. 'It's all interlinked. And it's not just about freeing Yolanda anymore. It's about the Daughter Eaters and Victor Diaz as well, and I'm going to nail them. At the center of all of this, like a big fat fucking spider, sits Solomon Gutiérrez - Gutman, the fat man. All routes lead back to him; he's the key; and he holds the evidence that will unlock it all.'

'You sure about that?' Ruiz said.

'Tell me about Gutman's son, Michael?' she said, lightly, completely throwing Ruiz.

'The boy?' Ruiz said, surprised. 'What about him?'

'Well, I only discovered he had a son today when I got an email from Christoff.'

'He's got a 8 year old kid? So what?' Ruiz said, exasperated she was straying away from the point.

'Well why all the mystery?'

'What mystery?'

'Well you never mentioned Gutman had any family, and the kid seems to be almost kept a secret. What's the story?'

'I don't know what you're talking about. Gutman has an eight-year old son who lives with him out at the ranch? What else d'you want to know about that?' Ruiz said.

'Isn't that a bit odd? And why doesn't he go to school? Did you ever see the kid when you went out there?'

'No, but why would I? It was business. I wouldn't expect to be introduced to his family. He would keep them separate.'

'Come on, Ruiz? What did you hear? This detail of the kid

intrigues me, and I always trust my instincts. They're rarely wrong.'

Ruiz shook his head, still perplexed, but trying to summon up any details he might have heard. He stood up and got the half empty bottle of tequila from the night before and poured them each a shot, handing Pascal hers.

'Okay,' he said, sighing. 'All I heard was the kid was very bright, like some kind of prodigy - he obviously inherited his dad's brains - and he was home tutored. Sol and the kid were apparently inseparable and barely ever left the ranch. Gutman apparently spent a fortune on excavating underneath and building a state-of-the-art basement which is where I think the kid hangs out most of the time. I did hear they had all sorts of tutors in, like for math and computer technology, ferried out there to teach the kid.'

'And you didn't think it was worth telling me?' Pascal asked.

'No, I didn't think it was worth telling you, and I still don't,' Ruiz said, getting frustrated. 'What the fuck can any of that possibly have to do with Gutman's criminal activities and Sapphire's kidnap?'

'I don't know, but I'd sure as hell like to talk to that kid.' she said.

'You're mad.'

'Possibly, but there's a very thin line between that and genius,' she said. 'Could you tap into the vast resources of the DEA and their contacts with the *Federales*, and come up with the architects plans for the basement out at the ranch, and also identify and locate any of these tutors who went out there to teach the kid?'

Ruiz just looked at her, his mouth dropping open. Then he shrugged and knocked back his tequila. 'Forget the *federales*. We ask any questions, Gutman's gonna know within minutes. Forget it.'

'What about DEA?'

'Maybe. I'll have a go and see if I can pick up anything on the street,' he said, his eyes going flat and empty.

'Ruiz, I probably don't have to say this, but you better be damn careful out there.'

You're right. You don't have to say it,' he said, his eyes haunted by demons.

###

As Ruiz left the pension and got into his car a man watched from across the street. As the car pulled away the man raised a cellphone and spoke rapid Spanish.

Dante listened intently as he sipped coffee sitting on a high stool at the bar in Cantina Gold. He thought for a moment, then told the man to stay put and watch the girl but get a tail on Ruiz.

###

O'Hara pretended to listen as Jesse prattled on about 'Nam and the gooks and what a great warrior he'd been in America's forgotten war. O'Hara had ascertained the guy had no transport. He relied for his wheels on another veteran who lived about ten miles away. O'Hara ticked off in his mind the resources available. The old guy had the cheap mobile phone, plenty of food and water, the shotgun and a well cared for hunting rifle. He also had some cans of petrol in the cupboards under the sink

O'Hara sat in a hard wooden chair caressing and cradling the shotgun, admiring its polished stock while Jesse's voice droned on at him from across the table. O'Hara cracked the barrel and checked the load; it looked sweetly packed and ready.

Jesse looked up and seemed to divine the madness in O'Hara's eyes. He began to rise from the chair.

'What's the matter, old timer?' O'Hara said with a grin. 'I thought you were a hero, killing all those gooks in 'Nam?' He laughed as he raised up the barrel on the old guys midriff and pulled both triggers simultaneously. The load riddled Jesse's chest with red, picking him up and throwing him back against the wall cabinet where he half held, then slid down into a crumpled and bloodied smoking heap.

O'Hara leaned back and cracked the barrel again, watching the smoke rise, savoring the kill, then he was up and moving, dragging out Jesse's old army kitbag and chucking in some food and a canteen of water. He finished what he had to do and took the kitbag outside.

When he went back in the smell of petrol was almost overpowering. He flicked a match and dropped it on Jesse's petrol-soaked body and walked out. As he moved, mobile to his ear, he turned to watch the flames build as he asked the FBI to send in a chopper to pick him up and get his location from the mobile signal as he would be moving. As he walked away, he felt a whoosh as the tinder dry petrol soaked shack erupted in a fireball. He didn't look back. He had only one thought in his mind now: find the woman and the kid and kill them both.

###

Sapphire stood at the side of the well, leaning over, looking down into the shadowy depths. It looked as if a bunch of lazy and messy people had been throwing a lot of junk down there as it was chock full of trash. She straightened up and began to wander around the hard-standing area full of a happy kind of exuberance. She loved the place and wanted to make it her own private ranch, but she figured it would take a whole lot of work to make it nice again.

Greyeagle and Sia wandered over to stand with her as they all looked about at their new surroundings. Greyeagle said, 'it's just like I remember it from when I was a kid. Nothings changed.'

'And that's good?' Sia said with cackle. 'Boy this place needs some elbow grease and a year long spring clean.'

'Yeah, well, maybe we should get on with that as I think we may have to stay here for a while,' Greyeagle said. 'I'll see what Courtney says when I speak to her. I've scouted out a couple of the shacks, so let's clean them out, and then we can unload the mules.'

Sapphire skipped away, dust rising from her tracks.

Later they had a picnic lunch out by the well, all sweat stained and covered with dust, beef jerky and water, tasting to Sapphire like the best food she'd ever had.

After a while Greyeagle went and looked down the well. He studied the drop-bucket pole that was still in place running across the opening; it looked sturdy enough although the rope hanging down only extended a few feet and was rotted through.

'Hey, Sapphire, you're smallest,' he called out. 'You fancy dropping down the well to look around? Then we can start hauling the crap outta there?'

'You bet,' she said, already scrambling along the edge.

'Honey, you better be careful,' Sia said.

'Don't worry, Grandma, I'll be fine. I'll go get the rope,' she said trotting off towards the tethered mules.

It took around twenty minutes to get a sling tied around Sapphire and then Greyeagle was gently lowering her, the rope running over the pole. Sapphire wasn't frightened. She felt like she was Alice in Wonderland going down the rabbit hole, just a whole lot slower.

About forty feet down she had to turn on the small torch Greyeagle had given her. Soon she started running into some of the stacked rubbish; fencing poles, wood, brush, tree branches, an old broken saddle and some kind of engine, maybe from a car.

She shouted up to Greyeagle telling him what was down there.

'Okay,' he shouted down. 'Sounds like the engine is the biggest thing. We can haul that out with the mules. I'll have to come down and tie on the rope, so I'll pull you up now, okay?'

When Greyeagle had been down and tied on the ropes to what he believed was an electricity generator, not a car engine, they were ready to start hauling. Greyeagle had placed a blanket over the edge of the wall surrounding the well for the rope to run over, and now he signaled Sia and Sapphire who each held a mule, to start walking them away slowly, whilst he watched over the edge of the well.

They heard a loud crack and then some scraping sounds as the generator slowly began to move. The mules seemed to take the load quite easily. When the generator reached the rim of the wall around the well, Greyeagle had them stop the mules while he tied on another rope to the top of the generator. With one final pull, they rolled it onto the top of the wall, where Greyeagle wedged and tied it fast.

As they all stood looking at it, Sia said, 'these silver mines were played out over a hundred years ago, but this don't look so old?'

'It's not,' Greyeagle said. 'There's evidence around here, if you look hard enough, others have been here over the years, some not so long ago. Probably testing for other natural resources, precious metals.'

'Well can you get it working?' Sapphire asked impatiently.

'I doubt it,' Greyeagle said, running his eye over the rusting, muddy looking hulk of metal. 'But I can take a look later. First we'll clear the rest of the junk out the well. I want to see if there's any water in there.'

###

Pascal sat in the lotus position on the floor, her face blank as her mind drifted, sifting, trying to make order from the chaotic facts that seemed to swirl around the Dinks case. Gutman was the key she knew, but how was she to open the door and get in? A sound broke her out of her reverie, the door opening.

Ruiz came in. He was carrying a grocery bag that clinked, and another man was with him. They both looked a little the worse for wear.

301

'Meet one-time occasional home tutor of Michael Gutierrez,' Ruiz said, gesturing at the man, who was smiling in a rather shy and humble way. 'Ex-professor of math, Roque Garcia.'

Pascal raised an eyebrow, bemused and interested at the same time. She took the man's flaccid hand and shook it whilst she studied him. He was small, a bit wizened, late fifties with stubble that wasn't designer and shortish black hair graying at the temples. His eyes were dark and soulful, but also slightly bloodshot.

Ruiz continued, 'Professor Garcia lost his position at the university last year, and is not doing so well, but he accepted my invitation to come and meet us for a drink, and here we are,' Ruiz said, with a flourish. 'We had a couple of snifters on the way, but I guess a few more tequilas won't hurt, right?'

Garcia nodded enthusiastically, his eyes staying locked on the bottles as Ruiz removed them from the bag.

Pascal said, 'sit down, professor and make yourself comfortable.'

'Ah, thank you, yes,' he said, his first words. His voice was firm, his English virtually perfect, probably educated in the US, Pascal speculated. She could see the cuffs of his shirt were frayed and his jacket shiny from wear, and there were some food stains down the front.

He noticed her look. 'I am sorry my dear,' he said apologetically, 'for the state I'm in. I am currently sleeping in my car.'

Pascal nodded sympathetically. 'Many's the time I've done the same thing,' she said.

Ruiz handed Garcia his drink which he finished in two quick gulps. Ruiz placed the bottle on the table in front of him, and said, 'easier if you help yourself, prof. Save me keep pouring.'

'I'm sorry,' he said again, absently. 'I'm grateful to you, but what is it you wanted to talk about? My fall from grace is directly bound up with the part time job I had tutoring the boy.' He looked hunted for a moment, then added, 'and I really don't want any more trouble than I have already.'

'Look, professor,' Pascal said, 'we've got plenty of food and drink and you can even bed down here for a while if you like. We're not looking for scandal, just information. No one will know, and your name will never be mentioned by us.'

He nodded whilst pouring another drink from the bottle, his hand gently shaking. Pascal clinked her glass against his. '*Salud*!' she said.

He reciprocated, sipped his drink, contented. 'So,' he said, warm alcoholic glow enveloping him. 'What d'you want to know?'

'Why don't you just start at the beginning and tell us how you first got involved in tutoring Michael,' Pascal said. 'We got as long as you need, and plenty of booze.'

He nodded, sipping his drink. 'Well it all started about 18 months ago when I got a call at the university. Would I be interested in tutoring a kid in advanced math, once a week, out in the desert. When they said he was 7 years old I thought they were kidding, but they weren't,' he said, with a kind of surprised look on his face. 'The call was from Gutierrez's assistant, bodyguard or whatever you'd care to call him. Said a car would pick me up and take me out to meet Mr. Gutierrez and the boy. Normally I'd have declined such an invitation, but things hadn't been going so well,' he said, becoming pensive, looking down at his hands and then at the bottle.

Pascal reached out and poured him another.

'You see, I always had a drink problem,' he said, suddenly looking old and tired. 'But kept it pretty much hidden, but then around that time I got passed over again for head of department, and I'd been banking on that extra money, but it never came. So I guess I was ripe for their proposal. So anyway, I went out there and talked.'

'What happened?' Pascal asked.

'Well, they certainly have some set-up out there,' he said, eyes going flat as he remembered, grim smile on his face.

'What d'you mean? It's just a simple ranch isn't it?' Pascal pressed him.

'Well up top it is, but underneath, it's something else. It's not like a basement where you open a door and go down a couple of steps. For this you take a lift, and it goes a way down, don't know how far, but it sure felt like a lot. I don't know if the guy was scared of a nuclear war or whether it was to block eavesdropping. Anyway, that's where Michael lived most of the time and that's where I met them to talk.'

'What happened?' Ruiz asked.

'Well I could tell after about five seconds the kid was a prodigy, gifted at math. He went through my tests like they weren't there, like it was a kind of joke. I hadn't seen that in a kid so young, so I was immediately professionally interested, and I needed the money. He was going to pay me two and a half grand a lesson. They ran me out there and back once a week for just that one two hour lesson. There was nothing in writing, but confidentiality was Gutierrez's main concern. He made it pretty clear that if I ever spoke to anyone or provided any information about anything to do with my connection with him and the boy, the consequences would be, how should I put it, fatal. I had no problem with that, because I had no intention of telling anyone about anything. To me it was just an easy gig for a lot of money and the chance to tutor a potential genius.'

'What did you make of the kid and his father, and the set-up there? It's a little odd, isn't it?' Pascal said.

'Extremely odd,' Garcia said, frowning. 'I always felt the boy was scared of his father, and kind of pretended whenever he was around. And the boy rarely left the basement and as far as I could see, the ranch either. Early on I also got the feeling all the lessons were being taped and filmed, so I was a little circumspect with the kid and just stuck to my brief.'

'Describe the basement,' Pascal said.

'What do you mean? It's a basement.'

'Just describe the layout for me?'

Garcia held her eyes for a moment, thinking she was crazy, then shrugged. 'It's big, but I didn't see much. Lifts are at the back of the house. When you come out of them, the boy has a suite of rooms to the left, including a games room he took me in couple of times, so we could play video games. To the right were more rooms that I never went in, then at the back was a kind of lecture hall where I tutored the boy. And that's it.'

Ruiz interrupted, saying to Pascal, 'it's a dead end on the plans. Got nowhere. Sealed up tighter than a rat's ass, so this is likely all you're gonna get.'

Pascal nodded then turned back to Garcia. 'Why d'you stop

going? Doing the tutoring,' she asked.

He sat for a long moment, then slowly held his glass up. 'This, I suppose. I was worse for wear couple times I went out there. The bodyguard had a word, saying straighten out or they'd get someone else. By then I couldn't straighten out, so they got another guy in. Shortly after, I got terminated at the university - maybe he pulled some strings, I don't know - and now my wife's gone as well.'

He sat staring vacantly down into his empty glass looking intensely sad. 'But the boy, he was something else,' he murmured, almost to himself. 'It wasn't just the intellectual force of his intelligence, he also had a phenomenal memory, like photographic. It's like the guy in the old old movie, "The 39 Steps", Mister Memory Man. That kid could look at a page ten seconds flat, look away, and just recite away verbatim, until the cows come home. I've never seen anything like it. Once his father came down to ask him something. Usually they made me leave the room, but this time he was in a hurry. It was to do with crypto currency, something I know a bit about, but I guess Gutierrez assumed I didn't. He seemed to be asking the boy for the crypto keys for a Bitcoin wallet. Those are usually a long string of encrypted random numbers and letters that give completely secure access to your digital currency funds. The kid just reeled them off like it was a shopping list, and that was five different accounts. Gutierrez typed them into some kind of hand-held device, maybe a hard wallet. Boy, that was some kid,' he finished, awe in his voice.

As Garcia looked up, he caught Pascal and Ruiz looking at each other in a strange way, then they both began to smile.

CHAPTER TWENTY-THREE

Dante seemed to have made Cantina Gold his home for the moment. The place was closed, and he sat hunched on a high stool at the bar drinking coffee and fielding phone calls. As a call came in from Maria, he gestured for Alvaro Chavez to move away, to give him privacy. 'You made quite a splash with the mayor and prosecutor,' he said by way of a greeting.

'Glad you liked it,' she answered, playful laughter in her voice.

'But I have a question for you?'

'Uh-huh?'

'Where's the kid? Without you having custody and control, your strategy is actually quite dangerous,' he said.

'The kid is with her crazy grandmother somewhere on their mangy flea-bitten reservation in New Mexico, where the US Marshall's and FBI are about to run them to ground,' she said confidently.

'You sure about that, because the Pascal women is here in Juarez.'

Maria was silent for a beat. 'Are you sure?'she asked, less confidently,

'Positive. She's hanging out in a cheap pension with the dirty DEA cop, Ruiz, and they're cooking up something. Why else would they be here?' he said.

'What are they doing?'

'Well Ruiz has been asking questions on the street, and they just spoke to a guy who was tutoring Gutman's kid some time ago,' he said, sounding puzzled.

'Gutman's the bozo you subbed this out to, right? The guy who was meant to make her disappear, and yet she's still around, and in a position to fuck us over, right?' she said, unable to keep the anger out of her voice.

'We've been over that,' he said patiently.

She bit back on a caustic response and thought for a moment. Then she said as if musing out loud, 'so it's quite simple really, isn't it?'

'What is?'

'Take them out. You're in Mexico for Christ sakes. Murder capital of the world. They're not gonna miss a few more. Why run any risk when we don't need to? Pascal, Ruiz and Gutman. Can you do it?'

He sipped his coffee, a chilly smile playing on his lips as he wondered at the basic simplicity, and yet quality of her thought processes. Her logic was brutal but impeccable. Gutman was problematic though. Any move against him would have significant consequences locally with the delicate balance of power in play, so a subtle approach would need to be worked out.

'Yes,' he said, 'but I must think on it.'

'Fine,' she said. 'Last question: could the brat be with her in Juarez?'

'No. I'm certain she's not here in Mexico.'

'Must be with Grandma then. I better see what kind of a fire I can light under the US Marshall's service and the Feds. Ciao,' she said, terminating the call.

###

Across town from Dante, about three miles away in another bar, Hector Morales paced up and down in front of his new bodyguard, Pepe. The new man, a replacement for Morales's much lamented chainsaw wielding predecessor, Chico, was a slim giant with eyes as empty as a billy-goats.

As Morales paced a call came in. Cellphone clamped to his ear his eyes lit up as he got news that the woman who had humiliated him and would have killed him as well if he had been in the SUV she hit with the RPG in the park; this Pascal or Hansen or whatever she called herself was back in Juarez. 'And you're sure about this?' he said, speaking quietly, keeping his deadly rage in check.

He listened a spell then said, 'no!' loudly, moving his shoulders in exasperation. 'Don't touch her. Closely observe and find out why she is back here. Then report to me. Is that understood?'

'Good. It had better be,' he said, terminating the call. He stood for a moment savoring the thrill of anticipation at the prospect of having the woman back in his grasp.

###

309

O'Hara sat in a cheap hotel room in Window Rock, Arizona trying to keep his temper in check whilst he spoke to senator Diaz on the phone. 'I take full responsibility, sir. It was my fault. I underestimated her, but that won't happen again.'

'But this isn't the first time, is it, son? That car stop with the DEA should have taught you something about what you're dealing with here. I need to know you're solid. That you won't fail me again,' Diaz said, cranking up the pressure.

O'Hara took a deep breath to try and stop himself from shattering the cellphone in his hand. When he was under control, he said, quietly, 'I won't fail you again, sir. You can depend on it.'

'Good, and I believe you, soldier,' Diaz said, smiling to himself. 'Now, I've got priority clearance for you, direct access to intel coming into the US Marshall's and FBI, and full use of all resources in tracking these felons down. So, son, I'd like to know your thinking about how you propose to locate them and complete the mission?'

O'Hara let his breath out silently. He was still in the loop and ahead of the curve. 'Sir, first I'd like a full background check on the redskin she's running with, this Greyeagle guy. He's the sniper took out two of my men from about a mile away, at night. Shoot like that, he's gotta have been in the services, so I'd like to know who the fuck he is. Excuse me, sir, for the profanity. And especially if he's local as it might give a fix on where they're holed up.'

'No problem, son. You'll have an initial run through within the hour,' Diaz said.

'Thank you, sir. I'd also like access to drones and any satellite imagery we might have spanning out say twenty-five miles from where I was extracted from.'

'You got it. Anything else?'

'That's it for now, sir.'

'Good. I'm relying on you, soldier, so keep me informed.'

An hour later O'Hara sat in a hard chair in his room, laptop open, poring over an initial report on Greyeagle, as well as maps and aerial imagery of the desert area he had just been roaming through.

O'Hara scanned Greyeagle's bio, eyes full of interest. Funnily enough turned out Greyeagle actually was his name; John Greyeagle, currently listed AWOL from Fort Bragg. Guy had crashed out of sniper school and never come back. He'd had a few beefs with officers and other men, insubordination as well as a pretty bad disciplinary record. That was usually a selling point as far as O'Hara was concerned. He preferred guys who tried to fuck the system. Greyeagle was pure bred Navajo, apparently a skilled desert tracker, horse rider and marksman. O'Hara smiled; he liked to test himself against worthy opponents, and this guy was sure as hell that.

But then his thoughts turned to Pascal and Ruiz. He hadn't told anyone they were no longer with Greyeagle and the child, and he wondered where they'd gone. It didn't really matter, because he knew she would return, because, just like for him, the child was the key, the thing at the center of it all. In fact Pascal might already be back with them, and if she wasn't, she soon would be, and he'd be waiting for her.

He studied the aerial photographs and the maps and also a brief historical and geographical report appended to them. Moving between these sources he slowly plotted out positions: Sia's ranch, table rock where Greyeagle had taken his mile long shots, Greyeagle's camp from where he had escaped, the old man's burned out funeral pyre shack, and finally the chopper extraction point where they'd come and picked him up from.

That done he sat sipping scotch, his eyes crawling over the red connecting lines he had drawn on the map, trying to divine a pattern or link between the locations. He shook his head; nothing was coming back at him. He picked up the phone and put in a call. He wanted aerial drone searches carried out immediately. He reeled off the map coordinates. He wanted real-time footage fed back direct to his laptop, and he wanted it now, and if they had any problem with that, they needed to speak to Senator Diaz. At the mention of the name, the guy at the other end turned straight into ass-lick mode; he would arrange it right now.

Then O'Hara hit him with his final request; he needed an experienced Indian tracker, preferably an FBI agent, if they had such a man, or women. He needed that confirmed within the hour and the agent dispatched to him that day, because he needed to get back out in the desert so that he could complete the mission.

The ass-lick said he would get on it that very minute. O'Hara didn't doubt it. He smiled. The chase was on again, and nothing gave him a bigger kick than that, and what lay beyond it.

###

Sia and Sapphire stood some way off watching Greyeagle light a piece of paper and put it to the base of the pile of rubbish they had just removed from the well. The contents of an old can of kerosene they'd found helped and now the blue and orange flames were climbing through the pile of junk, crackling and spitting, smoke spiraling into the sky.

As Greyeagle wandered over to stand with Sia and Sapphire his burner buzzed. He clapped it to his ear. 'Hey, Courtney,' he said. He listened intently nodding his head a couple of times.

When he finished the call, Sapphire asked anxiously, 'what she say?'

'She said we're good to stay here for now and we should make ourselves at home but stay well hidden.'

'Is she coming?' Sapphire asked hopefully.

'When she's done what she's gotta do, she'll be here. She asked after you,' he said solemnly. 'Wanted to know you were okay, and I said you were, that you'd cleaned out the well, and she was pleased.'

'What else did she say?' Sia asked him, 'cause you're starting to look a might flustered to me.'

Greyeagle grinned unconvincingly. 'She said we should watch out because she'd just heard that O'Hara had made it back out of the desert, and now they would be coming looking for us in numbers with all the resources of the FBI.'

'So I guess making this big fire is not such a smart move, right?' Sapphire said

'Too late now,' Sia cackled, the fire reflecting back in her eyes.

'It'll take 'em a little while to organize,' Greyeagle said. 'But from now on, no more big fires.'

'So what should we do, Greyeagle?' Sapphire asked.

'What we've been doing. Blend into the desert, stay low during the day and be watchful all the time. I'm going to set up some surprises for them when they come, and they will come,' he said, ominously.

'Can I help?' Sapphire asked.

'Tell you what,' he said. 'Have a climb down the well, now it's clear, and have a look. Check if there's any real water down there.'

She trotted off, pleased to have something to do.

'What about me?' Sia asked.

Greyeagle looked up at the rock face against which their wooden shacks were set, his eyes hooded. 'If you can find a way, without breaking your neck, to get up top, it might give us a real good eye view of anyone coming in,' he said.

She nodded, eying up the imposing rock wall. 'I did some climbing once, out in Colorado, and I loved it,' she said. 'But, man, that was a long time ago.'

As she marched off towards the rock slope, Sapphire climbed over the edge of the well. They had fashioned a thick rope with large knots in it for hand holds and it was quite easy for her because of her light weight to clamber up and down.

She checked for the torch in her pocket and began her descent. Near the bottom there was a kind of shelf or ledge they had stood on to rope stuff up, and now she alighted from the rope there. She took out the torch and played it over her surroundings. Looking down she could see still black water. She picked up a handful of gravel and dropped it down, hearing it plop. She lay down on the ledge to get a closer look and try and judge the distance to the water.

It was difficult for her to get a true perspective and judge the distance to the water. She lent out as far as she could over the edge of the ledge, playing her torch all around. As she brought the beam back towards her, leaning over the edge, she played the beam under the rim, and was surprised to see there was no wall under the ledge; it looked like there was an opening there. She felt excitement stir; she'd always loved stories with hidden rooms and tunnels and now maybe she'd found one. She giggled happily, starting when the sound echoed back at her.

She didn't want to disturb the others, and it would be good to surprise them if she found something. She figured if she could hang down over the edge of the ledge, she could swing herself into the opening below and then go exploring, and wouldn't that be cool.

Just as she was about to climb out over the edge, she heard Greyeagle's voice booming down from above asking her to come up and help with something. She sighed and pulled herself back from the edge. She'd have to come back and continue exploring later. She reached for the rope and began climbing back up to the top.

###

Pascal snapped off her cellphone and looked across the table at Ruiz as he dug plastic chopsticks into a carton of Chinese takeaway. 'Greyeagle and the team are primed,' she said. 'Anyone comes looking they'll be hard to find but ready.'

'Where are they,' Ruiz asked through a mouthful of chicken chow mien.

Pascal watched him for a moment, her eyes guarded.

'Hey, if you don't trust me by now, we're gonna be in real trouble when we go after Gutman,' he said

'Where's my Chinese?' she said, looking around the room.

He pointed with chopstick at a large red carton sitting on the sideboard. She jumped up, grabbed it and tore it open. 'God I'm hungry,' she said, raising a large mound of steaming noodles to her mouth. She looked back at him, talking through it, and said, 'they're out in an old worked out silver mine miles from anywhere. Greyeagle apparently knew it from when he was a kid.'

'Sounds good,' Ruiz said. 'You tell 'em O'Hara's coming, and he won't give up? Especially after Greyeagle took out two of his boys with shooting like a Navy SEALS wet dream.'

'Thanks for that, Ruiz,' she said, deadpan.

'Hell, I'm just telling it like it is.'

'I know,' she said, concern etched into her eyes. 'Which is why we need to finish it here with Gutman and get back there before O'Hara, the US Marshall's or the fucking media get anywhere near them. Then I'll take Sapphire in, my way.'

Ruiz nodded. 'So what's the plan for Gutman?' he asked, loudly crunching through a prawn cracker.

'Well first, Ruiz,' she said, tossing her empty carton into the waste bin and turning to look at him meaningfully. 'I need you to give me a pro's rundown on Gutman's security set-up at the ranch. You went out there, what? Twice? So, what will we have to get past?'

She could see Ruiz was about to protest, but then he thought better of it, satisfying himself with the merest of shrugs. 'I'm not going to say you're fucking crazy again, but I think you know where I'm coming from,' he said mildly. 'So, okay, hot shot, you got one track going in through the desert. They got irregular patrols going out randomly, sometimes drones as well, I heard. Surrounding the ranch itself you got state of the art fencing designed to be unobtrusive, but bristling with security features; the guys super paranoid so what d'you expect?

'Then you got the usual security hub, manned by probably one guy, at the back of the house in the service area, which is where Garcia said the lifts are for the basement. This hub is manned 24/7, monitoring CCTV feeds and he controls all ranch security from there. On the CCTV, I only saw cameras outside, none in the house itself, although that doesn't mean there aren't any.'

Ruiz got up and selected a fresh bottle of Tequila from the sideboard, cracked the top, grabbed two glasses and poured them a couple. As he handed off Pascal's, she kept her eyes focused on him.

He sat down again and took a shot. 'I reckon there's probably four guys in the house at any one time who are specifically tasked with protecting Gutman and the boy. And that includes the guy sitting in the security hub. Now the actual ranch compound itself is big,' he said, reaching under his chair and pulling out a large A3 size piece of paper. 'As you asked, I've done a rough sketch from memory,' he said, spreading the paper out on the coffee table.

Pascal leaned over, engrossed. 'So you're not just a waste a space then, Ruiz?' she muttered.

He ignored her. 'You need to understand that it's actually a working ranch as well as being his base. I think he genuinely likes the outdoors, and they keep horses and some cattle. So over here,' he said pointing at has sketch plan. 'You have a large corral usually with horses in and here is the mess cabin where he's got guys, would you believe, who are actually real cowboys, but double as security. There's probably five, six of them at any one time, and then probably eight who live in a wing of the house, and these eight are the two double shifts of four who man the house. These guys in the house are his inner circle, protectors, and they are tough Hombre's. Guys he grew up with and learned to control when they were part of street drug gangs drifting between Sinaloa, Juarez and their offshoots.'

He sipped his drink and raised his eyes to hers. 'You still think you can just waltz in there and have a friendly chat with him?'

'Nope. But *we* can,' she said.

He nodded, defeated. 'So how we gonna do it?'

CHAPTER TWENTY-FOUR

They sat around the small fire on the hard-standing area outside of the wooden shacks. Greyeagle had snared another wild turkey in a string trap and they were eating it out of an old black pot Sia had found.

'Will you teach me how to cook one day, grandma?' Sapphire asked, burping contentedly and giggling.

'Maybe when you've learned some table manners I will,' she replied.

Greyeagle lay silent beside Sapphire. He was looking up at the night sky at the never ending galaxy of stars stretching away to eternity. He felt good, better than he had for years, out here in the wilderness with these two uncommon people.

'What deep thoughts are you thinking, Greyeagle?' Sapphire asked, breaking in on his reverie.

'I was thinking about our people, and the past,' he said quietly, his voice tinged with sadness. 'I wish I had been born maybe three hundred years ago, when our people ruled the desert and the plains.'

'You know,' Sia said. 'I used to think like that, but as you get older you realize you can't go back. That it's foolish to live in, or for the past.'

'I know that,' he said softly. 'I suppose it's the injustice of what was done to us that I can't get away from. It somehow keeps dragging me back. They made us foolish with drink, tricked us, took our lands and killed us. In the end, they took it all. And now? What? Living on the margins, dying of alcohol, drugs or hypothermia before you hit thirty. Some future.'

'Such despair, Greyeagle,' Sia said, compassion in her voice. 'It's not all so bleak. We are fighting back in Gallup and we are making progress. And what about the mid-terms? There are now two. That's right, two, elected native American congresswomen,' she said with pride in her voice. 'And one of them is the representative for New Mexico, our state. So how about that for progress?'

Greyeagle was silent so Sapphire chipped in, slowly, with a kind of question mark in her voice, 'Mama never looked back, did she, Grandma?'

Sia sighed, her face registering some pain in the moons glow, the firelight flickering in her eyes. 'No,' she said, gently. 'No. Your Mama never looked back, only forwards.'

'What was she like, Grandma? I hardly remember her now. I mean, I do remember her, but it's like old film in my head; its faded.'

'She was a lot like you, you know,' Sia said with a smile. 'Quick and clever. Very inquisitive about the world around her. And she'd argue with you until the sun came down if she believed in something. And she could ride like the wind. Never saw someone who could handle a horse like her. She was my only child, and when she died of the brain tumor I wanted to die also for a while. But I knew I had you and you would come back to me someday.'

'What happened to you, Sapphire?' Greyeagle asked quietly from the shadows, giving her a start. 'I mean, no one's told me exactly what happened, what was done to you?'

Sia looked quickly over at the young girl, ready to intervene, but she looked calm, unperturbed, and maybe it was time to try and lay some ghosts to rest.

'I was taken to Mexico and hurt by a man there,' she said simply.

For a long while no one spoke. The fire crackled and the moon and stars glimmered down on the small group, each person wrapped up in their own thoughts.

Sapphire broke the silence, speaking quietly. 'But Tilly-May was my friend there. She saved me in the end. She was the bravest person I ever knew. She saved me, because she got Courtney, but we couldn't save her,' Sapphire said, and then she began to cry quietly and Sia was up and over, embracing her as she wept. Sapphire said, stuttering through her tears, into Sia's breast, 'I don't want to go back to New York, Grandma. I want to stay here with you, and, and with Greyeagle, out in the desert.'

Sia hugged her tight, whispering that she would never let her go. As she looked over Sapphire's shoulder, she met Greyeagle's eyes, unreadable in the moonlight, but she sensed apprehension. Sapphire was thinking way too far ahead. First they would have to survive the onslaught that would surely come.

###

Pascal and Ruiz had been throwing it around for an hour or so without getting anywhere. Pascal went and stood at the window and looked out at the back-alley, still awash with dirty streams of effluent. 'Okay,' she said, turning back into the room, tired from all the back and forth. 'I agree, we can't go in full frontal, so you're going to have to get us in.'

'Fuck,' he said exhaling, and rubbing his face. 'How? What do I say?'

Pascal sat down opposite him. 'Tell him,' she started, stopped, then started again. 'Tell him that you've been on an unrelated DEA operation with a lock-down. So you couldn't contact him. The bait is, you got a line on me, I'm back in Mexico with the kid. You can take us both down right now, but need to see him personally first. He'll have seen all the media, so he's gonna bite, no question. You can pad it, say the Feds put out a false story in the media about our whereabouts to try and trick everyone.'

'So, say we get in, which, by the way, is one helluva long shot,' Ruiz said. 'What we looking for?'

'Why d'you smile when Professor Garcia told us about the incident between Gutman and his son?' she asked him.

'You smiled too. Great minds?' he quipped back.'

'The kid is his record keeper, right? You said yourself, Gutman's more paranoid than the crazy bat-shit guy in the movie, Treasures of the Sierra Madre. The guy thinks everyone's trying to steal his treasure. So what does he do? He hides it. And that's what I think Gutman's done, but his treasure is information, and he's hiding it in plain sight.'

'Yeah, maybe. But that's just a theory, and you'll have a helluva time trying to prove it even if we manage to get in. I mean, where do you start?'

'With the kid. Look Ruiz, we can keep kicking this around until the world freezes over but it won't get any easier. Let's just do it, because we, and Sapphire, are running out of time.'

Ruiz nodded, not entirely convinced by her arguments, but knowing there was nowhere else to go. 'And if he bites, how do we go in?'

'You got such a thing as a chop-shop around here? Place where I can get an SUV carved up and customized?'

'Sure we have. What d'you have in mind?' he asked.

O'Hara watched the drone footage coming in on his laptop. He'd smiled when he'd seen the old man's burnt out shack, but now his eyes were starting to hurt from looking at the screen. It was just endless shitty desert with hills and cactuses. It was like searching for a nigger in a black-out, and with the redskin's savvy, maybe he'd have to find another way.

He got up, grabbed a bottle of water and went back to the maps, poring over them again, tracing with his eyes the red lines he'd drawn connecting up the locations. His phone buzzed; the ass-lick from the field office.

'Sir, we got three possible locations based on this Greyeagle's background,' he said.

'Have we got pictures? Done any flyovers?' O'Hara queried.

'Affirmative, sir. Got some stills and the drones are on their way to all three as we speak.'

'Okay, good,' O'Hara said. 'Give me the details and coordinates.'

'Roger that sir,' he said. 'Locations are all old mines. Two are coal and one is silver. And sir, I'd just repeat, they're only at this stage suggested search areas. We got nothing solid on any of them.'

'I know that, fuck-head,' O'Hara said, flaring up. 'Just give me the coordinates.'

The grunt reeled them off then added, 'and, sir, we have an FBI tracker for you, name of Dawson Creedwell, on his way to you now.'

'Good. ETA?'

'About an hour.'

O'Hara snapped his phone off and went back to the maps. He traced out the three locations the ass-lick had given him, adding in his red lines. He turned to the laptop and booted up pictures of all three, slowly scrolling through, eyes crawling over the detail. He went back to the maps and looked again at the three locations. The red lines he had marked out now made the shape of a triangle, situated just above the location of the old tent camp he had escaped from. To the left he marked the first coal mine, "A", then the silver mine at the apex of the triangle, "B", and finally the third location, as coal mine "C". A was nearest and B furtherest.

O'Hara got up, humming to himself the old Jacksons song, "it's easy as a b c". For a moment he was transformed, dancing Michael

Jackson moves he remembered from his youth, segueing into a moonwalk across the polished parquet floor. The buzzer broke in on him, a guy looking at him around the edge of the door, smiling.

O'Hara straightened up stone-faced; embarrassment wasn't an emotion he suffered from. 'Who invited you in?' he asked.

'Sorry. I'm agent Creedwell, sent down to meet with you. I'm the tracker.'

O'Hara sized him up, then jerked his head, inviting him to step inside.

Guy looked solid; 6-foot-tall and trim, brown skin, brown eyes and a buzz-cut. O'Hara led him over to the table and the laptop and maps. 'Guy we're hunting is a John Greyeagle, a Navajo, ex-military, clever and resourceful. He knows the area backwards, but he's got a child and her grandmother with him. Sit down here and have a look at what I've got, pictures, maps, bio and Intel. Then talk to me.'

'Sir,' the guy said and sat right down, started looking straightaway.

O'Hara nodded and stepped away. The guy would do. Made a change for the FBI to send him someone functional, who wasn't a complete moron.

###

They stood in shadow from the rock face, shielded from the sun, watching as Greyeagle sharpened a huge hunting knife on the edge of a stone. Laid out on a blanket before him were his sniper rifle, a conventional hunting rifle, a handgun, a knife and a longbow with arrows. Earlier Greyeagle had patiently been trying to train them to use all the weapons, explaining how they worked, techniques in their use, loading and firing.

Sapphire was mesmerized and had been for the last two hours, despite having found the rifles almost too big to handle. For Sia it was easy as she had hunted from an early age. The bow was the most difficult. Sapphire had a very good eye, but found it hard to pull back the string, but she was determined to keep at it.

They all sensed something at the same time, Greyeagle dropping the knife and holding his hand up for silence. He motioned them to hunker down under cover and he moved to the edge of the shadowed rock face, peeping out around it and upwards. His eyes scanned the sky instantly locating the source of the faraway noise, a tiny speck.

He raised the powerful binoculars and watched for a while then moved back into the shadows. They watched him, waiting for him to speak 'It's a drone; looks military. Its hunting us,' he said simply.

'Did it see us?' Sapphire asked.

'Maybe. I don't know,' he said calmly. 'But it does mean they've whittled down the places where we might be. So they'll be back, soon, probably on horseback.'

'What do we do?' Sia asked

'We carry on making preparations,' he said. 'Incidentally, what's it like up top?' he said nodding at the towering rock face.

'It's actually great up there,' Sia said. 'You've got a couple of secluded spots with a fantastic view all around. Anybody trying to sneak in, you'd see them from miles away.'

'Unless they come at night,' Sapphire said.

Greyeagle looked at the girl with amusement. She was dressed in light fatigues and had brush for camouflage around her head, face colored brown from desert sand she'd wet and rubbed into it. She seemed a natural and had earlier helped him set up some basic man traps leading into the camp. Rope nooses tied to bent down tree branches, that would pull an unwary approacher up into the sky. They would dig some pits as well when it got dark and put some sharpened wooden stakes in them.

'Come on,' he said. 'Lets you have another go with the bow.'

She smiled and raced over to pick it up. They moved away to a range Greyeagle had set up. As Sia watched them she noticed Greyeagle's cheap burner dancing on the sand where he'd left it. She picked up and answered. It was Courtney. Sia raised her hand and beckoned Greyeagle, Courtney saying they mustn't keep the connection open, in case of tracking, but how was Sia and Sapphire?

'We're fine, thank you, Courtney, in the circumstances,' Sia said. Then in a sort of embarrassed rush, she added, in a lowered voice as if scared of being overheard, 'Courtney, I know this may sound ridiculous given what's going on and the fact that we may not get out of this…..

'What, Sia?' Courtney asked impatiently.

'A perhaps silly question for your lawyer man, could I apply for custody of Sapphire, if we get out of here?'

Pascal couldn't help laughing despite everything. 'Wow, what an idea, and while all this is going on. I'll ask him. Now, give me Greyeagle.'

When she had Greyeagle Pascal told him they were about to go into the darkness and try and get the guy who was at the heart of it all. It was going to be dangerous and she might not come out of it. If she did, she would come straight there. If not, he was on his own. She gave him contact details for Christoff and detective Daly of NYPD. She wished them all good luck and then she was gone.

###

As Pascal snapped her phone off still absently thinking about Sia's custody plan, Ruiz came back. He had a big black canvas sports bag that he dumped in the middle of the floor.

'We're in,' he said with a grim smile. 'Eight o clock tonight at the ranch.'

'How'd he sound?' Pascal asked

'Nervous, which is highly unusual for him; he doesn't like using phones, so he kept it short. Just said to come out at eight as he wants things sorted.'

'Okay, good,' she said. 'What about the wheels?'

'Outside.'

She checked her watch. It was 5.30 p m. 'How far's the ranch?'

'About twenty miles. Take us less than half hour to get there,' he said. He moved over to the sports bag and started removing items from it. 'Sourced off the street,' he said handing her a Glock automatic pistol and continuing to take out boxes of ammunition.

As she checked the action on the Glock her burner was buzzing and dancing on the table. 'Christoff,' she said as she placed it to her ear, 'what you got?'

'Very little, I'm afraid,' he said. 'Only additional titbit I have managed to glean from records that have clearly been sanitized is that Michael Gutierrez's mother was a US citizen who died soon after his birth, and that's it.'

'That's good. I had a feeling you wouldn't find much,' she said. 'Can you meet up with Calver. I don't think the FBI will be busting his balls anymore, now it's all out there over the media, so it should be okay. Couple of things,' she said.

After she finished outlining what she wanted Christoff chuckled softly over the connection. 'That should please Maria Dinks.' he said.

She checked her watch again. 'Christoff, we're going in tonight. I'll be in touch.'

'Stay safe,' he said.

'Always.'

She clicked off the phone.

CHAPTER TWENTY-FIVE

The SUV powered them along the desert track road, swirls of dust rising up around their wheels. Above them the starlit night seemed serene, the hills a smudge of shadow to the west, and in between the valley floor stretched away for miles.

The couple in the vehicle looked incongruous: Pascal in black combat fatigues, belt with knife and Glock, woolly hat pulled down and blacked-up face; Ruiz smart looking in a loose-fitting black suit, Italian silk tie and pale yellow shirt.

He said, 'we're getting close now, where the patrols come out.'

'Pull over,' she said.

A moment later Ruiz swerved into a natural rock alcove at the road side. They sat for a moment, engine off, ticking metal sounds and cicada's in the background. He pulled out a hip-flask, took a long drag, then held his hand out in front of him to see if it was shaking. He laughed nervously. 'Must be getting old,' he said. 'Never used to get nervous.'

'Nerves are good. They heighten perception,' she replied. She held her hand out and he passed her the hip-flask. She took a short nip and turned to look at him. 'I'm taking a risk trusting you, and I think you know that.'

He started to speak, and she held her hand up. 'Don't say anything, Fernando. This is crunch time. You've done a lot of bad things, so this is a chance to kick back the other way. Everyone. Everyone, even the worst of the worst, can have redemption. Otherwise what's the point?'

His expression looked haunted for a fleeting moment. He looked away out into the desert as if he were about to say something, but no words came.

'Some speech, huh?' she muttered. 'Okay, let's get to it.'

They both got out the vehicle, Ruiz holding a flashlight and carrying some thin cord. Pascal lay down on the ground whilst Ruiz shone the light underneath. He said, 'they had it up on the ramp in the chop-shop, and they got your measurements perfect. They've raised the chassis and wheel ground clearance, so you won't get your ass burned,' he added with a laugh.

Pascal rolled underneath and Ruiz passed her the flashlight. Ten minutes later they had her secured. Ruiz crouched down and looked at her. 'They've never looked underneath before, the times I've come out, and I don't think they'll start now,' he said. 'As I said, we'll stop and they'll search the vehicle and then I'll go park it round back, and they'll escort me in the building. Then it's down to you, and I guess we'll have to play it by ear. Good luck.'

As they'd agreed, Ruiz took the last few miles sedately, under thirty, until he got in sight of the ranch and then he speeded up, but by then the road surface was tarmac. Underneath, Pascal was securely fastened in place with cord, and foot and hand grips. The journey went uneventfully, apart from the dust clogging up her face and nose. She should have worn a face mask but managed to pull the woolly hat down over her mouth.

Then the vehicle was slowing and coming to a halt. She remembered from before, there was a kind of sentry box with a couple of guys and a barrier, and that was where they stopped. There was some Spanish banter as the vehicle lifted up and Ruiz got out. They began searching. She heard the rear hatch opening, more rummaging sounds, the passenger door, glove box, and rear passenger doors. All the time there was a kind of complaining banter from the searcher.

She heard sounds of other footsteps approaching, turning her head to watch. The walker came to a halt a meter from her. 'How you bin, Ruiz?' the guy asked.

'Good, apart from this fucking leg. It's killing me, man,' Ruiz said, and she could sense the tension in his voice. She hoped they wouldn't notice.'Hope you're not bringing a bomb in here?' the guy said, laughing. 'Maybe we better take a look underneath,' he added, starting to stoop down, but as he did so there was a shout from the house.

'Seems like the boss is anxious to see you, Ruiz,' he said, straightening up. Underneath the vehicle Pascal let out a long silent exhalation of breath.

Ruiz got back in, started the engine and they were moving again. The vehicle swung in a wide arc before coming to a halt again. As Ruiz got out there was a man each side to greet him.

One said, 'come on, we'll search you up at the house.'

They moved away leaving Pascal strapped underneath trying to get her breathing back under control. She drew her aching hands off the grips and sagged down in the rope sling.

###

Ruiz stood outside on the porch as the guy expertly patted him down. He glanced over at the SUV, thinking about the girl hanging underneath, and already the doubt was beginning to crowd in on his mind. He took a look around the place, the security and the men ranged against them, and he just knew. Knew for certain the whole plan was a crock - cuckoo shit and didn't stand a chance. He knew he didn't want to die. And why should he? Why the fuck should he risk his life just 'cause she was crazy? Already his mind was working angles. But the girl trusted him? She was relying on him, believed he'd turned a moral corner; maybe more fool her.

They led him into the house and on into the large living room. Gutiérrez was standing near the French windows that looked out on the front area of fountains and garden. He was dressed in a cavernous white suit and he was reading a sheaf of papers, but he looked up as Ruiz approached. He put the papers aside and held his arms out. 'Fernando, my friend, you have come back to me,' he said pulling Ruiz into a bear hug. 'Let me look at you,' he said, stepping back and running his eyes over him.

'Hey, Sol. How you doing?' Ruiz said, trying to keep the tension out of his voice.

'I am good, but your leg, my friend, it looks not so bad, eh?' he said, solicitous. 'It was fortunate my doctor was here so quick to attend to it, no? In gratitude for your return I have laid on dinner, in your honor. Steaks from my pure bred Mexican Longhorns. Come, the table is prepared,' he said with a clap of his hands.

They moved through to the dining room where a table was laid; silver cutlery, napkins and crystal glasses. A waiter in livery immediately approached as they seated themselves.

'A drink first my friend before we eat?'

'Scotch,' Ruiz said, eying the waiter. 'Make it a double.'

The waiter moved to the side of the room to mix the drinks

'So, Fernando. Tell me what happened?' Gutiérrez said, his voice subtly different, probing, with a hint of impatience. 'We have all seen the news. The child lives, soon to be apprehended in the New Mexico desert, if they are to be believed. And the woman, this Hansen, or is it, Pascal? You hinted you knew her whereabouts?'

Ruiz kicked back the scotch and held his glass out for another, trying to avoid showing the shakes in his hand. Gutiérrez sipped a glass of water, his eyes hard. He continued. 'You were about to apprehend the woman and child. At the border south of El Paso, and then I hear, what? Nothing,' Gutiérrez said, sounding as if he was trying to understand. 'You don't contact me? What am I supposed to think? Why did you disappear? If I didn't know you better,' he said, a conspiratorial look coming into his glassy eyes, 'I might have thought you were thinking of betraying me, turning on me, the one who has rewarded you so richly?'

'No, Sol. Never. You've got it all wrong, man,' Ruiz said voice still calm but an edge of fear creeping in, making his words come quicker. 'I was embarrassed at fucking up, didn't want to disappoint you because the stop went bad, and then the DEA took me away on an operation I couldn't get out of. I was waiting for a chance of recovering everything. Then I was going to come back to you, problem solved,' he said.

Gutiérrez held Ruiz's eyes. 'At this border stop she outsmarted you again, didn't she, but this time it wasn't just you, was it?' he said, voice accusatory. 'Now it's the FBI and US Marshall's, making it infinitely more dangerous for me, and now the whole world knows. How long before the heat starts getting back to me, Fernando?'

Ruiz looked down at the table. 'I don't know what to say, Sol, other than I am sorry,' he said. 'But I am here now with perhaps a way to recover the situation.'

As Gutiérrez studied him, the door opened and the waiter wheeled in a trolley laden with silver dishes. Gutiérrez clapped his hands again and smiled. He licked his lips, watching as the waiter removed the lids from the various dishes and offered them up for his inspection.

'Come, let us eat,' he said. 'We will continue our talk whilst sampling some of the finest beef in all of Mexico.' He turned to the waiter, 'and, Pepe, bring us the bottle of Chateau Lafite set aside for this very occasion. Good food and fine wines, Fernando,' he said, nodding sagely at Ruiz, 'will assist us in our deliberations of how you can redeem yourself and recover the situation to my advantage.'

Ruiz wasn't hungry. He toyed with the massive bloody steak that hung over the edges of his dinner plate, whilst Gutiérrez ate noisily, his mouth soon coated with blood and grease.

'You indicated,' Gutiérrez said between mouthfuls, 'you had a line on the woman? Yes?'

Ruiz looked around the room. It was decorated like an old-style hacienda, perhaps like they were back in the 1920's. There were two large wall cabinets of ornately carved wood, and old oils of forgotten wars on the walls, as well as stuffed animal heads. Ruiz felt trapped and scared as he glanced around, like one of the animals looking down on him from the wall. His natural inclination was always to take the easy way out, to lie, betray or run. It had always worked in the past, but then the day Tilly-May had jumped over the balcony he thought he had felt something change. And then Pascal had trusted him, and he couldn't understand why. He would never have trusted anyone with a track record like his.

All these thoughts passed through his mind in a heartbeat. He looked up and considered Gutiérrez, avidly carving away at a large slab of bloody steak and lifting it to his mouth, savoring the taste and texture as he chewed on it, then raising his eyes, fixing them back on Ruiz, waiting for an answer.

Ruiz swallowed his bile. He was never going to change. Couldn't he feel it deep inside? He looked at Gutiérrez, heart in mouth, and said, 'she's here.'

###

Pascal cut through the cords securing her to the chassis and silently lowered herself onto the hard-packed earth. She lay there for a few

336

moments turning her head, listening and looking around. It was silent, quiet as a tomb. She rolled onto her side, getting a closer look at the approach to the building. Ruiz had warned her any CCTV was outside, and now she checked carefully for cameras.

There appeared to be one trained on the center of the parking area, and Ruiz had parked right at the edge, possibly because he knew of the camera. Even though she was hyper with adrenaline she couldn't seem to stop her mind drifting and unerringly fastening on the issue she couldn't get away from: her judgment in trusting Ruiz. She'd trusted him once before, turned her back on him and he'd struck like a rattler, and Till-|May had died. He was weak, she knew, and if Gutiérrez threatened him, he'd fold like a hand of cards. Fuck it she thought. It was too late to worry now, best just get on with it.

She rolled out from under the car and slowly began to crawl towards a shadowed area at the side of the porch where the entry door to the house was.

###

'Here?' Gutiérrez said, incredulous, alarm and confusion in his eyes, slab of bloody meat hanging from his fork.

'Yeah, here in Mexico. In Juarez,' Ruiz said, letting out a long exhalation of breath. Okay, he wouldn't give her up, yet.

'Is the child with her?' Gutiérrez asked, his voice shrill.

'Yes.'

Gutiérrez started eating again. 'So why is she here in Mexico?

And why do the media and FBI say she is in the USA?' he asked.

Ruiz began to cut away at a piece of steak just to be doing something. They'd never got this far in their gaming strategies; what he should say if asked such a question. Now he'd have to improvise. He checked his watch, wondering where the hell she was.

Gutiérrez's eyes narrowed. 'You waiting for something, my friend? Or you have another more important appointment somewhere else?' he said, voice silky, insinuating.

'Not at all, Sol,' he answered, smiling. 'Just didn't expect you to invite me to stay for dinner, is all.'

'Well, Fernando, I'm going to go one better. I'm going to extend my hospitality and insist you stay the night as my guest. We have much to talk about, and I am sure you wouldn't wish to insult me by trying to refuse, no?' he asked, and there was no hiding the implication in his words.

Ruiz hesitated, but it was clear they weren't going to let him leave consensually. He held his empty glass out and Pepe immediately moved to refill it. 'Thank you, Sol. I'm happy to stay and talk,' he said, cursing inside. Now what?

'Good. I have a business meeting later tonight with another visitor when you may retire to the guest rooms. But now,' he said abruptly, 'I would like you to answer my earlier question. The one posed before you started to so nervously check your watch.'

'She wants a deal with you,' Ruiz said, calm now he had decided on a way forward. He sipped the Chateau Lafite enjoying the flavor, his heavy alcohol intake starting to take the edge off his nerves.

'A deal?' Gutiérrez repeated wonderingly. 'She has balls, this

Chiquita, I will give her that. Leaving aside for a moment her weak bargaining position - if she is here I am sure I could have her picked up this very evening - what is it that she has to deal?'

'Silence.'

Gutiérrez laughed, then said, 'go on.'

'She's not interested in you, Sol. To her, you were a handler, after the event. She wants the kidnappers, evidence to nail them down in a US court. She thinks you can provide it. For that, you'd get silence about your role in all of this,' Ruiz said.

Gutiérrez leaned his considerable girth back in his chair and muttered something to Pepe who immediately brought over a humidor. Gutiérrez selected a large cigar and carefully cut the end and waited as Pepe lit it. He re-positioned himself in his chair, drawing on the cigar hungrily, taking it out of his mouth and looking at the burning tip before placing his eyes deliberately back on Ruiz.

'Maybe if she could guarantee such a thing - silence - we might have something to talk about.'

'She thinks she can. She believes she will be able to control access to the child by law enforcement, such as questioning. Also the issue of whether the child would testify at any trial or retrial,' he said. He knew that didn't sound so hot, enticing, but the fat man was still listening.

'That is no guarantee, but I must think on it,' he said, watching the smoke spiral up from his cigar.

Ruiz felt calmer now as he watched Gutiérrez through the hazy cigar smoke. And now the red wine was mixing with the scotch and feeding through his stomach lining in a powerful cocktail making him lose his sense of caution. 'How's your son, Michael?' he asked casually.

In Window Rock, Arizona, O'Hara pulled a Bud from the hotel mini bar and handed it to Dawson Creedwell, the Indian tracker. 'So what d'you think?' he said.

'No thank you, sir, I don't,' Creedwell said, handing the bottle back to O'Hara who immediately put it to his lips.

Creedwell looked out of the hotel window at the setting sun then back at the maps and aerial photographs strewn across the desk. 'It's too late to organize anything today,' he said, 'but in the morning I'd take another look at point "B" on your map, the old silver mine. Maybe send another drone up for a closer look.'

'Why the silver mine and not the other two?' O'Hara asked, sipping the Bud.

'The drone images suggest there's been some recent activity there; small earth movements, subtle changes to the landscape when compared to earlier satellite images. Also, sir, Greyeagle's bio suggests a connection to the site; his family resided not far from there when he was an adolescent.'

'Good work, Tonto,' O'Hara said, slapping him on the back.

Creedwell didn't smile.

'Hey, don't mind me,' O'Hara said. 'No offense intended.'

'None taken. I been getting that shit all my life, especially from redneck assholes.'

'Hey, lighten up, chief,' O'Hara said, playfully slapping him in the face.

Creedwell didn't move a muscle.

O'Hara smiled, moving over to study the maps. 'Okay, Creedwell,' he said, serious again. 'Say the drone comes back positive tomorrow. How would you approach the mine? How would you go in?'

'Well, not in a helicopter, that's for sure,' he said smiling thinly. 'In that still desert air they'd hear you coming from miles away. One thing's for sure, they'll be waiting for you and they'll have prepared some surprises, because that's what I would do.'

'Yeah, but it's one guy with an old lady and a kid,' O'Hara said, oozing confidence. 'What can they do against the team we'll be fielding?'

'You'd do well not to underestimate this guy. That's his country out there, even with the women along, and as they're native American, they're not going to be bystanders. They'll fight as well.'

'A kid and an old lady,' O'Hara said, laughing. 'You're kidding me, right?'

Creedwell's face suggested he wasn't kidding him at all.

'Okay, I got it,' O'Hara said. 'I get it and I got it - no chopper. So how do we go in?'

'We go in on horseback, at night, six men tops, with back-up in reserve not too far behind.'

CHAPTER TWENTY-SIX

'Why your sudden uncharacteristic interest in my family, my son, Fernando?' Gutiérrez asked, his brow furrowed, eyes suspicious. 'You know,' he added, contemplative. 'I have sensed a change in you, and it worries me greatly.'

'I'm the same as ever, Sol,' Ruiz said, cursing that he'd mentioned the boy - the demon drink again. He projected out what he hoped was an expansive grin. 'Hay, you give me some nice hospitality, so I ask about your family. Just being polite is all. And the only family I know of is your boy.'

'Michael is well,' he said with finality. 'Now, I have a visitor shortly, so Pepe will escort you to the guest rooms, and I will speak to you later.'

As Pepe walked Ruiz from the room Gutiérrez remained seated, puffing on his cigar.

###

Pascal had been around the entire circumference of the house once, moving agonizingly slowly, pausing frequently to avoid people and light, and now she lay holed up in some bushes at the back. She had peeked in at the front window on the way around and seen Ruiz, apparently quite calm, sitting eating and drinking with Gutman. That was okay, she told herself.

The plan of the house and grounds Ruiz had drawn for her seemed to be accurate. She watched the back entrance from twenty feet away, surprised at how much activity there was, people coming and going, mostly the cowboys who worked the ranch and service people bringing stuff in and out. There was no security apparent on the door and it was unlit.

She knew the security hub was not far inside from the entrance, and she would need to avoid that. She checked her watch. There were now fewer people entering and leaving as the evening drew on. Time to move. She tensed, watching and calculating, then she was stooping and running through the shadows towards the entrance. It was a swing door and she smoothly passed through it, immediately cutting her speed to a walk, head down to avoid any cameras.

In front of her was an empty unlit hallway with an unmanned reception desk. She snuck up against the far wall, peeping around it into the house. So far so good; she got her breathing down to regular as she considered her next moves. It was still early and if Ruiz was making time with Gutiérrez, she'd take a bit herself to explore the house before trying to access the lifts to the basement.

She wondered about the CCTV and the security generally as she looked into the interior of the house. Apart from the original entry point where their vehicle was searched, security seemed lax. Probably because out here they simply never got any hostile activity, or attacks, and eventually that filtered through into reduced vigilance and awareness. It happened in the best of organizations. They got complacent and sloppy. She doubted the CCTV was monitored or recorded. More likely simply subjected to the occasional eyes on from the security guy in the hub.

It took her an hour to carry out one complete circuit inside the house, avoiding cameras and people, keeping silently to the shadows. She'd counted a cook, a waiter, then a kind of games room with snooker table, consoles, computers and three guys hanging out there, sipping beers, who she took to be part of Gutiérrez's security compliment for the shift. They seemed casual as hell. It looked like they did a lackadaisical sweep of the house every hour.

She watched the guy in the hub. It was a small room with a glass back wall she was watching him through. He had a bank of monitors in front of him but appeared to be looking down in his lap at a smartphone. She heard a sound and looked back and saw Ruiz being led along the corridor by the waiter. She flattened herself in the alcove as they walked past her, then watched them go through a door leading to one of the wings of the house. A few moments later the waiter re-emerged and came back down the corridor and disappeared through the door.

She stood for a moment undecided, watching the back of the guy in the hub. She rose up and began moving silently down the corridor towards the door Ruiz had just gone through.

###

In New York City Calver sat in a glitzy bar full of tourists on Times Square waiting for Christoff Wisliceny to show. Detective Daly from NYPD was there already, looking big and athletic, wearing a smart blue suit

They both saw Christoff approaching through the crowd at the same time - you couldn't really miss him. He was done up in a light brown and pale green English tweed outfit and he wouldn't have looked out of place on a Highland Grouse Moor.

They nodded and Calver managed to secure him a large double scotch to match their own. They clinked glasses.

Christoff looked about the place with distaste. 'Didn't trust the phones so thought here would be good.'

'It is,' Calver nodded. 'But not for drinking,' he sighed. 'So, any news?'

Christoff took a judicious sip of scotch and nodded his approval. 'I believe I know what you know. She's hidden the child somewhere in the New Mexico desert with the grandmother and an Indian tracker, and she's gone back to Ciudad Juarez, I think to go after this Gutiérrez character to get evidence sufficient to convict Maria Dinks and Dante Figueroa of kidnap and attempted murder, in a US court, and thereby exonerate Yolanda Lopez. She asked me for background on this Gutiérrez's son. He's an 8-year-old who lives with the father out in the desert, and he's apparently a bit of a prodigy.

'I know,' Christoff said when they both looked at him with vacant expressions. 'I don't know either.'

'You know,' Daly said, quietly. 'I did a bit of moonlighting after I spoke with you, Christoff. The L.A. kid, Lucy Collins, aka Tilly-May, and Tamara Hunt from Washington bear pretty striking similarities. Upper middle-class white kids 7, 8 years old go missing. There's no body, no trace and no ransom demand. So I did a sweep on the national database and picked up another five possibles countrywide based on the same criterion.'

Calver sipped his drink, pensive, thinking. Christoff said, 'it's like she hinted at, that its possibly a sophisticated kidnap to order operation, based outside the USA, that no one knows is there.'

'But Dinks wasn't part of it?' Daly said.

'My guess, which Courtney hinted at,' Calver said, 'is that they used Gutman for logistics and later on. Seems like Pascal stumbled on all this other stuff when she went looking for Sapphire.'

'And Victor Diaz is involved in this shit?' Daly said, his expression sour and incredulous at the same time.

'It very much looks like it,' Christoff said.

All three stood silent for a while, looking around the busy bar drinking their scotch. Christoff was first to speak. 'When I spoke to Courtney last, she raised a couple of points. She was speculating about Diaz and O'Hara and how O'Hara seems to be able to operate completely freely, with no oversight, whilst using all the resources of the FBI. She's wondering how is he able to do that?'.

'Influence and patronage,' Calver said. 'Diaz is on the intelligence house committee and he's apparently very tight with the FBI director. So that's created something of a lethal conundrum. Courtney's saying we should give it to the FBI, but she can't. She's a fugitive so they won't listen anyway until they have her dead or alive. And Diaz is gatekeeper to the FBI and virtually controlling what's happening on the ground in the New Mexico desert.'

'That ain't right,' Daly said slowly, his eyes smoldering with anger.

'Precisely my thoughts,' Christoff added.

'And, I can't get hold of her anymore on the burner,' Calver said.

'That's probably because she's at Gutiérrez's ranch, so we'll just have to wait and pray for now,' Christoff said.

'You got any contacts in the FBI, Daly, we could go to with this?' Calver asked.

Daly shook his head. 'Not at the level we'd need, but I can make some phone calls. Some of the guys I know might be able to get me to the right ear.'

'Good enough,' Calver said. 'Not much more we can do for now.'

They nodded, sombre, wondering what might be happening hundreds of miles away in Mexico.

'Oh,' Christoff said, 'the other point, Jonas, that Courtney asked me to run past you is a rather intriguing one. In a way it is predicated I suppose on all this current unpleasantness having been brought to a satisfactory conclusion.'

Calver waived his hand at the waiter and ordered another round, marveling at Christoff's gift for understatement. 'And what might this intriguing idea be?' he asked.

'Sapphire's grandmother asked whether it might be possible for her to apply for custody of the child as against the mother, Maria Dinks?'

Calver started to laugh, but then stopped as his legal mind started to work on the idea.

'Quite,' Christoff said. 'That was my initial reaction also, before I started thinking about it. It does have a certain elegance. But then again, legally, is it even worth considering? Is it possible?'

'I don't see why not,' Calver said. 'I'm no family lawyer but I'll hit the books when I get back to the office. Maria kidnapped and tried to murder her own child, allegedly, and that suggests a certain unfitness to be a parent, don't you think?' he said, smiling. 'But strategically it has great possibilities because it means we have a way of fighting Maria if they do recover the child and she tries to get her back.'

Calver stood up. 'I'll go back now and see how we might go about lodging a petition in the family court.'

Daly stood up as well. 'I got to go too. Good to see you, Christoff,' he said finishing his drink and squeezing Christoff's shoulder.

As Daly and Calver walked away towards the exit they looked back. Christoff was already deep in conversation with a startlingly attractive young man.

###

She scratched at the door, heard the clink of a bottle inside, then Ruiz's face was looming out at her. 'Jesus!' he said, grabbing her arm and pulling her into the room. He looked around wildly as if he thought someone might be following her.

'Relax, Ruiz. I watched the guy in the hub. Don't think he looked at the screens once. Too busy playing with his smartphone. And anyway, this room looks clean, no cameras,' she said, looking around at the luxurious setting. 'Saw you stuffing yourself like a pig earlier. So what's going on? Why are you stuck in here?' she asked.

'He's got a visitor, but we're gonna talk some more when he's finished his business. And he's suspicious as hell.'

Pascal looked over at the bottles of drink on the sideboard, checked her watch, her mind whirring away. 'I been watching the security hub and the lifts to the basement, which are right alongside. Only one guy used the lift, but it makes a noise and the guy in the hub can't fail to be alerted, if we try and use it,' she said, looking meaningfully at him.

'So?' he said.

'I need you to divert him so I can take the lift unobserved.'

'You're kidding, right?' he said, half-smile as if she really was.

'No, I'm not kidding, Ruiz, and I don't think we have time to fuck around,' she said, grabbing a full bottle of scotch off the sideboard and uncapping it. 'Come here,' she said.

He looked at her questioningly, shrugged and strolled over to stand in front of her, crooked half smile back in place. She poured some scotch into her cupped hand. 'Not that you need this,' she said as she slapped the liquid onto his face, around his mouth and rubbed it in, allowing some to spill onto his shirt collar and tie.

'Hey,' he said, startled. 'Watch the tie, it's pure Italian silk. Cost me two hundred fifty bucks.'

'Stop bleating, Ruiz. I think you know what I have in mind,' she said, leaning up, loosening the flashy tie and pulling it awry, stepping back and appraising him. 'You'll do. Let's go,' she said, handing him the bottle.

He took it and moved to the door.

'Go,' she said, pushing him out into the corridor. 'I'll be following, but just forget about me.'

She watched him amble up the corridor, getting into character, starting to weave, nearly full opened bottle of scotch in his hand. She slipped out and followed him just catching the swing door as he went through it. She stopped and watched him approach the hub.

The bottom half of the back wall was solid material the glass starting from about waist height. As Ruiz started engaging the guy in the hub with an angry request for another drink, Pascal stooped down and scrambled across behind Ruiz over to the lifts. She was now standing in line with him, but out of the eye-line of the guy in the hub.

She pressed the lift call button, Ruiz watching her out of the corner of his eye. He said loudly, drunken slurred voice, 'Lemme in, soldier. I need another drink, man.' He began moving into the hub.

As the lift arrived with a loud pneumatic hiss, she heard the sound of Ruiz scotch bottle smashing on the floor, and then the lift doors were opening and she was in.

There was a camera in the lift and she just hoped Ruiz would keep the guy occupied for long enough that he wouldn't see anything. The lift seemed to be taking forever to reach the basement, but then it was coming to a halt, and the doors were silently sliding open onto a corridor.

She cautiously slid out and flattened herself against the wall, floor plan spread out in her head. The boy's quarters, according to professor Garcia, should be a short way up on the left. She began moving towards a half open door near the end.

She looked into the room. It was vast, stretching the whole length of the corridor. At one end it looked like Vegas: flashing neon lights, slot machines, even a mechanical rodeo bull in a ring. The other end it looked like open plan living quarters with a load of game consoles spread around, then up on a kind of mini stage a small boy sat in a chair watching a large screen TV. He had his back to her and seemed to be watching cartoons.

Pascal stood for a while examining every inch of the place whilst trying to work out what to say to the kid. She began walking towards him. When she got close, he said, 'hi,' without turning around.

She stopped in her tracks about 2 meters behind his chair. He turned and regarded her solemnly. 'Who are you?' he asked, studying her closely, full of curiosity.

He was small for an 8-year-old and seemed to Pascal like a rather cute dormouse, self-contained and cuddly with guileless friendly eyes that were still full of curiosity. His hair was dark and swept across his head, his skin light brown, eyes slightly darker. He wore a small gray tracksuit top with hood hanging down his back and baggy black trousers with soft blue sneakers.

'Would you like to watch cartoons with me?' he asked tentatively.

'Sure,' Pascal said. 'My name's Courtney by the way.' Then

following her intuition, she added, 'I snuck in here. You won't tell, will you?'

He smiled. 'No way. I've been waiting for you,' he said mysteriously. He got up and said, 'you take the chair. I'll sit on the floor.'

'Okay,' she said slumping down. He sat at her feet but kept looking back up at her as if he couldn't quite believe he had a friend to watch with. It was a real old Tom & Jerry cartoon that was showing. Pascal had always loved them and was soon laughing out loud, the boy joining in, uncertainly at first, but then gaining confidence and then finally laughing full on and unrestrained. It almost seemed like a dam breaking to Pascal.

As the cartoon finished, he said, 'would you like some cookies, or something to drink? I've got everything down here, or I can order from Pepe?'

'No, thank you,' she said studying him. 'It's Michael isn't it?' she said, offering her hand.

'Yes, Michael Gutiérrez,' he said, solemnly shaking her hand.

She smiled at him. 'I spoke to Professor Garcia a few days ago,' she said. 'He said you are a very special young person. Very intelligent, wonderful to teach and he said to tell you that he misses seeing you and the talks you used to have.'

'I miss him too,' he said, puzzled. 'I don't know why he stopped coming. I guess it was my father,' he said warily, eyes alight with something, for a moment.

'Michael, do you ever leave here? Get out and play with kids your own age?' she asked gently.

He seemed to tense, and his face became pinched as if internal anger and conflict were raging inside him. 'My father says I am different, and will be a great man one day, but to do that I must stay here, and not be....' His voice faltered and faded as if he were no longer convinced of what he had learned to say by rote.

'Not be what? Pascal asked.

'Not be made impure by the outside world. I am strong here, where I can learn,' he said, again as if reciting words he had learned.

'Wouldn't you like to just sneak out of here with me? Go on an adventure?' she said, excitement in her voice.

'Yes, yes,' he said immediately, a yearning in his voice, but then his face dropped. 'But I can't,' he said.

'Why not,' Pascal asked gently. 'You keep your father's records, don't you? In your head. Is that why you think you can't leave?'

'Yes.'

'If you came with me, later we could sit down and record everything you have in your head and send it to him. There are secrets I know, but you wouldn't have to tell them to anyone unless you wanted to,' she said.

He looked at her with a kind of desperate hope in his eyes, wanting so much to believe her. He started to nod slowly.

She decided to let that idea germinate in his head, hoping it would bear fruit. she changed the subject. 'Did you know Tilly-May and Sapphire?' she asked lightly.

'Yes,' he said, excited again. 'Well, no. I didn't know them, but I watched them sometimes and father said I would get to play with them soon, but then they left. Are they coming back?'

'We could meet Sapphire outside, you know,' Pascal said. 'She's hiding, a bit like you, but she's up in the USA, in the New Mexico desert.'

'Cool,' he said shyly, trying the word out on his tongue.

'Michael,' she said, 'do you know who or what the "Daughter Eaters" are?'

'Oh it's just a funny name father uses sometimes for people,' he said. 'He told me some of the South American Indians who I may have blood from, in history, were cannibals and sometimes ate their daughters when there was no food.'

'Do you know how Sapphire came to be here?'

'Her step-mother is like the wicked witch,' he said, just as the door opened.

As Pascal heard the sound she was moving, diving silently and rolling, ending up behind a small leather couch, praying the boy would play along and keep schtum

'Michael, my boy,' Gutiérrez said, coming to stand over him. 'Why are you sitting on the floor? Come, give your father a hug and a kiss.'

'Yes, papa,' the boy said meekly, climbing to his feet. He smoothed his trousers down and glanced over at Pascal who he could just see peeking out from behind the couch. She had a desperate expression on her face and a finger to her lips. He smiled uncertainly at her and turned to embrace his father, his body rigid.

'What's the matter, dear?' Gutiérrez said, concern in his voice. He held the boy out from his vast girth so he could study him.

'Papa, when can I go out and play?' the boy asked plaintively.

'You said I could play with the girls, and that you'd take me out.'

'Soon, my boy. Soon,' Gutiérrez said absently, stroking the boy's hair, but then the boy pulled away suddenly and walked over to stand over the couch where Pascal was hiding.

'What's got into you, Michael? Why are you so restless, eh?' Gutiérrez asked, suspicion rising in his voice.

'You always say, Papa, I can go out, maybe to the city or to school, but I never do,' he said, maybe the first stirrings of rebellion in his young voice. 'When can I go, Papa?'

'In time, my boy, in time,' Gutiérrez said, and now there was a tone of quiet calculation in his voice. He walked over to stand over the couch with the boy. 'Michael, I have important visitors and business to attend to tonight, but tomorrow, Pepe will take you out riding in the desert. You used to like that. Then we'll talk about your future, yes? You do trust your Papa, don't you?' he said, pulling the boy around by his shoulders and looking into his eyes.

'Yes, Papa,' he replied with little conviction.

'Good,' Gutiérrez said and kissed the boy on the forehead. 'Michael, you are all I have, and I only want what's best for you. Always remember that,' he said, turning and walking away.

The boy watched him go, then as the door closed, he looked down at Pascal, his face sad and conflicted. She slowly got to her feet, saying nothing.

'He always says that,' he said wistfully. 'That we'll go out and do something, but we never do.'

Pascal stayed silent, letting the emotions now in play work on the boy. 'You said,' he started, falteringly. Then started again, voice firmer, 'you said we could go out and visit Sapphire? Was that true?'

'Yes,' she said firmly, 'but, it may be dangerous, and it will mean tricking or deceiving your papa. And it means leaving now, this very minute, with no goodbyes.'

She watched him, this small boy with a tentative, uncertain smile starting to form on his lips as he looked around his vast and lonely playpen.

'I am ready,' he said, 'but I still don't know your full name.'

She smiled. 'It's Courtney. Courtney Pascal. You said when I arrived, you'd been waiting for me. What did you mean?'

'Oh, nothing,' he said, embarrassed. 'It was just a silly dream, like a fairytale that someone would come and take me out of here.'

'Well, it wasn't so silly was it, because here I am. Dreams do come true you know, if you wish hard enough.'

He nodded, unconvinced. 'What now?'

She looked around with a critical eye. 'Lets get you kitted out, shall we?

CHAPTER TWENTY-SEVEN

She looked Michael up and down and nodded. 'You'll do,' she said, ruffling his hair. All he'd done was put on a jacket over his tracksuit top and got himself a can of coke. 'Isn't there anything else you want to take with you, Michael?' she asked him.

He looked around starting to shake his head, but then he was running to a small desk and rummaging around in it. He took out a small item and brought it over to Pascal. 'That's my mother,' he said proudly, showing her the inside of a small locket. It contained a picture of a young woman with a face just like his. 'I never knew her,' he said wistfully. 'But I sometimes think she's down here with me, watching over me.'

'She looks like a nice person, Michael,' she said.

He nodded, pleased. He put the chain around his neck and then looked at Pascal expectantly.

'If you want to go up top for anything, what do you do?' she asked him.

'I'm not supposed to, but I go up in the lift and talk to the man up there. My father doesn't like me going up, so I don't often. Its like for if there's an emergency, or something,' he said.

'Like if say you had a bad tummy-ache, yeah?'

'Yeah. I mean I've got like an intercom I can use, but I don't like the men my father has here, so I don't talk to them,' he said.

'Okay, Michael. We're going to go up in the lift, and then I want you to pretend you're ill to the guy up there,' she said.

He smiled, his face lighting up with excitement. 'You know, I can do that. I can make myself almost turn green, holding my breath. If I do it in the lift, I'll look real ill by the time I get there,' he said, laughing. 'This is fun, Courtney,' he added, marching towards the door.

She hesitated, wondering whether to calm him down and warn him of the danger, but then thought better of it; it would only frighten him.

In the lift, Michael clowned about, putting his hands around his neck, mock strangling himself and rolling his eyes. As he held his breath his face started to turn red and a sheen of sweat appeared on his forehead, and then the lift doors were opening.

Pascal motioned him towards the hub knowing the guy would have heard the lift. Michael staggered around the corner and Pascal waited, listening to him start to groan and then say, 'I…I'm not well, Ramon. I think I need the doctor.'

She heard a commotion, and a voice saying, 'sit down here, Mike. You look awful. I'll get you some water, then we'll get some help here.

'Okay,' Michael moaned, playing it to the hilt.

Pascal peaked around the edge of the wall. The guy, Ramon she assumed, had his back to them and was on the phone speaking loudly.

She slipped past Michael and moved silently down the corridor.

When she reached Ruiz's door she knocked quietly. His startled face appeared in the gap and he motioned her in, but by then it was too late to retreat. Sat on the four-poster bed was Sol Gutiérrez, smiling sadly. Behind him stood two of his soldiers, one with a sawn-off shotgun trained on Pascal, the other with a hand gun hanging down by his side. She felt Michael pushing against her back as Ramon shepherded him in behind her.

'Move away from Miss Pascal, Michael,' Gutiérrez said.

'*No!*' the boy shouted. Then sobbed, 'she's my friend, Papa, and you're not going to hurt her.'

'I promise you, my son, I will not hurt her, if you move away from her, okay,' Gutiérrez said gently, his tone cajoling.

The boy studied his father, weighing the words, then looked at Pascal. She nodded it would be okay, and he moved away to stand by the door.

Ruiz said, 'I didn't tell 'em, Courtney. Guy in the hub finally woke up and looked at his screens.'

'That's okay, Ruiz,' she said, turning to Gutiérrez. 'What now?' she said.

'We talk,' he said. 'And you can stay too, Michael,' he added, looking at the boy. 'It is time you were exposed to some of the hard realities of the world. And you need to be shown what Miss Pascal is really like, because you will need to be able to read people if you are to one day run the business.'

'Sapphires in the desert, Papa. You lied to me,' the boy said.

'I didn't know that until recently, my boy,' Gutiérrez said.

Michael nodded his head slowly, reluctantly, his face a mask. He sat down on the floor where he was and took the locket out of his pocket, opened it and gazed at the picture of his mother as if he were in a trance. Pascal studied him, wondering how much he could take, and guessing he would be okay for now, but also realizing she'd never get a better opportunity to question Gutman than right now, and that it might be the only chance they'd get to lay the mystery to rest. 'Tell me about Dante, Maria and the kidnap, Gutiérrez,' she said. 'I mean you got all the cards now, right? What you gotta lose? And as you say, Michael needs to hear it all, even the bad stuff, if he's one day going to run your business?'

He looked at her, calculating, seeming to nod his head imperceptibly as he came to a decision. 'As I think you probably now know,' he said tentatively, 'I was not involved in the original planning in the Dinks kidnap. They conceived it and came to me very late in the day for logistics; Maria procured the child for a street team I put together.'

'Who no doubt all miraculously disappeared in the desert soon after the child got to Mexico, right?' Ruiz said.

Gutiérrez ignored the interruption. 'I then acted as an honest broker between various warring factions,' he said, speaking like a lawyer.

'Tell me about the honest broker bit, because I still don't get that,' she said, eyes alive with curiosity.

'It's quite simple,' he said. 'Dante Figueroa had a mishap; I believe he misplaced a substantial shipment of product, and was asked, as is standard practice in the cartels, to make up the shortfall. He had liquidity problems of his own at the time and needed to raise $15 million at very short notice, to satisfy this obligation and placate his nervous and bloodthirsty compatriots. The alternative would have been, simply put - fatal.'

Pascal nodded, mind turning it over. 'So what's the connection with Maria?' she asked.

'Some men are lucky with women,' Gutiérrez said, cryptically. 'Maria Dinks grew up poor on the South Side of Chicago, a penniless teenager until she met Dante and went on to become a model, with some help from him and his connections. As I heard it, it was love at first sight on her part. And maybe it became an obsession, although I've heard its faded with time, but he was a good Catholic boy with a wife and family and wouldn't leave them.'

'So what happened down the line?' Pascal asked.

'Dante called her up with his problem and she suggested ransoming the kid?' Ruiz said.

'Something like that I believe,' Gutiérrez said. 'She married well, for money and to fund her fashion house, but then found the money had strings. And she hated and resented the kid who was to get all the money in a trust fund, so when Dante came a calling she was ready and waiting with a plan.'

'You said you played honest broker,' Pascal said. 'What did you mean?'

'You dealt with the money, right?' Ruiz interjected.

'Yes, for a small fee, and I was returning a favor.'

'How did it work?' Pascal asked.

'The ransom was to come to us, suitably veiled of course.'

'It was crypto, wasn't it? Bitcoin?' Pascal said.

'Yes. We facilitated the transfer; took receipt anonymously, then distributed the money in fiat.'

'You mean good old greenbacks, right?' Ruiz asked

'That's right.'

'So let me get this straight,' Pascal said. 'The 25 million bucks came to you in Bitcoin anonymously. You exchanged it for dollars, paid off Dante's angry associates, took your cut and what, split the balance between Dante and Maria?'

'That's it.'

'And Michael here,' Pascal gestured at him, still obliviously studying the picture of his mother, 'kept all the crypto digital wallet keys, account numbers, fine detail, all in his head, right?'

Gutiérrez didn't answer.

'You know, I came down here looking for Sapphire,' Pascal said, rubbing a hand across her face, looking tired and played out. 'And I found her. Trouble is I also found the Daughter Eaters, right, Sol?' she said, turning to study the big man. 'That's your real bag, right? Forget the Dinks kidnap, that was kindergarten stuff, wasn't it? And as you say, you weren't even the prime mover there. No, your real deal, your life's work is the Daughter Eaters. Abducting and pimping children for high rollers with no limits on what they can do for their bucks, right? Torture and killing, all part of the deal, if the price is right?'

Gutiérrez remained silent, his face unreadable, as if he hadn't heard her words or wasn't listening.

Pascal frowned, almost scowling at the indifference shown by Gutiérrez and his silence to the charges. She doggedly continued, determined to get a reaction from him. 'Two kids we can now ID. Lucy Collins, or Tilly-May, you admitted you sourced for a high-roller Hollywood producer. That's kidnap and assault. Okay no murder charge there, but what about Tamara Hunt from Washington? What was she, six, seven years old? That was for Victor Diaz, right? From his own daughter's school. He even made an appeal for her safe return, fucking murdering hypocrite,' Pascal said.

'Yeah, where's the body buried, Sol?' Ruiz asked. 'Her family might like to know.'

Again Gutiérrez didn't say anything, but his eyes had widened when Tamara Hunt's details were mentioned. But now he was studying Michael. The boy sat with his back to the wall and didn't appear to be listening to the back and forth between the adults; still looking at the picture of his mother in the locket.

Gutiérrez turned to Pascal and said, 'Ruiz says you have an interesting deal for me? But I struggle to see how you could make good on it, especially as you have just shown me that you know far more about my activities than I suspected. What is it he suggested you might provide me with? Silence?' He laughed, his frame juddering on the bed. As his laughter tailed off, he signaled to his two men.

Pascal quickly glanced at the boy, still looking at the picture of his mother. She said, with urgency in her voice, 'Michael. Your father said he wasn't going to hurt us but he's going to kill both me and my friend, Fernando, here. He'll dress it up and say we're going away for a while, just like Sapphire and Tilly-May, but you'll never see us again, just like them.'

Michael remained seated on the floor staring at the picture of his mother, still as if he was in a trance. Gutiérrez slowly edged his bulk off the bed and rose to his feet. He waived his men back and walked over to stand looking down at Michael with a strange look of tenderness on his face. He said, 'she lies, Michael. She came here to destroy us, but nothing will separate us, will it, my wonderful boy?'

Michael looked up at him for a long moment, then whispered, barely audible, 'you killed my mother, didn't you?'

'How? Why would you say that?' Gutiérrez said, suddenly surprised, fear showing in his eyes for the first time. 'You were a tiny baby when your mother left us'

'I know you, Papa. You think you can keep secrets from me, but I am not stupid.'

Gutiérrez watched the boy, his face bewildered and fearful.

There was a sudden movement as Ruiz swiveled around Pascal, drawing her gun out of her waistband as he moved, snaking his other arm up and around the fat man's neck and bringing the barrel of the gun up to rest against the side of his head. It was all done in one fluid, almost balletic move, so quick that Gutiérrez's men had no time to act.

'One move, from anyone, and I'll kill this fat tub of shit like stepping on a cockroach,' Ruiz said.

'Ruiz, what the fuck are—'

'No time to talk, Pascal,' he said, weary. 'Get the kid and go. This is my penance. Time to cash out. This is for Tilly-May and all the others.'

'Ruiz, you don't have to do this. We can make it out—'

'*How*?' he said, sad regret breaking into his voice. 'How you going to get out past the gate with Michael unless I hold them. There's too many here.' He drew in a deep breath. 'Now, I'm tired and I can't hold this gun on him forever. You have one chance, and there's people's lives riding on that chance, so shut the fuck up and get moving.'

She held his eyes for what seemed like an age, then she nodded. She turned to Michael. 'Come on. We must go.'

The boy got to his feet looking confused and dazed.

Gutiérrez said, 'you won't get far. I will have all of Mexico on you. Michael, my boy,' he begged him, 'don't go, please'.

'It's too late, Papa,' the boy said calmly, and moved to stand by the door. Pascal quickly frisked the two grunts and took their guns. She moved to stand in front of Ruiz and put the handgun in his pocket, keeping the sawn-off for herself. She quickly hugged him and started to say something but he angrily waved her away. 'Get going,' he said, 'and take this,' he added, flicking a card. 'That number will get you across the border. Now git.'

She stood watching him again for a beat, reluctant to leave him, but she knew he was right. She nodded and turned, moving away, Michael following. As they got to the door, she heard Ruiz say to one of the grunts, 'call out to the gate that she and the boy are to be let through.'

###

'What will happen to him?' Michael asked, quietly, after they had been driving in silence for twenty minutes. Pascal, deep in remorseful thought, was regretting that she had been so hard on Ruiz in the past, remembering the harshness of some of her comments and the fact that she had doubted him right up to the end.

'My father will kill him, won't he?' Michael said, in the face of her silence.

'He'll try,' Pascal said, 'but Ruiz is clever and resourceful.'

'But there's too many,' Michael said. 'He must be a brave man, to stand and fight like that when the odds are so poor. He seemed sad to me'

'Yes. He did a lot of very bad things, betrayed people, even friends, and now he wishes to atone for those sins.'

'I will remember him in my prayers,' Michael said.

'I think he would like that,' she replied.

As they drove on in the beat-up old SUV, the outer environs of Ciudad Juarez began to spring up around them, empty warehouses, billboards and telegraph poles laden with cables. The first faint pinkness of early morning sun had begun to nudge at the horizon.

Pascal yawned, and then Michael did as well. 'Well, my boy,' she said. 'I think you and me need to get some sleep.'

'I think so too,' he said.

###

Sapphire and Greyeagle sat in the entrance to one of the caves that pockmarked the rock face by the side of their wooden shacks.

'Why are they all filled in, Greyeagle?' she asked. 'I've checked them over and they are all blocked up.'

'It's because they were dangerous. Kids like you would go in exploring and get trapped or there'd be a rockfall. So they blasted them closed years ago. I can remember a kid I knew when I was about your age,' he said, his brow furrowed. 'A Pueblo. He got lost in one of the caves and never came out. So they got together and blasted them shut.'

Sia arrived with a plate of cornbread and a jug of coffee. 'Breakfast,' she said, putting the stuff down on a rock and turning to watch the sunrise. She turned back to them. 'When will they come?' she asked.

Greyeagle looked out over the small enclosed valley, brooding, his eyes hooded. 'I thought they might have come during the night,' he said.

They all heard the faint sound at the same time and looked up, veiling their eyes from the sun. 'And I think that's your answer.'

'Another drone?' Sapphire said.

'Yeah. A final check I'd guess. They'll come tonight, I'd bet my best horse on it.'

'So we better be ready,' Sia said.

'Yep. That's about the size of it,' Greyeagle said biting into a big slice of cornbread.

###

Hector Morales sat at the bar eating a late breakfast, fried eggs over a corn tortilla with plenty of salsa. He was watching the big screen TV over the bar. There'd been a shoot-out at a ranch outside Ciudad, many dead and the place surrounded by *Federales*. As he watched the pictures of agents milling around, police tape and camera crews, Pepe, his new bodyguard approached and whispered in his ear.

He smiled, the connection between the pictures on the screen and what he was being told coalescing in his mind, creating a mood of heightened anticipation. It was Solomon Gutiérrez's ranch - he may have been one of the casualties - and the girl, Pascal was back in town with a young boy in tow. Morales had been in a rage because his people had lost the girl, but now they had her back, apparently, holed up in another cheap pension in the San Antonio area of the city. There was no mention of it on the news report, but he was being told the boy with the Pascal woman was Gutiérrez's son.

Morales's keen mind parsed the possibilities. Gutiérrez was a flesh peddler of the worst kind, children, even babies he'd heard, lower than a cockroach, although the man did occasionally have his uses. Morales hadn't been aware he had a son. But there was also another intriguing strand coming in from the street; Dante Figueroa, the top echelon guy in the hated Juarez cartel, had lost the woman too, and was putting much effort into rectifying that situation, offering a huge price on her head. He would know too she had re-surfaced back in Ciudad.

No more watching, it was time to act. And if Dante and the Juarez still wanted her so bad, so did he. He had seen the national TV coverage about the missing Dinks child but could not see how that old kidnapping might involve Dante.

Morales mopped up egg yolk with some tortilla and popped it in his mouth, his mind slipping into a familiar trope of resentment at his perceived lowly place in the cartel. He had been a captain in the Sinaloa too long and wanted more, to move up to a level like Dante in the Juarez, a senior guy. His eyes flashed with ambition. And this might just be the chance he had been waiting for. Get the girl and trade her for something big, and that could open his boss's eyes to Morales' true worth.

He motioned Pepe over. 'I want the girl, Pascal and the young boy, taken now, immediately. Time is of the essence because the Juarez want her also and may be planning an operation as we speak. We must get there first. They must not be harmed. Then take them to a safe and secure place that Juarez will not be able to find. I want to be kept informed at all stages, understood?'

Pepe nodded. 'At once *jefe*,' he said.

'Good. Go!' Morales said.

###

Pascal rolled over on the cheap bedding, sitting up, looking around, rubbing her eyes and yawning. It was another cheap backstreet pension, but comfortable and functional. She looked down at the sleeping boy beside her as her mind filtered the last twenty-four hours. For a while driving into Juarez, she couldn't think of what to do or where to go, racked with feelings of guilt over Ruiz. Eventually she had found herself back in the San Antonio area of the city where she had originally stayed when she had first arrived. She couldn't chance going back to the house because Ana would immediately tell her boyfriend and it would be like announcing her presence with a loud hailer. So they'd found this anonymous pension and almost immediately fallen asleep, but just before that she'd phoned the number Ruiz had given her for crossing the border. She guessed it might be a DEA guy. She wasn't going to worry about being traced because this was Mexico and not the USA. She'd told the confused guy Ruiz was in deep shit, man down, then given the location of Gutiérrez ranch, terminated the call and removed the SIM card. As her eyes were closing, she'd felt better cause the guy who'd taken the call had sounded like a mover and shaker, someone who got things done.

She shook her head free of memories and got up and paced around the small room. The boy looked dead to the world like he'd sleep for a week. She grabbed a jacket and left the pension, exiting the rear of the block, sauntering onto the street, eyes oscillating and panning, moving slow. It was mid-afternoon and hot, siesta time maybe and she could feel sweat under her arms.

It was a secondary kind of retail commercial area, a row of dime stores, cafes and general stores. She got a coffee and sat at a table on the sidewalk watching the world go by. She took the burner out of her pocket and stuck the SIM back in and called the number Ruiz had given her.

Guy answered immediately, like he was waiting. She wondered whether he was dirty like Ruiz had been. Maybe he wasn't DEA anyway. Maybe he was just a friend of Ruiz. Guy said, 'Ruiz is in IC, touch and go whether he makes it. Only other news I have is that Gutiérrez's son, who no one seemed to know existed, seems to be missing.'

'How about that,' Pascal said. 'Ruiz said you would help me cross the border?'

'I guess I can do that, as you may just have saved his life, if he pulls through.'

'I'll pray for him,' she said, remembering what Michael had said in the car. 'Look, I need to move fast. Me and an 8-year-old boy. Can you help?'

There was a silence during which she thought the guy had gone. Maybe he was consulting. Then he was back. 'Call me back on this number in 1 hour,' he said. 'We can get you over, but we may have some questions for you. Like the boys ID?' he said with a soft laugh.

She wasn't going to argue right now. 'I'll phone in an hour,' she said terminating the call. She ordered another coffee and called Greyeagle. As she did so she happened to look up directly into the eyes of a man standing across the street with a cellphone to his ear. He moved his eyes away a fraction too quickly. Pascal pretended not to notice.

As Greyeagle picked up, he said, simply, 'they're coming. How you doing?'

'I did the business, and I'm on my way, but can't guarantee how soon. Can't you run? Find another place?' she said.

'I don't think so. Anyway, this is a pretty good place to make a stand, and we're ready for them.'

'Good luck, Greyeagle. Take care.'

'*Yah ta hey*,' he said, and clicked off.

She looked up. The guy had gone, but now there was another watcher other end of the street. She got up and began walking away, past an alleyway. She looked down it, but it was a dead end. The next one wasn't and as she reached it, she turned into it, out of sight, then began to sprint, power running at maximum effort, eyes bulging, breath whistling out of her throat.

CHAPTER TWENTY-EIGHT

As Pascal got her breath back, leaning against the back fence of the block, she checked around, trying to order her thoughts. It didn't seem like anyone was following. She wondered who they were. The two watchers hadn't looked like law enforcement. Then it hit her: Michael!

She began moving fast through the back yard, dread welling up inside her. She'd been thinking too much about Ruiz, Greyeagle and Sapphire and forgotten about the boy. She flattened herself against the wall, peering around the edge. The landlady was busy washing in the kitchen. Pascal slipped past the doorway and up the stairs to their room.

It seemed deathly quiet as she approached the door. She put her ear to it listening intently; there was no sound. Maybe he was still sleeping. She pulled the door handle down and silently pushed the door open and entered.

The bed was empty. She sensed movement behind her a fraction of a second too late. The brutal blow struck the sweet spot between her neck and the back of her skull. The world exploded and she went down cold.

###

It was sundown and O'Hara was still too hot, but Iraq had been a lot worse he remembered. He sipped water from a canteen. They were camped about 10 miles away from the silver mine. Military style Humvee vehicles were drawn up creating a small circular arena where Dawson Creedwell was briefing the men on the upcoming mission. As most of the grunts couldn't ride, they'd be going in on foot.

On a foldaway table the redskin tracker had a scaled model of the valley and the silver mine and he was painstakingly going over the geography of the area and the hazards they were likely to face going in. The four other guys around the table were super-fit bonehead marine types, chewing gum, pumped up with testosterone, and they weren't taking the lecture too seriously.

'Sounds like a Turkey shoot, chief,' one said.

'Yeah. What the fuck are we doing here, man?' said another. 'An old lady and a kid?

'Ain't that a job for social services, Cochise? Or the reservation police?'

'Rag all you want,' Creedwell said, refusing to rise to the race-baiting. 'But this guy you're laughing at? He was a sniper out of Bragg. Other day took out two guys from a mile away, at night.'

'That don't scare me none,' said one, full of bravado. 'Bring it on. Night scope. Anyone could do it,' he said hopefully.

'Hey. How about some fire water, chief?'

'All right. Let's break it up,' O'Hara said. 'We go in, one hour.'

As O'Hara moved away his cell was buzzing. Diaz. He frowned but snapped the phone to his ear. 'Sir?'

'Soldier, things are starting to get critical,' Diaz said. O'Hara could hear the tension in the guy's voice. 'When you going in?'

'Within the hour, sir.'

'Good. Look, I'm coming down there to be on hand, so I'm just about to leave for Table Rock. I'm going to pass you over to my guy if you will give him the coordinates of your camp.'

'Yes, sir,' O'Hara said. 'It'll be a pleasure to have you aboard, senator.'

###

Pascal dreamed she was being suffocated. Something was over her mouth, and she couldn't draw breath. She struggled to free herself, then awoke, bathed in sweat, a terrible ache in the back of her head. It felt like a whiskey hangover, but much worse. She groaned, slowly opening her eyes.

She was trussed up in a hard wooden chair with black masking tape over her mouth. Sitting next to her was Michael also trussed and taped. His eyes were open, watching her, scared.

She looked around; they'd been moved and were now in a warehouse surrounded by pallets of stuff covered over and roped. The place looked eerily familiar; she noticed new brickwork and paint on an office area annexed to the building. Then it registered. It was where she had killed Chico when he was about to carve her open with a chainsaw.

So it was a pretty safe bet she was being held by Morales, of the Sinaloa.

She jiggled her hands around, and tried her feet, but she was bound up tighter than an Egyptian mummy. They were clearly not going to take any chances with her this time around.

She looked over at Michael trying to reassure him with her eyes, keeping them calm and smiling, as if she hadn't a care in the world. She looked over as the door at the back opened and Morales entered with a new guy in tow, a tall black-eyed figure. Morales approached and stood in front of her, the tall man standing back, eyes uninterested. Morales reached down and ripped the black tape from Pascal's mouth. She couldn't help letting out a yelp of pain.

Michael immediately started struggling, straining at his bonds, his eyes full of anger.

Morales laughed, leaned down and slapped the boy hard across the face. 'Be still, or I will get Pepe here to teach you some manners.'

'Leave the kid alone, Morales,' Pascal said. 'Your beefs with me, so take it out on me, not the kid. Anyway, how d'you miss getting roasted when I lit up your SUV with the RPG in the park? Some shot, huh?' she said, riding him. 'Bet you didn't expect that? I guess you sent your boys in to face me cause you're too scared to do it yourself?'

He smiled, ignoring her words. 'Tell me, Ms Pascal. What exactly are you doing here in Mexico, and why is Dante Figueroa so desperate to make your acquaintance?'

Pascal watched the guy, her mind turning it over, running the angles. She said, to give herself a spell to think it through, 'look, can't you untie the boy and take the tape off. He's not going anywhere. And how about a drink? Then I'll talk to you,' she said.

Morales watched her, then gestured to Pepe with a couple of words of Spanish. The giant man ambled over to Michael and removed his bonds and the tape on his mouth. The boy rubbed his wrists and his face.

Pascal said, 'it's okay now, Michael. We'll be fine.'

The boy nodded, unconvinced. Pepe brought a tray with coffee on which he passed around. Pascal asked Michael to hold her cup so she could take a sip.

Morales looked at her expectantly. So?' he said.

'So,' she sighed, leaning back in her hard wooden chair. 'I guess even drug dealers watch the news, right, Morales?'

'I've seen the stories about the Dink's girl. You obviously came here to get her. Now there's a manhunt going on in the USA. They think she, and you, are somewhere in the New Mexico desert, and they're apparently closing in on her. So what?' he said. 'Why d'you come back here? And why does Dante want you so bad?'

'Try joining up the dots, Morales,' she said.

He looked at her, uncomprehending.

'Dante Figueroa was one of the original kidnappers,' she said. 'I need evidence, because physically having Sapphire Dinks alive is not enough. That's why I came back.'

Morales looked thoughtful for a moment. He moved over and stood with Pepe, speaking quietly in Spanish, Morales intermittently nodding his head. 'We always wondered how Dante found the money back in the day,' he said. 'We knew he'd lost a big shipment and had to make it up. So that's how he did it, eh?' Morales said, nodding and smiling to himself.

He rubbed his chin, then barked an order, 'Tequila, Pepe.' As the tall man lumbered away to get a bottle and some glasses, Morales looked down at her, his eyes calculating. 'So, maybe we can help each other?' he said.

'Gimme a drink,' she replied. 'And a coke for the boy.'

When they were settled with drinks in their hands - Pepe had untied one of Pascal's - she said, 'so what did you have in mind, Morales?'

###

In Cantina Gold Dante sat at the bar sipping Rémy Martin. He watched as Chavez entered in a hurry and approached. The man looked nervous, the bringer of unwelcome news.

'What?' Dante said.

'We have located the woman, Pascal,' Chavez said, trying to get his breath back and cover his nervousness. 'Or perhaps, I should say, we know that she is in Ciudad, but we don't know exactly where. She is being held by—'

'What d'you mean?' Dante said, menacingly. 'You don't know exactly where? You were tasked with watching her, but you couldn't even do that satisfactorily. You lose her, and now you say she's back, but you don't know where?'

'*Jefe*, we have men all over town,' Chavez said, voice close to pleading. 'She slipped by us, we still don't know how, but we do know she was at this shoot-out at Gutman's ranch, that was all over the news, and now she's back here.'

'I worked most of that out myself, so why do I need you, Chavez? Or your useless men?' Dante said, glaring at the frightened man. Chavez stood silent, perhaps divining it would not help his case to say anymore.

Dante held the man's gaze for a moment longer then nodded at Dominga standing behind the bar. 'Give him a Rémy. Make it a double.'

Chavez gratefully took the drink and disposed of it in one shot.

Dante cocked his head, his mind fastening on what Chavez had said earlier. 'You said she is being held, I think. By whom?' he asked quietly.

Chavez looked down, not daring to meet Dante's eyes. 'By…By Morales.'

Dante just looked at him, his eyes going flat.

Chavez mumbled, 'and Gutman's young son is with them, we believe.'

Dante smiled mirthlessly, sipped some more Remy. His phoned buzzed. He irritably clapped it to his ear.

'Have you dealt with the woman yet?' Maria Dinks silky and insistent voice asked.

'No, I haven't dealt with the women yet,' he replied, barely able to keep the rage out of his voice. As they spoke, he watched a runner come in and speak urgently to Chavez, who then approached tentatively.

Dante said to Maria,' just hold a second.' Then to Chavez, 'what is it?'

'Hector Morales wants to meet. Says he'll trade the girl, and the kid of you want him?' Chavez said.

Dante was silent for a beat, ruminating. He said into the phone, 'it's under control. Just had word where she is. I'll have this wrapped up in 24 hours, believe me.'

'You said that before, and it didn't happen.'

'Yeah, well now I got extra reasons for doing it, if Gutman's been singing like a canary. So you can depend on it - she'll be gone, come the morning,' he said.

'I hope so, because that fucker is really beginning to burn me,' she said, her voice turning harsh.

'Chiquita, its unlike you to lose your cool. What could she possibly do to you when she's stuck down here in Mexico?' he said.

'That low-rent lawyer Calver has lodged a petition in the Manhattan family court on behalf of the grandmother, seeking custody of the brat, from me. Her mother. Can you believe that?' she said, incredulous. 'I mean how the fuck can that old women do that when no one even knows where she is?'

'Why is this a problem?' he asked, unconcerned. 'I don't see it.'

'It's a fucking problem because if they ever get that little bitch out alive from the desert it means she may not come straight to me. And if I don't have control, the FBI and Justice might get a free run at her as a witness, so you should worry, buddy. You should really worry. We need to nail this now.'

'So the answer must be what we already agreed: get rid of both of them, yes?' Dante said, calm now.

'You got it buster,' she said. 'You do Pascal, and I'll see what I can do about the brat. Ciao,' she said, terminating the call.

Dante sipped his Rémy and looked over at Chavez. 'Where's the meet with Morales to be?' he asked. 'We need to set something up?'

At last Chavez smiled. There might yet be a chance to redeem himself.

###

Detective Daly was sitting in a cop's bar not far from his Manhattan precinct house, supping back a malty beer when his cell buzzed. No caller ID but he picked up reflexively, phone to his ear. 'Yeah.'

Silence, then low hesitant voice. 'Daly? Its Fernando Ruiz, man.'

Daly blinked, surprised. 'Thought you were dead and gone. Where you bin?'

'Long story, man. Look I'm just out of ICU, gunshot wounds,' he said, his voice sinking to a whisper. 'Can't get a hold of Pascal and she's in danger. Look I just wanted to put on the record, case I don't make it. She did not kill the kid, Tilly-May, or Lucy Collins. Kid jumped a balcony. Suicide. You got that, Daly?' he asked in a desperate kind of last gasp. Daly could hear a nurse squawking in the background, and the phone went dead.

Daly took a pull on his bottle of beer, thinking, then he dialed up Calver.

###

O'Hara, Dawson Creedwell and the four grunts stood at the entrance to the narrow valley that contained the old silver mine. The men were silent. Creedwell held the night vision glasses to his eyes. He passed them to O'Hara. 'Dead as a tomb,' he said. 'But they're there all right. I can sense them.'

O'Hara held the glasses to his eyes slowly scanning the dark and silent terrain, only a fading half moon providing a faint glimmer of light. 'Okay,' he said. 'Sorenson and Baker, you come in either side of myself and Creedwell, and we fan out and go in. Ortega and Markeson, you stay here as reserve back-up. We'll call you if we need you.'

O'Hara took a last look around the group. 'I want absolute radio silence going in. And guys?' he said with a smile. 'No half measures. Hint of a problem, shoot to kill. Let's go.'

###

High up on the ridge, at the back of the valley, Sia lay on a rock ledge watching and waiting. She wasn't scared or fearful anymore. She'd had a long and fruitful life, lately tinged with sadness from the death of her daughter, but Sapphire's return had made her so incredibly happy. Now she enjoyed the quiet and peaceful night air.

Down in the valley Greyeagle sat in the entrance to one of the caves. He was completely motionless, his body like stone, only his eyes moving. From a short distance away, you'd never see him or know he was there. Then he moved, raising the sniper rifle, adjusting the night sight and then panning slowly across the valley floor.

Nothing. But he could sense something out there; a minor disturbance in the still night air that lay across the valley. A flicker of something indefinable that he felt in his soul. Some said his people had a developed a sixth sense over the centuries from living so close to the land, so that they knew it, and it spoke to them.

The scream when it came was loud and piecing; shocking and unnerving, slicing through the night air. At first you couldn't tell whether it was male or female, or indeed even human.

Sorenson, to the left of the approaching phalanx, had hit the first man trap. It was an axe tightly strapped to a thick tree branch, pinned back by a rope. The branch, freed from its restraining cord by Sorenson's foot, swung in a sideways parabola, in a vicious arc, the sharpened blade smashing and cutting through Sorenson's Kevlar tunic, then his rib-cage and finally slicing his heart in half. He was dead before his scream finished echoing around the valley.

Baker was next. Ironically his coon catching daddy had died the same way out in Nam in 68', at the hands of the Vietcong. An awful slow way to die. It was a simple camouflaged pit containing sharpened wooden stakes. Baker now lay fatally impaled on them, screaming and screaming, one bloodied spike standing right up through his guts, the other through his left shoulder.

Dawson Creedwell took one look in the pit and put a bullet through Baker's head and the screaming stopped abruptly. Then it was silent again.

O'Hara broke that silence speaking urgently into his face mike.

'Ortega, Markeson, move up. Party's started,' he said.

'Roger that,' both men said in unison, and started moving forwards.

Greyeagle, watching from the mouth of the cave, knew there were two close by, and that they were probably leaders, as they moved far more carefully than the two dead men had. He guessed one of them might be O'Hara; he hoped so. He also guessed they'd have back-up they'd call in, and with that in mind he began slowly sweeping his sniper rifle night sight across the terrain.

Up on the rock ledge, Sia looked down the sight of the heavy hunting rifle, its barrel resting on a small rock pile she had erected earlier. The half glimmering moon played light across the hard-standing area where the circular walled well stood and she could see this area quite clearly.

Greyeagle heard movement further back in the valley, guessing it was the back-up guys moving forward as carelessly as their dead colleagues had. But then it went quiet again, and the moments began to stretch out with no sound or movement discernible. Greyeagle surmised they were probably regrouping and reshaping their plan of approach, given their casualties.

It looked like a stalemate for the moment. Maybe he should think about moving position.

###

Pascal looked around the luxurious hotel room with approval. It was a marked improvement on the warehouse. The hotel was on Boulevard M. Gomez Morin, like Cantina Gold where she had worked the bar, seemingly an age ago. The hotel was a front for the Sinaloa and Morales had installed her and Michael there, under heavy guard, whilst he set up the meet with Dante.

Unfortunately the grunts guarding her were extremely jumpy and trigger happy. Morales had emphasized that she might not look much, but she had cut a swathe of hurt through tough street soldiers and law enforcement, and they must watch her carefully. He made it plain that if she escaped, each man on shift would pay with his life, and no one doubted him.

She had watched them carefully, hand-overs, the sweeps, bringing of meals - and it was tight as a drum, with no cracks to slip through. If she waited, she knew they would slip up eventually and give her an edge, but she couldn't afford to wait. She knew O'Hara would be mercilessly running down Sapphire, and she needed to get there and help them before it was too late. And she only had one hand free to do it with, the other was handcuffed around her back, to her belt. Michael was okay though, with access to a computer for the first time, but it was hard to drag him away from it. Now he sat in a chair at the window completely engrossed in something on screen.

Pascal got up and walked over to the window to look out over the city, worry about Sapphire and what was happening in the New Mexico desert furrowing her brow. She had to get out, and with the boy, but just how the fuck was she going to do it?

She sipped a whiskey she had been given earlier, and walked over to the door where Pepe, Morales's giant bodyguard stood, blank-eyed and uninterested. She knew though he was a pro and acutely aware of her every move. He wouldn't have risen to his current status if he hadn't been sharp and dangerous. 'Where's Hector, Pepe?' she asked.

'Mr. Morales is busy,' he replied.

'Go get him, errand boy. I agreed to play along with his little scam on the understanding he'd move his ass, but nothing's happening?' she said, applying the needle.

'Maybe you'd like another drink, lady,' he said. 'You ain't quite finished the bottle yet.'

She laughed. 'So you have got a sense of humor, Pepe. How about you join me for one?' she said. 'Come on, man. Hector won't know, and I won't tell.' She knew the guy liked a drink. He licked his lips

She walked over to the sideboard and poured him generous slug and carried it back to him. For a moment he just looked through her, but she remained standing holding out the glass. He reached down and took it, almost reluctantly. Pascal went and got her half full glass and came back.

They regarded each other. She said, '*Salud*,' and clinked her glass against his, and took a shot. He waited a beat, nodded and did likewise, savoring the taste.

'Come on, Pepe. Tell me what's happening?' she said, not expecting a response.

'It's no secret. The meets here, in this room today. They're just ironing out the details, security. Morales will come soon to fill you in.'

'Thank you, Pepe,' she said.

'No problem,' he replied, smiling for the first time. 'I always like to have a drink with the people I'm going to pop. *Salud*,' he said, draining his glass.

CHAPTER TWENTY-NINE

The valley had been silent for nearly fifteen minutes since the screaming had stopped with the single gunshot. Sia remained prone on the rock ledge, lying comfortably spread out in the pale moonlight, her eye trained down the gun sight of the hunting rifle.

She had been watching the same spot of brush at the outer edge of the hard-standing area around the well for an age. She blinked, and looked again down the sight, thinking she had seen movement. Maybe it was just the wind. But there was no wind down in the valley. A wisp of cloud drifted across the half moon, and she looked again. There was something there she was sure. A deeper shadow in the bush where before it had seemed sparse branches with few leaves.

She centered her sight on the middle of the darker area of the bush, letting her breath run down, her arm holding the rifle stock rock solid, her body as if it were part of the stony ground on which she lay. Her finger was firm on the trigger. Greyeagle had said that if she got the opportunity of a shot, she must take it. The odds were so stacked against them, they had to take every chance that came their way, however slim.

But to kill a man? Even if he was hell bent on killing them? It was not something she could do lightly. Her mind drifted and she thought of the stories she'd heard at her mother's knee about the five tribe's migration north and the Trail of Tears. She thought about her own people, the *Diné*, and their Long Walk in the 1860's when they had been forced from their lands at gunpoint. And she thought about the ongoing marginalization of her people, even today. But most of all she thought about blood and family; about a daughter taken away from her way too young, but since leavened by the gift of a grandchild she had never expected to see again. An image of Sapphire, beautiful repository of all her dreams flickered momentarily in her mind and her resolve hardened like the rock she lay on.

She re-sighted down the barrel, dead center on the dark shadow, her finger tightening on the trigger. She offered up a silent prayer to the Spiritual Earth Mother and pulled the trigger.

The sound of the shot was deafening to Sia and the recoil vicious, the rifle butt slamming into her shoulder. For a second nothing happened. Then the bush moved and a man, Ortega, stood up in it and began to stagger forwards holding his groin, moaning. He took a few more steps into the moonlit hard-standing area around the well and collapsed in a heap where he lay quietly moaning. Sia watched the earth around him darken with blood.

Thirty meters back from the wounded man, Creedwell, hidden in heavy brush, spoke into his face mike. 'O'Hara? You catch the muzzle flash? He's up on the top?'

'You take him,' O'Hara said. 'I'll move in down here.'

'Roger that,' Creedwell said, already moving silently towards the rock face.

In the cave entrance Greyeagle had watched the wounded man's death dance. He smiled to himself. The old lady was one helluva shot and would have made a great sniper. There were three down now and he calculated from what he had seen, three left. That evened things up a bit; three against three. Or, he thought with a grim smile, three against two and a half.

They would have seen the muzzle flash and he hoped Sia would be moving as he'd told her to do after taking a shot. Maybe it was time he made a move too.

Pascal watched with heightened interest as Dante Figueroa entered the room. He was with his captain Alvaro Chavez and another man who carried a sawn-off shotgun. Across the room Hector Morales, his captain, Pepe and their man with a sawn-off waited for them. Pascal surmised the security deal was two men a side, Chavez and Pepe with concealed side-arms and the two grunts with shotguns. Each side would have been extensively searched before the meet and the building and environs put under a microscope. She couldn't work out though why Dante would have agreed to meet at a hotel that was so clearly controlled by the Sinaloa. Maybe he had guys in place. She guessed they'd find out pretty soon.

Dante was flashily handsome and well dressed, looking super calm although that was probably an act. Chavez looked nervous though. He nodded to Pascal and said, 'nice to see you again. Maybe you wanna come back and work for me when this is all over, huh?'

'Maybe, if you're still alive,' she said, winking at him.

She turned and raised her glass of Tequila towards Dante. He was studying her with an amused expression on his face. 'So, we meet at last,' she said. 'Dante Figueroa, great drug lord and incompetent kidnapper of children. Sapphire sends her regards.'

For a second Dante's slick smile faltered.

'That's right,' Pascal said. 'You should never have visited Maria Dinks that day on Central Park. You know, day Sapphire came home early. Caught the two of you love-birds playing house. That's a lethal connection, Dante, and it's gonna get you life,' she said. She toasted him, '*Salud.*'

'Can it, Pascal,' Morales said, from across the room. 'We're here to talk business with Mr. Figueroa, so button it.'

'No,' Dante said. 'Let her talk herself into an early grave. I want to know what she thinks she has, because it sounds like dick. Kids ID wouldn't stand a chance against the kind of attack-dog lawyer I'd let loose on her - if she made it to trial, which she won't.'

'Fine,' Morales said. 'Talk away. Anyone want a drink, help yourselves.' He gestured at a trolley laden with bottles.

'I'll have another,' Pascal said, sauntering over to the trolley. She mixed herself a scotch. 'How about you, Dante? I'll be mother. What's your poison?'

He smiled, enjoying her chutzpah. 'I'll have a Rémy Martin if you have such a thing,' he said.

'Oh, we got everything here,' she quipped. 'One Rémy coming up.' She measured out a generous double. 'How about you, Chavez?

Maybe you need a bit of courage to come in here without back-up?'

Chavez stood silent, ignoring the barb. She handed Dante his drink.

'You'd have made a great cocktail waitress,' he said, looking her straight in the eye. 'That's quite a trick mixing drinks with one hand hooked up behind your back. What, don't you trust her, Hector?' he said, turning back to look at Morales.

'Come on, Dante,' he said, getting impatient. 'We're here for business and we ain't got all day to drink, so let's get to it.'

'Okay,' Dante said. 'But first I think your new man, Pepe here, might have something to say.'

As Morales turned, saying, 'what?' Pepe raised his gun, which now had a silencer attached and shot his own grunt twice in the head, the two shots making a soft phutting sound. At the same time Chavez raised a hand-gun and held it on Morales. The dead guy's head lolled on the floor, crimson starting to leak out into the thick pile carpet.

Morales stood staring at Pepe in disbelief. Dante said, 'don't you do due diligence, Hector? When you promote a new guy?'

Morales, still staring at Pepe, said, 'I raised you, Pepe, from a street kid. Looked after you. Gave you everything you have, and you betray me? Why?'

'You shouldn't have taken my woman, Hector,' Pepe said calmly.

'Enough,' Dante said. 'Pepe, go out and tell them we're all coming out and we're going on a trip to one of my warehouses for further discussions.'

Pepe moved away. Dante nodded at Pascal. 'Get the boy,' he

said.

She didn't move. 'What's going on here?' she said. 'I mean, I know what's going on, but where do I fit in?'

'Oh, didn't I tell you?' Dante said, mock forgetful. 'We're going to the New Mexico desert, so you can show me where Sapphire Dinks is.'

She was about to go back at him when she realized that was exactly what she wanted. She nodded. 'Fine,' she said.

'I got a plane waiting and clearance across the border,' Dante said.

'And what about me?' Morales said. 'You don't want another war, do you, Dante,' he said, hopefully.

'You're coming with us, for now,' he replied.

Pepe came back into the room. 'We're ready to go,' he said. 'And I got guys coming in to get rid of the body. We've given them a story about a little local difficulty,' he added with a grin.

Morales said to him, 'whatever happens, Pepe, you're dead.'

'We'll see,' he replied.

As Pascal returned with Michael in tow, Dante took a last look around. He said to Morales, 'one squeak out of you while we're going out, and you get it first.'

Morales nodded, face like stone.

Dante said, 'let's go.'

In the best hotel in Table Rock, senator Victor Diaz listened as one of his personal assistants reported to him. She was a seventeen-year-old unpaid intern, a bit too old for his tastes, but he could still derive considerable pleasure from admiring her jutting breasts as she spoke.

He was sat at a table in his suite. He had come down here because he knew he needed to be near the action, to oversee the removal of the threat that was facing him. He now knew the full extent of it, or most of it, and Sapphire Dink's was peripheral at best. He had enjoyed raping her, but the fat man had insisted she stay alive, so he was in the clear on any murder charge there. No, it was the woman Pascal who represented the main threat. She had been to Gutman's hacienda and must now know extensive detail about the operation. But more intriguingly she had taken the man's son, whom Diaz had not even known existed.

The question then had to be, why had she taken the boy? He had ordered an immediate report from trusted sources, and now he believed he knew the answer. Also he had learned that someone had accessed FBI data on missing girls, and in particular, Tamara Hunt, the enchanting child from Washington he had so enjoyed. He smiled wistfully to himself as he recalled his time with the child. He felt the familiar urge rising up in him but knew he mustn't succumb to it at this critical time. He needed to be fully focused if he was to neutralize the threat. One thing he was sure of; eventually Pascal and the boy would turn up wherever the Dink's girl was, and so he'd be waiting. He smiled when he thought of O'Hara and his team. The net was closing.

He turned back to the girl, his eyes moving up from her breasts to her face.

'And most of the media are camped out in Gallup, and they don't seem to know you're here yet, sir,' she said. 'We have the vehicles ready outside with your team and a couple of local trackers who know where Mr O'Hara's camp is.'

'Good,' he said. 'I'll be incommunicado in the desert for now, unless it's a national emergency.'

'Yes sir,' she said.

###

The small Pilatus PC-12 passenger plane flew low over the New Mexican desert. On board, Pascal and Michael sat at the back quietly talking, Dante with Chavez and four of their men plus Pepe and Morales were at the front.

Inside, the plane was surprisingly luxurious, with soft gray leather seats, thick pile carpet and plenty of room to move about. Pascal had been on a PC-12 before and knew it had capacity for around 10 passengers with a spacious hold for baggage. This model had two doors, one at the front, just after the cockpit for entry and exit and another larger one about half-way down, often used by skydivers.

She had been watching the activity at the front of the plane for a while now, guessing that having Morales with his betrayer in chief, Pepe, cooped up together would lead to friction. Now she could see words were being exchanged between Dante and Morales and she could feel the tension radiating back to where she sat.

She said to Michael, 'stay here. I'm going up front to see what's

395

happening.'

The boy nodded happily. He'd never been on a plane before and he was fascinated. He sat glued to his seat looking down through the window, his eyes traversing the desert as it unwound below them.

Pascal got up and made her way upfront. There seemed to be some kind of a stand-off. Dante was leaning back against the wall of the toilet cubicle, his arms crossed. He was enjoying Morales's distress and fear. Pepe stood in front of Morales, who had his back to the planes exit door. Dante nodded, saying to Pepe, 'it is time.'

Pepe nodded and now Pascal could see he had a huge hunting knife in his hand. Morales shrank back. Dante moved away from the wall, walked over and pulled open the door. Immediately the cabin was filled with sounds of the wind ripping by outside, although the plane was now quite low and traveling at a moderate speed over the deserted desert.

Dante walked back saying to Morales, 'your choice amigo. The knife or you can practice your skydiving skills. Without a parachute of course.'

The men around Morales chuckled and Pepe leaned forward threateningly, brandishing the knife at Morales.

For a second Pascal felt for the guy, but then it was gone. Morales was a murdering psychopath and the world would be a better place without him. They all knew the score when they joined the cartel; unimaginable riches and pleasure on the one hand; likely a short life and a highly unpleasant death on the other. And it looked like Morales's time had just run out.

He turned to the open doorway and looked out for a moment. He turned back and studied the men facing him. He seemed calm now, perhaps resigned to his fate. 'You know,' he said, addressing Dante. 'I have a feeling your time is up too, Dante.'

He tipped his head at Pascal. 'She's coming for you, and I wouldn't bet against her.' He bowed to Pascal. 'It was at least a pleasure knowing you,' he said. Then he turned to the open doorway and jumped.

As he sailed out of the open hatch Pepe walked forward and stood in the opening watching Morales's fast receding body. As he did so Pascal caught a movement out of the corner of her eye, Chavez stepping forward and delivering a violent kick to the center of Pepe's back, sending him tumbling out of the hatch in Morales's wake.

'That's what we do with the rubbish round here,' Dante quipped, to laughter, as Chavez slid the hatch back in place immediately cutting off the sound of the roaring slipstream.

'Honor among thieves, eh?' Pascal said.

'If he would betray his own boss, over a woman, what good is he to me?' Dante said

The pilots voice interrupted them suggesting that they were about to land, and they should all take their seats and buckle up. Pascal made her way back to Michael.

Sia stood silent, back in the bushes adjacent to the rock ledge she had been lying on. She had been there for what seemed like an age, immobile and silent, standing as if she were a bush or a tree. And there had been no sounds from down below. What could be happening? Maybe the attackers had withdrawn, she thought hopefully.

The click of the gun immediately behind her sounded implausibly loud. 'Place the rifle on the ground and no sudden movements,' the calm and careful voice said.

She hesitated for a moment, then slowly lowered the rifle and placed it on the ground. She straightened up and stood waiting for the bullet in her back, silently praying that Sapphire would survive. More moments passed before a shape materialized in front of her from the shadow, moving silently to stand before her.

'You Navajo, Granny?' he said in his quiet careful voice.

She studied him in the pale moonlight. Average height, military build with short dark hair. She said, 'yes. I am Navajo, but I sure as hell ain't your granny. And you?'

He smiled, his teeth startlingly white in the moonlight, a counterpoint to the dark smudge of his face. 'I am Mescalero Apache.'

She nodded. 'Why do you chase us? Your own people?'

'You're wanted for murder of FBI agents, and I'm an FBI agent,' he said.

She laughed softly. 'Man, they singing you a song,' she said. 'If'n you listening to that O'Hara, he's crazier than a rattler and twice as crooked. They came on my ranch to kill us and take my baby girl, and we defended ourselves. And they weren't no FBI agents.'

'What d'you mean?' he said

'How many Feds you know covered in street gang tats?'

He kept looking at her, his eyes boring in, looking for shadow or truth. Then the spell was broken as he spoke into a face mike, answering a question coming in through his ear bud. He said, 'roger that. It's the old lady and she's secured. I'll bring her down.'

He stooped and picked up the rifle.

###

Down in the valley Markeson watched the hard-standing area around the well, ignoring Ortega's dead body lying beside it. If Creedwell had neutralized the old woman that left just Greyeagle, and O'Hara must by now be awful close to taking him out.

Markeson was about to move when he sensed a stirring of the dense foliage around him and then O'Hara was there, beside him.

O'Hara said, 'he's up in the cave beside the shacks. I know he is. I've got a night sight on the entrance. You move up carefully to the left and make some noise, low like a scrape of a foot. It'll bring him to the entrance, and I'll take him.'

Markeson said, 'I'm on it boss.' He moved away silently at an angle to the cave entrance.

CHAPTER THIRTY

It was just a light scraping sound, but very close, and Greyeagle was immediately alert. They couldn't know he was in the cave as he hadn't shown himself. He moved silently to the entrance, staying in the shadow at the side, looking out. The moon was gone now.

He heard the sound again, closer, to the right of the cave entrance. He inched forward until he stood right along the opening, but still with no part of his body breaching that invisible line. There he remained, acutely aware of every sound around him, listening for that discordant note, that ripple in the night air that might tell him something.

He sniffed, and it was there; the very slight smell of aftershave. Someone was at the entrance to the right. He waited, then he heard a light scuffing sound, this time as if the guy was moving away. He smiled to himself and moved his head silently through the opening, scanning to the right. He could see a darker area in the air moving away, and he stepped out, raising the rifle, and knew in that instant they'd suckered him.

He sensed disturbance in the air above him as O'Hara dropped onto him, knocking him to the ground and winding him, all the breath gone from his lungs. He didn't struggle so O'Hara climbed off him. Greyeagle rolled onto his back as Markeson loomed out of the night fixing a red sniper dot on his face. 'Game's over, chief, Markeson said. 'One move and you'll go back to your ancestors hunting grounds quicker than you can whistle Dixie.'

'Where's the kid?' O'Hara said

'What kid would that be? Greyeagle said, rubbing his neck.

'Have it your own way.' O'Hara said. He nodded at Markeson. 'Get him up.'

As Markeson manhandled Greyeagle to his feet Sia appeared out of the darkness with Dawson Creedwell walking behind her.

O'Hara pulled a cellphone out of his pocket, switched it on and pressed a speed-dial number as he moved away from the group.

###

Victor Diaz was sitting in the back of a large black SUV powering its way through the desert in a convoy of three vehicles when the call came in.

'What you got for me soldier?' he said.

'We've secured the site within the last ten minutes, sir, and the two adult individuals. But there is no sign of the girl. I will question them robustly and organize a search immediately,' O'Hara said.

Diaz looked at the Indian tracker in the front passenger seat and asked, 'how long?'

'Ten minutes,' the guy said, studying a map on his tablet.

'We'll be there in ten, soldier. I'll question them but you can start a search right away,' Diaz said into the phone

'Roger that,' O'Hara said, but Diaz had already disconnected.

###

O'Hara wandered back to the group. He said to Creedwell, 'secure the prisoners.' Then to Markeson, 'start a sweep looking for the kid, and watch out for booby traps. Senator Victor Diaz will be arriving here soon and then we'll question the redskins.'

Markeson hitched his rifle and loped off towards the well and the hard-standing area. The sun was just starting to peep over the horizon bringing on the early morning. It was still quite cold, and Markeson shivered as he got to Ortega's stiff and dead body. He moved on, eying the well as he passed it, moving slowly towards the tree-line.

As he moved away a small shape rose up out of the well. She held a large bow the string of which she proceeded to draw back with an arrow. She took a line on Markeson's retreating back, held her breath and let go the string, immediately ducking back down into the well. As the arrow left the bow, Markeson must have sensed something, because he turned back so that the arrow struck the fleshy underside of his shoulder, going in deep, the force knocking him to his knees.

He looked down in disbelief at the arrow sticking out near his breast. Fury, outrage and pain driving him, he screamed, '*Goddamn it*! I'm hit.'

O'Hara hurried down to the hard-standing area, scanning all around as he moved. 'What the fuck happened?' he said.

'I don't know. Came from nowhere. Couldn't have been the kid, could it?' Markeson said, uncertainly, his face bathed in sweat.

'I don't know,' O'Hara said, 'but I'm going to find out.' He moved over to the well and looked down inside. The rope with the large knots hung down over the side disappearing into the black hole. He moved back, stooped down and picked up a couple of largish stones and dropped them in, listening. Not too deep O'Hara calculated. He shouted down into the well, 'hey, kid. If you're down there, you better come out now or I'm going to start shooting.'

Silence greeted him, but in the background the sound of vehicles up on the ridge. He looked up as the fronts of three black SUV's poked over the top. He turned to Markeson. 'Stay here and keep an eye on the well, case she's in there. Those are our guy's up on the ridge. I'll get you some first aid. Stay alert soldier.'

Markeson nodded, grimacing, looking down at the arrow.

Up on the ridge O'Hara greeted Diaz. Looked like he'd brought along two grunts and two Indian trackers. O'Hara asked one of the men to see to Markeson, then he walked down to the camp with Diaz, briefing him on the situation.

Inside the cave Dawson Creedwell had positioned Greyeagle on a large rock with his hands bound by wrist ties. Sia's hands had been left free so she could make some coffee over a fire they had started. Creedwell stood, back against a large rock as Diaz and O'Hara approached.

'Okay, soldier,' Diaz said, angry that all they had was the old woman and the tracker. 'The girl, Sapphire. Where is she? That was the mission.'

'She's here, sir. Likely in the well and we're sending someone down now, and starting a full scale search,' O'Hara said.

'I don't have time for that, soldier,' Diaz said, studying Sia and Greyeagle as if they were some exotic form of wildlife. 'Every minute I'm away from Washington there's people asking questions. We need to finish this now. Question the old woman,' he said. 'And if it kills her, that's one less mangy Indian, right?'

'Right, sir,' O'Hara said, his eyes gleaming with anticipation. He snapped an order at one of Diaz's trackers to get some lights and go down the well. The man moved away. O'Hara walked over and grabbed Sia's wrist and pulled her up against the rock wall. She stood, calm.

'Where's your granddaughter? Where d'you tell her to hide? What d'you tell her to do?' O'Hara asked.

The old lady held his gaze. 'We knew you'd come, so we told her to go out in the desert and hide, that's all. I have no idea where she is right now.'

O'Hara's fist shot out catching her completely by surprise, the punch hitting her face with a cracking sound and smashing her head back against the rock. Greyeagle was moving at the same time, but Creedwell calmly swung his rifle butt down on the back of his head knocking him unconscious. Sia shook her head, blood flicking off her nose and jaw, but her eyes were still clear, and calm.

'Wrong answer,' O'Hara said. 'You know, grandma, I watched an old western once. Called something like Run of the Arrow, or some such, maybe with Kirk Douglas. And in the movie, they had this Indian torture that I loved. I think the VC may have used it in 'Nam as well.'

'Yeah?' Sia said, unconcerned.

'Yeah,' O'Hara said, smiling, getting into it. 'What they do, is they cut a strip of flesh like at the top of the chest, so it's like a flap. Then what they do, and this is the good bit. What they do is they take a hold of that strip, and they just rip it, tear it down, so they rip off this long strip of flesh.'

'Fuck you,' Sia said.

'Gimme your knife,' O'Hara said to Creedwell.

He hesitated.

'Gimme your fucking knife, chief. Or your next,' O'Hara said.

Creedwell looked at the ground, shook his head as if he were going to refuse, but then slowly drew a long hunting knife from a sheaf on his belt and handed it to O'Hara.

###

Down in the well Sapphire held onto the ledge, looking up forlornly at the circle of rapidly brightening light as the morning began to break. She knew it was bad up top, but she had faith in Greyeagle. She knew he would come for her. She heard scrabbling sounds up above, and as a shape loomed into the circle of light she ducked back down.

She leaned over the edge of the ledge and looked at the misshapen jagged opening in the rock-face she had seen last time she had been down there. She'd felt then that maybe it was a tunnel of some sort, but it was so small, maybe it had been made by an animal. She heard more scrabbling sounds and the rope began to move. Someone was coming down. If it was Greyeagle he would have shouted to warn her.

She reached her hand down underneath to the opening in the rock face, but she just couldn't reach it. Now the rope was taught, and someone was moving slowly down. A light played and flickered over the walls of the well. She looked desperately around, her mind frantically looking for escape. She thought of falling back into the water, but then she'd just drown. Now she could hear him only a few meters away, relentlessly coming on.

She tried to edge a bit further along the ledge with her elbows, and now she was leaning right out, stretching down and around, but it seemed hopeless. She desperately reached out again, straining every sinew. Then just as she was about to give up, collapse in on herself, her fingers felt the edge of the rock. She grasped it firmly but then realized it was no use. The only way in would be to hang down from the ledge and swing into the opening and hope it was big enough, that she could gain some kind of purchase before she fell into the water.

Now she could hear the man very close, coming on. She wanted to scream and call for help. She quickly put her bow over her head, took a deep breath and rolled over the edge of the ledge so that she was hanging down over the water. She began to try and swing her body into the small entrance. She could feel her fingers slipping and losing grip; she began desperately scrabbling at the rock with her fingers to hold on as her body sluggishly swung over the water. She lashed out with a foot, to try and get a foothold, but just got a sore toe. She knew she wasn't going to make it, better to just give up and drop in the water now her hands were aching so much. As she prepared to let go her flailing foot suddenly made contact, on a tiny shelf. She immediately put weight on the foot and removed one of her hands to reach under and feel around for a handhold. The rock felt smooth and she couldn't find anywhere to grip and now she could hear the man's breathing as he came down the last couple of feet.

As he alighted her hand finally found a grip and she let go the ledge and swung under, hauling herself into the tiny opening. She clung onto the edge looking inside into the gloom. She could see it stretched away inside the wall of the well, but hardly looked large enough for her to squeeze through, and what if she got trapped, and couldn't get back out?

Now she could hear the man almost on top of her. She took a deep breath and plunged her small body into the opening, forcing loose rocks and debris aside as she squeezed into the tight space, almost burrowing her way in. She felt stuck with no wriggle room, and the bow string was caught tight around her neck, her breathing so loud she was sure the man would hear her. She could just see, looking down her body that her feet were still sticking out, and he would be sure to see them. She pushed with all her might, wriggling and squirming and could gradually feel the soft earth around her giving way, allowing her to move. She worried about the air. Maybe she would suffocate, but it was too late to stop now.

###

Sia screamed, piercing the bright morning desert air, the sound more animal than human. Blood dripped down her bare chest from the six-inch horizontal cut O'Hara had just made along the top of her breastbone.

He turned to look out of the cave entrance down the valley, long-bladed bloody knife in his hand. He raised it to his lips and tasted the blood, and bellowed down the valley, 'come to daddy, Sapphire. You don't show yourself, your grandma's going to suffer a world of pain.'

Silence greeted O'Hara's threat. Sapphire couldn't hear anything from up-top now. O'Hara turned back to Sia.

Above the valley up on the ridge Dante's group arrived, drawing their two black SUV's quietly to a stop behind Diaz's three deserted vehicles, out of sight of the camp down in the valley.

As they got out of the vehicles Dante said, pointing at Pascal, 'you. Come with me. Rest of you stay here.' He turned to one of the grunts and asked for field glasses which were handed to him. He beckoned Pascal to follow him up to the edge of the ridge. They lay on their stomach's and edged forward, Dante slowly scanning the valley.

He wordlessly passed the glasses to Pascal. As she looked through them, she began murmuring a commentary. 'Two dead bodies that I can see, and a camouflaged pit that's probably got another one in it. There's a thin stream of smoke coming out of that cave to the right of the two wooden shacks. Looks like there's been a war down there, Dante. You sure you want to go charging in?'

'I want the kid,' he said. 'And she's down there.'

'Yeah? So's Diaz, his crew and O'Hara. I tried to tell you about Diaz in the car, but you didn't want to listen,' she said, pausing as she focused the glasses on the cave entrance. 'There he is, Diaz, at the mouth of the cave. And down there, near the hard-standing area you'll see another guy just climbing out the well. Looks like he's been using a drilling rig down there,' she added, passing the glasses back to Dante.

He took a look, lowered the glasses and turned to Pascal. 'So what d'you think we got here?'

'You asking me? This is your play, Dante.'

He smiled. 'You don't fool me, Pascal. You're here 'cause you want the kid as well, and you think you're going to waltz out of here with her. So let's just skip the hard to get routine?'

She returned his gaze, her face calm, but underneath her nerves were screaming. Where the hell was Sapphire? And Greyeagle and Sia? Maybe they were all dead. But the fact that Diaz and his crew were all still there suggested they hadn't finished. Maybe they were all in the cave, and why the drilling in the well? She needed to find out and quick.

'Just like you, Dante,' she said, her mind working feverishly. 'Diaz wants the kid, 'cause she can link him to kidnap charges that'll destroy him. But he also wants something else, and maybe that gives you something to trade?'

'And what might that be?' he asked.

'Me. Diaz wants me, for the same reasons you do, 'cause I can put it all together and sink the both of you,' she said, hoping Dante wouldn't grasp the fact that it was actually Michael who would be far more lethal to their interests than her.

Dante studied her. He checked his watch and the sky.

'Get one of your guys to go down there with a white handkerchief. He can tell 'em you have me and want to talk, do a trade,' she said.

Dante carried on looking at her, turning it over. 'Okay,' he said. 'Let's do it.'

###

Sapphire could hear muffled sounds of drilling coming through from the inside of the well as she slowly tried to worm her way forward through the earth and debris clogged tunnel. It was desperately slow progress and it sometimes felt like she wasn't moving at all, but she was sure she could feel a faint breath of fresh air coming from in front of her and it lifted her spirits a little. But then perhaps she was just imagining it, to make herself feel better, as it was more likely she would just get stuck and suffocate. And now the dark enclosed space was bringing back terrible memories of the black casket she had been imprisoned in when she had first been taken from her home.

She stopped moving forward for a moment as the terror gripped her, freezing her in the earth, immobile, so she couldn't move. But then a thought popped into her head unbidden. Long ago her mama used to tell her stories about the Earth Mother who was worshiped by the

Navajo. Wasn't she in the earth now, in the Earth Mother? Perhaps the Earth Mother would watch over her and keep her safe. The thought cheered her, and her grimy muddy face set into a determined expression. She began to move forward again, pretending she was a mole with powerful front paws, forcing herself on through the earth.

She started to make quicker progress and the earth seemed less hard-packed. She stopped to rest again, breathing deeply. She lay her head down on her hands for a few moments. When she raised her head, she was sure she sensed a faint light up ahead through a small gap in front of her. It energized her and she began scrabbling the earth violently, hauling herself forward, dragging the long-bow underneath her through the muddy earth.

She was sure she was about to burst through into the open air when she heard a deep far away rumbling sound. The earth seemed to move above her, and she could feel a great weight pressing down, getting heavier and heavier, squeezing all the air from her body. It was all around her now as earth cascaded down in front of her as well, entombing her, closing off the air and knocking her unconscious in a rain of stony rocks.

Sia was now collapsed against the rock wall, held up by a rope around her neck. Blood ran down her breasts onto her stomach from the gaping wound at the top of her chest where O'Hara had cut it open. She was barely conscious. Greyeagle had come around and was sitting on a rock, hands bound, his head down, eyes half-closed.

O'Hara stood a few steps away with Diaz, sipping coffee, taking five from their exertions. They both looked up as the grunt came back from the well. 'There's no one down there, sir,' he said. 'And the opening under the ledge is too small for an adult, and even a kid would struggle to get in there. And if she could get in, where would she go - get trapped and suffocate most likely. Its full of loose earth and debris. I've drilled in the rock around it, to get in, but that's gonna take forever. I reckon she never went in the well, just ran. Only way you can figure for sure, quick, would be to dynamite it,' he concluded.

O'Hara nodded and looked at Diaz.

'I think the old woman knows where the kid is,' Diaz said, with a thin murderous smile. 'Let's get on with it, soldier.'

'Someone's coming, sir,' the grunt said, pointing down the valley. 'With a white flag.'

'Who the fuck is that?' O'Hara said, cocking his weapon. 'Cover me,' he added as he moved out to meet the approaching man.

CHAPTER THIRTY-ONE

Dante snapped the phone to his ear, holding his other hand up for silence. As he listened, he looked at Pascal, standing on the ridge staring down into the valley. He nodded his head and issued a burst of quick-fire Spanish, then said to her, 'Chavez, he say Diaz agrees the meet, and maybe they trade some? They can't find the kid, Sapphire. They're still looking.'

'Good,' Pascal said. 'Can I suggest you don't play all your cards face-up.'

'Meaning?'

'Keep Michael back in reserve.'

He pondered that a moment, then called a grunt over. 'We'll secure the boy in the back of the truck while we go down to talk,' he said.

Pascal said to Michael, 'don't worry, it won't be for long, and I'll be back for you soon. That's a promise. Sapphire may be down there as well. You'd like to see her again wouldn't you?'

'Yes I would,' he said solemnly. 'I'll be okay. I'm used to being a prisoner,' he added.

Pascal tussled his hair as the soldier came over. 'I'll tie him,' she said.

The grunt looked at her for a moment, unsure, then shrugged and nodded. He watched as she secured Michaels hands and ankles and carried him to the back of the vehicle.

The grunt said, 'sorry, Mr Figueroa insisted,' as he placed some masking tape over Michael's mouth.

She looked the boy in the eye and said, 'just relax, Michael. I will come back for you.'

His eyes looked calm and untroubled. She hated to leave him like that, but there seemed to be no choice.

###

She was dreaming of a cartoon she'd watched where a steamroller driven by Jerry the mouse runs over Tom the cat and flattens him into the road surface, but then he bounces back into his old cat shape with a sound like a large spring being released. She tried to giggle but her mouth was full of mud, her laughter turning to terror as she felt the awful weight pressing down on her back, bringing her awake with a start, snuffling and coughing into the black earth.

She desperately started scrabbling at the muddy earth around her face as the reality of where she was reasserted itself in her mind. She was stuck, buried in the earth alongside the well, and no one was coming for her. The rumbling sound of the man with the drill had stopped and she was completely alone.

She rested her head on her hands and began to cry, her soft sobs echoing in her ears.

After a while she stopped, her mind returning to the stories about the Earth Mother. Surely she was safe here inside the earth and no harm would come to her? Her young mind mulled the idea for a while. She wiped her muddy face with her fingers. She tried to shake herself and was surprised to feel that the earth covering her body had loosened, and she could move again.

She took some deep breaths in the confined darkness, then began to squirm forward through the soft and crumbly earth. Again as she cleared the earth in front of her she felt that tiny fresh feel of air on her face. After around ten minutes of laborious worming along like a snake she was just about to stop for a rest when her leading hand burst through the earth into fresh air. She poked her head through and couldn't quite believe what she saw. It was a large cavern with a pool of water. She looked up and could see, way up above, some gaps showing light slanting through from the surface. She looked around in wonder, drawing in deep breaths.

She dragged herself out of the earth with her bow now covered with mud and debris. She stood up and moved down to the edge of the water where she quickly washed her face in the ice cold water. She cleaned the bow and checked inside her blouse that her last arrow was still there undamaged. She sat down at the side of the water and looked around the cavern.

She soon noticed on the far side of the pool there was a path that seemed to lead upwards. She looked around and noticed there were drawings on the walls of animals, buffalo and deer. She looked down at the water; it looked deep and she knew it was very cold. She shivered. To get to the path she'd have to cross the water, but she was a good swimmer.

She looked up at the light slanting through the high domed roof and said out loud, 'thank you Earth Mother.' She put the bow over her head once more and slowly edged her way into the water. Her breath caught in her throat as the shock of the ice cold temperature hit her. She let the air seep from her lungs, took a slow deep breath and pushed off from the side into the water, immediately slipping into a rhythmic and powerful breast stroke. Now she was a beaver, powering her way through the water.

After a little while she could feel the ground come up under her as she got to the other side. She hauled herself out and stamped her feet and shook as much water from her clothes as she could. Still shaking the water out, she began to walk up the pathway, her shoes making a rather unpleasant squelching sound.

Pascal stood in the mouth of the cave, nausea and ice cold fury passing through her as she took in the scene. Sia was roped to the rock wall, her head lolling as if she were asleep, held up by the rope passing under her chin. The wound across the top of her chest was bloody and raw, a flap of skin pulled away in a horizontal line above her naked breasts. Thick blood had congealed along the wound and flies crawled over it feasting whilst a trickle of fresh blood dripped and ran down her stomach. Pascal swallowed hard, exerting every ounce of self-control to stop herself from rushing to Sia's aid, but cold hard logic told her she had to stay calm.

Greyeagle sat near Sia, his back against the wall and head down as if he were sleeping, but she knew he was watching.

Pascal coldly analyzed what she could see and what she had seen whilst walking down the valley. There was Dante, his captain, Alvaro Chavez and two soldiers. And then there was Diaz with two of his close security team plus two local native American trackers. O'Hara's team seemed to have been reduced to just a tracker they referred to as Creedwell, and one other guy with an arrow sticking out of his shoulder. The odds looked decidedly bad. And where was Sapphire?

Diaz chucked some coffee he had been drinking into the ground and walked up to Dante; each man studying the other. 'So, Mr Figueroa, what we seem to have got ourselves here is what you might call a Mexican stand-off,' Diaz said with a chuckle.

Dante didn't smile. 'Senator, this is no stand-off. We have a temporary common purpose is all. It will serve us both to join forces, and then we can end it here. Simply put: I can help you and you can help me.'

'And how can you help me, Mr Figueroa?' Diaz said.

'I have Ms Pascal here,' he said gesturing at her, and at Chavez who now held a sawn-off shot-gun pointed in the general direction of Diaz's men. 'Whom I believe you have been searching for?'

Diaz nodded, his face deadpan. 'Well, son, I reckon its possible you might just need her to disappear a might more than me. But tell me,

Mr Figueroa. Do you have Solomon Gutiérrez's son, Michael?'

'I do. And he's hidden away safe and sound where you'll never find him,' Dante said. 'So perhaps it is, as you say, a Mexican stand-off?'

Diaz nodded again, continuing to study Dante, sizing him up. He glanced at his watch. 'Okay, we'll put that aside for now, and lets just find the girl first. Then we can finish the job.'

'Sounds like a plan,' Dante said. 'So where is she?'

'O'Hara,' Diaz barked.

The name was repeated outside, and O'Hara ambled back into the cave.

'We're going to join forces temporarily with Mr Figueroa here and his crew,' Diaz said. 'The mission is to find the Dinks kid. Where is she?'

O'Hara eyed Dante up and spat in the ground. He rubbed his face, tired after his nights work. 'We suffered heavy losses coming in here 'cause they were well prepared. No one saw the kid until the end of it, and we're not even certain it was her, although I believe it was. We believe she was hiding in the well. She pops up with a bow and arrow and hits Markeson in the shoulder then disappears again,' O'Hara said.

'Into the well?' Dante said.

'We're not sure,' O'Hara said.

'What do you mean?' Alvaro Chavez asked.

'We've carried out a careful sweep and search of the area and can't find her or any tracks. She's not in the well drowned, but there is a small gap in the wall of the well small enough for a child to squeeze through, and there may be a space there or even a tunnel of some kind. We've had a guy down there with a drill who tells us it'll need dynamite, unless we want to spend the rest of the year here.'

Now Diaz was speaking quietly into his cellphone and nodding his head. He finished his call. 'I need this to be over now, so I can head back to Washington,' he said. 'Put the Indian up with the old woman and then lets ask them both where the kid is. And I mean let's really ask them. One of them will know. Meantime get some C4 in the well and blow it.'

O'Hara nodded, pleased to at last get some definitive orders. He walked over to Creedwell who was sitting beside Greyeagle. He said to him, 'get him up on the wall.'

Creedwell didn't move. O'Hara said, 'you hear me soldier?'

'I hear you, sir,' he said, then more softly, 'but tell me, who were the guys in your team who hit the old lady's ranch, 'cause it sounds like they were mercenaries. And this,' he said gesturing around the cave with his hand. 'This bullshit. Is this all official, sanctioned?' he asked.

O'Hara looked at him, his eyes flaming with anger. 'You disobeying an order, boy?' he said. 'An order by the way sanctioned by a US senator on the intelligence committee, who's a close buddy of our own FBI director?'

Creedwell looked down at the hard-packed earth for a moment, contemplating his options. He looked up, unsure. 'I guess not,' he said reluctantly. He slowly got to his feet and pulled Greyeagle up.

As Creedwell moved away, hustling Greyeagle in front of him, O'Hara watched him with a calculating eye.

###

O'Hara walked slowly up and down in front of the rock wall against which both were now roped. Sia seemed as if she were sleeping, her head still lolling, whilst Greyeagle looked straight ahead, ignoring the pacing O'Hara. A few feet away Dante and Diaz watched.

Despite her desperate concern for Sia, Pascal remained preternaturally alert, her eyes constantly scanning the interior of the cave and the state of readiness of the soldiers ranged against her. Most of the men had gone out to search and organize the blowing of the well. But Alvaro Chavez remained, standing with a shotgun that seemed to waiver between Pascal and Diaz. Then there was one grunt from Diaz's personal security detail, and one of the Indian trackers, plus O'Hara and Dawson Creedwell. Not great odds, and even her natural optimism was starting to fade.

O'Hara came to a halt in front of Sia. He slowly lifted he head up by the hair and studied her bruised face and closed eyes. She seemed asleep. 'Wakey-wakey,' he said, slapping her face playfully. 'You're gonna miss all the fun.'

Sia's eyes struggled open, slowly bringing O'Hara into focus. She moved her head slightly, taking in Pascal's presence and Greyeagle roped up beside her. She smiled through cracked lips. 'Can't say I'm glad to see you, my dear, in these circumstances,' she said, addressing Pascal in a croaky voice and ignoring O'Hara, 'but I am.'

'Good to see you too,' Pascal said. 'And don't let this inadequate little psychopath frighten you. He couldn't cut it in the FBI so now he's gone rogue, playing at soldiers.'

'You think I'm—'

'Can we get moving, O'Hara?' Diaz said, impatiently cutting in. 'I haven't got all day. The old woman's broken so concentrate on her and get what we need. The other one will talk as well, to save the old lady. So let's not be squeamish. Get to it, soldier.'

'Sir,' O'Hara said. First he walked over and got an iron bar like a poker lying near the fire. He lay the end of it in the glowing embers. Then he went and got a cup of water and approached Sia again. He lifted her head and threw the water in her face. She sluggishly shook herself, clearing her eyes, focusing on him.

'Tell you what, O'Hara,' Pascal said, desperate to keep the guy from hurting Sia anymore. 'Instead of beating and torturing an old lady who's got her hands tied, why not you and me go head to head? I'll even let you keep the knife, 'cause I don't need anything against a pussy like you. Last guy standing wins,' she said.

Now the audience was focused on O'Hara, some grinning, wondering how he was going to try and save face. But he ignored them. Instead he slid his fingers into the bloody flap of skin at the top of Sia's chest, working his fingers in, getting purchase. She moaned deep in the back of her throat, the pain she felt palpable in the air.

Pascal instinctively began to move towards Sia, until Chavez cocked the sawn-off, stopping her in her tracks. She cursed under her breath, desperate to find a way to end Sia's suffering.

'You like that, Greyeagle?' O'Hara said. 'Old lady can't take much more, especially when I tear a strip off. So, folks, I want to know where the brat is, where you told her to hide.' He looked around at them.

###

Sapphire walked up the path humming to herself the old lullaby her mother had taught her. In places the track was worn out and she had to edge her way forward, and in others there was no light coming through, so she had to feel her way. The path seemed to be rising steadily upward, but then suddenly she could go no further because it was blocked off by a rock fall. It was reasonably light, and she was able to study the obstruction carefully; it was a wall of gravel and debris stretching up to the roof of the cavern.

She sat down tired and hungry. What was she to do now, she wondered? Seemingly she couldn't go forwards and she didn't think she could go back, because even if she made it through, they would be waiting for her. She lent back, studying the wall of rock rearing up before her, her eyes crawling up, down and across.

She lifted the bow from over her head and began to clean it. She also took her one remaining arrow out of her blouse and smoothed the shaft. The arrow was special because the tip was coated in scorpion poison Greyeagle had helped her get and apply, and she had covered it with masking tape. She carefully put the arrow back in her blouse and continued cleaning the bow. From time to time she looked up at the rock face, resenting it, and hating it for blocking her way. This time as her eyes idly traversed the rocky crags, she thought she saw a gap or hole near the top. He eyes stopped their tracking and returned to the spot,

422

excitement rising in her. She jumped up and ran at the wall, scrabbling her way up like a small mountain goat.

By the time she reached the spot her fingers were bloody and raw. She was on a kind of ledge and she peeked over the top of it. It looked as if there was yet another small opening at the back of this ledge, but again it appeared to be blocked with earth and debris. She scrambled across and lent down to the opening. She stopped, stiffening; she was sure she had heard the faint sound of voices. She listened again, intently, her ear at the opening, then the hair on the back of her neck rose. She could definitely hear indistinct sounds of speech coming through. She leaned into the hole pushing her hand into the earth, and it was loose and gave way easily, so she began to shovel it aside, forcing herself into the tight space, and then forwards again.

After a couple of feet, she came up against a large rock blocking the soft earth. She was soaked in sweat and mud, now mingling with the blood from her fingers, and she could barely breathe. She folded her hands in front of her and rested her head on them, despairing of ever getting through and out.

After a while she began to hum her lullaby again and once again the specter, unbidden, of the Earth Mother rose in her mind. She smiled through the mud, placed her hands against the rock and pushed with all her might. She felt a very slight give in the rock. She stopped, and then tried again, applying every sinew and all her strength, and very gradually the rock began to move, centimeter by centimeter.

Then earth was falling off the rock and she could see a chink of gloomy daylight, and then her head was poking out, and she could hear distinct voices from below. She silently pulled herself out of the hole.

She was in another cave on a ledge high up. She crept to the edge of the ledge and looked down.

She started at what she saw, horrified, her stomach churning, and she nearly cried out. Sia and Greyeagle were roped to the wall like animals, and blood was dripping down Sia's bare chest. A group of men stood around Courtney, and they were watching. With another start she recognized Victor Diaz amongst them, and there was the hated O'Hara with a knife in one hand and in the other a poker with a red glowing tip.

As she watched, horrified, O'Hara walked down in front of Sia and Greyeagle, toying with them, teasing the knife blade across their faces, leaving trails of blood. He put the knife down and held the red-hot poker, close to their faces, pulling it away at the last moment, and all the time questioning them about her. Her! She must give herself up immediately she thought, to stop the torture.

Now O'Hara stood in front of Greyeagle, threatening him. He held the poker and suddenly he was pressing the glowing tip against Greyeagle's forehead, and she heard the sizzling flesh and Greyeagle's cry. She lifted the bow from over her shoulder and removed the arrow from her blouse, picking the tape off the tip, tears running down her face leaving tracks in the caked mud.

O'Hara, smiling, pulled the poker away from the blistered and burning flesh, leaving Greyeagle hanging unconscious in his ropes. 'I just branded myself a new steer,' O'Hara said, driving the poker down into the sand and leaving it there.

He moved on and stopped in front of Pascal. She stood silent, hatred radiating out from her eyes like laser beams. 'You don't know where the kid is so you can wait for yours,' he said.

He moved on to Sia. 'This time it's for keeps, granny' he said, moving his fingers back into the bloody flap of skin, feeling around then gripping it tightly. He looked at Sia. 'Where's the kid?'

'I don't know,' she whispered.

O'Hara looked around at the watching men, all engrossed in the spectacle, apart from Dawson Creedwell who looked sickened, his eyes full of doubt and questions.

'Wrong answer,' O'Hara said, and viciously ripped down on the strip of flesh. As it came away, with a sickening tearing sound, Pascal screamed.

CHAPTER THIRTY-TWO

Sapphire cried out when O'Hara tore Sia's flesh away, but no one heard her, and now she was weeping unrestrained, the tears blurring her eyes so she couldn't see properly. She knew it was all her fault. She should never have taken Courtney to Grandma's ranch; that's what started it all.

She wiped a hand across her eyes, clearing her vision. Like in a dream she studied the tip of the arrow in her hand, still smeared and moist with scorpion venom. She carefully placed the flight feathers against the string of the bow and drew it back with all the strength she had left. She focused her eye on the center of O'Hara's head as he smiled and clowned around with the strip of Sia's flesh, still held in his hand, holding it out in front of his laughing men.

Eyes locked on O'Hara, Sapphire offered up a prayer to the Earth Mother, asking her to guide the arrow true, then she let go the string. As the arrow whistled away, Sapphire stood up on the ledge and let out a war cry, the long piece of cloth she had tied around her mud caked hair trailing in the air behind her.

The arrow traveled at great velocity striking and going through

O'Hara's left eye deep into his brain killing him instantly. His head flicked up with the arrow still embedded, his face turned up toward the roof of the cavern, then he dropped to the ground.

###

As O'Hara fell the only one moving was Pascal; just as Sapphire had let go the arrow, Pascal had spotted her rising up on the ridge. Now she dived for the knife O'Hara had dropped, picking it up as she rolled, then throwing it underarm as she came up into a crouch, the knife taking Alvaro Chavez in the stomach. As he slumped, she was around behind him lifting the sawn-off out of his hands and lining it up on Diaz and Dante.

As she did so there was a huge blast outside as the well was dynamited.

For a moment nobody stirred. Pascal had Diaz and Dante covered, whilst Diaz's grunt, his Indian tracker and Duncan Creedwell all had their guns trained on Pascal.

'Looks like stalemate,' Diaz said, already recovering his composure. 'But with our guys outside, you've got no chance.'

Before Pascal could come back at him, Dawson Creedwell said something in native American to the Indian tracker. The man looked at Creedwell for a moment, his expression uncertain, then he nodded his head. Creedwell turned to Pascal, 'what happened here ain't right,' he said. 'So I'm with you, and I'll take my chances. This man is Mescalero Apache like me and he's with us also.'

As they turned their guns on Dante, Diaz and his guy, another blast came from outside. Pascal said, 'We need to take down the guys blowing the well, so let's get this lot in here put away first.'

As the Indian tracker disarmed Diaz's man and moved to secure all three, Creedwell moved to Greyeagle and cut him loose. Pascal ran to Sia who was now unconscious, hanging in her ropes. Starting between her bare breasts O'Hara had torn away a strip of flesh that was about three inches wide and nine inches down, the wound angry and red. Pascal could barely stand to look at it. She was about to pour water on the wound when Creedwell said, '*No!*'

He had retrieved the strip of flesh from O'Hara's dead hand, and now he came over with some green leaves. He placed the strip of skin back in place over Sia's wound and pressed the leaves against it, telling Pascal to hold it in place. He brought the first aid kit over and they bandaged Sia's chest and gave her an injection of morphine, before Creedwell moved on to Greyeagle to treat the burn

Pascal turned to find Sapphire charging at her and throwing her arms around her. Pascal gave it a few moments before breaking away and moving up to the cave entrance, realizing they were still far from safe. Dante, Diaz and company were bound and gagged. Pascal said to the tracker, 'move the prisoners behind that rock and then call the other guys in. Tell them we've found the girl. When they're all in here we get the drop on them.'

The man nodded, immediately moving away.

Within twenty minutes they had all the grunts accounted for and all weapons and cellphones taken from them. They set up a sick bay for the wounded and injured, including Markeson, then brought Michael down to the cave. Diaz and Dante were gagged and roped to the wall just as Sia and Greyeagle had been, and now Pascal slowly paced up and down in front of them. Neither man seemed scared, their eyes simply watchful.

Pascal stopped and turned to them. 'So, guys,' she said. 'True confession time. We already know what you did, but we need to hear it from you. So Dante, you're going to tell us about the kidnap, ransom and attempted murder of Sapphire. And you, Diaz,' she said, looking at him. 'Are going to tell us about the abduction to order and murder of Tamara Hunt.'

She removed both their gags.

'Man, are you storing yourself up some grief?' Diaz said, back full of confidence despite his circumstances. He continued, 'It's you, sweetheart, who should be worrying. You're wanted by the FBI and US Marshall's to answer for an ever increasing list of the most serious crimes on the statute book, and you're threatening *me*? And with what? You have no evidence against me and the allegations you make are false.'

'Dante?' Pascal prompted him.

'Fuck you, Pascal,' he said. 'Senator's right. What you've done here just compounds your crimes, and you still have no evidence against me that would stand up in court.'

'Fine,' Pascal said, 'but as your friend O'Hara was fond of saying, its the wrong answer. Now, you guys seem very convinced of the efficacy of using physical threats and pain as a means of getting someone to speak. So we're going to carry out our own little experiment to see if you're right.'

'What is this bullshit?' Diaz said.

'My friends here,' Pascal said, nodding over at the two trackers and Greyeagle, whose head was now bandaged. 'Are going to take you a little way into the desert. Say, Diaz,' she said suddenly, turning to face him. 'You ever had your hand laid in the embers of a red hot fire and smelled it roasting?'

He just looked at her, maybe still thinking she was kidding.

'Guys,' she said. 'When you're ready to talk, they'll bring you back.'

'You're crazy,' Diaz said. 'FBI already know you're here. Only a matter of time before they show up, and then your toast.'

'Well you better hope they turn up real soon?' she said, nodding at the two trackers. They moved Diaz and Dante to the cave entrance where the horses were waiting.

A moment later Greyeagle, sitting astride his mount, said, 'there's a small culvert about half a mile away that's perfect. I'm guessing we won't be long.' He tipped his hat and coaxed his horse forward.

As the small troupe moved away, Sapphire said, 'why can't I go with them, Courtney?'

'Because I have other plans for you, sweetie,' Pascal said. 'You're going on TV, so let's make you beautiful. Come on.'

As they walked down towards the well, the child looked up at her to see if she was kidding, but Pascal already had a cellphone clamped to her ear.

'Calver?' she said. 'Things are moving fast, and we don't have much time. I need you to contact the federal prosecutor, Daniels urgently and the two FBI guys who visited you, and this is what I want you to do.'

She spoke for around five minutes

As her call to Calver finished, she dialed the number she had for Fernando Ruiz, on the off chance he might still be around and talking, and he was, albeit still in a hospital bed. She spoke for around five minutes to him also, telling him what she wanted him to do. He said he'd get on it.

###

It was nearly two hours later that Greyeagle returned with Diaz and Dante. Now both men looked almost like ghosts, faces white and drawn, eyes haunted.

'What the fuck did you do to them?' Pascal asked. 'No,' she added. 'Better you don't tell me.'

'Believe me,' Greyeagle said. 'It's better.'

Diaz and Dante were studying in a kind of dazed but interested way the table and chairs Pascal had set up near to the well. Dante said, licking his dry lips, 'so we tell you what you want to hear. Then it's over, right?'

'That's about the size of it,' she replied.

'Why not,' Diaz said. 'Any testimony from us obtained under torture is inherently unreliable and will be laughed out of court.'

'Good. So you won't mind going first then, Diaz?' she said

gesturing at the chair.

He hesitated. To the side of the table a few meters away the two Apache trackers had made a small fire and now Greyeagle placed some large stones in the embers. He looked up at Diaz and said, 'in case you get kinda tongue tied.'

Diaz swallowed, looking at the stones heating in the fire. He straightened up, walked over and took a seat at the table. Pascal sat down opposite him.

'Senator Diaz, we haven't got all day, so we'll keep it nice and brief,' Pascal said, placing a cellphone on the table and pressing the record button.

Fortified by the fact that Pascal was not filming him, only recording his voice, Diaz seemed to puff himself up slightly in the chair and adopt a more confident pose. He knew with his deep pockets, network of connections, his influence and access to the best lawyer's money could buy, whatever he was forced to say could be instantly retracted, wiped away and neutralized.

Sitting behind Pascal on either side of the wall of the well were Michael and Sapphire, each holding a concealed cellphone directed at Diaz.

'You raped Sapphire Dinks, yes?' Pascal asked casually.

Diaz hesitated. Away to his right Greyeagle lifted one of the glowing stones out of the fire with a piece of wood.

###

In Calver's spare office in Brooklyn Federal Prosecutor Daniels sat with Maria Dinks beside him. 'This better be worth it, Calver,' he said with an impatient glare. Maria looked studiedly bored.

Hettie pushed the door ajar and poked her head in saying, 'agents Calhoun and Monroe are here, Jonas.'

'Good. Show them in,' he said.

'With guests,' she added.

First to enter was Yolanda Lopez, chained and shackled, dressed in an orange jumpsuit with Bedford Correctional stenciled on the back, followed by the two FBI agents, and behind them came Isabel Lopez.

Calver said, 'take a seat guys.'

There were chairs laid out in the room and up front a big screen. Yolanda's chains and shackles sounded strange and incongruous echoing around the room as she was led to a chair and seated.

'Had to get the prisoner a special flight up here, Calver,' agent Monroe grumbled. 'So you better not be jerking us around.'

Before Calver could reply there was a loud blowing sound coming through the speakers, and Pascal's voice saying, 'testing, testing.' A blurred picture appeared on the screen. It looked like some people on horses approaching through a desert valley. But then the sound stopped, and the screen went blank.

Maria who had been moodily watching Yolanda, stood up and said, 'this is bullshit, and I have a fashion house to run, so I'm out of here.'

As she started for the door the screen suddenly came alive again, this time with a clear image of senator Victor Diaz, and Pascal's voice boomed out once more through the speakers. 'You raped Sapphire

Dinks, yes?'

Maria, face conflicted as she listened, hesitated for a moment, but now her curiosity was piqued. She sighed heavily and re-took her seat.

Diaz's gaze was imperious as he looked around at the people watching him. He said, in a firm voice, 'yes I did.'

'Thank you, senator,' Pascal said. 'That wasn't so hard was it? But could you repeat it louder so the tape can pick it up?'

'Yes, I did.'

Whilst Sapphires phone was connected to Calver's spare office in New York City, Michael's phone was connected to an office in Ciudad Juarez where a heavily bandaged Fernando Ruiz sat translating the feed into Spanish. Alongside him sat two senior, and clean, *Federales* officer's as well as a guy Ruiz could trust from the DEA.

'Tell us about Tamara Hunt?' Pascal said.

Diaz looked down at the surface of the rickety old table they'd brought out of the shack, closely examining the scars and stains. For a long moment he said nothing. He looked up and smiled at Pascal, but his eyes were empty as if he were running remembered images in his head and was watching them rather than the person facing him across the table. When he spoke, his tone and manner seemed divorced from the look on his dull face, his voice animated and strange.

'That little miss came like a sultry harlot, oozing her temptation, and I was too weak to resist,' he said. 'With the Lord's help, I tried to teach her the error of her ways. We had spiritual and wonderful conjugal relations, but I am a flawed man. But sweet Jesus, I fought it. Oh, yeah, I fought it with the help of the Lord,' he said. 'And I stopped that temptress from casting her spell on others.'

Pascal studied Diaz, wondering whether the guy was simply hedging his bets, laying the groundwork for an insanity plea down the line, or if he really was stone crazy. She'd leave that for the courts. 'You're a righteous man, Victor,' she said without irony. 'And you first saw this temptress, Tamara, at your daughter's school in Washington, right?'

'That's right,' Diaz said, sounding surprised. 'You know I was worried she would be a bad influence on my daughter. Had to get her away from that school.'

'And for that you employed the Daughter Eaters, right?' Pascal said.

Diaz smiled beatifically. 'What an outfit,' he said. 'Solomon Gutiérrez handled it all. Served up that little miss like a box of candy.'

In Calver's New York office FBI agent Monroe, shorn of her

mobile, began to scribble furiously in an old style notebook.

Pascal continued her questioning. 'You said earlier you stopped Tamara Hunt from casting a spell on others. How did you do that?'

'I sent her screaming back to the Lord,' he said. He looked around at the watchers as if he were awaking from his dream, his eyes clearing. He said, 'now I've said my piece. I need to get back to Washington.'

'All in good time, senator,' Pascal said. 'First, we're going to hear from Dante here,' she said, nodding at him. Dante got up and ambled over to the chair that Diaz had just vacated.

'This is bullshit, Pascal, and you know it,' he said. 'We're talking under duress. Soon as we're out of here it'll be withdrawn, and they'll add another couple of charges to your rap sheet. Kidnap, assault with a deadly weapon, you name it.'

'You let me worry about that,' Pascal said. 'Start talking.'

Dante sighed. 'Okay. I was in a hole. I needed $15 million dollars. Maria Dinks suggested kidnapping her kid, so we did. Later I used Gutiérrez's network to handle the brat and distribute the funds. That's it,' he said.

'Well that's not quite it, is it?' Pascal said. 'Gutiérrez pimped her out to upstanding guys like senator Diaz here, right? And your instructions to Gutiérrez were actually to kill the child so there'd be no evidence, right?'

'Wrong. I knew nothing about that. If Gutiérrez had orders to kill the child, they came from Maria Dinks. And if he had such orders why didn't he carry them out? As we know, the kids still here, so no harm done.'

In Calver's office, Maria had let out a gasp at Dante's betrayal. She started to angrily protest her innocence, but Daniels quieted her with a a sharp comment and an authoritative wave of his hand. She sank back into angry silence.

Pascal ignored Dante's last comment. 'So let me get this straight,' she said, moving to the whole purpose of her mission. 'Yolanda Lopez, the Dinks maid, had no involvement whatsoever in the kidnapping of Sapphire Dinks, right?'

'Yeah, that's right. Ain't you been listening?' Dante said.

'Thank you, Mr Figueroa,' she said.

'No problem,' he replied. 'Now, can we go?'

'Have patience, my friends,' Pascal said. 'We're nearly there. We're just going to hear some brief testimony from two more witnesses.'

She looked over at Sapphire. 'Sweetie?' she said, gesturing to the chair across the table.

Sapphire passed the cellphone to Greyeagle, then took the seat offered.

###

In Calver's office, as Yolanda caught sight of Sapphire, she let out a high-pitched whoop, and said, 'there's my baby-girl.'

Isabel asked, 'anyone got any popcorn?' She went and sat with Yolanda hugging her as they both watched spellbound. In contrast, Maria's face held a horrified expression as Sapphire began to speak unprompted.

###

'I saw my stepmother, Maria at our home in New York with this man,' Sapphire said, pointing at Dante. 'That was a few weeks before I was kidnapped. I believe Maria drugged me and placed me in one of her fashion house trunks and I was shipped to Mexico where I woke up in the fat man's house.'

'That's the house of Solomon Gutiérrez, right?' Pascal interjected.

'Yes. I saw other girls there as well: Lucy Collins from Los Angeles, who we called Tilly-May, and Tamara Hunt from Washington. Victor Diaz raped me, and I saw him with Tamara there as well, and then I never saw her again,' Sapphire said.

'Thank you,' Pascal said to her. Then, looking at Michael, she said, 'ready?'

He nodded, handed his cellphone to Sapphire and then took her seat.

'You are the son of Solomon Gutiérrez, right?' Pascal asked him gently.

'Yes, that's right,' he answered, looking calm. 'I held all my father's records in my head, because he didn't trust tech. I am told I have a very high IQ and a phenomenal memory, and my father made use of that.'

'What sort of records are we talking about, Michael?' Pascal asked.

'Oh, lots of things. Passwords, crypto currency wallet access codes, bank accounts, phone numbers. All sorts of things,' he said.

'Are you able to give us the financial details surrounding Sapphire and Tamara Hunt?' Pascal asked, not holding out much hope.

'Of course,' he said, sounding surprised. 'Sapphire's father transferred the $25 million ransom in Bitcoin into a wallet controlled by my father, and these monies were then distributed to the Juarez drug cartel and Mr Dante, and my father took a cut. And I can also give you all the dates and accounts into which the monies passed.'

Pascal beaming, said, 'and what about Tam—'

'What is this?' Diaz shouted, moving towards Michael, but then being restrained by one of the trackers. 'This kid is crazy,' he continued, straining against the guy holding him. 'His father kept him locked away because of it. Thousands and thousands of dollars on doctors and psychiatrists and they couldn't cure him, and now you want to rely on what he says?'

'Yes,' Pascal said. 'Now shut the fuck up, and sit down, or we'll put the gag back in.'

Diaz held her eyes for a moment, then shrugged and sat down.

Michael continued, 'Mr Diaz paid my father $5 million in Bitcoin to abduct Tamara Hunt from her school in Washington. Then I believe he raped and murdered her.'

'Yeah. So where's the body?' Diaz asked, supremely confident.

'Underneath the corral outside the house,' Michael said.

For a second no one reacted to the words, but Pascal was first to recover. 'What d'you mean, Michael?' she said.

'My father went away for a short trip just after Victor Diaz had been at our Hacienda, which was at the same time Tamara disappeared,' he said. 'One of my father's security men I didn't get on with was ragging me. I thought he was kidding me when he said he had orders to take Tamara's body out to the acid vats in the desert. Then he laughed and said he wasn't going to because he couldn't be bothered, so he'd put her under the corral instead. When I later looked, I saw there was some freshly turned earth there in the corner, so I believe if you dig you will find her body and plenty of DNA. He said that Victor Diaz had made a real mess of that little girl.'

In the office in Ciudad Juarez, as Ruiz's Spanish translation of Michaels words was finishing, the senior *Federales* guy was issuing orders for a team to swoop on Gutiérrez's hacienda with forensics and a digger.

And now Diaz and Dante had noticed the cell phones. Dante looked resigned, but Diaz was shouting, until the tracker stuffed a bandanna in his mouth, cutting him off mid-flow.

In the back of the New York office Calver was hugging a weeping Yolanda Lopez, whilst at the front, as Maria tried to leave, agent Monroe blocked her path and began to read her her rights.

Back in the New Mexico desert Pascal raised the cellphone to her mouth and gave FBI agent Calhoun their coordinates for an immediate pick-up.

Epilogue

The six dancers wore tribal costumes, the three women in long dark skirts with blue trimming, the men more colorful in white tops, blue wraparound skirts and elaborate feather headdresses. In their hands they held ceremonial bows and arrows. As the ululating chants rang out and the drums beat the dancers moved, slowly at first, little clouds of dust rising up around their feet, then gathering pace, hopping and swooping, rising and jumping and swooping again, always moving, the dancing mesmeric and affecting.

Around them and spread out across Sia's ranch were many people from the community. There were trestle tables laid out with food and drink and people moved about or stopped to stand and watch the dancers. It was a celebration of sorts, giving thanks for the safe return of Sapphire and the release of Yolanda Lopez from custody.

On the veranda, Sia asked Jonas Calver, 'so how d'you like our bow and arrow dance?'

'I love it,' Calver said, leaning back in his chair and sipping a coke, basking in the sun and soaking up the atmosphere.

'Good. I'm glad,' she said.

There was still a faint tremor in her voice, but it was fading. It was six weeks since the horror at the silver mine and Sia was getting better every day. 'So,' she said tentatively. 'Any news?'

'Yeah, been saving it until last,' he said with a smile. 'The court have granted you interim custody of both Michael and Sapphire, pending a full hearing which may not in the end be necessary. We'll have to see. With both Gutierrez and Maria Dinks facing trial they've probably got more pressing things to deal with than where the kids live.'

Sia smiled softly and placed a hand on her chest, gently pressing where the wound had been, remembering briefly that day and how it had changed everything, for the better.

'And that's not all,' Calver continued. 'The Trustees of the fund that was settled on Sapphire, that's her aunt and uncle on her father's side, want you to become a Trustee as well, so you can help to distribute the trust fund as your daughter might have wanted. Obviously some can be directed towards Sapphire and Michaels education.'

Sia nodded, pleased, but then a shadow fell across her face. 'What will happen to Maria, d'you think?'

Calver sighed. 'She'll fight like crazy, and she might just beat it, because there's only circumstantial evidence against her, and Dante will no doubt retract. But thing is, whatever happens, she'll be tied up in lawsuits for the next few years, so you and Sapphire can forget about her.

'What about Victor Diaz?' she asked.

'He's going down,' Pascal said, hopping up onto the veranda with a drink in her hand. 'He's posted $10 million bail and he's on the street, but he's toast, along with Dante Figueroa who's already behind bars. But the best thing is, Diaz won't get anywhere near the levers of power. His political career is over whatever legal shenanigans he engages in.'

As she finished speaking Fernando Ruiz with Michael on his

shoulders, and Greyeagle with Sapphire on his, climbed up on the veranda.

'Hey, Ruiz, we don't allow dirty cops on the tribal lands,' Pascal said, her expression mock serious.

'Leave him alone, Courtney,' Sapphire said quietly.

'Yeah, leave him alone, Courtney,' Michael echoed her more loudly. 'He saved my life. He was a bad man but he's going to do jail time and probation, and I think he's already learned his lesson. We should all have a chance at redemption.'

'How about that,' Sia said. 'The kids teaching us oldies a lesson.'

'Maybe,' Pascal said, her face set.

Calver dipped his fingers in a glass of tequila and flicked some in her face. 'Lighten up, Pascal. You're spoiling the party.'

THE END

About the Author

Mark Young is a bookseller, a lawyer, a guitar player and a writer whose works include *Explosive Verdict* and *An Eye for Justice*. This is his third novel. He lives in Suffolk, England.

www.mark-young.com